MW00830111

Lorelle
of the DARK

LEGACY OF SHADOWS

Lorelle of the DARK

LEGACY OF SHADOWS

TODD FAHNESTOCK

F4 PUBLISHING

DEDICATION

For Lara,

My *Lorelle. It all begins and ends with you.*

THE CHRONICLER
LORELLE OF THE DARK

The man in the stocks had been there for longer than anyone could guess.

He stood on a rise before a valley that contained broken buildings, collapsed walls, and a single metal tower. The ancient city behind him had been abandoned in another age, but the man remained, bent over, gnarled hands and gray-haired head stuffed through the holes of his forever prison.

He was a storyteller, and since he'd first begun telling his tales months ago, the crowds had grown:

"Do you know the story of the Second War of the Giants…?" the old man asked. "I have told you about Khyven the Unkillable, how he came into his power, how he discovered his magic.

"But I have not told you about his paramour, the one who stood in the shadows beside him. Khyven would eventually rise like a wave that crashed over our enemies, but Lorelle was the moon.

"How do I know? Oh, I know, my dear esteemed learned one. I know because I was there.

"I was there the day Queen Rhenn of Usara turned the tide of darkness. I was there when the great wizard Slayter Wheskone outwitted an elder dragon at his own game. And I was there when the Luminent Lorelle went into the Dark, when she made it a part of herself…

"The seeds of Khyven's victory began with her. She did not think twice about giving her own life for those she loved. She was as selfless as Khyven had once been selfish. Because of this, she was destined to die. The great weaver of events, Nhevalos the Betrayer, had consigned her to oblivion, but she slipped her fate. And because she did, so did we all.

"I'm going to tell you her story, the true story of the Luminent who determined the course of the war by embracing the Dark…."

ACKNOWLEDGEMENTS

Becca Gardner and Hailey Gregor: My Alpha Readers! Thank you for reading this lightning fast and reassuring me that it was ready.

Elowyn Fahnestock: Thank you for helping me work through the plot points, and for helping me shape Slayter and Vohn into the fantastic characters they are. I can't wait for Slayter's book. It's gonna be a blast.

Marie Whittaker: Thank you for going through the Save-the-Cat beat sheet with me in Albuquerque. The novel didn't turn out *at all* like those initial scribbles on that legal pad, but it started the process.

Quincy J. Allen: For being so receptive to every single crossover idea between Noksonon and Daemanon. You're not just receptive, but you RUN with them. I can't wait to get to the point where our stories are actively crossing. It's gonna be badass.

Rob Howell: For having faith in this story, and in Khyven and Lorelle, from the very beginning.

Chris Kennedy: Our fearless leader. Thank you for championing the Eldros Legacy! We could not do this without you.

Mia Kleve: It **seemed** the moment you sent the manuscript back to me—and so quickly—I **leapt** to the task. Your editing was **golden**. ;)

Becky Busch: Thank you for all the amazing conversations and your astonishing ability to quote all the best movies. ALL THE BEST MOVIES. (Or maybe just ALL the movies…?)

Mark Stallings: Thanks for being that calm presence that keeps pushing this project forward, and for… THE COINS!

Chris Mandeville: My avatar! You're always there for me. Every book. Every time. Thank you!

Lara Wirtz Fahnestock: Always. Always. Always. (Say it thrice, the bond is forever). Thank you for your unceasing support of all of this crazy writer rollercoaster stuff. You are the best. "I think I'm gonna keep ya."

MAPS

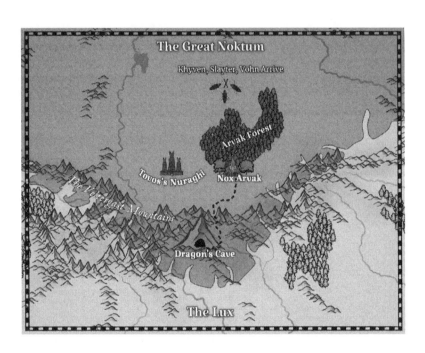

1. Palace
2. The Night Ring
3. Reader Library
4. Mariner's Rest
5. Shkazat Den

THE CROWN CITY OF USARA

PROLOGUE

ELEGATHE

Elegathe entered her study and waited just inside the door like some servant girl. The floor-to-ceiling bookshelves lined every wall, filled with the wisdom of Noksonon. She had read every word on every page of every book in this room. She had used that knowledge to elevate herself, to secure her place as the High Master of the Readers of Noksonon. This was her sanctum and her general's tent, all in one. Just the smell of polished mahogany and old tomes filled her with serenity and confidence.

And Darjhen had wasted no time in making it his own again.

He and the tall stranger had cleared her quills, her missives box, and her box of ready scrolls from her mahogany desk. They stood on either side of it, pointing at a huge map, talking in low tones.

And of course, they'd already begun without her, though she was here precisely at the stroke of six o'clock. He'd given her the wrong time.

No. He'd given her the time he'd wanted her to arrive.

Senji's Fist, she hated everything about this. Darjhen had also told her to join the meeting but remain silent unless he or his guest talked to her. The old man was making her feel like a little girl again—the fresh apprentice—and it scraped her pride like a jagged piece of granite. This was the room of the High Master of the Readers of Noksonon—*her* room. Yet here she was, invited late to the meeting and standing like a servant by the door, quiet and unseen.

She pushed her glasses higher on her nose, drew a deep breath and let it out. Darjhen had gone through the reasons with her. The stranger was important, a traveler of the Thuroi who had visited places Elegathe could only imagine, knew things even Darjhen seemed to hold in awe.

Darjhen believed the mythical Giants were surfacing again, bent on war. Somehow this tall stranger was involved. He knew about the upcoming war and was apparently a key resource. Darjhen's brief conversation with her earlier today had indicated the man was either oddly skittish or ridiculously arrogant.

"Don't speak, unless he speaks to you," he had said. "Then make your answers short. Don't show off."

"If you don't want me to speak," she had said. "Perhaps you should have your secret meeting elsewhere and cut me out entirely."

Darjhen either hadn't noticed, or chose to ignore, her scathing sarcasm. "No. I want you there."

"Either include me in your plans or don't. I don't care," she had lied. "I'm not your apprentice."

"And your attire," Darjhen had said as though she hadn't spoken. "Conservative, please. I understand the reasons for your usual appearance, the allure of beauty can make some opponents predictable. Not this time. You do not want to draw attention to yourself, especially—"

"Through sex appeal?"

"You do not want to draw attention to yourself," he had repeated and left it at that.

So, she had donned her most conservative dress and robes, the front open only to just below her collarbones.

The tall stranger looked up when she entered. His dark eyes shone gold for a moment, but so quickly she wasn't sure she'd even seen it. Was the man a mage? Or had it been a trick of the golden light shining through her study's window?

The stranger was one of the largest men she'd ever seen, six and a half feet tall, but he was far younger than she'd anticipated. When Darjhen had told her about their visitor, coached her, she'd thought he was talking about someone as old as Darjhen, but the stranger was Elegathe's age.

"She is of the blood," the stranger said, still looking at Elegathe. "You didn't mention that."

"Two lesser lines," Darjhen said casually, still focused on the map as though the stranger's statement wasn't particularly important.

"It's an opportunity, Darjhen. Why didn't you tell me?"

"She is positioned where she will be most effective when the war comes."

The stranger kept his unsettling gaze on Elegathe, and she found herself compelled to look down, focusing somewhere on the man's chest.

That was unacceptable. She forced herself to look upward, but found that holding the man's gaze was like putting her eyes close to a hot stove and trying to keep them open. Senji, what was *that* about?

"She will fight in her own way." Darjhen looked up from the map, still trying to make it sound like this topic was far from important. He was a consummate actor when he had to be, but she knew him as well as anyone and she caught a glimpse of his true emotions. Worry.

You do not want to draw attention to yourself...

This was what he'd warned her about. The stranger had not only noticed her but taken an interest.

"You favor her," the stranger said.

"She is well trained. I need her is all."

"Sentiment will not win this war."

"Humans are bound together by sentiment, Nhevaz, by how we feel for one another. *That* is what will win the war."

So, the stranger's name was Nhevaz. She felt she knew that name from somewhere, but she couldn't place it. That was frustrating. Elegathe was meticulous about remembering important events and names. Why did that name sound familiar?

Nhevaz's gaze bored into her, and the gold sheen flashed over his eyes again, flickering and vanishing. So, he *was* a mage.

His eyes returned to their depthless black, and Nhevaz looked down at the map again.

"Khyven should be our focus," Darjhen said.

Khyven the Unkillable. *That* name she knew. Elegathe took reports from all over Noksonon, from every Reader on the continent, and she was well aware of the coup in Usara. The daughter of the previous king, Rhennaria Laochodon, had unseated the usurper Vamreth, the man who'd killed all the Laochodons ten years ago—or so it had been believed. Queen Rhennaria had been assisted by a handful of Usaran nobility, a Luminent, a Shadowvar, a Line Mage, and a renowned Ringer named Khyven the Unkillable.

If Khyven was the topic in this room, he was important to the Giant war somehow. The lion in Elegathe's mind tore into the information, putting pieces together. The renowned Ringer was in his early twenties. Ten years ago, he would have been ten or eleven.

… just like the boy she and Darjhen had found when she had been his apprentice.

Senji's Spear, was *that* boy Khyven the Unkillable?

Ten years ago, Darjhen had pulled her—a newly indoctrinated Reader—to the first major crossroads in her life. She hadn't been ready. She'd been a girl, but her fate as a Reader had been decided that night. Darjhen had performed the most powerful Lore Magic she'd ever witnessed—before or since—and it had pointed to a ten-year-old boy who had just leapt from the burning manor of Duke Chandrille.

The line of Chandrille died that day. No one had survived.

None save the boy…

Coincidentally, the usurper Vamreth had risen to power that same year. Except there was no coincidence when it came to

Darjhen. The boy's survival and the usurper's rise had almost certainly been spun by the old man.

Maybe both of these men. Who *was* this Nhevaz?

And why was Khyven important? Why not Queen Rhennaria instead? That seemed far more likely. That woman was going to change Usara, perhaps even the entire face of the Human lands of Noksonon.

Elegathe's internal lion wrestled with a half dozen other questions, but she turned her focus to the men at the map. She didn't want to miss anything.

Yes, she was dancing to Darjhen's tune again. Yes, it stung her pride. But she had to admit, if reluctantly, that the last time she'd followed at his sleeve it had led her to this place, to being the High Master.

"You risk much," Darjhen said. "Khyven could have easily died in that confrontation. He almost did."

"He survived," Nhevaz said. "The battle for Usara was nothing compared to what is coming. He came through the fire; that makes him our primary."

"And the others? Are they ready?" Darjhen asked.

Nhevaz said nothing, like a man used to keeping his own counsel.

"Never mind," Darjhen said, and she saw his hope for an answer wither, uncontested, on his face. That stunned her. Darjhen behaved like a supplicant for the information this stranger possessed. She'd never seen that before, not once in all the time she'd known him.

"He wielded the Helm of Darkness," Nhevaz said. "Neither of us saw that. Rauvelos sometimes has… an uncanny intuition."

Rauvelos… Another name Elegathe felt she should know. She was certain it wasn't any of the top three tiers of nobility in Usara, Imprevar, or Triada. Damn it! She hated feeling like an apprentice again.

"He survived because his blood was pure enough?" Darjhen asked.

"The Luminent bonded with him."

Darjhen's eyebrows went up. "Did she?"

"Your Human sentiment at work. Khyven is on the path now, and I took steps to ensure Tovos is looking elsewhere."

"Rhennaria?" Darjhen guessed.

"I removed her from the board."

"You took her?"

Nhevaz nodded once.

Took the queen? Elegathe had had no reports that Queen Rhennaria was missing.

"Is she safe?" Darjhen asked.

"As safe as anyone in this time."

"It's still a long road," Darjhen said.

"The Luminent is now the problem," Nhevaz said. "I've read the *kairoi*. She will interfere. There are… many possibilities that spring forth from her. She is too much of a risk."

"Must we separate her from Khyven?"

"No. Not us. If we play our part Tovos will do the job for us. He has taken the bait."

Tovos! She knew *that* name. Tovos had been a Giant, long ago. Could they actually be talking about *that* Tovos?

"Tovos wants the queen."

"I took her to engage his interest, to keep his eye off Khyven. He can't reach her, so I predict he'll grab for the next best thing."

"Rhenn's best friend."

Nhevaz nodded.

Darjhen hesitated.

"Tovos will kill her," he said at length.

"Eventually," Nhevaz said without a scrap of remorse, his dark eyes cold. "When the Luminent is removed, the threat is removed, and Khyven will move toward his destiny."

"Nhevaz…" Darjhen swallowed. "That will have an effect on him."

"Yes."

"A poor effect," Darjhen clarified.

"She will serve him far better as a martyr than as a living distraction. We trained him to cleave to a singular purpose. When he realizes Tovos is behind her death, she will become an icon in his mind. He will fight the war with the memory of her driving him. Forever."

"He can still do that without her death," Darjhen said.

"Being bound to the Luminent divides his loyalties."

"She didn't know that when she bonded with him. She did it to save his life."

"Of course."

"She is the reason you still have him at all."

"She is."

"Letting her die seems a poor repayment for that," Darjhen said.

"We are not here to repay anyone. We play the board as it is set. Wishing we had different pieces wastes time. She sealed her fate when she bonded with him; she accepted that."

"She didn't accept *this*. She doesn't know the larger picture."

"She's already dying. Luminents who fail in their soul bonds do not last."

"He might bond back with her, Nhevaz."

"No."

"There *is* a chance. He loves her—"

"This is the path, Darjhen," Nhevaz cut him off. "I have read the *kairoi*. If she falls to Tovos, she will be of use to us."

"If you remove Khyven's attachment to his friends, you could lose more."

For the first time, Nhevaz's brow wrinkled, showing a glimpse of annoyance. "You've lost your perspective. You're thinking like a Human."

"That's why you need me."

"I need you because you are a Reader, because you prize foresight and judgment over emotion. Right now, you're sacrificing that judgment for the imagined happiness of one man. Happiness is not a factor. Tovos and the others will destroy your kind if we let them. When the war is won, bask in all the happiness you want."

Elegathe watched the exchange with dumbfounded surprise. Darjhen was deferring to Nhevaz like a boy deferring to a teacher. Who *was* this man?

"I think you're missing a vital piece."

"I am not," Nhevaz said. "We trained him. Then we threw him to the wolves and he made pelts of them. That is the man we need."

Darjhen let out a breath. "I will read the *kairoi*. There may be—"

"Waste your magic on sentiment and you may be removed from the board as well," Nhevaz said.

Elegathe bristled. That sounded like a threat! She'd had about enough of this.

"You'd do well to listen to him," she interjected. "He knows more than you do."

Nhevaz raised his head, the black eyes cold as he glanced at her, this time not simply with cool appraisal, but with a cold, inevitable hunger.

It stole her breath.

Men had looked at her with hungry gazes before. She had built her teasing appearance upon that very thing, but this was different. There was no passion in Nhevaz's gaze. No fantasies lurked behind his eyes that could unbalance him and give her the edge. He looked at her like he already owned her, like she was a stringed doll beneath his hand, and he would move her when and where he wished.

"No, Elegathe," Darjhen said.

"You talk of reading the *kairoi*..." She ignored Darjhen and took a step toward the stranger, forcing herself to look him in the eye, trying to throw off the pounding intensity of his gaze. "Darjhen has *walked* those paths. He's sacrificed for those paths. I don't know who you are, but when you speak to him, you speak with respect and understand that he—"

"Elegathe, shut your mouth!" Darjhen barked.

The force of his words startled her and she glanced at him. His eyes blazed with emotion, but she couldn't tell if it was anger or fear.

She swallowed, longing to finish what she had to say to this irreverent stranger, to put him in his place, but she hesitated, suddenly feeling like she'd completely misread the room.

Darjhen held her gaze until she stepped back. Each footstep seemed a betrayal, but she made them one at a time.

"Is this what you meant by Human sentiment making us stronger?" Nhevaz asked softly, as though Elegathe's outburst had just proven some point. Heat rose in her cheeks.

"She is young," Darjhen said. "She is learning."

"She doesn't have time to learn. The moment is upon us. She will be more use as a—"

Darjhen slammed his hand flat on the table, making a thunderclap in the room. "She stays here, or you find another ally!"

Darjhen's explosion made Elegathe jump, but Nhevaz didn't even twitch. He continued looking at Darjhen with that cold gaze.

"The board is scattered with stones," he said softly. "Do not trip, Reader."

Muscles stood out in Darjhen's jaw. His internal struggle played over his face, but he mastered himself. "We keep our eyes on what is vital," he said, his voice barely a breath.

"Yes," Nhevaz agreed, drawing the word out as though he doubted Darjhen's sincerity.

"Khyven is vital. We focus on Khyven."

Nhevaz gave one last look at Elegathe then turned back to Darjhen.

"You say the Luminent has to go," Darjhen conceded, as though holding the Luminent out to Nhevaz like a raw piece of meat before a hungry hound. "How does it happen?"

"A Nox comes for her."

Darjhen nodded. "What must we do?"

"Remove the Plunnos from the library in Usara."

That seemed the oddest of choices, but Elegathe had long since learned that moving the future required orchestrating seemingly unconnected items.

"I will send Elegathe," Darjhen said.

Nhevaz turned his gaze on her one final time. "Very well, Reader."

"Is there anything else?" Darjhen asked, his tone clear that he was done with this conversation.

In answer, Nhevaz stepped backward, to the left of the hearth, where the slanting golden sunlight had created a dark triangle of shadow. She expected him to collect something, perhaps something he'd leaned in the corner between the hearth and the wall. But he stepped into the shadow and did not step out. She knew exactly where he was standing—there was just enough room in that triangular shadow for a man of his size, but she suddenly realized she couldn't see any part of him anymore, no sleeve or the tip of a boot to catch the light.

She leaned her head, changing her vantage and squinting so her eyes could catch sight of him.

He was gone. There was no one in the shadow.

"He's a mage," she said to Darjhen.

"Indeed," he said, and he sounded tired.

"Who is he?" she asked bluntly. "Why do I know that name?"

"He's an ally."

"He doesn't act like it."

"Sometimes it doesn't seem like it, but trust me, he is."

"He talked to you like you were—"

"That is not your concern. Your concern is to do your part."

"Like killing the Usaran queen's best friend?"

"We're not going to kill her. You are going to go to the Reader Library in Usara. You are going to take the Plunnos and bring it back here. You're going to do it tonight. That is all."

"Don't talk to me like I'm stupid," she said, her anger re-igniting. "We move a Plunnos here and Lorelle is slain by someone named Tovos there."

"You know her name," Darjhen said, glancing sidelong at her. She thought she saw a flicker of pride in those haunted eyes.

"Of course, I know her name," she snapped. "They're the confidants of a key ruler on my continent. I know all their names."

"Your continent." He smiled.

"I have many questions, old man," she said. "And by all the gods, I'm going to get answers."

His weary face sharpened and the lively glimmer came back to his eye. "Are you now?"

"What happened to Queen Rhennaria?"

"Nhevaz took her through the Thuros."

"Why?"

"To throw suspicion off Khyven."

"Because of Tovos," she said.

"Yes."

"Is he actually the Tovos I'm thinking he is? Is this creature a Giant from thousands of years ago?"

"Yes."

Elegathe's heart skipped a beat. She cleared her throat. "Where did Nhevaz take her?"

"Never mind the queen. She is beyond our reach."

"I thought you said you wanted the kingdoms of Noksonon to be stable for the coming conflict. How is Queen Rhennaria's absence going to ensure stability in—"

"Nhevaz is taking care of that part. We must take care of ours."

"What's going to happen to her?"

"Concern yourself with your own tasks. Leave Queen Rhennaria to Nhevaz—"

"I don't trust Nhevaz!"

Darjhen shook his head. "I cautioned you to control your emotions. I told you to observe, to stay silent, and to keep from drawing attention to yourself. You failed on all three counts."

"What's going to happen to her?" she demanded.

"Whatever Nhevaz chooses!" he shouted, and she fell silent. Darjhen never shouted, and yet he had done so thrice today. "I'm warning you and you are not listening. We all have our parts to play, and you need to stay out of Nhevaz's way or..." He trailed off.

"Or what?" she said.

He didn't say anything.

"Or what, Darjhen? What will he do to me if I step out of line?"

"Elegathe…" Darjhen began, but for the first time he didn't seem to know what to say.

"Do you think I'm blind? You protected me from this man. He scares you. What in Senji's seven hells has ever scared you before now? Who is Nhevaz? The man is like a doom hanging over you. If I'm in danger, you have to tell me how. Give me the information to protect myself."

Darjhen ran his hand across his scalp and mumbled something she couldn't hear.

"What?"

"You can't protect yourself. Not against him."

"Oh, I think I can." Elegathe had three thin daggers strapped on her person right now. She had two packets of paralytic powder and a needle coated in *somnul* hidden in pockets within her robes. She had thin, invisible sheens of choking paste applied to both sides of her neck and at the cleft between her breasts. And she was as talented as any—save perhaps Darjhen himself—at Lore Magic. Had he forgotten who he was talking to? Did he only see the child she had been when she'd apprenticed to him?

If that arrogant, cold-eyed interloper had tried to do anything to Elegathe, he would have instantly regretted it.

Darjhen looked up. "Elegathe, please. You are looking at this from the wrong side."

"If I am, it is only because you're not showing me all the sides. Show me. Let me choose. I think I've earned it."

He closed his eyes, and suddenly he looked as old as she'd ever seen him.

"Sometimes I think…" he said in a weak voice, a voice that didn't belong to him, "that I am an evil man." He looked up at her, his eyes glistening with unshed tears. "But never more so than when I dragged you into this."

"I *chose* to be here."

"That's what they all think," he said raggedly.

"Listen to me." She grabbed his chin and lifted his face. "I understand about the *kairoi*. I understand how we manipulate people, and I'm telling you I chose this, and I choose it still. I knew the path, the danger of it, even back then. So don't look at me like I'm yours to protect because I'm not. I'm not your daughter or your granddaughter. I am the High Master of the Readers of Noksonon, and I will die to save this world. How *dare* you think I would be frightened by some foreigner from another land just because he's somehow gotten his hooks into you!"

"Nhevaz is a Giant," Darjhen said.

Elegathe's mind, alive with fury, froze. It was like a winter wind had turned flames to icicles.

She swallowed. Her glasses slid down her nose and she didn't push them back.

"What…" was all her mouth could manage.

"He is the Giant known as Nhevalos."

"Nhevalos…" she murmured, and the frustrating mystery of his name slammed into place. "Nhevalos the Betrayer."

"That is what the other side calls him, yes," Darjhen said.

"What is he—Why is he…?" She tried to formulate the question she wanted answered.

"To help us," he said. "To ensure we win."

Elegathe took an involuntary step back. Every time she thought she had grasped her situation the floor fell out from under her again.

The Giants had indeed returned.

And one of them controlled her mentor.

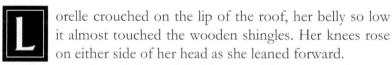

CHAPTER ONE
LORELLE

Lorelle crouched on the lip of the roof, her belly so low it almost touched the wooden shingles. Her knees rose on either side of her head as she leaned forward.

Her ragged soul burned inside her, filling her body with flames, but she forced herself to ignore the pain.

She waited half a breath, then dropped to the second story window without a sound. Her toes perched on the windowsill while her fingers pressed against the top of the recessed frame to hold herself in place over the three-story drop. She tested the latch. Unlocked.

The secret society known as the Readers tried so hard to keep itself hidden. An unlocked window seemed strangely out of place. Perhaps they felt the whispered stories of their vengeful reputation were enough to dissuade thieves.

Well, not this thief.

She opened the window and slipped inside. Just below the windows, a decorative, six-inch ledge ran around the interior of the tall room. She crouched low and slid quickly to the side so her silhouette didn't show against the open window. The ceiling curved over her, requiring perfect balance to remain on the narrow ledge without falling. The most acrobatic of Humans couldn't have accomplished it.

But Lorelle wasn't Human. Her muscles, her bones, even her blood, were less dense than her heavy counterparts. A Human woman Lorelle's size would weigh at least a hundred and fifty pounds. Lorelle weighed eighty while her physical strength remained comparable, which meant she could leap higher, move faster, and balance her body in ways Humans could never match.

She looked at the huge library below. It was exactly as the thief master had described it, but even at that it barely seemed real. How could this place be here, practically in the center of the city, and no one knew about it?

Books and scrolls and bound sheaves of paper lined every wall. Large bookcases stretched across the length of the room, creating seven aisles filled with untold knowledge. She surmised there were more secrets in this room than in the royal library.

Neither Rhenn nor Slayter had known about this place.

But the thief master of the Thin Alley Thieves' Clutch, a man named Zenghi, had known. One of Zenghi's thieves—the last person who'd dared to enter this secret library uninvited—had also known. He'd died for breaking into this place and stealing the mythic Plunnos Lorelle also sought. The Plunnos was the only way to open the Thuros in the basement of the palace that had swallowed Rhenn.

And Lorelle was going to find it and take it.

Since Rhenn's abduction through the Thuros two weeks ago, she had hunted for the key to follow. Her single-minded drive had pushed her to interrogate Vohn and Slayter, to tear through the palace library, and to visit every noble house that possessed rare books that might contain some hints about the mystical Thuros. It had driven her to every dirty gambling house, *shkazat* den, and brothel where even a whisper of secret knowledge might be spoken. She'd barely slept, barely ate, and the ragged edge of her soul had tried its best to burn her alive in that time.

But she'd followed the alley gossip. She'd uncovered a

promising whisper about Zenghi's now-dead thief. According to rumors, he'd held the Plunnos in his hand, had sold it, and had reveled in his riches. Those stories had led her to Zenghi, the master of the dead thief's clutch. Of course, thieves were secretive. Zenghi hadn't wanted to talk.

She'd made him.

With her fist squeezing his throat and her knee pressing on his groin, Zenghi had finally panted out his secrets. He'd told her the story about the Reader Library.

Three years ago, a thief of the Thin Alley Thieves' Clutch had snuck in, even as Lorelle was doing now. He'd stolen a small casket of jewels, a book with a gold-and-jewel-encrusted cover, and a thick, oversized coin with the royal Usaran symbol engraved on both sides. The thief had brought the jewels to his thief master—Zenghi's predecessor at the time—who had taken a substantial cut as leader of the clutch. After the clutch's fence turned the items into gold, the thief had run to the lure of gambling and wenching to spend his earnings.

Five days later, he'd died in an accident. Drunk after a night of gambling, the thief slipped in the alley outside the gambling den, struck his head on the corner of a building, and passed out.

That was unremarkable in itself. Drunks passed out in alleys every night in Usara. But in a twist of fate, the thief fell face first into a puddle created by a huge divot of missing cobblestone. He drowned there, his head in half a foot of water, and that was the end of him.

Bad luck, Zenghi had thought at the time.

Five days later Zenghi's predecessor, the master of the Thin Alley Thieves' Clutch at the time, also died.

One might have thought his death a murder if there hadn't been five witnesses in the room of the brothel. There had been a silk scarf on the floor, tied around the base of a bedpost. Zenghi's predecessor slipped on the free end while his other foot shot back to catch his balance—and caught on the now-taut scarf. He stumbled and slammed into the window. It might have ended there with a broken window and some cuts, except the window was open. Without a sound, the thief master tumbled through, plummeted three stories to the cobblestones, broke his neck, and died.

Bad luck, Zenghi had thought without much remorse. After all, it opened the way for him to take leadership of the clutch.

Exactly five days after the thief master's fall, like the workings of an insidious clock, the fence who'd handled the sale died.

On a trip to the butcher's market, the fence stepped awkwardly off a poorly built curb and turned his ankle. The resulting stumble made him lurch in front of four draft horses hauling bars of iron. The horses' hooves mangled the fence and the steel wheels nearly cut him in half. Grisly. A hundred-to-one fluke all the bystanders said.

Zenghi got the message that time. There was too much coincidence between the deaths to assume it was just "bad luck." All three dead men had handled the items lifted from the Readers Library.

The next day, Zenghi's first edict as thief master was: Leave that building alone. Any thief coming back to the clutch with goods from the Reader Library would be expelled from the clutch and thrown into the street with his eyes put out.

"It was Readers what killed 'em," he had gasped painfully to Lorelle as she leaned on his groin. "With magic!"

Lorelle had heard of Readers. In her ceaseless search for knowledge about the Plunnos, the term "Readers" had come up several times. She'd also heard it back when she and Rhenn had lived in the Laochodon Forest. Rhenn and Vohn had been obsessed about anything concerning the noktum, which had included stories about the history of Giants, magic, and the Human-Giant War at the beginning of known civilization.

The Readers were a notable part of that history. As keepers of knowledge, they had been instrumental in defeating the Giants during the Human-Giant War. After the Giants vanished, the Readers had promised to stay vigilant for their return. Except the Giants had never returned, and the last recorded instance of a Readers' Conclave was centuries ago. Like the

Giants themselves, the Readers seemed to have vanished.

Except, apparently, they hadn't...

After extracting the information from Zenghi, Lorelle had returned to the palace to question Slayter. As usual, the mage had eagerly regaled her with everything he knew.

Slayter was easier for Lorelle to be around these days than either Vohn or Khyven. The mage didn't comment on the dark circles under her eyes, her gaunt frame, or the fact that she was always away from the palace. He didn't look at her with soulful, hurt eyes. Slayter acted like every day was a fresh adventure and he didn't seem to notice, or care, about Lorelle's state of mind. When prodded, he would talk until he was blue in the face about anything regarding history or magic. It was as though his ten years as a spy in Vamreth's court had driven him near to mad with the need to reveal secrets. Now he did so with abandon whenever he could.

According to him, the Readers might never have actually vanished. They might simply have... removed themselves from the public eye.

"Could they make people become unlucky?" she had asked him.

"Unlucky?" Slayter's eyes had lit with interest at the question. "Lorelle... Did you meet a Lore Mage?"

"Just tell me about Lore Magic."

"Oh, well, it's fascinating. Lore Mages pay close attention to moments and objects that seem inconsequential. They move trinkets from one place to another for no apparent reason. They give warnings that seem like gibberish. All because they have 'read' bits of the future. Lore Magic is the art of knowing what is going to happen so far in advance that a person can move these seemingly inconsequential things to a more favorable position by the time the mage interacts with the events they've predicted. Then, by the time the future catches up with them, they are in the most favorable position to get what they want."

"So, Lore Magic makes a person lucky."

"No." Slayter had shaken his head. "Not at all. But it would *look* like that to the uninitiated. Lore Magic is the opposite of luck. It's knowledge. It is strategically using what no one else knows. It is thinking two, twelve, a hundred steps ahead." His eyes had glittered. "So, tell me. Did you meet a Lore Mage?"

She had left him with that eager look on his face and dove out a window, back into the night.

Obviously, it was dangerous to offend a mage, but Lorelle had almost beaten her hands bloody on the Thuros in an effort to get it to work. She wasn't about to pass up a chance to get to Rhenn, no matter how dangerous.

If the Readers punished those who stole from them—reaching them wherever and whenever they wanted—it was a sure bet they'd also taken back what was theirs.

But even if the Readers no longer possessed the Plunnos, they certainly *knew* about it. That, small though it was, could be another lead, and Lorelle was running out of time. Her insides felt bloody and tattered, like a red-hot saw blade was being dragged back and forth across her vitals. Every day, the saw dragged deeper.

The pain, exquisite beyond anything a Human could understand, was meant to drive her toward Khyven. It demanded she do anything to finish the bond, to convince Khyven to attempt to give half his soul to her.

She'd begun the bond by giving half her soul to him to save him from the Mavric iron's destructive effects. During the months of his unconscious convalescence, the pain had been manageable. But since he'd woken it had been torture, and the pain wouldn't stop until she capitulated.

She'd been willing to try the soul-bond, frightening though it was, before Rhenn was taken. Now it was simply impossible. Until Lorelle brought Rhenn safely back through the Thuros, Lorelle's life wasn't her own. She couldn't afford to risk it.

She estimated the chances of a Human successfully bonding with a Luminent at less than one in ten. If Khyven tried to give half his soul to her and failed, as he almost certainly would, her life was over. The search for Rhenn was over. The pain would subside, and a hollowness would grow in the center of her chest. Soon, she'd lose all care for the usual mortal passions. Her desire for Khyven. Her dedication to her found family. Her care to eat or drink. Nothing would matter, including Rhenn.

She couldn't allow that.

So here she was, perched on the windowsill of the Readers' secret library, flirting with the wrath of Lore mages who had already proved they wouldn't hesitate to kill those who stole from them.

If she could just get her hands on the Plunnos, though, let the Readers chase her. Let them follow her through the archway of the Thuros. Let them kill her five days from now. None of that mattered.

She silently closed the window so no one would accidentally notice it and raise the alarm. From her vantage point, she could see down the aisles and across the small foyer at the entrance of the room. The place was empty. It wasn't late, but only one person in black robes moved through the stacks, cowl up.

That struck her as odd. Why would he wear his cowl inside the building?

She unsheathed her blowgun and carefully inserted a special dart. This one was coated with a rare herb called *verit*. When mixed with honey and the smallest dose of *somnul*, *verit* had a startling effect upon its target, especially for her current purposes. Once pricked with this dart, the victim would feel as if they'd quaffed six beers. Within seconds, they'd experience a glorious euphoria, relax all reservations, and tell her anything she asked. Shortly after that, they'd slip into sleep.

Lorelle raised the blowgun to her lips. It was a long distance, maybe a hundred feet, and she couldn't see the neck of the person through the cowl. It was a tough shot, but at least there was no wind.

She fired.

The dart hit the back of the Reader's neck and stuck. They jerked and hastily batted the dart from their neck. They always did that, as if they could save themselves if they just pulled out the dart quickly.

The robed figure spun around, floppy cowl twitching as they searched desperately behind themselves. The batted the cowl back, blinking and rubbing at his neck. It was a man with wavy brown hair and shocked eyes. He opened his mouth to shout…

And the *verit* went to work.

His horrified expression froze and he blinked like he'd forgotten why his mouth was open. An easy grin spread across his face.

Lorelle dropped from the ledge, caught it with her free hand, and swung. Her momentum carried her above the first line of bookshelves, and she dropped, pivoted, dropped again, and landed a hundred feet in front of the man.

She strode toward him, her golden hair streaming behind her, glimmering in the dim room. She was having more and more difficulty controlling the glow of her hair since Rhenn had been snatched, but she didn't care now.

"You're a Luminent." The man grinned.

Lorelle had never enjoyed violence before. But grabbing someone and shaking them, pinning them, seemed to quench the ragged burning in her chest. It had felt wonderful when she was leaning on Zenghi.

Unfortunately, she couldn't use that tactic here. The *verit* required a different approach. Befriending a *verit* victim would get them talking about anything. Whereas pain could jolt a victim out of the drug's embrace.

"I need your help," she said in a soft voice.

"I would like to help you," the man said dreamily. "It's a library. That's what it's for. Everyone who comes here is always looking for something."

"Do you know what a Plunnos is?" she said.

"Yes," he said.

"Have you seen one?"

"Yes," he said. "In many books."

"Have you seen one in real life?"

"Only once. Today. They have one here."

She felt electrified with hope. "Where is it?"

"Well, it *was* here, but the pretty Reader took it. She was very pretty…" He sighed, then blinked as though remembering something unpleasant. "But kind of mean."

"Who took it?"

"*She* did. She said someone was going to try to steal it. A woman with golden hair. I think they meant you."

"What?"

"The Readers were talking about you."

"You're not a Reader?"

"Oh," he giggled. "No. I'd *like* to become a Reader, but they don't tell you how to do that. It's a secret, like everything else. So, I just do what they tell me and hope…" he trailed off, looking at her with half-lidded eyes. "You're so pretty."

Lorelle clenched her teeth. The drug was working faster than usual. In the first stages of *verit*—the first five minutes or so—the victim was talkative. But the second stage could make them amorous; *verit* was sometimes called "the love potion."

"Tell me about the Plunnos," she insisted.

"They moved it."

"Where?"

"They don't tell me things like that. The pretty Reader took it. She was so…" He sighed. "Did I mention her?"

"What does she look like?"

"Her neck was smooth and long…"

"How tall was she?"

"Oh. She was little. Barely up to here." He lifted his hand to his shoulder, which Lorelle gauged to be less than five and a half feet tall. "But she had the nicest, roundest—"

"What color was her hair?"

"Black, with a few streaks of brown, you know? And her eyes were *so* blue. She saw me when I caught them talking. She only looked at me once, but I could see the blue of her eyes. It was like she was looking at me the whole time, even though she was actually talking with Lekoff and Menzel."

"She took the Plunnos?"

"That's what they do. If something is in the wrong place,

they move it to the right place. I want to be a Reader some day."

"Where did she go?"

"They let me see her. Does that seem funny to you?"

"*Let* you see her? What do you mean?"

"She was in the Reader's office and I was told to go up and deliver a scroll to them. They'd never asked me to deliver a scroll to them before. I think that was intentional. I think everything the Readers do is intentional. I think they wanted me to see her. Then they sent me down here; told me to bring them the Canwell Compendium. You know the Canwell Compendium?"

"No. Why do you think they wanted you to see her? Why do you think it was intentional?"

"Oh! You've never read the Canwell Compendium? It's fascinating. It's the Triadan book that records the list of allies during the Human-Giant War."

Lorelle wanted to shake him. Some people were more susceptible to drugs than others, and the *verit* had moved through him fast. In less than a minute, he'd gone from talkative to amorous to babbling about everything and anything that entered his head. The trick now would be getting him to focus.

"Who was the Reader?"

"She was exquisite and small and the front of her robes were kind of open and you could see—"

"Who *is* she?"

"She was the one who told me to put my cowl up. She said, 'Walk down the center aisle and search for the Canwell Compendium.'"

"Her *name*. Did you catch her name—" Lorelle stopped. "Wait, she told you to wear your cowl up and walk down this aisle?"

"That's what she said."

An alarm gonged in Lorelle's mind. She pieced several things together that had been niggling at her since she'd entered. The empty library. The raised cowl. The unlatched window. Almost as though they were encouraging her to come in.

Almost as though they had planned it.

Her keen ears caught the shuffling sound of a foot behind

her and she heard a soft puff.

She dropped to the ground.

The dart that would have hit her in the back of the neck stuck into the acolyte's throat instead.

The acolyte gurgled and snatched the dart from his throat. She didn't know what it was coated with, but she wasn't going to stay here long enough to find out.

She sprang straight up to the top of the bookshelf.

"Senji's Braid," a voice cursed softly behind her, no doubt fumbling to insert another dart. "She's a Luminent!"

Another *puff* alerted Lorelle and she threw herself sideways, leaping over the aisle to the next stack. The second dart—from the other direction this time—buzzed by her ear.

Luminent hearing was superior to Human hearing in every way. Not only could she hear at a much greater distance, and not only could she distinguish nuances in sound a Human ear could not, Luminents could triangulate distance on a specific noise just by hearing it once.

So, after the two puffs sounded she knew exactly where her assailants were hiding.

She sprinted noiselessly to the end of the stack, leapt off the edge, flipped in midair, and landed softly right next to the second blowgun owner.

He was a red-headed man about her age, and his eyes flew wide when he saw her suddenly standing right next to him.

He opened his mouth to shout, but she struck him in the throat, paralyzing his vocal chords. She dragged her pinkie sheath across his cheek as she withdrew. The needle was covered with pure *somnul*. He had about five seconds.

He grappled with his throat, sucking a breath, and she slapped his blowgun aside. The weapon clattered to the floor even as the red head stumbled backward. She followed him and grabbed his tunic.

"Who told you to attack me?" she demanded. "What is her name?"

"She came… from the Great… from the Great…" But the

somnul took him. He slid down and slumped at her feet.

The Great *what?*

Her keen ears heard the approach of others. Not only was her first attacker closing on her, but now there were more, coming from all around.

Slayter's words about Lore Magic rose in her mind.

"Lore Magic is the art of knowing what is going to happen so far in advance that a person can move these seemingly inconsequential things to a more favorable position by the time the mage interacts with the events they've predicted."

If she'd been a fraction of a second slower, they'd have tagged her with the first dart and she'd be asleep. The only reason they'd missed was because she'd moved faster than they'd expected, because they hadn't known she was a Luminent.

The ragged saw on her soul suddenly ground back and forth and the fire arced through her. She stifled a gasp. The red haze of agony burning in her chest spread through her entire body, covering her vision in red. She clenched her teeth.

It was a trap, and if she didn't turn this around they were going to capture her or chase her out of here. Without the Plunnos.

"No," she growled.

The woman who took the Plunnos could still be here. She'd just sent the acolyte to look for the book. She could still be in this building.

The Readers were on alert now. She'd never get another chance to get this close to the Plunnos. If that woman escaped the Plunnos was gone forever, and Rhenn with it.

Lorelle ducked around the side of the stack and into the shadows. She had no cloak, but her tight leather tunic had a cowl. She flipped it up to hide her glowing hair and slid silently along the side of the bookcase. Ahead, she saw the shadow of a man with a blowgun in his hand waiting at the end of the stack.

She broke into a silent sprint. The man turned the corner when she was almost upon him. He saw her and his eyes went wide. He whipped up the blowgun, but he was only Human.

She leapt into the air and, turning upside down as she arced over him, caressed his cheek with her pinkie sheath. He cried out, but she didn't care now, the time for stealth was gone.

He fumbled at his waist for his dagger, but she paid no attention. The dagger cleared the sheath in shaking hands, and then the man collapsed. She spun past him, pausing with her back against the stack to steady herself. She deftly drew out a vial of *somnul*, carefully dipped each pinkie sheath into it, capped it, and slipped it back into its case. She silently sprinted toward the sound of shuffling feet behind the next stack. Like the whisper of a breeze she launched herself up and landed atop the bookcase even as the man turned the corner, aiming his own blowgun where the shout had come from. She dropped on him.

He never saw her coming.

Shouts went up from the remaining attackers.

"It's a Luminent!"

"She's attacking!"

"Where's Guzan? Where's Guzan?"

"He's down!"

"Where *is* she?"

Each shout let her know exactly where each man was. There were three more...

... And a quieter sound, a fourth person trying to be stealthy. Not rushing to attack, but to get away. Soft boots, expensive boots, making for the door.

Could Lorelle be so lucky? Those boots could belong to a small woman. Was it this visiting Reader, this woman of importance?

Lorelle sprinted down the aisle. The entrance was before her, and the other three men were lost in the stacks behind her.

The woman appeared, running quietly for the door. She *was* small, nearly a foot shorter than Lorelle, and her black hair—with brown streaks—flowed behind her.

She made it to the door, and Lorelle paused in a shadow as the woman, wide-eyed, turned to give one final worried glance at the room. Obviously, this hadn't turned out the way she'd wanted.

The woman closed the door softly, quietly, and only when

she was gone did Lorelle resume her pursuit.

"Senji's Spear, she got Madri, too!" one of the men said behind her.

She opened the door and silently slipped through. The edge of the woman's black robe disappeared to the left around a corner.

With the men flailing around in the giant library, Lorelle might be able to get a moment alone with the fleeing woman.

The woman who had Lorelle's Plunnos.

She sprinted up the hallway. Closing the distance between herself and the woman would take only moments. No Human on Noksonon could outrun a Luminent.

She rounded the corner, saw the Reader's cloak fluttering as she hastened to the door at the end of the hall.

She never reached it.

Lorelle took five powerful steps and launched herself into the air. She arced across the distance and landed at the feet of the running woman. Lorelle snatched the Reader's ankle, exerting just enough force.

The woman cried out as she tripped, hit the floor, and slid unceremoniously against the wall. Lorelle rolled to her feet and padded toward her opponent like a stalking Kyolar.

The woman fumbled to pick up her glasses, which had fallen next to her, and pushed them onto her face.

"Give me the Plunnos," Lorelle said.

"It was not meant for you," the woman said.

"Give it or I'll put you to sleep and take it."

The woman's lips pressed together in a defiant line and said, "It won't serve you, Lorelle. I know what you're doing and why. In your place, I would do the same, but it won't work for you."

Lorelle's eyes narrowed. "How do you know my name?"

"Knowing things is what I do."

The woman was playing games, stalling for time, hoping her fumbling protectors would come in time.

"Last chance," Lorelle said.

"I will never relinquish the Order's property."

Lorelle moved like a tree bending in the wind, forward and

backward so quickly the woman barely had time to jerk away, and certainly not fast enough. Lorelle left a light scrape just below the woman's chin.

"I'm sorry," Lorelle said as the pure *somnul* went to work. She hadn't had time to dilute it. The woman's eyes dropped to half-mast, and she sank back against the wall. Her arms and legs went limp.

Lorelle knelt next to her. The woman wore a black cloak and, beneath it, a low-cut dress belted at the waist. Three pouches hung from it and Lorelle searched them quickly.

She drew a breath. The second pouch contained the Plunnos, a silver coin four inches in diameter with the symbol of Noksonon—a sun being devoured by tentacles of darkness—on one side and the head of a demon with five horns on the other.

Lorelle's heart beat faster. She turned the coin in the light of a window that let in a shaft of moonlight. It glimmered.

"I will return it," Lorelle promised, tucking it away into her own pouch as she glanced up at the window. "If I am able."

The woman's hand closed around Lorelle's ankle, startling her. She shouldn't have had the ability to move at this point, considering her size and the purity of the *somnul*. The one advantage Humans had over Lorelle was their greater weight and the brute force that came with it. The worst thing a Luminent could do was let a Human get a grip on them.

Lorelle tried to wrench her leg free, but she couldn't. The woman held fast with a burning intensity in her quickly dulling eyes. She looked up at Lorelle.

"Beware the Nox, Lorelle," she whispered through numb lips as her eyes tried to slide shut. "The game... is... larger... than you think..." Her head bobbed forward, but she yanked it up through sheer force of will. "Don't... trust..."

But the *somnul* took her. Her grip slackened and her eyelids slid shut before she could finish.

Lorelle stood there, stunned. That sounded like a warning.

She was actively stealing an artifact from this Reader—an artifact for which men had been killed—and the woman was *warning* her?

Her keen Luminent ears heard footsteps approaching. Obviously, the fumbling men in the library had exhausted their search and were heading this way.

Nox?

She shook her head. It didn't matter. Only Rhenn mattered. And for the first time, Lorelle had a way to reach her friend.

She sprang to the nearby window and escaped into the night.

CHAPTER TWO

ZAITH

Zaith smiled at the look of fierce concentration on his sister's face. She walked the rail at the western edge of the training ground for Glimmerblades. It was the first part of a difficult course made for adult Nox, but E'lan put one delicate foot in front of the other, up the narrow band of steel like she had walked it all her life.

She was grace personified, and only nine years old.

"When can I take the test?" she said.

"The earliest, if you are ready, is twenty," he said. In order to become a Glimmerblade, one had to first be a Shadow, then a Shadowmaster, then finally a Darkblade.

Zaith had become a Glimmerblade at age twenty. He'd been ready at nineteen and every bit as impatient as E'lan, but Aravelle had refused to let him take the test. No one took the test before twenty.

He'd just returned from his tenth mission in the world of the Lightlanders. They'd given him an entire week to simply enjoy the comforts of Nox Arvak, and he'd chosen to spend this day with E'lan. Of all his seven brothers and sisters, she was the most like him, and he loved that she wanted to follow in his footsteps.

"I am not going to wait that long," E'lan said, now ten feet in the air on the ribbon of steel. She still hadn't so much as wobbled.

"You must," Zaith said.

"I will train three years. Then I will be ready."

"But the law will still be the law," he said.

"So, change it. You are First Glimmerblade. Can't you change it?"

"Some laws are absolute."

"It's a dumb law."

"Perhaps. But it must still be followed."

"Why?"

"Sometimes there is wisdom in the laws that we cannot yet see. Those who made them are wise."

E'lan made it to the top, thirty feet in the air now. She reached the end and jumped into the air even as she turned. Zaith leapt to his feet, thinking he would have to sprint forward to break her fall.

But she turned in midair, grasped the ribbon of angled steel, and slid down, her sleeves wrapped around her hands. There were two support posts that held the tiny walkway aloft, but she gracefully swung one way, letting go with one hand while she grasped with the other, then swung the other way, dodging both posts.

When she was halfway down, she thrust her legs straight up in the air, did a back flip, and landed on the ground a few feet from Zaith.

He couldn't suppress his grin.

She bowed to him.

"Impressive."

"Impressive enough for you to change the law?"

"I told you, I cannot—"

A boom shook the ground, and eldritch lightning crackled overhead.

E'lan's eyes went wide, and she took a step back. Beyond the training ground, in the city of Nox Arvak, shouts and screams arose.

Zaith turned, baring his teeth. Was it the Orvektu? There had been intelligence suggesting the longtime bestial Nox enemies were beginning to organize, but the scouts had indicated no impending attack. And the Orvektu were not mages. They couldn't create lightning—

Zaith's breath caught in his throat. Looming behind the city stood a castle.

It hadn't been there a moment ago.

It towered over Nox Arvak, dwarfing the city, so vast it overwhelmed Zaith's imagination. He stared at it. Thick walls encased the monolithic pentagonal structure and five spires thrust into the indigo sky. If even one of those towers had been laid flat upon the ground, it would have been longer than the entire city of Nox Arvak. Zaith just looked up and up as though he would never see the end of it.

"E'lan, go home."

"What is it—?"

"Run home. Tell Mother and Father what you saw."

"But I want—"

"Go now!" he barked at her. He'd never shouted at his before, and she jumped.

He turned toward the Nox palace, nestled beneath the sudden castle like a pebble at the foot of a great Shadowtree. Aravelle would be there. If anyone would know what this castle was, or what it meant, the Shadowweaver would.

Zaith was about to launch into a sprint when he realized he hadn't heard his sister's footsteps fleeing toward home. No doubt she harbored hopes of glory at Zaith's side, running toward danger rather than away. He turned to reprimand her again—

His gesture and his command withered as his throat constricted. Standing behind E'lan—unbeknownst to her—towered a giant of a man.

The enormous figure—he had to be twice Zaith's height—wore all black and a long cloak that blended with the shadows. He had pale skin like the Lightlanders, with hair like a Nox, and deep, indigo eyes like the sky overhead. His muscled torso was wrapped with black, skin-tight scale mail. He wore a giant sword as tall as Zaith at one hip and a dagger on the other that could have served Zaith as a short sword.

Zaith leapt at his sister, landed next to her, and pushed her behind him even as he drew his own long, slender blade.

"Step back," Zaith warned, "or you'll wish you had."

The enormous man's brow wrinkled in rage, and fear shivered through Zaith. It was as though the skin between his eyebrows bunched and bunched and bunched until it was simply impossible that it could fold anymore, but somehow it did…

Zaith had faced Orvektu with their long limbs and crude, barbed spears. He'd slaughtered the frightening Zek Roaches, avoiding their venomous teeth. He had traveled to the Lightlanders' world and hidden in their sparse shadows. But not once had he feared for his life. Zaith had been born willing to die for his people.

But this man's expression made his heart trip faster. The stranger's fierce look heated Zaith's face and made his eyes go dry. He forced his gaze away.

"Kneel," the enormous man said.

Zaith might not be able to look the stranger in the eye, but there were ways to attack without eyesight. As a Glimmerblade, he'd learned them all. Going to the world of the Lightlanders meant Zaith could be blinded at any time by the broiling, naked sun.

Zaith felt the shadows like he felt the blood in his veins, and he slipped into the nearest, vanishing from the stranger's view.

He hated to leave E'lan behind, but threats demanded immediate action. To hesitate was to die, and Zaith gambled she'd be safe long enough for him to finish this stranger.

He rushed through the shadows, through the life's blood of the noktum, slithering from one crooked patch of blackness to another until he was behind the enormous man. He crouched and prepared to leap straight up. The man was easily fourteen feet tall, but that was an easy jump for a Nox—

The shadows around Zaith suddenly became as tangible as canvas and wrapped him up tight. He huffed in surprise as they spun him and threw him into the open.

Zaith turned his crashing tumble into a graceful roll and came to his feet at the heels of the enormous man. High above, the malevolent face turned and looked down.

"If you've forgotten your place, I've truly been gone too long," the enormous man said. "Throw down your weapons, now."

Zaith swung at the man's calf—

His sword turned to water as it struck the enormous man's wide leg. Silvery metal splashed to the ground.

Zaith rolled, came to his feet, and drew a long, thin dagger—

The man whispered and shadow tentacles shot from the nearest crooked patch of blackness and slithered around Zaith's throat, constricting. The tentacles lifted Zaith into the air as he struggled, legs kicking. He pulled his dagger and slashed at the tentacles, but hit nothing.

"You purpose is to serve," the enormous man said. "Submit or I will jog your memory."

Zaith choked and struggled, and his gaze fell upon E'lan. She hadn't frozen, wide-eyed, like another child might have. Instead, like the Glimmerblade she aspired to be, she had thought strategically and retreated. She hid quite well in a sudden crooked shadow by the trees.

Stay there, he thought. *Stay hidden, little E'lan.*

"You will be my voice," the enormous man said, "and my hands, Glimmerblade."

"I... will... not..." Zaith choked around the shadow hand.

The enormous man's indigo eyes flashed.

"I will not be forgotten," the enormous man said. "If I must I will remind you who the Lords of the Dark are."

Lords of the Dark!

The scattered tales of Zaith's childhood came together in his mind. The Lords of the Dark were giant men who had supposedly ruled the Nox long ago, the makers of the world, but they were myths. Misty legends.

"You… are no Lord," Zaith choked.

The man glanced to the side. The shadows hiding E'lan turned into tentacles, wrapping her up and thrusting her forward.

She screamed in fear as the tentacles held her aloft.

"No!" Zaith choked. "Let her go!"

"I am Lord Tovos," the stranger said, his face swiveling back to Zaith.

The dark tentacles dropped Zaith, and he landed on his feet. He drew another dagger from his boot and—

And froze. His muscles locked up and his brain suddenly felt like there was a weight pressing down upon it.

"Today, you will remember me," Lord Tovos said. "And you will remind the rest of your ungrateful kind about their place in *my* noktum."

As a Glimmerblade, Zaith had bonded with the noktum years ago. He had put his hands upon the Cairn and married his soul to the Dark. It was this that made him a Glimmerblade. It was this that allowed him to move unseen through the shadows more completely than any of his fellows. It was this that allowed him to know when others approached him through the shadows.

The Dark whispered where they were. The Dark flowed through his veins like blood, moved him with confidence like his own muscles. It permeated every part of him, and it had always stood at the ready to serve him since that glorious day.

Now, the Dark turned from servant to master. It clenched his entire body, as though a thousand tiny tentacles had suddenly flexed inside his own muscles, holding him still.

Then the Dark moved him like a puppet.

Against his will, his arm brought the dagger up before his eyes and tested the edge. A thin line of blood trickled down his thumb. Zaith always kept his weapons razor sharp.

"You will remember why we are your Lords," Lord Tovos said.

Zaith's body jerked forward and walked to where E'lan hung, whimpering, completely immobile in the grip of the tentacles. His body raised the dagger to E'lan's throat.

"Zaith?" E'lan cried, frightened. "Zaith!"

He screamed denial inside his mind, but no sound emerged. He fought with every ounce of his strength, but his body no longer obeyed him. It belonged to the Dark. It belonged to Lord Tovos.

"You will serve me willingly," Lord Tovos said.

Yes, gods! Please! Yes, I will serve. I will serve! he shouted into the quiet, but his mouth made no sound. And if the Lord could hear him, he ignored the pleas.

"Or unwillingly," Lord Tovos said.

Zaith's muscles jerked. The dagger slashed sideways, cutting down to the bone. E'lan jerked. Her eyes flew wide with surprise and blood poured down her neck and chest. Horror squeezed Zaith's sanity and he screamed inside the prison of his mind.

The light faded from E'lan's beautiful eyes and her head fell forward.

"But you *will* serve," Lord Tovos said.

CHAPTER THREE

KHYVEN

Khyven kept his cowl low as he stalked through the gritty streets, trying to let his anger drift away on the chilly air. He was still groggy from the *somnul* Lorelle had shot him with. Again. The woman had become inconsolable since Rhenn had vanished. The moment Rhenn had been abducted, Lorelle had slammed shut a gate between herself and the rest of them.

So yesterday, Khyven had cornered her in her room—a rarity because Lorelle didn't seem to be sleeping in her room anymore—and he'd refused to move until she talked to him. So, she'd raised her blowgun and shot him.

He'd looked at her incredulously as he slid to his knees. She'd walked past him, her eyes haunted.

He'd woken to Vohn's worried ministrations, which had faded instantly when Khyven told the Shadowvar what had happened.

"Well, what did you do to her?" Vohn had asked angrily.

"Nothing! I just wanted her to tell us what she's doing!"

"We agreed that *I* was going to talk to her."

"Well, I—"

"Did we agree on that or didn't we?"

"Look, I—"

"We work as a team, Khyven. and when we agree on something, we stick to it." Vohn had stalked away in disgust, leaving Khyven on the floor, still woozy, to follow as best he could. "Come on," he said over his shoulder, "Slayter has found Shalure."

Now Khyven was striding through the seedy side of Usara just north of Umberland Street. He'd frequented this part of town when he'd first won his freedom after forty wins. This was where he'd drunk his first sip of ale since his capture.

And this was where Slayter had identified the *shkazat* den known as The Dreamweaver.

He didn't make eye contact with anyone and kept his face shielded by the cowl. He thought he'd been famous *before* the Battle of the Queen's Return, as they were calling it, but that had been nothing. It seemed everyone knew Khyven the Unkillable now.

He slowed at the mouth of the alley just beyond Hornway Street. In the dark recesses, on the left-hand side, a short staircase led down to a door. Loitering beside the door, leaning against the wall, was someone who was supposed to look like an alley drunk, but that wasn't true. Khyven knew a guard when he saw one. Despite his ratty clothes and the bottle in his hand, the man's eyes were watchful.

Khyven turned up the alley.

"I'm looking for Shalure Chadrone," he said to the guard.

"And I suppose I should know this person," the guard said without even a hint of slurred speech.

"This tall." Khyven held up his hand, palm down. "Auburn hair. Doesn't talk much."

"Piss off. Do I look like I'm hiding her in my armpit—?"

Khyven grabbed the guard and slammed him against the wall. "No. You look like a man who's about to bleed."

A dagger flashed into the man's hand and he tried to stab Khyven. Khyven twisted, avoiding the point, but he caught the man's fist.

"Bad move," Khyven said. He wrenched the wrist and it snapped.

The guard gagged. Khyven kicked the man in the groin and cross-faced him with an elbow. The dagger clattered to the stones and the guard collapsed next to it. He curled into himself, holding his broken wrist and twitching. Khyven kicked the dagger into the shadows, crouched, and put his face next to the whimpering man.

"You could've answered the question," Khyven said in a low voice. "Could've made this easy."

"Inside…" the man grunted. "She's inside. Just don't hurt…"

"Thank you." Khyven stood, sized up the small door and kicked it in. He stepped quickly down the two steps and into the smoky room.

The *shkazat* den burst into a flurry of action. Three men and a woman playing Senji Stones jumped straight up like they'd been hit by lightning, upending the board and scattering pieces everywhere.

A scantily clad woman dancing on a tiny stage at the back squeaked and cringed, covering herself with her hands. The drunk men watching her turned and threw bleary glances Khyven's way.

Everyone at the bar to Khyven's left sat up, and one man fell off his stool, pitching his beer over his shoulder. The raucous noise of the den dropped into silence.

The bartender reached beneath the bar and came up with a cudgel and a snarl. Two bouncers—one on the far side of the bar and one close—came for Khyven.

He pivoted. The nearest bouncer threw a wild haymaker, no doubt intending to punch Khyven's head all the way to the Hundred Mile Sea.

He lunged inside the punch, which was still on the way, and planted a palm squarely in the man's chest with all his strength.

The bouncer flew backward, crashing through a table and a chair before hitting the wall and crumpling. He groaned, barely moving.

The second bouncer pushed his way through the now shrieking and running crowd, dagger in hand. Khyven instinctively put his hand on the pommel of his own dagger and half drew it, but he managed to stop himself.

He was angry enough to kill someone, but that wasn't why he was here. This wasn't the Night Ring, after all.

He heard Vohn's voice in his head.

You can't just go around killing people you don't like. That doesn't work when you are the authority instead of the oppressed. Diplomacy, Khyven. Use diplomacy.

Khyven, of course, wasn't the authority. He didn't want to be an authority. But since Rhenn had been abducted and Lorelle had effectively become a ghost, the kingdom of Usara was down to few options, and Khyven was one of them.

He jammed the dagger into its sheath and stepped back as the man closed with him, dagger high overhead for a downward strike.

Of course, Khyven's retreat was a feint. Once the dagger went up he scissor-stepped in, pinning the hand high and snake-striking the bouncer in the throat.

The man's arm went slack and he choked and doubled over. Khyven gripped the man's neck and wrist, pivoted, and slammed him into the wall. The man miraculously held onto his dagger.

"Drop it," Khyven commanded.

He didn't.

"Drop it or I drop you." Khyven squeezed the man's wrist to the breaking point, feeling the bones bow.

The dagger thunked to the floorboards.

"Good choice." Khyven threw him to ground and turned in time to face the bartender, who'd come up behind Khyven, brandishing the cudgel.

Khyven threw back his cowl. He gave an iron smile, then gestured, welcoming the man forward.

Whispers shot through the crowd. Khyven's scarred face, a memento from his battle with the Helm of Darkness, was easy to recognize.

"That's Khyven the Unkillable!" one of the patrons murmured.

"It's Khyven the Unkillable," another chimed in at the same time.

"Khyven the Unkillable is here!"

The bartender hesitated, cudgel lifted high. He glanced at the broken door, then at the two fallen bouncers. His befuddled mind seemed to do the math.

"Shalure Chadrone," Khyven said.

The bartender narrowed his eyes. There was defiance there. He opened his mouth to lie, but Khyven cut him off.

"Don't," he said menacingly. "No one's dead yet. Don't be the first."

The man's defiance flickered and faded. He lowered his cudgel and the tip clunked against the wooden floor. He reluctantly jerked his thumb over his shoulder. "In the back."

Khyven nodded tersely.

See Vohn? Diplomacy.

He strode to a small door to the left of the stage. It was about half the size of a normal door, like the hatch to a cellar or crawl space. He opened it and ducked through.

Inside was the *shkazat* den. The smoke in this room was tinged blue and it hung thickly in the air. A number of divans and pallets for the patrons who smoked the mind-numbing drug were scattered beneath the low ceiling.

Khyven narrowed his eyes and kept his lips shut to keep from inhaling any more of the hallucinatory blue smoke than necessary. He had no wish to see his nightmares come to life, or to be lulled into the dim euphoria that held the half dozen people strewn on the pallets in thrall.

He searched the room and spotted Shalure immediately. She lounged on a divan in attire as scanty as the woman on the stage. A man lay next to her, chest-to-back, stroking her arm. He saw

Khyven and he sat up. He didn't have the dull-eyed gaze of the rest of the patrons, and Khyven suddenly knew he wasn't a patron at all; probably the owner.

The man was snuggled up to her, caressing her arm—and who knew what else—while she lay insensate in the grips of the *shkazat*. Khyven clenched his teeth.

The blue wind swirled through the room, and a half dozen blue funnels opened up on the man, all dark blue. All killing strikes.

Barely aware that that he'd crossed the room, Khyven suddenly loomed over the divan, dagger in hand. He wanted to stab it into this feckless cur, wanted it so badly the blue wind whipped about in a frenzy. A roar filled Khyven's ears.

You can't just go around killing people…

Khyven managed to stay his hand and regain his senses. The man was babbling, holding his hands up in a pacifying gesture.

"… she came to us! She offered payment!"

Khyven grabbed the babbling man by his tunic and hurled him toward the open door. He crashed into one of the empty pallets, rolled, scrambled to his feet, and lunged out of the room.

Khyven knelt next to Shalure. Her eyes were rolled halfway back into her head.

"Shalure," he said softly.

She smiled dreamily at him, reached a languid hand up and caressed his cheek with fingers so light they might have been made of blue smoke themselves.

"Kah eh," she said. A small line of frustration wrinkled her brow at the sound of her own voice, like she'd forgotten she couldn't speak. She came to her senses a little, as if realizing where she was and who he was. She shook her head. "Go," she said, one of the few words she could articulate since Vamreth had taken her tongue.

He removed his cloak and wrapped it around her.

"Go, Kah eh," she said, pushing ineffectually against his chest.

He gathered her into his arms and stood, bending over a little to keep from hitting his head on the low ceiling. She went limp and didn't fight him.

He wanted to scream in frustration, wanted to ask her why she would debase herself by coming here, addling her wits, and letting some stranger paw at her.

But he knew why. He knew why…

And it was his fault.

He held her protectively as he carried her out of the *shkazat* den. Everyone wisely got out of his way.

CHAPTER FOUR

KHYVEN

Khyven strode through the streets with Shalure in his arms. She soon recovered from her disgruntlement at being taken away from the *shkazat* den and nestled into him with a dreamy smile. Apparently, *shkazat* was like that. It pulled a person's thoughts away from what they didn't want to see and submerged them in a blind and ignorant fugue.

He took her to the palace, to the room she'd been given by Rhenn before she was taken, and laid her gently in her bed. Shalure ran a slow caress down his arm like she could feel every thread in his long-sleeved tunic. She maintained the dreamy smile, but her eyes slowly slid shut and her hand fell away like a feather, floating to the coverlet. He tucked her under the covers. She would sleep for now, drifting in a haze of the *shkazat* that was apparently more bearable to her than her actual life.

He stood over her, a frustrated frown on his face. He was good at killing people who were trying to kill him, not making someone live who apparently wanted to die. He had to fix this, but he had no idea how.

In a sensible world, this would have fallen to Lorelle. The beautiful Luminent was a master healer. If anyone could cure Shalure, it was Lorelle.

But it was almost as though Lorelle had been abducted along with Rhenn. Lorelle was here, somewhere in the city, but she flowed in and out of the palace like a ghost. She never seemed to sleep, almost never spoke to Khyven directly, and while she attended the council meetings Vohn had assembled to discuss the fraying state of the kingdom, she rarely stayed long.

The tall grandfather clock in the hall at the top of the stairs chimed midnight, and Khyven let out a long breath. He was late for the council meeting right now, in fact.

He left Shalure, shut the door softly behind him, and walked swiftly up the lantern-lit hallway. There were no servants in this part of the palace at this hour. Everyone but the guards had gone to sleep.

In the Night Ring, Khyven had had his share of problems. His life had always been in danger, for one, and the masters had tried to trip him up constantly. But those problems usually came one at a time and often from one direction. In the palace, problems came unpredictably, plentifully, and they came from all angles.

And the worst part was that almost none of them could be solved with a sword.

According to Vohn and Slayter, Rhenn had run the kingdom seemingly effortlessly during the months Khyven had been asleep and near death. He couldn't fathom how that could be true. Of course, Rhenn hadn't had to do it in secret like they did. They lied about her whereabouts—and the lie held up for now—but they were going on the second week since Rhenn had been abducted. It wouldn't hold much longer.

Khyven corralled his thoughts and brought his focus to the present as he opened the door to the queen's meeting chamber.

Bright lanterns lit the room, and two maps had been rolled out on the table, kept from curling with ornate little brass dragons. One was the map of the crown city of Usara, the other—which Khyven hadn't seen before—looked like a map of the entire continent of Noksonon. Vohn stood beside the table with a slender hand perched like a bony black spider atop the city map.

Slayter sat at the back of the room, to the right of where Rhenn would be if she were here. He'd propped his stump on the table and was tinkering with the metal prosthetic leg he and Vohn had crafted.

Khyven crossed to the table and sat down in the nearest chair, which was four chairs away from Slayter. There should be a dozen people at this table discussing the fate of the kingdom. But since the queen had vanished, there was only their secret little cabal of four.

Or, well, three. Lorelle the ghost hadn't yet shown up.

"We have a problem," Vohn said as Khyven entered.

Slayter chuckled at that.

Vohn glared at the mage. "A *new* problem, then. *Another* problem."

Khyven put on an easy smile, though he didn't feel it. He'd discovered early on that Vohn could easily whip himself into a frenzy and that remaining calm was the best way to keep that from happening.

"Nope," Khyven said breezily. "I think today we have to simply say there are no new problems."

Vohn's frown deepened. "We can't say that. It's not true."

"I was joking."

He blinked. "Oh. All right. I understand now. That's funny." He nodded tersely.

Slayter laughed. Vohn shot him another glare.

"Where's Lorelle?" Khyven asked, but he already felt that familiar sinking feeling in his stomach. Whenever he expected to see Lorelle, he felt a growing euphoria. Whenever she failed to show, it pulled at his guts.

Ever since he'd awoken, since she'd kissed him, it had lit a fire within him that he could barely tame. He wanted to grab her, kiss her, but the Lorelle who had leaned over him and said she owed him a kiss had vanished these past two weeks. She seemed to go out of her way to avoid him.

"She's… well, I couldn't find her," Vohn said.

"Don't tell me that, Vohn." Khyven ran a hand through his hair, checking his frustration as best he could.

Vohn raised his voice. "Well, what would you like me to tell you? That she's here?"

When Khyven was moving, when he was throwing people against the wall and punching them like in the *shkazat* den, he almost felt like his old self again, but in moments like this his body ached like he'd been torn apart and put back together, except the glue they'd used hadn't dried yet.

He thought back to the night he'd awoken, the night Rhenn had vanished. Slayter had come to Vohn and said he'd detected magic in the palace. When they'd realized both Rhenn and Lorelle were missing, they'd all gone searching. They'd found Lorelle frozen by the Thuros. After Slayter had painstakingly—it had taken him most of an hour—dismantled the spell, Lorelle had frantically told them the story.

Of course, they'd tried to get the Thuros to work. Slayter and Lorelle had tried for two full days while Khyven and Vohn had scrambled to plan some kind of government for a kingdom that suddenly had no queen. In an exchange of frantic ideas, they had spun a story about Rhenn traveling to a secret meeting with the king of Imprevar to cement relations between the two countries. They'd actually sent a half dozen envoys and a dozen guards on a ship to Imprevar the next morning to cover the lie. It was as solid a lie as could be. After all, the king's daughter had been halfway to Usara to marry Vamreth when Rhenn's coup had toppled the usurper's reign. A face-to-face meeting was one of the only things that could smooth that over.

They'd taken Rhenn's honor guard, the mute knights Orig and Chellit, into their confidence. With Lorelle's reluctant help—she hadn't wanted to leave the Thuros even for a second—they'd convinced the knights of the truth of the story.

But they would have to think of somewhere else for the queen to not-actually-be, and soon.

There were only so many people they could confide in before their shaky facade came tumbling down. Frankly, only a few people would even believe such a wild story. A magical traveler. A Giant's portal. A queen vanishing into thin air.

Four scant months ago, Khyven himself wouldn't have believed it.

Since it became obvious that they couldn't make the Thuros work, they rarely saw Lorelle. She was never in her room, never in the palace. As far as Khyven knew, she never slept. Vohn had been tasked with finding out what she'd been up to.

"So… you lost her," Khyven said.

Vohn's temper flared. "*You* try following a Luminent, Khyven!"

"I can't turn invisible in shadows. That makes you the—"

"Can you jump on rooftops? I can't jump on rooftops."

"What?"

"She's jumping on rooftops!"

"Vohn, we can't just—"

"Are you saying I didn't *try*?" Vohn said, clearly working himself into a fit. "Is that what you're saying?"

Khyven held his hands up. "I didn't mean it that way."

"Her legs are twice as long as mine!"

"I'm sorry."

Vohn frowned at him.

"Do you know where she *might* have gone?" Khyven asked.

"She's looking for a Plunnos."

Plunnos… Slayter and Vohn had done the research and discovered that the only thing that could open the Thuros and make it usable was a "key" in the shape of a giant coin, some magical artifact created by Giants long ago. Such a key was called a Plunnos.

"In the city?" Khyven said. "I thought we agreed there weren't any in the city. Where would she go to do that?"

Vohn exploded again. "Well, if I knew that I'd know where she'd gone, wouldn't I?"

Khyven held up his hands again. "I'm sorry."

"She asked me about Lore Magic," Slayter offered. He was considering one of the brass dragon map weights, and he picked it up contemplatively. He was prone to distraction and his mind constantly wandered. The mage was a walking library, but you never knew if the information he spouted was going to be helpful to the topic at hand or if he was going to talk about how to safely cook raw meat.

"She wanted to know about Lore Magic? Why?" Khyven asked.

"Oh, and Readers."

Khyven sighed, feeling like he had to pull the information from the mage. He didn't know what a "Reader" was. "Is that relevant to this conversation?" he forced himself to ask.

Slayter, now toying with the brass dragon, finally looked up, seemingly startled. "Oh, well... it certainly could be. Actually, knowing Lorelle, it is. The Readers are the keepers of ancient knowledge since... Well, as far back as recorded time. If anyone has an artifact like a Plunnos, it would be them."

"And these Readers are in the city?"

"They certainly could be. They're probably all over the place. Most people think the Readers vanished a long time ago, if they think about Readers at all, but I'm fairly positive that the Readers still exist yet remain hidden."

"That's a helpful bit of information," Khyven said, trying to keep his temper. It was so helpful, in fact, Slayter should have mentioned it the moment Rhenn had vanished.

"In fact..." Slayter turned the brass dragon left and right, inspecting it from both sides. "Anything crafted by Giants, if it still exists, could be stewarded by the Readers. It's the kind of thing they would do. I heard of a Reader who possessed a working Dragon's Chain."

"A what?"

"You've never heard of a Dragon's Chain? It's a powerful artifact made by the Giants, of course, long ago and with such vast and powerful magic it makes me shiver. A Dragon's Chain has the power to trap and keep an elder dragon. Isn't that amazing? An elder dragon." He glanced up at Khyven. "And the trigger is so uncomplicated, even you could do it. It was just a simple chain with a manacle at one end. You snap it on the back of the dragon's leg and that's it. The magic in the Dragon's Chain came to life, so powerful it could actually hold the dragon, would hold it for eternity no matter how many spells the dragon cast, no matter how he clawed at it." Slayter set the weight down, marveling at it as though it was actually a mythical Dragon's Chain. "Unless, of course, you touched the dragon. Once you clamped the manacle on, you couldn't touch the beast. If you laid even a finger on it, the spell would break, and it would instantly devour you because—"

"Slayter," Khyven interrupted. "Does this Dragon's Chain have anything to do with Lorelle?"

Slayter blinked, then chuckled. "Well, no. Why would a Dragon's Chain have anything to do with Lorelle?"

Khyven sighed.

"We're talking about Lorelle," Vohn said through his teeth.

"Oh, the Plunnos!" Slayter said.

"Yes, the Plunnos."

"Well, she's probably doing exactly what she said she would do. I'd say she's hunting for Readers, looking for a Plunnos. She mentioned something about kicking and choking a thief, as I recall."

"And you didn't think to tell us?" Vohn asked.

"Should I have?"

Vohn was exasperated. "Yes, you should have. She's not acting normal!"

"Am I to know this?" Slayter looked from Khyven back to Vohn. "I thought maybe she was bloodthirsty."

"What?" Vohn said incredulously. "She's a Luminent!"

"Well, Khyven is," Slayter said. "You don't seem angry about that."

"Lorelle is not Khyven."

"I'm *not* bloodthirsty," Khyven interjected.

"How do you *know* she's not bloodthirsty?" Slayter ignored Khyven's statement.

"I'm not bloodthirsty," Khyven repeated.

"She uses a blowgun," Vohn said.

"And?" Slayter said, nonplussed.

"With sleeping potion on the darts."

"So?"

"Why do you think she does that?" Vohn practically shouted.

"Style?" Slayter offered.

"She doesn't kill people," Vohn said. "She's never killed anyone in her life."

"Well, now I know that," Slayter said.

"What's a Reader?" Khyven tried to turn the conversation back to something useful.

"A secret order." Vohn glanced at Khyven, though the little Shadowvar looked like he wanted to continue glaring at Slayter. "Keepers of lore. Librarians with a secret handshake."

"Librarians?"

"And most of them are mages," Slayter interjected.

"Most? How many mages are we talking about?" Before Khyven had actually seen behind the throne, in all its imperfect workings, he'd thought King Vamreth had two dozen mages in the castle working with him in secret. In reality, Slayter was almost unique. He had an apprentice he described as "an incompetent duke's son whose cranium is comprised primarily of wood." There was also an ancient mage who Slayter had described as "a mediocre talent in his prime. In his dotage, a doorstop."

That Slayter was the only real mage in the palace explained, in part, why his deception of King Vamreth had been so successful. The king hadn't *wanted* to believe Slayter was a traitor. He'd needed him too much.

"I thought mages were as rare as an ice storm in summer," Khyven said.

"They are, but when you can predict the future, you can find the best talent. Readers know what we don't. That is their hallmark. And they have been at it a very long time, longer than most kingdoms have existed."

"Longer than Usara?" Vohn asked.

"Usara is very old," Slayter said.

"How is it I've never heard of the Readers before?" Khyven asked.

Slayter spread his hands. "Readers take great pains to ensure you do not. King Vamreth knew about them. And Rhenn. They might both even have had liaisons within the Order. But if Vamreth did, I didn't know about it."

"So Lorelle is looking for these Readers because she believes they have a Plunnos."

"Yes," Slayter said.

"Where would she go?"

"Probably to their hidden library in Usara," Slayter said.

"They have a hidden library in Usara?"

"Undoubtedly."

"Undoubtedly?"

"Without doubt," Slayter clarified, then narrowed his eyes as though he might have to explain the word to Khyven again. Khyven wanted to punch him.

"I mean," he said, measuring each word. "Do you know where this library is?"

"No. It's hidden."

Vohn snapped his fingers. "The interrogation of the thief. That's why she did it. Slayter, did she mention a name?"

"Zenghi," Slayter supplied. "A thief master, now that I think of it. She said she interrogated a thief master."

"And he's a Reader?" Khyven said.

Both Slayter and Vohn turned disappointed frowns at Khyven like he'd said something stupid.

"No, he's a thief." Slayter continued. "But thieves go everywhere. He probably knows where the Readers' hidden library is."

"So, we interrogate Zenghi again," Khyven said. "Find out where she went."

"I have no doubt you'd scare him more than Lorelle," Vohn said. "But you'd probably also kill him."

"I don't just go around killing people!"

Vohn began ticking off fingers. "Txomin, Ferbasi, a half dozen of Vamreth's knights at Rhenn's camp, most of Vamreth's honor guard in the Thuros room, at least fifty people in the Night Ring—"

"That's not—I'm not bloodthirsty," Khyven said. "And I didn't kill Ferbasi."

Vohn rolled his eyes.

"Well, bloodthirsty or not, Lorelle wouldn't wait," Slayter said. "So, whatever she intended to do, I would guess it's already done. And since she's not at this meeting, I would speculate one of two things has happened: either she has the Plunnos or the Readers killed her."

"Killed her?"

"That is the most likely," Slayter confirmed.

"They didn't kill her!" Vohn flared.

"Oh, they probably did," Slayter said. "Even I know you don't steal from Readers. They kill you."

"How can you be so callous?" Vohn said.

Slayter raised his shoulders. "I'm just stating the likeliest possibilities."

"Well, we need to find this place and we need to find it now. She's in danger. I mean, if she'd found the Plunnos, she'd be at this meeting," Khyven said.

"Oh, I hardly think so," Slayter said. "She'd be at the Thuros. If she was successful—unlikely, but let's just say—then she wouldn't wait."

That realization smacked Khyven like an iron pan to the head. "Of course!"

"You could have just said that," Vohn said.

"I *did* say that."

"In the beginning!"

Slayter opened his mouth, then shut it. "Should I have?"

"Slayter!" Vohn snapped. "Yes, damn it!"

"Oh." Slayter seemed genuinely mystified. "Well, now I know that."

"So, she could be there right now," Khyven said. "At the Thuros. She could be trying to use the Plunnos to go wherever Rhenn went."

"Assuming she didn't die," Slayter said.

Khyven pushed away from the table and headed for the door.

"Khyven—" Vohn said.

Khyven slammed through the door and sprinted up the hallway.

CHAPTER FIVE

LORELLE

L orelle climbed the dark, winding steps up from the Thuros room. She should be sprinting. She should return to the library and throttle that Reader, but she couldn't muster any rage at the moment. The heart had gone out of her.

The Plunnos didn't work.

It hadn't opened the portal. Lorelle had flicked it at the surface like she'd seen Nhevaz do. She'd pressed it against the surface. She'd slid it around in a circle, clockwise and counterclockwise. She'd hammered the damn giant coin against the portal so hard she'd scarred and dented it. Her knuckles were scraped and bruised.

She reached the top of the stairs, pushed through the painting into the study, and fell to her knees and pushed her hands against her head. It didn't work!

Her ragged soul chewed at her insides with flaming teeth. Only the piercing need to find her sister rose above the pain, but it was slowly being engulfed.

It was possible Rhenn was dead, anyway. Whatever Nhevaz had in mind for her, surely two weeks was enough time to carry it out.

Dead… like Lorelle's family was dead. Like Rhenn's family was dead.

The last thing Lorelle wanted at this moment was to think of that night, but it came anyway, the last conversation she'd ever had with her parents…

◆ ◆ ◆

"I heard something today, dewdrop," Mother said as she arranged her dress on the hangar, making sure every fold hung just so.

Lorelle's heart sank. She knew immediately what it was going to be. Yesterday Rhenn had taken Rogan, the stable master's son, behind the stables. It was all because Lorelle had said something she shouldn't have in a moment of confession: she'd never kissed a boy before. Rhenn had thought that was simply a crime, and despite Lorelle's protests, she'd been determined to remedy it.

So, with Lorelle in tow, Rhenn had dragged the clueless Rogan behind the stables and planted a kiss full on his lips, showing Lorelle how to do it. The boy had turned beet red as Rhenn turned to Lorelle and said, "Now you try." Lorelle had hesitated. It was then that Rogan's father, Stablemaster Vhendin, had come around the corner and caught them. Laughing, Rhenn had grabbed Lorelle's hand and fled.

Lorelle swallowed, glad that Mother was turned away. Lorelle knew she wouldn't be able to meet her gaze.

"Can you guess who told it to me?" Mother asked.

"Master Vhendin," Lorelle said glumly.

"Master Vhendin," Mother agreed.

"I didn't kiss him."

"The boy?"

"Rogan. I didn't kiss him," Lorelle said.

Mother paused arranging the pleats and glanced over at Lorelle. There were many rules in a Luminent household, but foremost among them was telling the truth. Lorelle had never lied to her parents. Not once. But Mother looked like she was trying to decide if this was the first time.

"You almost did," Mother said.

Lorelle couldn't refute that. She probably *would* have kissed Rogan if his father hadn't come along. Rhenn would have insisted, and Lorelle found it hard to say no whenever Rhenn insisted.

"Would that have been so bad?" Lorelle murmured.

"For a Human, no," Mother said. "You are a Luminent."

"Rhenn insisted," Lorelle said, but as soon as she heard the words aloud, she felt heat in her cheeks and realized how silly the words sounded.

"Of course, she did. She is the princess of this kingdom. This—these kinds of situations—is one of many reasons we brought you here. We want you to experience new and different cultures."

"Then I don't understand."

"Just because you're friends with a Human doesn't mean you act like a Human."

"I don't know," Father said conversationally from the other side of the room, entering the discussion late in his usual fashion. Father never spoke first; it was always Mother who reprimanded Lorelle, who calmly laid out the expectations of a Luminent in Human lands, then Father would jump in and offer a more moderate perspective. Almost always, he was on Lorelle's side, which she loved. She thought this should annoy Mother, but it never seemed to. Mother always looked placid.

It wouldn't occur to Lorelle until much later that her parents had planned these coming-of-age conversations.

"Now is the time for her to be a little wild," Father continued. "She's eleven."

"Eleven," Mother said calmly, giving a critical eye to the dress as though it was her top priority and this conversation was a distant second. "And next year she'll be twelve. And the year after that, thirteen. Will we leave her naked against the world? Or do we give her the skills she needs *before* the critical moment she needs them?"

"You're probably right," Father said. "But she's not in danger of going through the Change today, is she? Perhaps we start in a couple of weeks?"

Mother hung the dress in the wardrobe, gave the line of dresses a last appraising look, as though they should live up to her expectations, then closed the wardrobe door. She glided to the bed and sat down.

Lorelle came closer as though drawn by gravity. Mother always did this. When she sat down, it meant Lorelle now had her full attention, and Lorelle loved Mother's full attention. It always felt warm and full of love, even though it often came with lessons. She stood before Mother, her hip bones pressing against Mother's knees. Mother took both Lorelle's hands in hers.

"The Change will be difficult," Mother said. "But your control will be superior to it. We will help you. We will show you how Luminents master their gifts and therefore their world. By this time next year we will be back in Lumyn so that, when the Change comes upon you, you will be among your kind. At that point, you will get to choose a mate and you will soul-bond."

"But I don't want a mate. I just want to play with Rhenn. The only reason Rogan was a part of it was because I told Rhenn I'd never kissed anyone. He isn't usually there."

Mother's warm and genuine smile filled Lorelle. There was also a kind indulgence in the look, like she recognized Lorelle's words as if they were an old friend she had known a long time ago. Lorelle suddenly wondered if a mother had said these same words—or something similar to them—to her when *she* was a child.

"Of course, you don't," Mother said. "As well you shouldn't. But the Change will come swiftly when it comes, and you will feel different before you realize it, before you even want to realize it. By then we must be safely back in Luminent lands so you may choose."

"I have to leave Rhenn? Why can't I just choose a Human mate? Why not Rogan?"

Mother glanced at Father, for the first time with a flicker of concern. It was quick and gone in an instant, but Lorelle saw it.

"Luminents cannot choose a Human mate," Mother said calmly.

"Why not?"

"We are not… compatible."

"What does that mean?"

"Human souls are different. It is *possible* to join with a Human, but very dangerous. For generations Luminents have honed their souls specifically for the exchange of the soul-bond. Humans have not. In attempting to bond with a Human, even if they tried their best, only a fraction of your soul could make that bond. The rest would be left frayed and burning, and it would eventually shrivel and die, taking you with it. For a Human, the consequences of this failure are small. But the price for us is catastrophic."

"Isn't there another way? Perhaps I could find another way, bond with something other than a Human, something with a larger soul, and set myself free?"

Mother hesitated. She glanced over Lorelle's shoulder at Father again. Lorelle craned her neck and caught Father's hesitation, then he nodded.

Mother looked at Lorelle again. "Lorelle, this is the way. It is the Luminent way. It is the only way. And there is danger in thinking what you are now thinking, though you may not know it. When Lotura created the Luminents long ago, he imbued them with great powers. Our ability to see at a great distance. Our ability to hear things no Human can hear." Mother delicately touched the point of Lorelle's right ear. "And Lotura put the light of the sun within us. It lifts us up, such that we are not drawn so strongly by the earth like other races."

"That's why I can jump so much higher than Rhenn."

Mother nodded.

"And my hair glows when I'm happy. Or sad."

"Just so. But these gifts, they come with a price. Control and vigilance. We must maintain control over our soul-bond or we can lose our way, we can fall from the light."

"Rhenn doesn't have to maintain control."

Again, Mother hesitated, but she didn't look at Father this time. Instead, she asked solemnly, "Do you remember the stories of the Nox?"

"The bad Luminents," Lorelle whispered. Mother and Father had only told her one story about the Nox, about how they were a group of Luminents who had turned evil. They left Luminent society to live in the noktum. Their glowing hair and fair skin had turned as black as coal and they had vanished within the noktum, never to be seen again. But Lorelle had heard half a dozen other stories from her friends in Lumyn before her family had come to Usara. The Nox were still in the noktum somewhere, and from time to time they would emerge into the world of daylight and steal children because they couldn't have children of their own. She heard that the Nox killed Humans and feasted on their bones with teeth as sharp as needles. "Are the Nox really real?"

Mother nodded. "They were Luminents who did not listen to Lotura's warning. They sought other ways to use their soul-bond and the darkness took them. You see, a Luminent who relaxes her control becomes a slave to her own passions and to her own powers. Once those powers are wild, they will pull her in directions she does not wish to go. The Nox were pulled into the darkness. Do you understand?"

Lorelle nodded, her eyes wide.

"I do not say this to scare you, little dewdrop, only to remind you that we are different from your friend Rhenn. As Luminents, we stand upon a bright but narrow bridge. If we stray too far to one side or the other, we will fall. Like the Nox."

Lorelle nodded again.

"Remember…" Mother squeezed Lorelle's hands, "you must master the situation on your own. You cannot rely on Humans to do it for you because they will not. They are not bound by the same rules. Only when you have achieved this mastery can you then help others. Your mastery. Not Rhenn's. Not Rogan's. Not mine nor your father's.

"Control and mastery will allow you to do wondrous things. It will protect you and those you love. It will allow you to take your own destiny in hand, to shape and mold the world around you in ways Humans cannot even dream. Lose that control and the darkness will find you. The darkness hungers for our kind. Never forget."

"Yes, Mother."

Mother moved her hands lightly up to Lorelle's shoulders, gave them a squeeze. "I want you to let my words sit. Think about them, and do not worry. Your father and I have already mastered this control and we are looking out for you. We will begin your training in earnest in…" She glanced at Father.

"Two weeks," he said.

"Two weeks," Mother agreed.

"Thank you, Mother."

"Now off to bed. A Luminent also needs her sleep." Mother winked.

Lorelle scampered off to bed…

❖ ❖ ❖

Lorelle opened her eyes and the memory dissipated. That had been the last time she'd talked to her parents. That night, Vamreth had attacked the palace.

Since then, not a single day had passed that Lorelle hadn't heeded Mother's advice. Even hand in hand with Rhenn, through that first terrifying trip through the noktum and the ten years of rebellion that followed, Lorelle had managed her and her situation. Control and mastery. Not a day went by that she hadn't kept herself and her world in complete control. Not a single day…

Save one.

The night Rhenn was taken Lorelle had let her mastery slip. She'd indulged in fantasies of Khyven, of a life with a Human.

She'd imagined him overcoming the impossible and overturning the laws of Luminent biology just as he'd overturned Vamreth's rule in Usara. She'd believed it because Rhenn believed it. She'd slipped and seen herself as Human, and she'd forgotten Mother's wisdom. She was a Luminent. Control and mastery alone had to guide her.

And Rhenn had paid the price.

Lorelle saw the truth now. She saw what should have happened that night. If she had maintained mastery over her emotions and the situation, she'd have been alert. If she hadn't been indulging in fantasies she had no right to indulge, she'd have noticed that the Thuros was acting strangely and would have pulled Rhenn from that room immediately. She'd have had her blowgun with her, at the ready. She'd have darted that bastard Nhevaz before he'd had a chance to move. She'd have been ready as a shield for her friend.

She went to the window and looked out at the dark, starless night as despair tried to drag her down. She felt like she couldn't catch her breath.

I should have kept my own counsel, she thought. *Not been swayed by Rhenn. I should have remembered that, in the end, I am the only Luminent and no one here—not Rhenn or Khyven or even Slayter or Vohn—can help me with that.*

But she was still alive. So, it was still possible to take control of the situation. No one else would be hurt again because of her lapses. What Khyven wanted, what Vohn and Slayter wanted, didn't matter anymore. She couldn't allow her need for them, or their need for her, to confuse her. If she maintained mastery, she could retrieve Rhenn. Lorelle could set things right. And she was close. This frustration and despair were just distractions. She *had* the Plunnos. She had the key. She must take it in hand and *force* it to work—

Her keen ears caught the sound of footsteps pounding up the hall. Someone was coming. One person.

Khyven.

No. He couldn't find her. Not now. Not when she was so weak.

She took a quiet breath and stepped into the shadows as Khyven reached the door.

CHAPTER SIX

LORELLE

Lorelle inwardly cursed her luck. Why was Khyven coming here, now, panicked like he had to hurry?

Because he thought she was going away. Because someone had put together that Lorelle had found a Plunnos, so of course he was rushing to catch her before she could use it to vanish through the Thuros and leave him behind.

Slayter had probably put it together. It had to be. He was the last one she'd talked to, and the mage was a genius at associating seemingly random elements to make a picture. Now Khyven was coming to save her. Or stop her. Or join her.

The ragged edges of her soul burned as he approached.

She almost gave in. She almost ran to him, kissed him, wrapped herself around him.

Lotura, it would be so easy.

Then she saw Rhenn in her mind's eye. She envisioned her sister holding her hand as they fled through the noktum as children. She saw Rhenn at their camp, raising her head with that mischievous grin, glancing sidelong at Lorelle and making a crude joke about men and spears. She felt Rhenn's arms around her, hugging her as she fought to keep her emotions locked away, Luminent hair glimmering gold.

"No…" Lorelle growled softly. Rhenn wasn't dead. Not yet. She wasn't dead until Lorelle saw a body. Until then, she had to fight.

She flipped her cowl up just as Khyven burst through the door. Her soul burned hotter, searing her, and she clenched her teeth.

"Lorelle!" He looked straight at the open painting-door. She forced herself to remain still while he practically dove down the stairs. "Lorelle!" he shouted again inside the tight spiral of the staircase. He shouted her name again, his voice fading as he descended the steps.

She gave one last, longing look toward the opening, then she moved to the window and climbed out. She clambered easily onto the roof and ran swiftly across the clay tiles.

She dropped from one level of the palace to the next as she reached the northern wing, finally leaping to the top of the wall and over, into the city.

The darkness of the alleys fit her mood, so she stuck to them, wending aimlessly through the crown city of Usara. Slowly, the fierce flare of her incomplete soul faded to a dull burn.

"It's not real…" a whisper said from behind her.

She spun and scanned the alley. Nothing moved. Only the still, squat hulks of a half dozen broken wood barrels filled with rotting lettuce and carrots tops, boot scraps, and torn strips of grimy cloth. No bulges in the shadows where a bulge shouldn't be.

Someone had crept up behind her. Except that was impossible. Humans were far too loud and slow to sneak up on her.

She scanned the roofline two stories above—

And spotted something.

The night was dark, a starless sky, but her Luminent night vision picked out an irregular bulge against the roofline. Someone was trying to hide there.

She reached back with her left hand and unholstered her blowgun. Quick and fluid, she brought the long tube to her lips and blew.

The bulge vanished and the dart soared over the edge of the building, just missing whoever it was. For a split second, she thought the intruder had pulled back, then she heard the soft *thump* as someone landed in the darkness ahead of her, deeper into the alley.

She crouched and loaded another dart. They had jumped from the roof! They'd jumped and landed more softly than even she could have managed. How was that even possible? Who was this Human?

She still couldn't see anyone, so she raised her blowgun to the precise point where she'd heard the thump and said, "Come out, or I *will* shoot you."

"Are you always hostile to the well-meaning?" the soft voice emerged from the dark.

"Who are you?"

"A friend."

"I don't need a friend."

The voice laughed.

"If you mean no harm, step out of the shadows and let me see you," she said.

"You should already be able to see me, Lorelle," the voice replied. "Maybe you need to step *into* the shadows."

She paused. "How do you know my name?"

"I know a lot about you."

She shot a dart in the direction of the voice. It vanished into the shadows and clinked ineffectually against bricks.

"You're pointing in the wrong direction," the voice whispered, now suddenly to her left, by her ear.

She spun and leapt back, loaded a dart and shot in a single, smooth motion. Again, the dart clinked on the wall, wasted. She hadn't even seen him move! Hadn't heard the slightest footstep.

The chuckle came again from the depths of the alley, and she peered down its length.

"I am your friend," the voice said. "Though you don't know it yet. And when you turn away from your friends, you sacrifice their knowledge, their strength, and what they can show you."

She loaded and pointed again but didn't shoot. She needed a secondary confirmation, something other than his voice. She needed a glimpse of something, anything.

But there was only darkness.

"You don't have to be confused," the voice came from her left again, and she jumped backward, landing lightly ten feet away. A Human simply could not hide in the dark. Not from her. How was he doing this? Was this a Reader mage?

His chuckle came from the depths of the alley again. "I will stop toying with you, but you must admit to your need."

"What need?"

"You struggle. Lost. Alone. Torn. Burning. What you need is family."

"You're *not* my family."

"Only your *true* family can help you with what lies ahead."

"And what is that?"

"Transformation."

"I have no intention of transforming," she said, wincing as the burn in her chest flared.

"Oh, but you do. You already are. The only question is, will you emerge alive?"

"Who are you?" she demanded.

The darkness in the center of the alley seemed to… coalesce, as though it was being compressed, growing darker somehow, then it suddenly lightened and a silhouette formed.

The man was tall, slender, and broad-shouldered. He wore a cloak that covered him from head to ankle and he threw back the cowl to reveal his face.

Lorelle gasped.

His ears were tall and pointed, but his eyes, his skin, his long hair were all as black as the night sky between the stars, as black as the noktum. He looked like a Luminent swallowed by shadows.

He was a Nox.

CHAPTER SEVEN

LORELLE

eware the Nox...

Beware the Nox...
A chill ran through Lorelle. The Reader's warning had seemed like gibberish when she'd spoken it, and yet now this creature stood before her.

Slowly, she rose from her crouch. Her hair glimmered like gold reflecting sunlight.

"Your time grows short," the Nox said, slipping from the shadows like he was floating. Lorelle had become so used to the way Humans clomped around that it stole her breath to watch the Nox move. She wondered if Humans saw her this way. Untouchable. A wisp of wind. His black cloak trailed behind him, still clinging to the shadows.

"Who are you?" she repeated.

"Your friend. Your family."

"You're a Nox."

"So, you do recognize me. That's a start." He tipped his chin at her. "Your hair is glowing."

"It does that when I'm suspicious."

"Ah... So, you cannot control it."

Heat crept into her cheeks and her hair glimmered brighter. She tensed, but tried not to show him how rattled she was. She was easily a match for just about any Human, but she had never fought someone with Luminent abilities before. He could have snuck up behind her, stabbed her with a dagger, and she wouldn't have known it until her heart was pierced.

She searched her memory for the scant scraps she could remember about the Nox. The only thing that resounded over and over was that they were evil.

Beware the Nox, Lorelle... The Reader's words echoed in her mind again.

"What do you really know about your people, Lorelle? Luminents," he murmured. "You're running around on rooftops, threatening Humans, but I suspect you know very little about your true potential."

She raised her chin. "And you're going to tell me, I suppose," she said, gauging his movement. She didn't like how this conversation had spiraled out of her control. But he'd made a mistake. He'd revealed himself, and that was all she'd needed.

Quick as a blink, she lifted the blowgun and shot at him.

He became a blur, his cloak swirling, and the dart vanished into its darkness. He closed the distance between them so quickly she barely had time to move. He grabbed her fist holding the blowgun and twisted. She gasped as pain shot through her wrist and she dropped the weapon.

She spun, twisted out of his grip, and leapt twelve feet backward into the alley. In midair, she deftly unsheathed her dagger—

The Nox was gone.

"Your speed impresses the Humans, I bet," he whispered, his words tickling her ear.

She lurched sideways, but his hand closed over her fist again, forcing the dagger up. Lorelle wasn't a brawler like Rhenn or Khyven, but she threw an elbow at his face anyway.

He blocked it. "If running on rooftops and impressing Humans is enough for you," he whispered, "just say so and I'll leave."

She yanked her hand free. His cloak swirled about him, and he seemed to melt into the shadows.

She hunted for him, gripping her knife as she turned and turned. The Nox reappeared at the mouth of the alley.

Lorelle's hair brightened and a cold certainty oozed over her scalp: she was no match for this Nox. Not even a little. He wasn't a slow and bumbling Human. He was every bit as fast as her, and he possessed magic she didn't understand.

She couldn't fight him, and she couldn't run. He could catch her. He'd caught her twice already.

She suddenly wished Khyven were here. She'd spent the last weeks doing anything to avoid him, but of all the people she knew only Khyven might be a match for this man. He had magic, too, a knack for making impossible challenges possible.

"I think you are beginning to comprehend where we stand if this were a real fight. So, no more games. I'm here to help you, Lorelle, whether you believe me or not," the Nox said. "Your Luminent parents raised you to be blind and deaf. I can show you how to open your eyes and lengthen your ears. Am I wasting my time?"

Lorelle felt like she was spinning.

"I watched you bang that coin against the gateway. Do you want to know why it didn't work?" he asked.

A cold foreboding filled her. He had been there. He'd been in the palace, in the Thuros room, and she'd never noticed him.

"Why?" she said.

"Because it's a fake," he said in a stage whisper.

She thrust her hand into the pouch and pulled out the Plunnos. "I took this off a Reader."

"I know."

She swallowed. He had been there, too! How long had he been watching her?

He seemed to read her mind. "Yes, I have been following you. I wanted to see what kind of woman you are."

"It's not a fake," she said through her teeth, clutching the coin in her hand. She just couldn't believe that. It *had* to work.

"Look at it. Look at the scrapes on it."

She glanced down at the scars on the coin, the scratches and dents she'd made slamming it against the Thuros.

"A Plunnos is one of the most powerful artifacts the Giants ever made," the Nox said. "No sword or axe or hammer made by mortals could scar it. Only five mages working the five streams at once could hope to affect it. Do you really think *you* could dent it like soft gold?"

"The Reader said—" Lorelle whispered.

"Did she?" He interrupted her with a wry smile. "What else did she say?"

She could barely breathe. He'd heard the Reader's warning.

"Readers want you to jump at glimmers. They want you to look at their left hand so you don't see what they're doing with their right. So, if you want to listen to her, go ahead. Go back and bang that coin against the Thuros. You'll get the same results."

Hot shame warmed her cheeks.

"This is your choice. Stumble about, blind in the dark, or let me teach you how to see. You want a Plunnos? I'll take you to one." He held out his hand.

Her heart hammered.

She glanced down at the Plunnos clutched in her hand. Had the Reader lied? Or was the Nox lying to her now?

"I see you need time to think," the Nox said. "I will offer you three chances. This was the first." His cloak of shadows swirled as he turned.

"Wait!" She raced after him. He turned the corner before she could reach him, and she dashed after, emerging from the alley into the darkened street. It was empty.

The only thing she saw was a hundred silent, mocking shadows.

CHAPTER EIGHT

KHYVEN

Khyven slowly climbed up the steps and walked the long hallway back to the meeting room. He hadn't found Lorelle. He'd run to the Thuros room, but she hadn't been there. He had, however, found a sleeping pallet and some blankets. She'd been sleeping in that room, beneath that eerie archway. That he, Slayter, and Vohn didn't know that didn't bode well. Lorelle was slipping away from them.

Plagued by his thoughts, Khyven silently opened the door to the meeting room and found Vohn and Slayter arguing, as usual.

"... not to mention you have two outsiders running the kingdom," Slayter was saying in his lackadaisical way.

"Outsiders?" Vohn bristled. The Shadowvar was facing away from the door and Slayter, if he noticed Khyven at all, was too involved with what he was saying to care.

"A glimmery Luminent and a shadowy Shadowvar," the mage said. "Running a Human kingdom. Outsiders."

"Lorelle has been at the queen's side since the usurper killed her parents, and I've been with the queen for years!"

Slayter waved that away. "I'm not talking about loyalty. I'm not talking about truth. I'm talking about perception. Those people out there—" he waved a vague hand at the wall "—they look at you and see horns. Your noktum-y skin. They think Shadowvar are demons. Vicious, brutal, violent eaters of Human flesh."

"My culture is far more peaceful than any Human civilization!"

"No need to convince me. I know that. They don't. Even if they could get their sluggish thoughts to come 'round to the truth, do you think they care that Shadowvar culture is more peaceful than ours? No. They care that you look different, that you have horns and they don't. Someone says 'a demon sits on the throne' and they believe it. Because they want to."

"I've never sat the throne."

"It's a metaphor."

"Well, you can take your metaphor and—" Vohn finally noticed Khyven standing in the doorway and cut himself off. "Khyven! Did you find her?"

Khyven shook his head. "She had been there. She's been sleeping in that room, apparently. But she wasn't there when I arrived."

"Do you think she used the Thuros?"

"I don't know," Khyven said.

"No," Slayter said.

Vohn turned an annoyed look at him.

"The last time the Thuros was used it tripped my guardian spell."

"When Rhenn was abducted," Khyven said.

"Correct. And now I've specifically set a guardian spell next to the Thuros, just in case this Nhevaz returns. If she'd successfully opened it, I'd know."

"Then the Readers have her?" Vohn asked.

"It is one of the possibilities."

"I hate this." Khyven clenched his fists. "She could be in trouble and we have no way to find her."

"I could put a tracking spell on her," Slayter said.

"You can?" Khyven perked up.

"It will take a little time, but yes."

"But then… what if she *isn't* in danger?" Khyven asked.

Slayter looked blankly at Khyven.

"My point is, I don't think she'd like being tracked; us using magic against her," Khyven said.

"Against her?" Vohn said. "We're using it *for* her. She's acting irrational. I, for one, think we might be past what she likes or doesn't like. She isn't talking to us. The most responsible thing we can do is to find out what she's up to and where she is. She certainly isn't telling us."

"Her recent transformation has been intriguing," Slayter mused.

"By Grina, not everything is an intellectual exercise for you, Slayter!" Vohn blurted. "Something's gone wrong with her."

Slayter raised an eyebrow as though he didn't understand why Vohn was upset.

"Rhenn's disappearance has been hard on her, that's all," Khyven said, but his gut told him Vohn had the truth of it.

"Have you considered alternate theories?" Slayter asked.

"Slayter—" Vohn began.

"I mean, aside from the trauma of Rhenn's abduction, could something else have caused a change in her personality?"

"What do you mean?" Vohn asked.

"Well, there are four major thresholds in a Luminent lifespan. Each can profoundly change a Luminent's personality."

"You mean like life stages?" Khyven asked.

"Exactly like life stages. Except with Humans, the only predicable threshold is from childhood to adulthood. There is a general two- to four-year age span in which that Human transformation happens. All other Human life stages happen at wildly different times for each individual because they are linked with social behavior and opportunity more than with physical makeup. But with Luminents, everything is tied to their bodies. Their developmental thresholds are all very predictable based on age, and not only do these transformations profoundly affect their bodies, but each comes with a magical discharge."

"Discharge?" Vohn asked.

"Luminent bodies are magical."

"What are the thresholds?" Khyven asked.

"The Change, the Soul-bond, the Birthing Cycle, and the Release."

Khyven held up a hand, trying to keep his temper as he realized this might just be a fascinating brain teaser for the mage. "Slayter, does this matter to what we're talking about?"

"I think she bonded," Slayter said.

"What?" Vohn said.

"Bonded. Mated. Paired." Slayter threw out alternate words.

"I know what it means," Vohn growled.

"Oh." Slayter looked confused. "Then why—"

"Bonded?" Khyven said. "You mean the Luminent bond?"

"Ah, you know of it," Slayter said.

"Rhenn told me," Khyven said. "But I thought a Luminent could only bond with another Luminent."

"Wait," Vohn said. "You actually think Lorelle has soul-bonded with someone?"

"Just so," Slayter said. "It makes sense."

"It makes no sense," Vohn said. "There are no other Luminents in Usara."

"Luminents *are* known to stay within the borders of their kingdom, but odds dictate there must be at least a few wandering about."

Vohn shook his head. "Impossible."

Slayter raised an eyebrow again. "It's actually the most natural, possible thing I can think of. Mating rituals and all. Look at Humans. They'll bond whenever they—"

"You're telling me," Vohn interrupted, "that amidst the battle and the coup, the abduction of Rhenn and our subsequent cover-up, she found time to fall in love with some Luminent and bond with him? Where? When? Who is this mystery Luminent?"

"Actually, it's probably not a Luminent," Slayter said. "With the loss of her best friend and the subsequent turmoil, Lorelle's emotions have been running at a peak. I'd wager she accidentally bonded with some Human. A failed bonding. A random accident."

Khyven's heart sank. "She wouldn't do that. Not Lorelle. She has more control than anyone I've ever met."

"Let's look at the facts," Slayter said. "Most Luminents stay in their kingdom of Laria, surrounded by other Luminents. If you're a normal Luminent, young and unbonded and you undergo emotional distress, the Luminents around you take note and take steps to protect you from an accidental bond. An accidental soul-bonding in Laria is rare, I would wager. But an accidental bonding could easily happen here. Let's imagine Lorelle was surrounded by a series of factors likely to cause trauma. Like being immersed in a swirling pot of emotionally volatile Humans. Like staging a coup and toppling a kingdom. Like losing your best friend to a Thuros-traveler with Line Magic."

"How can you be so casual about this!" Vohn barked.

"Casual?" Slayter said.

"Would you two stop fighting?" Khyven said. "What does this mean for Lorelle? The way Rhenn described a failed bonding, it... It's not good."

"Oh, it certainly isn't. Imagine ripping your body in half and giving that half to someone. First, it would be excruciating. Second, you'd bleed all over the place. Third, you'd die. But then imagine there's one thing that can save you: if the recipient of your gift rips themselves in half and gives you half of their body in return. Then imagine if they don't. Rather than connecting with half of their body, you cauterize your remaining half instead. You might live for a time. But it wouldn't be pleasant. And it wouldn't be long."

"That's grisly." Vohn looked horrified.

"Now replace every time I said 'body' with 'soul,' and that will give you a good idea what Lorelle is going through."

The front of Khyven's head began to throb. A failed soul-bond would explain a lot. Why Lorelle was distancing herself from them. Why she was so single-minded about finding Rhenn. If Lorelle thought she was dying, she would drive for her goal like an Imprevari ox.

"You're saying she's going to die?" Khyven said.

"Yes, but probably not quickly," Slayter said. "It's the soul, not the body. She'll likely start with a fracturing of her personality. At first, she won't quite act like herself, then she'll settle into her new role as her life light fades."

"New role?"

"From what I've read, a Luminent attaches to the first powerful emotion that strikes her *after* the failed bonding. Most commonly depression. Then, once that sets in, they drift toward the dregs of society. Usually Human society. They can't stand to be around normal Luminents anymore, so they end up as beggars, thieves, prostitutes… Humans pay a lot for a Luminent—"

"We get the point," Vohn said angrily.

"Lorelle does *not* seem depressed," Khyven said. She seemed enraged, actually. She had seethed beneath the surface every time he'd talked to her.

"What do we do about it?" Vohn asked.

"We help her," Khyven said.

Slayter shrugged. "A failed soul-bond is a permanent condition. It can't be undone. In the thousands of years of Luminents, there's never been a single report of a Luminent undoing a failed soul-bond."

"To Senji's hell with logic," Khyven said. "We save her. That's what we do." He felt a tightening fear for Lorelle, but he also felt ashamed, guilty for the other emotion that rose within him: jealousy. Who had Lorelle bonded with? Was there someone out there in the city right now holding half of Lorelle's soul? It made his stomach twist.

"You don't actually know that she soul-bonded," Vohn said. "You shouldn't say something like that unless you're sure." The Shadowvar shot a worried look at Khyven.

"It is the superior speculation, though. It explains many things."

"Can you stop speculating and be Human for a moment?"

"You're upset," Slayter said.

Khyven let their bickering fade into the background as he imagined Lorelle during that first day he'd awoken. He could see her leaning over him.

"I believe I owe you something."

Her soft lips pressing against his. It had been exquisite. It had felt... destined.

"For being... more than I imagined you could be."

And now she had bonded with another. Some stranger on the street who's only qualification was that he'd been standing near her when she'd lost control.

"It's a permanent condition. It can't be undone..."

Slayter's comment swam in his mind and rage built within him at the unfairness of it all. Losing the kingdom after all they'd sacrificed to take it. Losing Rhenn. Losing his new family so soon after he'd found them.

Losing Lorelle.

Khyven slammed his fist on the table. Both Vohn and Slayter stopped their argument in mid-sentence. Vohn started, and even Slayter looked surprised.

"We find a way to help Lorelle," Khyven growled.

Vohn nodded. Slayter shrugged.

It was easy to mistake Slayter's behavior as flippant or uncaring. Certainly, the easily-pricked Vohn fell for it time and again. Slayter didn't cover his knowledge in honey. But the mage had lost his leg in service to the queen and he hadn't uttered a word of complaint. For years, Slayter had hidden in the palace, practically pressed to Vamreth's breast, and he'd convinced the king he was a loyal servant so he could choose the one moment where his betrayal would mean the most. Most men couldn't keep up that kind of facade for even for a week. Khyven certainly wouldn't have been able to. Watching what Vamreth did—like cutting out poor Shalure's tongue—would have sent Khyven into a murderous rage.

A man couldn't do what Slayter had done without deep conviction.

It was because of him that Rhenn and the rest of them had survived, and Khyven would never forget that. It astounded him when he thought about it. There was a deep, powerful undercurrent to Slayter. He would do anything for Rhenn and her people. He'd proven it.

"Lorelle has served the kingdom faithfully her whole life, has served Rhenn her whole life," Khyven said. "We aren't going to turn away from her because a few books tell us that what she needs is impossible. How many times have we done the impossible together? Traveling the noktum, toppling Vamreth's reign, using Mavric Iron and the Helm of Darkness." He looked at Slayter. "Don't say 'can't' to me. The impossible is what we do."

Slayter raised his eyebrows. "Nice speech. Perhaps *you* should be king."

"We're going to help Lorelle. We're going to find Rhenn. We're going to set things right," Khyven said.

"As you say, Sir Knight." Slayter smiled wryly.

"We save Lorelle," Vohn affirmed softly. "Whatever it takes."

"Are you talking about me?" a voice interrupted.

Khyven spun and Vohn jumped.

Lorelle stood in the doorway.

CHAPTER NINE

KHYVEN

Khyven's breathing sped up at the sight of her. He felt invigorated, like a little lightning bolt had hit him. She stood in the doorway in the tight black clothes she always wore now with only her face, hands, and her pale ankles showing above her slipper-like shoes. Such attire was designed to hide a person, the garb of thieves and cutthroats. Before, Lorelle's quiet way of walking had seemed unintentional, like she couldn't help being graceful and therefore quiet. Now it seemed intentional, like she was trying to sneak about.

Dirt smudges marked her face and hands, but her golden hair looked newly washed. It always did, as though dirt couldn't cling to the magical hair of a Luminent.

She glanced at each of them in turn, then she came in and took a seat next to Slayter, which was as far from Khyven as it was possible to be and still be at the table. This was the kind of thing she did now. It was like she couldn't stand to be in the same room with him, could barely tolerate his presence. He swallowed hard.

Vohn looked uncomfortable. "Well, we were discussing…" he began, but faltered.

Slayter smiled. "We were talking about you. We wanted to know where you were."

"You were talking about how to save me," she said.

"You were listening at the door?" Khyven asked. Annoyance bubbled up inside him. "You could have come in. We're not hiding anything."

Lorelle took one look at Vohn's downcast face, then back at Khyven. "Clearly not."

"Where have you been?" Khyven asked.

"Do I report to you now, Khyven the Unkillable?" Her eyes had dark shadows underneath them, like she hadn't slept in days.

"Lorelle, we're your friends. We're trying to help you—"

"Good," she interrupted. "Where is Rhenn? Have you found her?"

"We're trying."

"And failing," she said. "Two weeks, and we still have nothing."

Khyven opened his mouth, but no words came out.

"We are doing things," Vohn said, his voice calm now that he was talking to someone other than Slayter. "Slayter has been scouring the histories for the last known locations of Plunnoi."

Lorelle's searing gaze stayed on Khyven. It was like she didn't want to look at the other two, like she blamed him for Rhenn's disappearance.

"What would you have us do?" Khyven asked.

"Do? Maybe you could have told us she'd be attacked."

"What?"

"You brought Nhevaz down upon us," she accused.

Vohn's eyes widened, and he looked at Lorelle as though she'd said the moon was purple. Slayter's smile faded, and his brows came together.

"He was unconscious," Vohn said quietly.

"Nhevaz's message was for *you*," Lorelle said to Khyven, still ignoring Vohn. She blinked, as though she was looking at a light that was too bright. She clenched and unclenched her fists like she couldn't stand to be in her own skin. "He took Rhenn and gave *you* a message."

After they'd found Lorelle and undone the spell that had frozen her, she'd told them about Nhevaz's final cryptic words: *"He lived, and that means things will move quickly now."*

"We don't know that was about Khyven," Vohn said. "It's only speculation. Why would he say that to—"

"Who cares why!" She stood up, knocking the chair over. "If Khyven had died, Nhevaz wouldn't have come for Rhenn!"

"Maybe I should have died, then," Khyven said softly.

She lifted her chin and he saw tears in her eyes. She turned away, like she wanted to banish them all from the room by simply not looking at them. One fist clenched at her side and the other moved up to push at her chest, massaging it like it was bruised.

She turned back and let out a strained breath. "I didn't mean that," she whispered, swallowing hard. "I-I don't mean that, Khyven."

She stumbled back, disoriented, looking clumsy for the first time Khyven had ever seen.

He came around the table, wanting to help her, to hold her in his arms, but Vohn was already there steadying her.

"It's all right," he said soothingly. "It's going to be all right."

She glanced at Khyven, sorrow in her eyes. She opened her mouth as if she was about to apologize, but then turned her head away.

"Please. Sit down," Vohn said softly.

"No," she said. "No, I—You don't need me here. I can't help you here. I'll... go see about Shalure. She needs... There are herbs that can counter the *shkazat*."

She glided to the door without another word and left.

"How did she know about Shalure?" Khyven turned to Vohn.

"I think maybe she's watching us. Hiding. Listening in on our conversations," Slayter said, his head cocked to the side like he was contemplating a particularly engaging puzzle. "Her clothes are made exactly for that."

Khyven didn't want to say his next thoughts, didn't want to acknowledge them, but he said them anyway.

"I think you're right," he said to Slayter, "about the soul-bond. The way she's acting… I think you may be right."

"Why?" Vohn asked. "Because she's angry?"

"Because she's in pain," Khyven said. "Physical pain."

Vohn glanced at Slayter in surprise, then back at Khyven. "She is?"

"I've been injured enough to know when someone's trying to hide a wound. Did you see how she pressed her hand to her chest? How she could barely sit still?"

"Ah," Slayter murmured.

"If we're going to help her, we have to find this person she's bonded with," Khyven said.

"We do?"

"I want to know who it is."

"What exactly will that accomplish?" Vohn asked.

Khyven felt his cheeks grow warm when he realized he didn't have a good answer to that. He wanted to know because…

Because it wasn't him. Because Lorelle had chosen a Human to bond with and it wasn't him.

"If we're going to find out how to reverse this thing she has done to herself," he said, "we have to start somewhere."

Vohn and Slayter exchanged a glance, and were silent for a long moment.

"How are we going to do that?" Vohn finally asked. "Obviously none of us can follow her."

"I'll do it," Khyven said.

Vohn blinked. "Khyven…"

"What?"

"You're about as stealthy as a bull."

"Then I'll get better at it."

Vohn and Slayter exchanged another glance, but Khyven didn't care. And he wasn't going to wait. He turned and left the room.

CHAPTER TEN

LORELLE

Lorelle walked swiftly along the hall and leapt up the steps until she reached the next floor.

She was a fool. She should never have gone to the meeting. It was increasingly pointless, and dangerous. Being that close to Khyven nearly drove her mad from the pain, and she could barely manage it already without tempting fate.

She paused at the door to Shalure's room, bowed her head, and pushed inside. The room was dark, and Lorelle breathed a long sigh. She didn't know why, but the darkness soothed her pain, just a little. She far preferred darkness to daylight these days for that sole reason.

She looked down at the half-dreaming Shalure, sprawled on the bed. The baron's daughter had removed her clothes and Lorelle saw a fresh tattoo on the woman.

Lorelle moved closer to look at the illustration on the angry red flesh. It couldn't have been made more than a day ago. It was a beast of some kind. It had the face of a barn owl with Shadowvar-like horns sprouting from its head. Its body was that of a powerful cat—like a Kyolar—with skeletal wings reaching up from its back and surrounded by an inky mist.

The image of the creature coiled around Shalure's arm, the rear of its body resting along her back. The claws curled around Shalure's upper arm like black bracelets, and the owl head rested on her shoulder, seeming to look directly at Lorelle.

She had no idea if this was an actual beast from the noktum, cataloged in some obscure tome somewhere, or if it was simply the wild imagination of the tattoo artist.

Shalure moved a little, as though the sensation of slithering across the covers felt good to her. The woman's life had been upended during the fight to reclaim Rhenn's kingdom. Her dreams had been dashed, her social standing crushed, and her body mutilated. Shalure was a baron's daughter from the far north who had bet everything on her journey to the crown city of Usara. According to Khyven, she'd hoped to secure a landed husband with her quick mind, clever tongue, and the lure of her body.

That hope had been crushed when Vamreth cut out her tongue.

Now, apparently, Shalure thought her life was over and that *shkazat* was the perfect conduit to hasten her end while immersed in an enjoyable fog. Lorelle knew the drug well. *Shkazat* washed over the body in a wave, exciting the senses and burying the mind.

But it was poison.

The wonderful effects Shalure was now experiencing were slowly, methodically destroying her body. Only the first month of *shkazat* usage was this pleasurable. Once the drug took root, the pleasurable sensations came less frequently, lasted shorter spans, and the need for the drug strengthened. In another month or two, Shalure would be smoking *shkazat* daily, not to feel good, but to keep from feeling horrible. A few months after that, it would claim her. Either she would continue smoking it until her body experienced vital organ failure, or she would stop smoking it, at which point her body would experience vital organ failure. Once the drug took root, there was no escape.

But Shalure wasn't there yet, and Lorelle could help.

During her and Rhenn's time in the Laochodon Forest, Lorelle had mastered Usara's local herb lore. She had come across *shkazat* root, and its users, many times during that decade in the woods. As with all the other roots, leaves, berries, and barks she'd experimented with, she'd made herself understand *shkazat*'s effects.

And how to counter them.

She had found a purple leaf which, when combined with a pinch of ground *shkazat* root, formed a counteragent. In the right amounts, Lorelle had created a potion that could purge the body of the drug. But it only worked if it was delivered before the *shkazat* took root.

She pulled the strap of her herb satchel, bringing the pouch around from where it rested against the small of her back to the front, so she could open the flap. She pulled out a small glass vial of the purple liquid she'd called *nettoye* after the Luminent word for "clean."

She sat on the bed and Shalure shifted, drawing a breath and seeming to sense Lorelle's presence for the first time. *Shkazat* was like that. Nothing existed five or six feet away from the user, but everything within that small sphere was vibrant and compelling.

"Mmmm," Shalure said, reaching up and touching Lorelle's elbow. The tattooed owl-creature's claws appeared to reach for Lorelle, the owl's intense eyes glaring. Shalure's fingers lingered, moving down toward Lorelle's hand as though the tight cloth over Lorelle's arm was the most fascinating thing she'd ever felt.

Lorelle held up the vial of purple liquid. It glimmered in the scant starlight from outside the window, and Lorelle knew that in Shalure's vision the bottle would seem like a dazzling purple gem, flickering with fire.

"Mmmm!" Shalure purred, reaching out for it.

"If you think it looks nice," Lorelle said softly. "Wait until you taste it."

Lorelle dramatically uncorked the vial.

Shalure sat up, leaned back her head, and opened her mouth. Gently, making sure every drop went into Shalure's mouth, Lorelle poured out the contents of the vial.

Shalure swallowed and shivered at the sweet flavor, then lay back against the soft pillows. Lorelle had made sure the concoction first sent shivers of pleasure through a *shkazat* user. An addict might reflexively spit out something bitter, and Lorelle had learned long ago that there was more to herbalism than just the effect of the drug.

Unfortunately for Shalure, that would be the end of the pleasure. *Nettoye* worked fast. It didn't just leach the poison from the blood, it transformed it. It would take about as long for the *shkazat* to be purged as it would take for Shalure's blood to circulate throughout her body.

The transition, Lorelle had been told, was like jumping into a pool of icy water.

Shalure gasped and her eyes flew open. She sat up and glared at Lorelle in horror.

"Goohhhh!" she exclaimed as the indulgent fogginess of the *shkazat* vanished. She grabbed Lorelle's arm with both hands, wide eyes beseeching. "Ease!" she begged. "Ease!"

Please.

Lorelle put a soft hand on Shalure's desperate claw.

"I'm sorry," Lorelle whispered.

"Oooh!" Shalure shook her head.

No.

"It's for the best," Lorelle said. "Though I know it doesn't seem so."

Shalure's lips curled into a snarl and she looked like she wanted to slash Lorelle with her fingernails and march straight back to the *shkazat* den. Which, unless Khyven and the others watched her all day was probably exactly what she would do.

"I know you think your life is over, but I would ask you to consider something." Lorelle corked the empty vial and slid it back into her satchel. "Why are you in this bed?"

Shalure's auburn eyebrows crouched angrily over her eyes.

"You're in this bed because Vohn asked Slayter to find you," Lorelle answered her own question. "And then Slayter told Khyven about the *shkazat* den. And then Khyven marched into a guarded basement and took you by force."

Lorelle paused to let that information sink in. Shalure crossed her arms like a petulant child.

"You have many friends for someone whose life is over." Lorelle stood to leave.

"Ah onk oo aye!"

I want to die!

She glanced down at Shalure. "Your life will never be easy again, Shalure. That much is true. If an easy life is all you are capable of living, then perhaps it is best if you run back to the *shkazat* den the moment Khyven's back is turned."

"Ah ang ohgkess!" she shouted.

I am worthless!

"You have been wounded," Lorelle said. "And I'm so sorry for that. But it is only a wound."

Shalure slapped her bare chest with a hand. "Ah angok eek!"

I cannot speak!

An idea rose within Lorelle then, but she didn't want to do it. She almost turned to go again, but instead she opened another pouch and withdrew a weathered, leather-bound book. It was small, barely the size of her hand. She carried it with her everywhere, had carried it since she and Rhenn had learned it almost a decade ago.

It was a book of annotated hand positions for a silent language. It was old, with a strange, gray paper, and Lorelle wasn't sure in which kingdom it had originated, but it had been invaluable to the two girls.

In their ten years learning to live in the woods and later as they began building Rhenn's rebellion, the two friends had used these hand signs to communicate silently, a skill of great usefulness when sneaking into the city or dodging patrols sent to kill them. After a year of inventing and practicing, they could carry on an entire conversation without opening their mouths.

Lorelle didn't need the book anymore—she'd long since memorized its contents—but she had kept it, a loving memory of two scared girls who had bonded so strongly that they could speak without saying a word.

Lorelle squeezed the book with both hands and mentally let it go.

"This is for you." She set the book on the bed.

"Ah ig ik?"

What is it?

"A new language. A different way to speak."

"Ah ong ang ik!"

I don't want it.

"That is your choice, but the book now belongs to you."

Shalure picked it up and hurled it across the room. The precious catalog of Lorelle and Rhenn's silent language hit the wall and fell to the floor. For Lorelle, it felt like her heart had struck the wall. She wanted to turn on Shalure and scream at her.

Instead, she clenched her fists and held her anger.

She knew what it was to be in pain, to feel your whole life slip away like you'd dropped through a hole in the floor. Lorelle had precious little compassion to give right now, but Shalure needed it even more than she did.

Lorelle took a deep breath and turned to face the blazing rebellion in Shalure's eyes.

"Vamreth's cruelty was monstrous." She raised her arm and pointed directly at Shalure's mouth. "He did that to you. You didn't make that choice." Then she gestured at Shalure's skinny body, at her bedraggled hair, and finally at the little book laying in the corner. "But you are making this one. Your friends care about you. Let them help you."

"Ah ave oh oiyses!" she gargled.

I have no choices!

"After I lost my parents, I thought the same. I felt helpless, spent, scared. I wanted to lay down and die. But Rhenn picked me up and saw me through that time even though she had lost her family as well. She made me see that I still had so much left to give and to live for—an entirely new life. With her help I found my way again."

She walked to the door and paused, turning a final time to regard Shalure. "You may feel alone, that you're the only one feeling so much pain, but you aren't. Rhenn, the last scrap of family I have, has been taken from me, and I swear I'm going to find her or die trying. What will you die trying to do?"

She left the room.

CHAPTER ELEVEN
LORELLE

L orelle closed the door, leaned on the wall, and pressed her hand to her chest, pushing at her breastbone as though that would quiet the flames inside. She felt she could have handled that better with Shalure, but it was so hard to concentrate. It took so much effort to simply stand and not scream at the pain. She needed rest, but she couldn't sleep. It was like trying to sleep while someone was branding her with glowing hot iron.

Enough, she thought. *Feel sorry for yourself after you rescue Rhenn.*

She strode up the hallway. What she needed was more experimentation on the Plunnos. The Nox said it was fake, but Nox were liars. The Plunnos was where she needed her concentration. Not on Khyven. Not on the Nox and his silver tongue.

Her tattered soul suddenly flared as she reached the intersection of the corridor. She gasped, pulled up short, and looked to her left.

Khyven was leaning against the wall, one leg cocked up behind him, his arms crossed over his powerful chest. He exuded the power of a crouched Kyolar. Lotura, the man was only a few weeks from his sick bed, and he already looked like his old self.

At the camp, Rhenn had called him "Khyven the Pretty," and that's all Lorelle could see now. The light scars on his face from the Helm of Darkness only served to make him more compelling, just as Rhenn had joked. His carved jawline, the muscles in his neck, and the hollow of his throat drew her eye. His rough, capable hands, large and callused from years of sword wielding made her want to put them on her body. She wanted to run her fingers through that careless mess of his thick, brown hair that looked just right on him. She wanted to let those rich brown eyes warm her with their intensity.

Since she'd given half her soul to him, he seemed perfect in every way.

She hesitated, glancing to the side, and thought about bolting. He would chase her, of course. In the Night Ring, he had been trained to stalk his objective, trained never to stop.

If he found out the truth of their half soul-bond... he would take charge, take the decision out of her hands, attempt to complete the soul-bond immediately and damn the consequences.

She'd managed to hide it from him to this point, but he wasn't an idiot. He'd sensed something was wrong, and now he wouldn't relent until he found out what it was.

The fire inside her heightened, and she wanted to scream. She bit her lip.

She had to break away from him, come up with a good excuse.

But the pain kept her from thinking clearly. She couldn't think of anything clever, anything he would believe.

"Khyven," she said, every muscle in her body clenching as she tried to make her voice sound normal.

"How is she?" he asked.

His question startled her and she came to her senses. He was talking about Shalure.

"She's... fine now. I purged the *shkazat*," she said quickly.

"Thank you." He smiled, and it melted her. She wanted to rush to him, throw her arms around him. She took an involuntary step toward him.

"Of course," she said through her teeth, stopping her advance.

"You're a bit of a miracle, what you can do with those herbs."

The frayed half of her soul burned through her, rising to a new height, urging her to take another step, to leap across the distance between them. She held it in check.

"What do you want?" she demanded.

"What do I *want*?" Khyven's compassion hardened. "To know about Shalure. To know about the welfare of my friends. To know about you, for Senji's sake. You're in pain. Why are you trying to act like you're not?"

The flames seared and scorched her and she knew the moment she touched him the pain would vanish. All she had to do was—

"I have to find Rhenn," she bit out the words. She had hoped to say something to convince him to leave her alone, but she simply couldn't think straight long enough to formulate it. She turned away.

His hand closed on her arm, soft but firm. She jerked, staring at him in horror. He'd moved so fast, so silently, she hadn't even heard his approach. She'd forgotten how fast he was. He was gentle, but with his greater mass, his grip stopped her dead.

The raging fire vanished, and she gasped. Instinctively, she put her hand over his. The skin-to-skin contact tingled joyously. She drew a quick breath.

"S-stop," she managed weakly.

He put his other hand on her arm. She shivered. Gods! She felt like a rabbit trapped in a hutch. Their gazes locked, there was only a foot between them. The frayed tendrils of her soul reached out to him, going into him.

"Let me go," she whispered again, without conviction. She didn't want to go. She wanted to melt into him.

"Let me help you," he said softly. "You're in pain. You're hurting so badly you're barely able to talk. The look on your face... I'd do anything for you, Lorelle. Anything. Don't push me away."

Her heart blossomed with joy and the flames vanished. She drew a long breath like she'd been holding it in for minutes. This was it. The tendrils of her soul reached out, touched him, going deeper, trying to re-attach to that piece of herself that now lived inside him. Her thoughts scattered. Her resistance crumbled.

"Khyven, I'm... I did something—"

"Slayter told me," he interrupted. "It's all right. We're going to help. We'll find a way to undo the soul-bond."

His words shocked her, snapped her out of her euphoric slide. She blinked.

"You don't need to hide it from us," he continued. "There's a way to fix this, no matter what anyone says. And I don't..." He faltered. "I don't care who it is. I just want to help."

She heard the lie in his voice, saw the anguish on his face at the idea of her bonding with someone else. The half-bond was working on him, too, pulling him inexorably toward her, even though he didn't know it.

"I will find a way." He touched her cheek with those big, rough hands, and she closed her eyes—

"No!" She twisted out of his grip and backed away.

Fire flared inside her, consuming her as she disengaged. It hurt so much dark spots appeared in her vision and the room began to spin. She reached out to catch the wall, to steady herself. Lotura, the pain!

Khyven's large hand closed over hers again. "I've got you." He slid an arm around her waist, steadying her. "I've got you." The fire vanished and pleasurable tingles shot through her again. "Please, Lorelle. Rhenn's not the only one who loves you. Slayter, Vohn, me... We're all here to stand beside you no matter what. We *will* solve this."

"Khyven... let me go," she begged. "You don't understand. You have to let me go."

"It's not just—"

Khyven hissed and released her. He held up his left hand—the hand that had been gripping hers. A thin line of blood marked the back of it.

"The maid asked you to let her go," a familiar voice said from the dark. "That's thrice now. Best do it."

Lorelle spun, saw a thin, silver sword poking out of the shadow by the window. A tiny spot of Khyven's blood shone on the tip. The shadows shifted, showing the barest hint of a silhouette.

The Nox!

His dark cloak looked like it was made of the hallway's shadows. She couldn't see his face or even most of his body, only his hand and that thin silver blade. She heard the Nox draw breath to continue his verbal reprimand...

But this Nox didn't know Khyven.

Khyven had trained for two years to respond to threats lightning fast, to roll with pain, to get to his enemy at all costs, because failing to do exactly that meant death.

Khyven spun, a dagger appearing in his hand like he'd been holding it all along. The Nox grunted and Lorelle realized Khyven had *already* thrown a different dagger and it had hit its mark.

He leapt into the shadows, slashing where the Nox had been, but the blade passed through empty air.

The Nox's dark chuckle emerged from a shadowed alcove six feet up the hall, and Khyven faced the noise. His dagger jumped expertly from his right hand to his left, and he drew his sword. Steel rang in the quiet hallway.

The Nox half emerged from the shadows, a hand on his side. He watched Khyven with glittering eyes.

"Khyven stop!" Lorelle shouted.

"Well, well, well," the Nox said. He held up a black hand, blood shining on the tips of two fingers. "Fairly exchanged,

Khyven the Unkillable. Blood for blood. You're fast for a Human."

Khyven stepped smoothly in front of Lorelle and she felt a rush of cool air over her skin as though a wind had blown up the hall behind them, flowing over her and Khyven toward the Nox.

Except the hallway was still. That wind hadn't come from... anything natural. She didn't know *where* it had come from.

Then it hit her. That wind was coming from Khyven himself! Or... not *from* him, but *because* of him. She felt it through the half-made soul-bond. She was feeling... his magic, whatever made Khyven nearly invincible in combat.

He was going to kill the Nox.

And the idea terrified her.

You want a Plunnos? I'll take you to one. The Nox's words echoed in her mind.

"Khyven wait," she said.

But he was already stalking his prey, his body loose, ready. His sword levitated in front of him like it had a mind of its own. He held the dagger close to his side, ready to block or throw. A trickle of blood snaked from the back of his hand to his wrist.

"Listen to her, Human." The Nox faded into the shadows, disappearing from view. "She's trying to save your life," the Nox said from their left, at least twenty feet from his previous location.

Lorelle started, but Khyven barely flicked a glance in that direction. He stared at the alcove of shadows ahead.

She peered into the thin shadows where the Nox's voice had last come from, next to an open window. The Nox wasn't there. He couldn't be. The shadows weren't large enough to hold a person.

His voice! Lorelle thought. *He can throw his voice!*

That's how the Nox seemed to be all around her in the alley. She'd kept turning, following her ears. He'd been taunting her.

But whatever magic flowed through Khyven wasn't fooled. Somehow, despite the Nox's magical abilities, Khyven knew exactly where he was.

"You know him?" Khyven asked tightly, moving forward half crouched, his gaze fixed on the shadows.

"I..." She didn't know what to say. "We've met."

"You let him into the palace?"

"He's... my friend," she lied. She didn't know why. She didn't know this Nox, and he could be every bit as dangerous as Khyven was treating him.

But she felt compelled by the Nox. She'd denied him the first time he'd come for her, but if she was honest with herself, she had to know what he knew. Even if it was a lie, she had to know for sure. His offer had seemed, against all rational thought, like a line to a drowning person. She couldn't afford to let Khyven kill the Nox.

Khyven spared a quick glance over his shoulder, narrowed his eyes as though he scented the lie.

"Please," she said.

He hesitated, then shook his head. "He cut me, Lorelle. What if he'd cut you?"

"He isn't going to cut me."

"What about Vohn? Slayter? What about everyone else in the palace?"

"He thought... you were trying to hurt me," she said. Her heart pounded harder with each lie, and the burn seared through her. "He doesn't know you."

"Doesn't know *me*?" Khyven focused on the shadows ahead again.

"Just let me talk to him."

Khyven's posture shifted, and he rose slowly from his fighting crouch. His sword arm stayed at the ready, but the hand with the dagger lowered.

"He's gone," Khyven said.

"How do you—"

"Who is this creature? All I could see was a dark blur..." He trailed off, and his eyes went wide. "Is he...?" He lifted his chin like he was preparing to get punched in the face. "Is he the one?"

He meant the failed bond. He thought this Nox was the one she'd attempted—and failed—to soul-bond with.

She almost blurted, *"No!"* but stopped herself.

That could be perfect. If she confirmed his guess, it would keep him from guessing the truth. It might make him stop chasing her.

She opened her mouth to say it... but she couldn't. She just couldn't bear to lie to him again. Not about that. She sensed that if she lied to him about the soul-bond a door would close in her heart forever. And maybe in his as well. It might ruin any chance she ever had to...

"Just... let me handle this," she insisted.

"I can't." He shook his head. "You've allowed this creature into the palace—"

"Creature?"

"What is he?"

"If he is a creature, then perhaps so am I," she said.

"What does *that* mean?" Khyven asked, frowning. "Are you saying he's a Luminent?"

"He and I have more in common than you think." She leapt a dozen feet away and landed lightly on the windowsill. The pain flared inside her as she distanced herself, but she gritted her teeth and grabbed the stones of the sill.

"Lorelle!" Khyven spun and stalked toward her like he wasn't going to let her jump out the window.

"He won't hurt anyone," she said, not knowing if that was true at all. "Trust me." He lunged toward her.

This time, she was faster. His hand closed over open air as she jumped out the window.

She dropped to a balcony two stories below and glanced up.

He didn't shout after her, didn't leap after her. He just looked down at her like a boy who'd lost a footrace competition. His shoulders slumped and he let out a breath. She jumped from the balcony and landed softly on the cobblestones of the courtyard.

"Lorelle..." Her keen ears caught his heartbroken whisper four stories above.

Soul burning, she ran into the night.

CHAPTER TWELVE

ZAITH

Zaith D'Orphine closed his eyes, fell backward into the embrace of the magical cloak, and left the Human palace. He felt the cold wind of the noktum flow over him, felt the darkness breathe through him. The cloak was a gift from Lord Tovos, an artifact that enhanced Zaith's ability to move through shadows, but that wasn't its greatest power.

As long as its wearer was completely shrouded in shadow, or standing inside a noktum, the cloak could be used to teleport.

Only certain Nox could bond with the cloak. Only those who had inextricably bound their souls to the Great Noktum through the Cairn and become one with the darkness. Only Glimmerblades.

Zaith could jump from one shadow to another within a room, or around a building. If he took time and concentrated, he could move distances much greater than that.

Now he teleported from the shadows of the daylight world into the nearest noktum. From there, he traveled far away from the backwater Human kingdom of Usara. He traveled south almost two thousand miles.

The Lightlanders thought they knew about their world. They saw the noktums as splatters of leftover darkness of a bygone age, magical remnants, nuisances to be avoided. But the Lightlanders were like Frovian ticks on the back of their giant host. They thought they ruled their little patch of hide, all the while completely ignorant of what a Frovi even was, let alone where it was taking them.

Unbeknownst to the Humans, all noktums were one noktum. They didn't seem connected, but they were. The darkness seeped below ground, flowed like rivers. It spun like webs above ground with strands so thin a mortal eye could not perceive them. The blotches the blind Humans saw were the organs of the Great Noktum, yes, but they were all connected by veins the Humans could not see.

Zaith traveled those veins now, squeezing through them with the powerful magic of the noktum cloak.

He arrived at the base of the great nuraghi, and the pain nearly tore him apart. Zaith clutched his stomach and fell over at the base of a tall, gnarled Varka tree. In his days as a Glimmerblade he had been stabbed and sliced, hit with clubs and rocks, but he'd never felt pain like this before.

He opened his mouth as he tried to master it, writhing on the ground in the wake of the cloak's magic. His black hair flared an incandescent purple.

Then the pain was gone. Zaith lay on the dark grass, shivering and panting.

That had never happened before. What could have caused it? The only thing he could think of was that he'd never used the cloak wounded before. It was as though the darkness had sensed his wound and tried to rip him apart.

Grina's dark eyes, he wouldn't try that again! The next time he was wounded in the Human lands, he would simply stay there to tend the wound.

Of course, he hadn't expected the Human to be able to hit him, either. That should not have happened.

The Human could not possibly have seen him. Zaith had shifted from shadow to shadow. He had even thrown his voice with the Tallyx. Lorelle had far better hearing and dark vision than the Human, and she hadn't been able to find him.

But the man's dagger had come straight at him. If Zaith had been even a fraction slower, it would have lodged in his chest just beneath the breastbone, a killing strike. He'd have died tonight.

Zaith had lingered after, the dagger deep in his belly, and bantered to allay suspicion as to how badly he was hurt, but the moment he felt he could retreat, he had done so.

He clenched his teeth, pulled the dagger out, and dropped it. Keeping one hand tight to his belly, he maneuvered himself to his hand and knees. Grina's bloody nails, it felt like all his guts were going to spill out.

The man... this "Khyven the Unkillable" was a local hero of the Usaran Humans and supposedly a talented killer, what they called a "Ringer" because he'd learned his trade in the Night Ring of Usara. Zaith had barely given this "hero" any thought. Humans were Humans, after all. They were slow and blind.

He'd have to be more careful. Even as stupid and sluggish as they were, even Humans could score a thousand-to-one lucky shot every now and then.

Zaith levered himself to his feet, closed his eyes, and let the darkness of the Great Noktum fill him. It seeped into his soul like thick oil, filling him, reclaiming him, bringing him back into the fold, although the wound remained.

He took a deep breath and made the light of his hair wink out.

He opened his eyes to the city of Nox Arvak. The tall, muscled arms of the oak trees spread out before him. The Darkwood Palace rose in the distance, alerting any travelers that this was home to the Nox.

The Great Noktum wasn't just mother to the Nox. All manner of beasts and races lived within its eldritch embrace. There were creatures far older, far more powerful—and smarter—than the Nox. Thank Grina that most of the smart ones seemed entirely uninterested in boundary skirmishes or preying upon the Nox. As long as the Nox didn't invade the territory of those ancient beings, they stayed where they were.

There were plenty of predatory beasts, though. The Lightlanders lived with creatures called "herd animals" whose purpose was purely to eat grass and feed predators. There were no herd animals in the noktum. Every creature was a predator here, and even some of the plant life.

Zaith started toward the welcoming oaks, dreaming of the Nox healer Caelera's gentle hands, the hot bowl of water she'd use to clean the wound. Her deft hands as she stitched him up.

Suddenly, the darkness yanked at his soul. It felt like fingers plunging into the coils of his entrails and squeezing. He hissed, holding his belly and clenching his teeth.

"Zaith," Lord Tovos said through the dark, his presence vibrating into Zaith's mind and translating into words.

For a futile moment, Zaith clung to the thought of Caelera's gentle ministrations and healing. But there was nowhere in the noktum Zaith could resist the Lord. He had tried, and his sister had paid the price.

"My Lord," Zaith replied. Though the Lord's voice was internal, Zaith spoke aloud. He had not yet mastered how to create that vibration through the dark, how to speak as Lord Tovos spoke.

"Why have you returned?" Lord Tovos asked.

"It is only a brief stop, My Lord—"

"Why have you returned?" The Lord repeated.

Zaith clenched his teeth. There was no conversing with Lord Tovos. All he gave were commands and questions. And all he wanted was action or immediate answers.

"I was wounded."

Silence.

"By a Human?"

"It was a bit of luck, My Lord. Nothing more. It won't happen again."

"Come to my tower."

"My Lord, I must tend to my wound—"

The cloak engulfed Zaith and he hastily prepared himself. He squeezed through the darkness again, screaming as it wrenched his wound.

CHAPTER THIRTEEN

ZAITH

The trip was far shorter this time, and the pain far less. But Zaith still fell to his knees at the base of a massive wall. His hair flared again, throwing purple light across the grass and black stone. He snarled and put it out. He climbed to his feet, his fist tight against the hole in his belly.

Controlling his breath, he looked up at the monolithic castle that had shown up at the edge of Nox Arvak last week like an angry father who'd finally found his disobedient children.

The five thin towers with their conical roofs pierced the sky like black spears. The black grass of the courtyard was trimmed to perfection. Lord Tovos didn't like artwork of any kind, including sculptures, so there was nothing but the wrought-iron fence with its spikes pointing in the same direction as the towers.

There were no shortage of naguils, though. The giant owl-headed lions wandered the courtyard. Their skeletal wings never fully folded against their backs, instead extending high above, trailing wisps of smoke.

They'd sensed him, of course. The monsters were intelligent, loyal, and they could smell intruders. No one entered the environs of the nuraghi without the naguils noticing. They instantly recognized him and left him alone.

Zaith belonged because Lord Tovos said he belonged, because Zaith wore the Lord's noktum cloak. The silky black fabric could not only spirit him through shadow and noktum, but it changed Zaith's scent to the monsters.

If Zaith had been an intruder, the naguils would have pounced and disemboweled him, rending him apart with their mighty claws and beaks before he could scream.

He turned and entered the castle through the servant's door. It was a long hallway, wide enough by Nox standards but narrow to the point of insignificance to one of the Lords, stretched out straight before him. To the right and left inside the door were two stairways in equally "narrow" corridors. There was no foyer, only the most brief and utilitarian architecture for servants to enter, quickly do the Lords' bidding, and leave without being noticed.

He took the left stairway and leapt up them six at a time, holding his side and growling through the pain as the movements pulled at his wound.

The Lord, of course, hadn't told him where to go, but Zaith had never visited anything in this castle except his own room on the third floor of the castle proper—which was about six floors worth of stairs to a mortal. Only the most useful servants were given quarters so high up, so there were only a half dozen rooms in the small wing. He'd seen a Wergoi up here once, two doors down from Zaith. The squat, muscled dwarf had given Zaith a dour glance before leaving without speaking a word. Zaith imagined the Wergoi as a representative of his people, like Zaith was a representative of the Nox, but he really had no idea. The Wergoi must hate it up here, though, so high in the air. From what Zaith understood, the whole race preferred to spend its time digging beneath the earth.

Zaith entered the room, unfastened the black enameled clasp on the noktum cloak and threw it at the shadows behind an overstuffed black chair. The cloak spread out like a giant bird's wings and melted into the darkness. In moments, it was gone and only the black enameled clasp remained, glistening on the shadowy wall like an ornament.

Zaith crossed to the cabinet on the north wall. The Lord could have teleported him anywhere, but he'd tossed Zaith at the base of the castle by the servant's entrance.

He plucked his wound kit from the wrought iron night cabinet and sat on the edge of his bed. He gingerly pulled the bloody pieces of tunic from his wound, wincing, then peeled his ripped tunic over his head and laid it next to him. He looked down at the wound: a two-inch puncture just beneath his ribs, laying open meat to the bone.

The strike had been true and had very nearly succeeded.

He measured a length of thread, cut it with his dagger, and fixed it to the needle. Uncorking a clay jug, he splashed Arvadian dark gin on it and clenched his teeth as the pain came.

The air in the room shifted. It was subtle, and if Zaith hadn't experienced the effects of the noktum cloak firsthand, he wouldn't have noticed.

He glanced at the corner by the door.

Lord Tovos stood there, towering over the furniture in the room, more than twice Zaith's height. His nose was long and pointed, his eyes like black slashes in his face, and his expression, as ever, was angry. His arms were long and as wide as tree trunks, his legs the width of gin barrels. He wore loose black leggings, a thick black belt, and a tight shirt of black scale mail that looked like it was made of actual dragon scales. Zaith had been in Lord Tovos's presence a half dozen times now and it never got easier. His hatred of the Lord always fled in the wake of the Lord's presence as Zaith felt he was shrinking to the size of a mouse, becoming smaller and smaller. That angry gaze leached away Zaith's confidence, leaving behind only fear and a thin thread of silent rebellion.

"I did not order you back," Lord Tovos said. "Yet here you are."

"I told you why. I need to fix this before I can continue." Zaith applied a russet-colored paste to his wound, feeling the lightly magical salve enter the wound and begin to do its job. He picked up the bandage.

Lord Tovos flicked his finger and a hundred invisible needles stabbed Zaith's side, working into his flesh around the edge of the wound.

Zaith turned his face to the ceiling and clenched his teeth, stifling a scream as the needles stabbed him over and over. A growling noise escaped him and his body shook, but he would not give the Lord the satisfaction of the scream he so clearly wanted.

The pain vanished. Zaith gasped and looked down at his bare torso. A crooked gray scar zigzagged across his skin, ugly and efficient.

"The Luminent girl, what does she know?" Lord Tovos asked.

Zaith bared his teeth, his limbs trembling with the Lord's callous handling of the wound. He longed to draw his daggers and slash Lord Tovos's throat until it was nothing but tatters.

But Zaith had attacked the Lord before, and he'd lost his sister. Zaith had other family to protect.

"Nothing," Zaith replied. "She seeks her friend, Queen Rhenn, but she can't work the Thuros."

The Lord's lips tightened. Clearly not the answer he'd wanted. "Then we need her to come here."

"Yes," Zaith said so quickly he nearly stepped on the Lord's words.

Lord Tovos raised a cold eyebrow.

"I have already begun," Zaith continued.

"Bringing her here?"

"Yes."

"Where is she?"

Zaith turned his head away from the frigid eyes of the Lord. No matter how hard he tried, he couldn't hold Tovos's gaze for more than a few moments. It felt like the coldness inside that gaze would frost him down to his bones if he looked for even another moment.

"I am baiting the hook," Zaith said.

"Are you."

"Lightlanders are stupid, blind, and slow," Zaith said. "But they are also stubborn. If I simply kidnap her, she will resist. If she thinks she is betraying her friend, she'll die before she'll say anything. We need her to *want* to be here, to follow me willingly into the dark."

Tovos raised his head and looked out the window over Zaith's head.

"Why is Lorelle's friend so important?" Zaith asked. "Why chase this queen? This Rhenn Laochodon?"

Lord Tovos moved past Zaith to the window, as though he could see the object of his search on the horizon.

"Why chase Rhenn Laochodon?" Lord Tovos murmured contemplatively. At first, it seemed like the Lord wasn't going to answer. Then he began talking, almost as though Zaith wasn't even in the room.

"Because I think I know what Nhevalos is doing," Lord Tovos said. "And I'm going to catch him this time. I'm going to kill him."

Nhevalos. The Betrayer. The Lord who had turned on his own kind, who had turned on the darkness. When Lord Tovos returned, Zaith had scoured the books in Aravelle's library, had read everything about the Giants that he could, and Nhevalos was a name noted often. He had betrayed the other Lords when the war with the Lightlanders began.

"He is joining Human bloodlines," Lord Tovos murmured. "Thickening the original concentrations of our experiments from ancient times."

"Concentrations?" Zaith asked.

"Humans, Nox, Taur-Els, Shadowvar—every mortal race that creeps across the land and supposes themselves self-determined... All were created by us. And for certain Humans we went further. The masters mated with servants, mingled the potency of our blood with theirs, long ago. Which means the legendary heroes of their kind have Giants' blood in their veins.

These select groups became the leaders, of course. Naturally, they took command because of the potency of their blood and the strength of their souls. They formed the first kingdoms of the daylight lands. And even now, millennia later, some Human royal families still have our blood flowing in their veins."

"And the more of the Lords' blood they possess—" Zaith murmured.

"The more powerful they are," Lord Tovos finished his sentence. "How do you think Humans learned to wield magic in the first place? Traces of our blood attuned them to the magic. The higher the concentration, the more potential power they can wield. This is at the core of Nhevalos's plan. I think he is joining ancient bloodlines."

"To challenge you with these Humans with the blood of the Lords? To make an army of them?"

"Possibly. But I doubt it. That is what Nhevalos did last time, and he never takes the same avenue twice. He sneaks like a cockroach, scuttling into cracks that have not yet been seen. But I see him. I know what he is trying to create."

"Powerful Human mages?"

"Of a specific kind. There is a Human legend of a warrior named Ora Lightbringer. Supposedly, Ora single-handedly battled one of my kind to the death. I did not see this battle firsthand, so I dismissed it as ludicrous, a tale trumped up by the victorious Humans. I thought there was no chance a single Human could undertake such a feat. But I have had seventeen centuries to ponder it. I have had seventeen centuries to grow my own arcane powers and I finally stumbled across something interesting. Suddenly, the tale does not seem so far-fetched."

Lord Tovos went silent, as though his external musings had gone internal.

"What was it?" Zaith prodded.

Lord Tovos turned his head and glanced over his shoulder at Zaith before turning back to face the window. "Do you know what Lore Magic is?"

Zaith searched his memory. "One of the five streams, My Lord. Rare."

The Nox did not use any of the five streams of magic. They had not received that particular gift from the Lords. Instead, they'd been blessed with the ability to join with the Dark. Zaith had done some research on the abilities of Humans. He knew the basics of the five streams of magic. "It predicts the future, doesn't it?"

"It manipulates the future. Of the few Humans who have talent for magic at all, even fewer have the ability or the patience to use Lore Magic. Human lives are like brief flickers of flame. Effectively utilizing Lore Magic requires long vision, patience, and a soul that burns low and lasting. Most Humans lack this capacity. But…"

Zaith waited, feeling that to interrupt the Lord again might cause him to stop his verbal ruminations.

"During my long contemplation, I read the journals of one of my Noksonoi sisters, Avanisos. She died in the Human-Giant War, but beforehand she stipulated something interesting, an unorthodox application of Lore Magic. Her initial thought was that it was ludicrous for Humans to attempt Lore Magic at all. Their lives flamed out so quickly, how could they possibly live long enough to see their plans come to fruition? From this basis, she explored, experimented, and observed. In the end, she postulated a wild idea: What if Lore Magic might be used in a quicker fashion than was previously known? A battle fashion, if you will. Instead of planting and nurturing possibilities over decades, centuries, or millennia, Lore Magic could—if carefully twisted to this one purpose—be used to predict tiny events. Immediate events. Like if a sword was about to skewer you, or an arrow come at your face, or to predict when your opponent was going to leave themselves open for a killing strike. A warrior with this kind of ability could avoid being hit, could find every weakness in an opponent and exploit it." Lord Tovos glanced at Zaith over his shoulder again. "A warrior with this kind of ability could possibly even kill a Noksonoi single-handedly."

"Ora Lightbringer."

"Ora Lightbringer," Lord Tovos echoed. "It would, of course, take a high concentration of our blood to allow a Human to utilize Lore Magic in this way."

"And the Betrayer is joining bloodlines."

"I think he is trying to create more Ora Lightbringers. And I think Queen Rhennaria is one of them. She stormed the Usaran palace in one night, at the one place where Vamreth could not bring his potent army to bear, and where he foolishly fought her personally, at the one time she might have succeeded. Her coup reeks of Lore Magic. Everything in the perfect place at the perfect time. And Nhevalos knew I was watching, which is why he spirited her away."

"To protect her." Zaith marveled at the scope of it.

"That is why I want Rhenn Laochodon, Glimmerblade. He's made her a Greatblood—joined at least three bloodlines of old—and somehow taught her this experimental, accelerated Lore Magic. I think he is planting these Greatbloods throughout Noksonon for the coming conflict. Giant Killers, if you will. So, I must have her. I must peel her like an onion to find out how Nhevalos has accomplished this."

"Why not just kill her?"

"And how many more just like her are there?"

"Destroy Usara then," Zaith said. "Kill them all."

"Kill them all..." Lord Tovos stared out the tall window again. "Yes, that's exactly what we tried seventeen hundred years ago. Nhevalos baited us into that trap as well, and we... lost. We rushed around, stepping on Nhevalos's little fires of rebellion. But the more we stamped, the more rebellions flared up. Kill them all? Nhevalos may *want* me to kill his little pets in Usara. These incidental Humans are but pawns littering my path, each one leading where Nhevalos wishes me to go. Each a piece to be sacrificed to draw me further into his game. No." Lord Tovos shook his head. "Nhevalos feints and withdraws. He lures and lies. The lives of his pawns mean nothing. The Greatbloods... *that* is what must be uprooted. His plan for them, *that* is what must be killed."

"The rebellions. You mean the Human-Giant War."

"In the war, Nhevalos flicked sparks at dry tinder and we went running after them. But he had piled that tinder to draw our attention. He *wanted* us running around stamping out fires. If I slaughter those Humans in Usara, the news of my reappearance will spread across Usara to Triada, to Laria, to Imprevar. The mortal kingdoms will awaken. The rallying cry will go up. No, I will not walk into Nhevalos's traps this time. I will dig carefully until I uncover every spidery root of his plan. Then I will rip them all out at once and watch the hope drain from his face. My allies are secrecy and darkness. There will be time to blaze a path of destruction—and I look forward to that time—but I will not trumpet my position just yet. Not until Nhevalos's plan is exposed. Not until I have the upper hand…"

Lord Tovos turned and brought his burning gaze down upon Zaith, who held the stare as long as he could before bowing his head.

"Get the Luminent. Bond her to the darkness. That is your job, Glimmerblade. Your *only* job. Put aside these matters you cannot hope to comprehend."

Zaith ground his teeth. "Yes, Lord Tovos."

"And if you fail me…"

"I will not, My Lord. I need no more than a week to—"

"You have two days." Lord Tovos seemed to fall into his noktum cloak, and he was gone.

CHAPTER FOURTEEN
LORELLE

Lorelle landed on the cobblestones and ran for all she was worth. She might not be able to break Khyven's grip once he had ahold of her, but by Lotura she could outrace him. Even if Khyven could have made the jump without breaking his legs, he'd never catch her.

She clenched her teeth as the burn roared through her, making her feel like her skin must soon blacken and curl at the heat from within. She ran blindly, turned down this alley and that, running and running until she skidded to a stop, breathless, at the edge of the wharf. A dimly lit pier ran out into the water, a half dozen boats hitched up to it.

She'd never spent any time at the Usaran docks. She had not spent time at any docks since her family had left Laria. The ports of Lumyn were grand, and she'd seen them every day as a child, but when her parents traveled to Usara and made friends with the king and queen, all the interesting things seemed to be inside the palace. With her new best friend. With Rhenn.

She walked onto the pier, pushing a hand to her chest and biting her lip. She looked at the dark waters glimmering with silver moonlight. Far offshore, those glimmers abruptly ended where the darkness of a noktum swallowed the light, and she stared at that consuming darkness. Something about it seemed... peaceful. She had always feared the noktums ever since her harrowing escape with Rhenn. But these past days, the sunlight only seemed to heighten the burn within her. She stayed out of sight during the day. Nighttime, on the other hand, soothed her, and she wondered how much more soothing it might be inside a noktum, in a place where there was never any light.

The noktums were scattered over the whole continent of Noksonon, seemingly at random, and it didn't matter if it was the top of a mountain or the depths of a cave, the Laochodon Forest, or the middle of the Claw Sea. The noktums could be anywhere. Lorelle had heard that far away—much too far to see from here—there was a noktum that swallowed almost an entire quarter of the sea.

"You long to be free," the Nox said from behind her. "Your need radiates out from you."

She forced herself not to start this time. Instead, she turned, and this time she saw the whole of him.

He stood on the dock behind her, tall and lean and wide-shouldered. His dark hair lifted to the side on the light breeze, as did his rippling cloak. There were no pockets of shadows to hide him on the pier, and he cut a black silhouette against the wood deck, the quiet buildings behind him, and the moonlit sky. He was taller than her. Lorelle stood at six feet, which was tall for a Human woman but only slightly above average for a Luminent female. The Nox himself was six and a half feet—taller even than Khyven, though much more slender.

"Free..." she said, and longed for it. How glorious it would be. Freedom from the pain. Freedom from the burning bond. It was right at her fingertips, if she tried to finish the bond with Khyven. She could have peace at any moment if she simply capitulated. "No," she said roughly. "I want my friend."

"Rhenn Laochodon."

The name cut through the constant pain, woke her senses. The Nox had said Rhenn's name like he knew her, like he knew

Lorelle's situation. "What do you know about Rhenn?"

He held out his hand. "Come with me and I'll show you."

"Come with you where?"

"To a cessation of your horrible pain. To the life you were meant to lead. To the life that has been denied you by lies." He paused. "To freedom."

"Denied me by lies?"

He tilted his head. "I know the tales told by Luminents. I can guess what you believe the Nox to be."

"And what is that?"

"Evil. Malicious. Killers. Luminents who fell from the light," the Nox said.

Lorelle lifted her chin as he enumerated exactly what the legends said about the Nox.

"Would you like to know the truth?" the Nox asked.

"Your forgot 'liars,'" she said.

He chuckled. "Ah yes... Evil. Malicious. Killers. And liars. But answer me this, beautiful Lorelle, if a liar calls another man a liar, who is to be believed?"

"You're saying my parents lied to me?"

"Your entire culture lied to you," he said. "And that has never mattered to you before. It was never relevant before, I would guess. But it is now." He pointed slowly and purposefully at her chest.

The raging fire inside her flared, and her eyes watered as she tried to push it down.

"Tell me," she said breathlessly.

"I will tell you all. You suffer needlessly. I know why you only come out at night, and why you stare at the noktum with such longing. Your instincts want to bring you home. Instincts that have been there since the birth of our race."

"*Our* race?"

"You were told the Nox were Luminents who fell from grace, who repudiated the light and embraced evil. As though evil and darkness are somehow the same. They told you to stand in their daylight and feel their sun on your face. They told you the light stood for goodness and to shun the shadows, because that's where the monsters are. Do you want to hear what they didn't tell you?"

Lorelle's heart hammered.

"The Nox did not come from Luminent culture. We did not repudiate the light and flee into darkness. We were born in darkness, in the noktum. We came from the Dark. The Luminents broke away from *us*. We did not flee into the noktum. *They* fled to the light—"

"That's a lie," she said.

"You're so certain, are you? Because you've heard your Luminent stories. Because you've read your Luminent histories. Tell me, have you read any Nox histories?"

"I'm sure their lies are just as slippery as yours."

"Those who do not explore the world themselves are reliant on others to shape their views. Who do you think wrote those histories, Lorelle? Who created those stories your parents so confidently passed off as fact?"

"More trustworthy souls than you, I'm sure."

"You don't sound sure." The Nox smiled wryly. "They rewrote their histories, Lorelle. They twisted the story around…"

"Shut up."

"… until the renegades who broke from the noktum convinced themselves that they'd always lived among the Lightlanders. That they were born into a land of blasting sun, pretending to be Humans."

"Lotura's Heart, you're exactly what the legends say you are."

"It is the truth. We are not the ones who fell from grace. You are."

"Shut up!"

"If you want proof, you need only look as far as your own soul." Again, he slowly and purposefully pointed at her chest. "They did that to you, the ancient liars of the Luminents. They told you this was your fate, inescapable, and you believed them because you didn't know what else to believe. But I am telling you there is more, and I can show it to you. The Dark calls you. I've seen it on your face. I know what that call feels like, and I know you resist it. But have you ever asked yourself why? Can you give me one reason other than, 'because they told me so'?"

"You're insidious," she whispered.

"I am trying to open your eyes. Eyes that have been burned by the light for so long that you cannot see the truth that lies right before you, resting in the shadows. You are so lost you will stand there and burn to death because of a nameless fear. You will stand there and burn to death because of a lie."

With a cry, Lorelle charged him and jumped high into the air. She leapt completely over him and landed on the dock beyond, running for all she was worth back toward the city.

"Rhenn Laochodon isn't on Noksonon anymore," he said.

That pulled her up short. She skidded to a stop at the beginning of the dock and spun around, eyes wide.

"What do you mean?" she demanded. *"Where is she?"*

"I do not know," he said. "But I do know there are other worlds besides this one, and the one who took your friend went to one of these other worlds."

She held her breath. Her heart stilled at the hope, her emotions tangled up in all the things the Nox had said. He'd woven a spider's web of everything she wanted to hear. That's what liars did. This was like everything else he'd said. False. Meant to trick her.

But... what if it wasn't?

"Why would you help me?" she said. "Say I believe you. Why are you doing this?"

"Because I am a Glimmerblade. In Nox Arvak, my home, we have specialized warriors called Glimmerblades. The sole purpose of a Glimmerblade is to go into the daylight world, to seek out Luminents who are close to seeing the truth, and to bring them back into the fold."

"I don't want to be part of your fold!"

"I know you believe that, but if you would just open your eyes, you would see there is more. If your decision, after you know the truth of everything, is to come back here and live in the light, then I will honor it. But until you know the entire story, how can you make that decision? Come with me and I will show you. And I will show you where you can secure a Plunnos—a real one."

He strode slowly toward her until he stood only a foot away.

"You need me." He looked down at her, his smooth midnight face hovering over hers. His dark hair swung forward, almost touching her cheek. "You don't know it, but you do. The aberration the Luminents created is burning you up. Even your blind Human friends can see it." He slowly lifted his hand, palm up, between them, an offering. It was near enough to touch her, but he didn't.

Part of her wanted to take his hand, wanted it so badly her fingers twitched. She needed to know if he was telling the truth, but she couldn't risk it. Everything she knew about the Nox told her this was dangerous. They lied. They cajoled, then they knifed you in the dark. Once he had her in his power, she'd be at his mercy.

"You can... end the soul-bond? How?" she managed to say.

He stared down at her for a long moment, his eyes compassionate. "I'm going to return for you, Lorelle," he said softly. His hand slowly descended, vanishing into the folds of his cloak. "I'm going to hold my hand out to you a third and final time. I pray you'll take it, for it will be the last time."

He leaned back into his cloak and it swirled around him, wrapping him in utter blackness. The blackness twisted into a knotted ball, and then there was only empty night before her.

Chapter FIFTEEN
LORELLE

Lorelle paused before the council room door. She'd left the wharf and roamed the streets for an hour before returning to the palace. The Nox's words wheeled across her mind like stars across the sky. All of it was twisted up in an indecipherable knot, impossible to unravel. Was any of it truth? And if even a portion of it was, could she risk not knowing? Even if he'd lied about her soul-bond and the Plunnos, if he actually knew something about where Rhenn had gone, it would be more than she currently knew.

She placed light fingers on the wooden door and her keen Luminent ears assessed the room. Not only could she hear the conversation, but she knew in an instant that only Khyven and Vohn were present. Slayter was not.

She silently opened the door.

The lanterns burned brightly, hanging from wrought-iron arms on the walls. Khyven and Vohn huddled over the map of the kingdom of Usara spread out on the table. They did not hear her enter.

"… problem is Lord Bericourt," Vohn said, tapping his finger on the map. "He almost has enough troops to make a go at the throne."

"I hate Bericourt," Khyven mumbled.

Vohn raised an eyebrow.

"He tried to have me murdered."

"Did he?"

"Well, I killed his son," Khyven said.

Vohn frowned. "Oh, and he was upset about that, was he?" He thumped the map with his finger. "He's the closest," he continued. "And he has allies. But the power dynamics have shifted wildly since Rhenn's return. Many of Bericourt's allies could be pulled away now that Rhenn sits on the throne. I'd bet some of them would enjoy crawling out from under Bericourt's shadow if the queen showed them even a little favor. Rhenn knew that. She'd started her inroads before she left."

"So, we need the queen to show them favor."

"I just said that. Except we have no queen."

"I wonder if we could make one."

"That may be the dumbest thing you've ever said. How did you ever survive fifty bouts in the Night Ring?"

"It was forty-nine, actually."

"We send Lord Harpinjur." Vohn ground his finger into the map for emphasis.

"No," Khyven said.

"Why?"

"Because I hate Lord Harpinjur."

"Well, who *don't* you hate?" Vohn threw his hands up.

"I don't hate you yet."

"We send Lord Harpinjur," Vohn repeated.

"And what do we tell him?"

"Everything."

"Oh no." Khyven shook his head. "We can't—"

"Lord Harpinjur was the first noble to come to Rhenn's side," Vohn said. "He came to her in the early days, when it was almost a certainty she'd be destroyed by Vamreth. That was an all-or-nothing risk for him. Harpinjur could have lost everything, but he stood by her anyway. If there's anyone we should bring into our little cabal, it's him."

"He's going to spit and curse and blame us for losing the queen," Khyven said.

"We have come to the end of what the three of us can do, of what we can hide. We are holding together a cracking dam with our bare hands, and unless we can actually 'create a queen,' as you so casually put it, we need an authority figure to continue this ruse. Lord Harpinjur is that man."

Khyven shook his head. "If more than two people know a secret," he said as though reading it from a script, "it's not a secret anymore. We already have four. I don't trust anyone else."

"You *never* trust anyone else!"

"That's why I'm still alive—"

"No, you're alive because of those you *did* trust."

Khyven opened his mouth, snapped it shut. "That's fair," he mumbled.

"So shut up and listen."

"Harpinjur would have let me die. I'm just saying."

Vohn rolled his eyes.

Lorelle's eyes stung watching them. Vohn, so passionate. He never gave up on any of them or any problem put before him. He simply kept working for a solution. And Khyven, the cynic, who somehow always saw hope anyway, who could make the miraculous happen.

The burn in her chest intensified seeing him. Lotura, she loved them all. In another moment in time, in another life where Rhenn was safe, this family could have worked. But without Rhenn… it was falling apart. Lords like Bericourt would move in when they discovered Rhenn was gone. They'd hang Slayter as a traitor. They'd kill Vohn as a demon. They'd throw Khyven back into the Night Ring, and a new Vamreth would sit the throne.

She cleared her throat.

"Lorelle!" Khyven spun. Of course, he immediately started toward her. She held up a hand and, bless him, he stopped.

"I'm going," she said.

They both looked confused.

"Going..." Vohn said. "Going where?"

"Away. Far away, I suspect."

"You don't know where you're going?" Khyven said.

She didn't answer, but Khyven put it together. The man's ability to judge people was uncanny.

"That Luminent," he said. "You're going somewhere with that shadow Luminent."

"Shadow Luminent?" Vohn said.

"He's a Nox," Lorelle said.

"What's a Nox?" Khyven asked.

"There's a Nox?" Vohn demanded.

"All you need to know is that I can't stay here," she said. "It's not... helping Rhenn. And I can't help you with what you must do. You're right, you have to run the kingdom. You're... you're doing what you have to do. We have to preserve Rhenn's kingdom until I can bring her back."

"Wait, what? Lorelle, if you know how to get through the Thuros, you have to tell us," Khyven said.

"I don't yet, but I will soon. I have a lead on where to find a Plunnos."

"I thought you had one."

"No."

"Well, where is it?" Khyven asked.

"The Nox. He knows. He's going to take me there."

"You're not going anywhere with that guy," Khyven said.

"Could someone catch me up here?" Vohn asked plaintively. "There's a Nox. And he has a Plunnos. When did this happen?"

"It's our best option, and I'm going to chase it down," Lorelle said.

"All right," Vohn said calmly. "Everyone needs to calm down and not go anywhere until we've discussed this. There is a Nox who has promised you a Plunnos?"

"Yes."

"Well, you can't go," Vohn said. "You should know better than anyone: Nox are liars. They're killers. They abduct Luminents, Lorelle."

"And yet it's the only avenue I currently have to find Rhenn."

"We all want Rhenn back," Khyven said.

"And I'm the one who can get her. There is no other way."

"Of course, there is," Vohn said.

"Name it."

Vohn opened his mouth but said nothing.

"I'll name it," Khyven said. "*Not* trusting someone who sneaks into the palace and who-knows-where-else and cuts me with a sword."

She averted her gaze from Khyven's intense eyes, focusing on Vohn instead. She just couldn't look too long at Khyven without the burn becoming unbearable. She was already panting with the effort of keeping the pain in check. She couldn't be in this room with him for much longer.

"One of us needs to look for Rhenn and *only* look for Rhenn," Lorelle whispered through the pain. "And even if this is the slimmest chance, even if I die in the attempt, it doesn't matter—"

"It matters to me," Khyven interrupted.

"And me," Vohn said.

"Stop it!" she shouted. "I made the mistake! It's my fault she's gone. If I'd been faster. If I'd... if I'd been paying attention, Nhevaz would never have had her!"

Vohn's eyes widened. Silence fell in the room.

"Lorelle, you realize that's ridiculous," the Shadowvar said.

Lorelle couldn't be here. She had to get out of here. Their words were like little hammers clinking on her head. She'd come here to say goodbye to them, but it was just getting twisted up. She should have known they wouldn't let her go easily. Why couldn't they see that this was the only way? Someone had to sacrifice themselves to get the Plunnos, to unearth the impossible and make it possible. And this time, it had to be her.

"He's lying about the Plunnos," Vohn warned again. "That's what they do."

"Why?" Lorelle shouted.

"Why?" Vohn asked.

"Yes!"

"Because he's a creature of the dark!" Khyven interrupted. "A monster with a face that looks like ours! Can't you see that?"

"A monster, is he?" she said.

"He's a beast of the noktum."

"So, what if I am, too?" she blurted. The burn in her chest flared so hot she gasped and pushed her hand to her chest.

"Hey…" Khyven said softly, his eyes filled with worry. "Let's just calm down and talk, like Vohn said. Let's just talk it out. Tell us what's happening, Lorelle. We are your friends. We will help you. We would *die* to help you." He started toward her like he was going to hug her.

She held her hands up and backed away. "You *can't* help me," she said brokenly.

"This Nox creature is twisting your mind and selling you lies. Clearly, he wants something from you. If he really wants to help us find Rhenn, then let him come here. Let him bring the Plunnos to us. There's no reason for you to go with him."

There was, but she couldn't tell him why. That was the last thing she could do.

"It's a *chance*," Lorelle whispered, repeating herself. "I have to take it. To find Rhenn. To protect you."

"Going alone into the arms of someone dangerous isn't the way to find Rhenn," Khyven said.

In the shadows behind Khyven and Vohn, who were both staring at her, a knot formed, unfolded, and revealed the black silhouette of the Nox. He reached up and pushed back his cowl, revealing his dark face. It was so subtle that if she hadn't been looking right at that corner, she wouldn't have seen him. Neither Khyven nor Vohn noticed.

The Nox opened his cloak and extended his hand, his third and final offer.

She'd wanted to say goodbye to this beautiful little family, maybe even risk hugging Khyven before pulling away from him. But they simply wouldn't allow it, and she had run out of time.

"I'm sorry..." she murmured to Khyven. The soul-bond flared and tears filled her eyes. "I'll come back with the Plunnos."

"If I see that Nox again, I'm going to kill him," Khyven growled.

She started toward Khyven and saw him react, saw the soul-bond pull at him. His arms twitched, coming up to take hold of her, but she used her momentum to move swiftly past him, toward the corner, toward the darkness.

Confusion crossed Khyven's face, and he turned as she passed him, his arms raised.

"It's my fault we lost Rhenn," she said. "I'm going to fix it. Just me. I'm not going to lose you, too. I-I can't risk that. Please understand."

"No. I don't understand," Khyven said. "If there's a Plunnos, *we* go after it. Not you. We do this together—"

Khyven and Vohn saw the Nox at the same moment, and it was like time slowed down. Vohn's jaw dropped. Khyven's confusion turned into rage and he drew his sword.

The Nox's arms closed over Lorelle's shoulders as she fell into his embrace.

Khyven leapt forward. By Lotura, the man was fast. He almost reached them.

"Khyven!" Vohn shouted. "Don't let him take her!"

The darkness of the Nox's cloak folded around her. She felt a cold wash of sensation, just like entering the noktum.

The room vanished.

CHAPTER SIXTEEN

KHYVEN

The blue wind swept from behind Khyven like a hurricane when he saw the damned Nox appear. Mind and body blended into one as he threw himself at the foul thing. He saw blue funnels, one on the right side of the Nox's neck, just behind Lorelle's head, and one on the Nox's left side, exposed behind the curve of Lorelle's waist. Khyven could reach them. He could stab those spots.

His body lengthened. His sword stretched, straight and true—

The darkness folded in on Lorelle and the Nox. They vanished.

Khyven's sword drove into the wall with a sharp ring and the crunch of marble. It jolted his arm and he twisted, hitting the wall with his shoulder.

He rebounded instantly, crouching and glaring at the other shadows in the room, waiting for the Nox to reappear. That cloak—or perhaps the Nox itself—could jump from shadow to shadow.

But the blue wind lost focus, became an indistinct haze, like a fog hovering throughout the room, searching for an opponent. The Nox was gone.

Lorelle was gone.

"No!" Vohn said again. "No, no, no!"

"Senji damn it!" Khyven whirled around, seeking, hoping. *Show yourself,* he thought. *Just show yourself once.*

But the blue wind didn't need eyes to see its opponent. There was nothing in the room. The Nox—and Lorelle—were gone.

"You knew there was a Nox in the palace?" Vohn accused.

"Where is Slayter?"

"No!" Vohn's voice cracked like a whip, and Khyven looked at him, surprised. "How long has that thing been creeping around the palace? How long did you know?"

"Vohn, this isn't the time—"

"You stone-headed Ringer!" Vohn said sharply. "You're not in the Night Ring anymore. We work as a team. Do you even know what it is that just grabbed our friend?"

"My next kill," Khyven growled.

"Oh, fine then." Vohn crossed his arms over his chest. "Go on. Kill him."

Khyven looked around the room, but the Nox and Lorelle were gone.

"No, you *won't* find him," Vohn said, coldly watching Khyven's fruitless search. "Because Nox are every bit as magical as Lorelle, and their magic has to do with shadows. He's gone. And you'd have known this if you'd thought of yourself as part of a team instead of the lone Ringer and shared this information with me. We could have taken precautions."

"I… met him earlier tonight," Khyven admitted. "Lorelle indicated that maybe he was a friend."

Vohn threw his hands up. "And you believed that?"

"I didn't even know what a Nox was," Khyven said. "I… honestly, I thought he was a dark-skinned Luminent."

"He *is.* The evil kind. That's why you tell me when something like this happens. You tell me and Slayter if a magical creature is suddenly walking around free in the Senji-be-damned palace. Do you know what Nox do to Luminents?"

Khyven felt a cold hardness growing in his gut as Vohn berated him. He hadn't wanted to say anything about Lorelle's paramour because he hadn't wanted it to be true. She'd fled from him and he was afraid if he angered her even more, she...

She what? Wouldn't like him anymore?

Vohn was right. He'd been foolish.

"I'm sorry," Khyven said.

"Good. Now answer my question, because frankly a little bit of education in that Ringer head of yours could have changed this entire mess. Do you know what they do to Luminents?" Vohn repeated pointedly.

"No."

"Two things. They kill them or they turn them. Clearly, this is the latter."

"Turn them?"

Vohn was as angry as Khyven had ever seen him. "Turn them into a Nox. Now you're going to tell me everything you know about that Nox, every single detail of your interaction, and we're going to try to piece together what's going on here. And just maybe we can save Lorelle."

"I think she bonded with him, Vohn. I think he's the one she—"

The door burst open and Slayter limped through. When he was strolling calmly in his full-length robes it was almost impossible to tell he'd lost his leg. But whenever he moved too fast, he limped.

Vohn and Khyven whirled to face him.

"I'm an idiot," Slayter said as though he'd been having a conversation with them seconds ago and was just now picking it back up. He breathed like he'd limped all the way up the steps from his laboratory.

"Where is Lorelle? Is she here?" He glanced around the room.

"Slayter—"

"Good, she's not here," he said. "I think it's better if I relay this to you first."

"Slayter," Vohn said. "Something has happened—"

"It's him." Slayter pointed at Khyven.

Vohn turned his angry gaze on Khyven like the Shadowvar wanted to say *"Yes, it certainly is him. He's ruined everything!"*

"I can't believe I was so dense," Slayter continued, shaking his head and hobbling toward his usual chair at the back of the table. "Right in front of my face, and I missed it." He glanced at them apologetically. "I don't usually do that, so I offer my apologies. I should have seen it. The important thing is that I *have* seen it now, I suppose, and maybe we can do something about it. Yes... Yes, I think we might be able to do something about it."

"Slayter," Vohn interjected. "Stop babbling! Tell us what you're on about."

Slayter looked up, confused, as though he *had* just told them. "Oh," he said. "Of course, it only seems obvious once you see it. I had the same problem—"

"Slayter!"

"It's him." He pointed at Khyven.

"You already said that," Vohn said with strained patience. "*What* is him?"

"The soul-bond. Lorelle's soul-bond. He's the one. It's Khyven."

Vohn's gaze snapped to Khyven, his eyes wide.

The bottom of Khyven's stomach dropped away.

CHAPTER SEVENTEEN

KHYVEN

Both Khyven and Vohn blurted out responses at the same time.

"I'm the one—That's impossible!—she bonded—He would—with?—have known!"

Slayter blinked. "Could you repeat that, please?"

Khyven blurted, "*I'm* the one she bonded with?"

Annoyed, the mage narrowed his eyes, as though he'd already gone over this ground. "Yes," he said with exaggerated slowness. Khyven wanted to punch him.

"That's impossible!" Vohn said. "He would have known."

"He was unconscious," Slayter explained.

"A Luminent can't bond with someone who's unconscious," Vohn insisted.

"She most certainly can," Slayter said. "Or rather, she can start the bond."

"Doesn't he have to look in her eyes and—"

Slayter waved that away like he was shooing a fly. "You're not understanding what a soul-bond actually is. A Luminent soul-bond can go one way. It's why Lorelle has always been so reserved, lest she accidentally start a bond with someone. If Lorelle had already formed feelings for Khyven, which I think is safe to say she had by then—we all had—letting them show while he was unconscious would actually have felt safer to her. She could have started the bond while he was incapable of refusing."

"I wouldn't have refused," Khyven said.

"Or trying to bond and failing. That too."

"I wouldn't have failed to bond."

"Actually, you probably would have," Slayter said.

"How do you know that?"

"Most likely you would have."

"Most *likely*?"

"It's so incredibly rare for a Human to actually succeed in a soul-bond with a Luminent that I only found one recorded instance in my library. Unfortunately, there are a number of instances of Luminents failing to soul-bond with a Human, then they wither and die." Slayter tapped his chin thoughtfully like he was considering a mathematically problem. "I'd give you one chance in a hundred maybe."

"So... still possible," Khyven said.

"Let me put it in terms you'll understand: Imagine Lorelle's soul is a tapestry with a hundred horizontal threads and a hundred vertical threads. She rips it in half, gives it to you. That now becomes part of your tiny Human soul."

"Tiny?"

Slayter held up his hand as he continued. "Imagine your soul is a tapestry. Except it's five horizontal threads and five vertical threads. Let's say you rip your soul in half and give that half to her. All right? Are you with me so far? Well now you've both begun the bonding. You've both acquiesced. There's still one more step. The remaining threads of your half-soul must then be tied to the remaining threads of her half-soul except... *you can't!* Because she has a hundred threads and you only have five. *That is how the bonding fails.*"

Khyven's belly felt cold. "That can't be true."

"I'm speculating, of course," Slayter said. "The odds could be much worse."

"Could they be better? Maybe you don't know… Maybe I have more threads in my soul than you think."

Slayter smiled. "I do like how you always believe you can win." He cocked his head. "I wonder how much of a factor that has played in your ability to win forty-nine bouts in the Night Ring—"

"Slayter…" Vohn warned, bringing the mage back to the present.

"Yes, of course." Slayter snapped out of his mental calculations and focused on Vohn. "Well, the good news is that with all of us working together I'd say we could improve Khyven's odds of a successful bond from one-in-a-hundred to one-in-fifty. Maybe one-in-twenty. Consulting with Lorelle, of course."

"Except," Vohn said. "Now we have a new problem—"

Slayter suddenly snapped his fingers. "Of course!" he exclaimed. "*That's* why the Giant's blood worked so well!" Slayter considered, marveling at whatever was happening in his mind. "Even I was surprised about how well it worked. I mean, the vial was two thousand years old, wasn't it? I didn't have many doubts that it was *real* Giant's blood—I was relatively certain about that—but I wasn't sure if it would actually *do* anything. It was the very essence of a gamble. But I had to try something, didn't I? I didn't say this at the time, but I didn't think it would actually bring him back to life. I even lamented wasting that precious vial on a lost cause—no offense, Khyven. I think my greatest hope was that the Giant's blood would slow the worsening of the poison. I knew it didn't have the ability to reconstruct your already-damaged tissues, but lo and behold, I was wrong! You started repairing yourself as though the Giant's blood was a miracle cure. I've been speculating ever since how it healed your body so quickly. But, actually, I was right. The Giant's blood made you more resistant to the ongoing damage of the Helm, but it was the vitality that Lorelle pushed into you that healed you. She literally gave you new life." He shook his head. "Right in front of me. Ah, I've been blind. I tell you, I don't remember the last time I'd so thoroughly failed to—"

"Slayter!" Vohn snapped.

Slayter sat up and nodded. "Right. Of course. Let's get to work. The poor thing must be in excruciating pain by now, standing so close to the balm for her woes yet resisting her impulses. Now that we know the problem, we can get started on the solution. Where is she?"

Vohn ground his teeth. "She's gone."

Slayter glanced around the room, then back at Vohn. "Clearly. Well, someone go get her."

"She's gone with a Nox," Vohn said.

"We have a Nox?" The mage's eyes lit with interest. "There's an actual Nox in Usara? In the daylight?"

Vohn threw up his hands in exasperation and looked to Khyven.

"A Nox took Lorelle away," Khyven said. "About five seconds before you burst through the door. She said he's going to give her a Plunnos to open the Thuros to go after Rhenn."

"*That's* a lie," Vohn muttered.

"Then the Nox wrapped her up in a cloak and they vanished," Khyven finished.

"A cloak?" Slayter's eyes glimmered with interest. "What kind of cloak?"

"Oh, for the love of Lotura. Lorelle has been kidnapped!" Vohn shouted.

That seemed to reach the mage. "Oh…" he said. "Oh, well that's no good. Yes, of course. Well, that's…" He tipped his head slightly back and forth. "Yes, that's bad. Nox and the Luminents don't… Well, they kill each other on sight, usually. Back a thousand years ago they did, anyway. Big wars and such. That was when there were still Nox to be seen. There hasn't been a Nox abroad in the world since—"

"Can we get her back?" Vohn interjected.

Slayter fell silent. He opened his mouth to speak, then shut it, then opened it again, then shut it again. "No," he finally said. "I don't think so, no. I mean, unless the Nox brings her back here."

"You can't find her..." Khyven waved a hand vaguely, "you know, magically?"

"Yes," he said. "I could probably do that. We certainly have enough of her personal items to possibly get a fix on her. I could do a location spell in the style of Life Magic. Just a smidgeon, you understand. Line Magic's version of Life Magic, as it were. So, it wouldn't be particularly strong and the range would be limited. Of course..." He tapped his chin thoughtfully. "I could increase that range by—"

Khyven sliced his hand through the air like he was physically chopping off the end of Slayter's sentence. "Then do it."

"Oh. Well, it wouldn't matter," Slayter said.

"Why?"

"I don't need a spell to tell you where she's gone."

"Then tell us!" Khyven said, exasperated.

"She's in a noktum. The Nox don't live outside the noktums. Moreover, I'd wager she's in the Great Noktum." Slayter's voice dropped to the lower tone he used when he talked to himself while working out some problem in his head. "All the texts I've read about the Nox say they retreated to the Great Noktum after the Luminent Wars. There may be scattered tribes and such in smaller noktums, like the one near us, but unlikely. In fact, I'm almost certain there are no Nox in the noktum near us. We'd have seen some sign of that when you were exploring the—"

"The Great Noktum is hundreds of miles away." Khyven didn't know much about Noksonon geography, but the map laid out on the table had it clearly marked, far below the Eternal Desert and the Rhaeg Mountains even. "Surely we can catch them before they get too far."

"Hardly. You said they vanished into his cloak?"

"That's what it looked like," Khyven said.

"Yes," Vohn confirmed.

"Well, he has a noktum cloak," Slayter said. "Wherever he wanted to go, he's already there."

"Then find her in the Great Noktum," Khyven interrupted.

"Well, that would hardly matter," Slayter said.

"Why," Khyven said through his teeth, "would that not matter?"

Slayter blinked. "You'd die."

"It would be nice," Vohn said in a calm-ish tone, "if you would slow down a little bit for us, Slayter. Explain to us what is happening in your mind. Sometimes you forget to do that."

"My apologies. I will explain. I could locate her. Probably. I might even be able to work a teleportation spell that would take us all the way to the edge of the Great Noktum—if I prepared for a few days. But even if I could do all that and we traveled to the Great Noktum in the blink of an eye, we only have amulets that last for an hour or so. Unless she is right at the edge—which I doubt—you could never make it into and out of there fast enough. The monsters would devour you the moment the amulets' power faded. Not to mention that, once inside, we would need a master guide to navigate the terrain. And we don't know anyone who is a master of *anything* inside the noktum."

Khyven felt a chill. Memories flashed unbidden through his mind. The giant raven leaning over him, his glistening black eyes watching Khyven, his chillingly lucid speech issuing forth from that long, sharp beak.

Rauvelos.

"Yes," Khyven said. "Yes, we do."

CHAPTER EIGHTEEN

KHYVEN

K hyven, Vohn, and Slayter stopped before the tumbledown gate of the towering nuraghi's courtyard. He hitched his pack—filled with foodstuffs and other useful things for a long journey—higher on his shoulders.

The Mavric iron sword whined in his mind.

Khyven didn't like that one bit. The sword had begun talking to him the moment he'd stepped into the noktum. That was new, and Khyven suspected it had everything to do with the Giant's blood Slayter had pumped into him. The sword whined like an insistent hound ready for the hunt. There weren't any words, though it "felt" like the sword was talking as Khyven understood the meaning exactly. The blade longed to be unleashed, and somehow Khyven could now hear its desires.

While Khyven had slept after the Battle of the Queen's Return, Slayter had occupied himself with studying the Mavric iron sword. To protect himself, he'd created a magical, protective sheath that would contain the melting, destructive effects of the Mavric iron—at least as long as the user didn't draw the blade. It was quite an amazing accomplishment. The magical sheath also made the unwieldy sword easy to draw. While the sword was six feet long, the sheath itself was only three feet, easily worn over Khyven's shoulder, yet the enormous sword could be sheathed to the hilt without the point bursting through the end.

Magic. Khyven was beginning to see the appeal.

So Khyven could wear the thing across his back without encumbering himself, but the insistent whine was new. It felt... intimate, like some kind of secret bond.

He had considered asking the mage about this new aspect of the sword, but in the rush to chase Lorelle, he hadn't wanted to stop and take the time. He knew Slayter well enough at this point to know the mage would want to study the effects immediately.

Of course, Khyven could have left the blade behind, but they were walking into a magical noktum to brace magical beings. The Mavric iron sword was the most potent weapon he had. The thing could cut through just about anything. It weighed less than a small dagger and it became one with his hand when he used it. In short, it was dominating in a fight. That was something they would likely need.

Wielding it could kill him, but that was a risk he was willing to run. Of course, he didn't intend to use it unless at utmost need. He'd brought his other swords—one of steel and the other of wood—to be used in normal situations. He only planned to draw the Mavric iron sword if an altercation got weird.

Khyven shoved the whine to the bottom of his mind and stared at the Giant's castle with Vohn and Slayter. This was the third time he'd come here, and the enormous thing still staggered his imagination. It dwarfed the Usaran palace—the largest building Khyven had seen before coming here—its worn and crumbling towers vanishing upward into the dark gray sky.

The first time Khyven had set foot in this forbidding place, he'd almost been eaten by a huge raven named Rauvelos.

The second time Khyven had come here, he'd returned to ask a favor. He'd been certain Rauvelos would take offense and kill him. But the raven had given him the Helm of Darkness instead, an artifact that could control the minds of the monsters in the noktum. It had been key to defeating Vamreth and helping Rhenn retake her throne.

The creature's behavior was mystifying, but it apparently hinged on Khyven's Amulet of Noksonon. After a single glimpse at the back of the amulet the raven had changed from polite murderer to reluctant host. From what Khyven could piece together, the amulet gave its wearer the protection of Rauvelos's master, a Giant called Nhevalos, whose name was suspiciously similar to Khyven's adopted brother, Nhevaz.

Nhevaz was the one who had spirited Rhenn away through the Thuros.

Khyven couldn't see the big picture yet. None of them could, though Khyven had told them everything he knew about Nhevaz and the old man.

Slayter suspected Nhevaz was a descendant of Nhevalos—or perhaps even the legendary Giant himself. Apparently, Giants lived for thousands of years.

Either way, Nhevaz's favor seemed to carry absolute authority with Rauvelos, and since Khyven's amulet had been a gift from Nhevaz, Khyven could walk the noktum unmolested.

But even though Rauvelos had told Khyven he was safe here, he'd never felt it. Rauvelos had never indicated that he served Khyven. The raven did what he did for his own inscrutable reasons, his own internal code. Khyven felt there were secret protocols being observed, and if he unknowingly crossed some unseen line his protections would vanish and the noktum would turn from sanctuary to nightmare.

Now he was returning to make another request, and he felt that unseen line out there somewhere, more acutely than ever before. The giant bird might welcome him and help, accepting Khyven's requests as part of his oath to Nhevalos.

Or he might not.

Khyven pulled himself from his grim doubts and back to the present. He glanced at his companions. Slayter's eyes were wider than Khyven had ever seen them as he looked all around. In the

Usaran palace, nothing fazed Slayter. Not Lorelle's soul-bond. Not the sudden appearance of a Nox. He'd even shrugged off the loss off his leg.

But during their walk through the noktum, it became clear that Slayter, while amazingly knowledgeable about just about everything, had never actually been inside a noktum.

At first, he hadn't been in favor of Slayter coming along. Khyven had worried they'd have to turn back after fifteen minutes and return the hobbling Slayter to the palace. Khyven had known two fighters in the Night Ring who'd had peg legs. They were not fast, nor did they have a great deal of stamina for staying on that false leg. He was sure the one-legged mage would only slow them down.

But while Slayter walked with a slight limp, he'd crossed the distance as fast as Vohn. The prosthetic leg Vohn had crafted was, apparently, far more sophisticated than a peg leg. The bottom was actually in the shape of a flat foot with a clever spring and hinge at the ankle. Whatever mechanism they'd used to secure it to Slayter's leg seemed quite solid. It hadn't fallen off yet, and it certainly hadn't slowed the mage down.

Vohn's attitude toward Slayter had changed since they'd entered the noktum. Vohn was constantly snapping at Slayter in the queen's meeting room for his lengthy tangents, but the Shadowvar started acting like a mother hen the moment they'd stepped into the darkness.

Both Slayter and Vohn stopped when they reached the top of the rubble pile of the gate, breathing hard. Slayter reached out a hand and Vohn moved closer so Slayter could set it on Vohn's shoulder to steady himself.

"Well, that's just... so different," the wide-eyed mage huffed.

"Different from what?" Khyven asked.

"My imagination. The drawings. I mean, I've seen depictions of this very nuraghi. But..."

"It is big," Vohn said.

"It's... mind-bending," Slayter breathed. "A monolithic testament to eldritch beings beyond the scope of Human imagination—"

"Let's write nuraghi poetry later," Khyven interjected. "The amulets got us this far, but they don't have enough to get us all the way back to Usara. If this goes badly, we're going to have to run for Rhenn's old camp."

He made his way down the stones between the gates and into the courtyard. Vohn and Slayter followed more awkwardly.

"Badly? How could it go badly?" Vohn asked.

"So many ways," Khyven murmured.

Rauvelos was hardly predictable. Khyven still didn't know exactly why the bird had lent him the Helm of Darkness. In fact, while Khyven had been asleep, the Helm of Darkness had vanished, as had the similar helm Vamreth had used in their final battle.

Slayter had locked both helms and the Mavric iron sword—when he wasn't experimenting on it—safely in a vault. When Khyven and his friends had decided to visit Rauvelos, Khyven thought it would be prudent to return the magical items to Rauvelos. So last night, Slayter had taken Khyven to his laboratory where he'd secured the deadly treasures.

Neither helm was there, though the Mavric iron sword remained.

Slayter had found that fascinating, of course. That vault had a heavy lock and three spells protecting it. The lock was still locked. The spells were still intact. Yet the helms were gone.

It had to be Rauvelos. The raven had somehow retrieved the items.

Khyven hadn't been sure if the remaining Mavric iron sword was a sign of favor from the giant bird or not.

"Wait. Badly? How could it go badly? I thought you said you knew this creature," Vohn said.

"Rauvelos," Slayter said reverently.

"Rauvelos," Vohn corrected.

"Steward of the realm of Nhevalos the Betrayer," Slayter said.

Vohn flashed an irritated look at Slayter.

"Nhevalos the Betrayer?" Khyven said, feeling a chill scamper up his spine. That name didn't bode well for Rauvelos's predictability. "You called him Nhevalos the Savior before."

"Well, he's both, depending on which side of the war you were on. Nhevalos is a fascinating historical figure. The idea that he might still be alive, still orchestrating events in the world…"

"I thought you said he was on *our* side."

"I said he fought for Humans in the Human-Giant War."

"That's our side," Vohn growled.

"In point of fact, it's the side of the mortal rebels who rose up against Giant rule seventeen hundred years ago," Slayter said. "Strictly speaking, that's not us."

"How is that *not* us?"

"Well, seventeen hundred years is a long time."

"You're saying he's *not* on our side?"

Slayter shrugged as he gingerly stepped onto the ground. "What I've read indicates he was a cunning Giant who was always a step ahead of his enemies. Who can say what Nhevalos is thinking." He gave Vohn a sidelong glance. "That's what makes it so fascinating. Are we his friends or his foes?"

"He stole Rhenn," Vohn said.

"Yes, he did. But to help us or hurt us?"

"How could that help—"

"All right," Khyven interrupted. "Discuss later. Keep your eyes open now. Slayter, whatever attack spells you have, have them ready."

"Of course, Sir Knight," Slayter said.

They marched across the long, flat courtyard. Khyven kept his gaze forward and did not look at the eerie statue that had frightened him last time. It was only when he and Vohn reached the enormous steps that he realized they'd lost Slayter.

Khyven whirled, his hand going to his sword, but the mage was in plain sight a hundred feet behind them, standing next to, and staring up at, the same statue that had tortured Khyven's mind.

"Slayter!" Khyven whispered harshly. When the mage didn't move, he cursed softly and jogged back. Vohn stayed at his heels.

Slayter seemed mesmerized. Khyven gripped the mage's arm, intending to pull him away.

"Khyven," Slayter said excitedly. "Do you know what this is?"

"A damned eerie statue," Khyven said, tugging Slayter's arm. "Let's go."

Slayter gently dislodged his arm from Khyven's grip. "This is…" he trailed off, his face alight with wonder. "This is alive."

A chill ran up Khyven's back. "It's a statue."

"No," Slayter said. "I think he's still alive, still in there. Khyven, this could be a real Giant!"

"Impossible." Khyven looked up at the statue's face. It began to change almost instantly, just like it had before. The haughty, noble brow creased in anger, folds in the forehead deepened to a frightening parody of rage. Khyven forced himself to look away.

"Slayter…" Vohn approached.

"Miraculous," the mage said, awed.

"This isn't your laboratory, Slayter. Almost everything in the noktum can kill you. Stop looking at it." Vohn took Slayter's other arm and tried to pull him away, but the mage shook his head and wriggled out of his grip.

"Imagine what we could learn…" Slayter whispered.

Khyven was tempted to pick up the skinny mage and carry him away, but he hesitated.

"Just… give me a second," Slayter said as he flipped open the cylindrical pouch at his side. His deft, slender fingers clicked through the stack of meticulously made clay disks and he pulled one out. "Ah," he lamented. "I wish I had more time. I should really craft a spell specifically for—"

"Slayter, we can't just stay here," Vohn said. "We don't have the time."

Slayter's head came up and he looked around as though just realizing they were in the middle of the noktum. "Oh, yes. Yes, of course. I'll be quick."

Vohn sighed and glanced around, but Khyven was intrigued despite himself. In the past, mysteries like the shifting expression of the statue were simply mysteries, unable to be solved. There were some things that mortal men simply couldn't know.

But Slayter seemed to look at mysteries like annoying masks to be removed. And he actually had the ability to pull those masks away, to discover the secrets beneath. His well of knowledge was so deep he could unravel mysteries no one else could.

Khyven had taken one look at the statue and run away like a wild animal running from fire, but Slayter wanted to understand it. Maybe Slayter couldn't wield a sword or lift a person and carry them away, but he could look past the inscrutable and see the workings of the world. That was amazing to Khyven.

"Give him a moment," he murmured.

Vohn raised his eyebrows, surprised.

Slayter placed the clay disk on the flat surface of the pedestal, which came up to his chest, then he hesitated.

"What?" Vohn asked nervously.

"I can't just..." He pressed his lips into a line, then glanced down at the charcoal dirt and black grass at his feet. "Yes. This." He knelt, managing his prosthetic awkwardly, and scooped up a handful of dirt. Vohn helped him stand, all the while looking worriedly at Khyven, perhaps hoping he would do something to stop this, but Khyven was fascinated.

Slayter scattered the dirt across the pedestal, up to the shiny black feet of the statue. He took out his little metal scratcher, a twin to the one he'd given Khyven when he'd first been sent to spy on the Queen-in-Exile.

"It won't be strong," Slayter murmured to himself, "but it'll do. I have to know."

The mage began his spell.

CHAPTER NINETEEN

KHYVEN

Slayter took a deep breath and slowly let it out. With steady hands, he scratched a line through the scattered dirt, carefully building a symmetrical symbol that meant nothing to Khyven. The mage's hands moved economically and confidently like he had done this a thousand times. He never raised the scratcher from the dirt. It took him less than a minute and the symbol looked complete except for one little line.

Slayter let out another slow breath, careful not to disturb his creation.

Khyven had never seen Slayter at work before. He'd never noticed how deft the man's hands were, his fingers long and agile. They seemed almost to have a life of their own as they handled the first scratcher, then produced a second from some pocket in his robes.

Even Khyven, who had relied on his reflexes and his sense of his body to save his life over and over again, didn't have the kind of manual dexterity Slayter now displayed. Every motion was intentional, every move through the air, every single shift of the scratcher in his hand, they all seemed to have a ritualistic purpose and Slayter was aware of each tiny movement.

"Slayter—" Vohn began, but the mage gave a curt shake of his head.

Khyven put a hand on Vohn's shoulder. The muscles in Vohn's jaw flexed, but he didn't say anything else.

"Vohn, hold this for me please," Slayter murmured, nodding at the coin resting on the pedestal.

"This is a bad idea," Vohn said.

Slayter remained completely focused on his dirt drawing and the coin beside it, never looking at Vohn, but his forehead wrinkled a little in frustration. Khyven moved forward and carefully touched the clay coin without moving it, holding it firm.

Slayter nodded, closed his eyes, and drew a breath, then opened them again. He lowered both hands simultaneously. The tip of each scratcher touched their respective symbols, one on the coin and the other on the dirt drawing. Slayter drew two lines at the same time, one an eighth of an inch long through the clay and the other two inches long on the dirt. He finished each symbol at exactly the same moment.

Blue light flared from the lines of the dirt drawing and orange light from the coin. The sudden color in the otherwise gray-and-black landscape was shocking. Khyven started, though he kept the coin pressed firmly against the black marble.

"Let go," Slayter murmured, and Khyven lifted his hand away.

"Lotura!" Vohn whispered harshly. "No light! You can't make light in here!"

Slayter ignored him.

The orange light from the coin slithered up the legs of the statue, circling around and around until it reached his waist. The blue light chased it like a little brother trying to catch up.

Slayter held his breath. He held both scratchers at shoulder level.

The statue moved!

Its hands clenched into fists, making a grinding noise. Vohn stepped back and Khyven drew his sword. The statue craned its neck, making the same grinding noise, and it looked down at them. The rage-filled expression hit Khyven like a blow. The statue opened its mouth as though he was yelling, but no sound came out.

Then the blue light caught up with the orange, wrapping around the Giant's throat, and a roar exploded from its mouth, shattering the silence.

"Release me!" the Giant demanded.

"Senji's Teeth!" Khyven exclaimed. He hadn't known what to expect, but by the abyss itself, he hadn't expected the statue to speak!

Slayter held up an imperious hand to Khyven, indicating he should be quiet.

"Who are you?" Slayter demanded.

"Cockroach," the Giant said through his teeth. He strained, veins pulsing in his stone neck as though he was trying to lift a boulder. His arm jerked forward an inch, popping and cracking. "Release me, Human!"

"Answer my question," Slayter replied calmly.

"I will *kill* you."

"Answer my question and I will release you."

Both Vohn and Khyven looked in horror at Slayter, but again he gestured that they remain still.

The Giant roared again, head tilting pitifully upward with the same popping and cracking sound.

"You attacked this castle, didn't you?" Slayter asked. "You came to do harm."

"Your bones will splinter as I twist them!" the Giant raged, painfully shifting his head as he looked down again at Slayter.

"You'll do nothing unless I allow it," Slayter said. "Answer my question and I'll release you."

The Giant's eyes blazed with blue fire and his stone lips peeled back from his teeth.

"What is your name?" Slayter insisted.

"I am Harkandos," the Giant ground out. "Which will be the last name on your lips as I crush you to paste, cockroach."

Slayter twitched as though he recognized the name, but the zeal in his eyes only increased.

"Who did this to you?" he demanded. "Tell me his name—"

The earth jumped, rippling like a wave, and threw the three of them away from the pedestal. Khyven shouted, launching from the sudden rock wave, flipping in midair, and landing on his feet. Slayter and Vohn tumbled like rag dolls.

The Giant raised a hand like he was holding a chalice by the bowl. Earth rose up on either side of Slayter and Vohn, throwing paving stones and showering them in dirt.

"Khyven!" Slayter yelled. The mage looked terrified. The earth rose high and smashed down on Khyven's friends.

"Slayter! Vohn!" Khyven yelled.

But the earth crumbled in a swirl of orange light. The dust cleared, revealing Vohn and Slayter, unharmed. Slayter's eyes were narrowed in concentration. Orange light emanated from two fingers, where crumbles of a broken clay disk sifted downward.

"Khyven!" he shouted. "The symbols. Break the symbols!"

Khyven looked at the pedestal. Despite the upheaval of the earth, the pedestal remained completely undisturbed. The disk still lay at the Giant's feet, as did the dirt drawing, completely intact.

But the Giant had changed. His arms were moving almost normally. The earth heaved again, rising like a wave over Slayter.

Khyven sprinted for the pedestal—

The ground launched him upward, twenty feet in the air. He yelped, dropped his sword, and flailed his arms. The ground rushed up fast and he barely managed to turn his fall into an awkward roll.

He tumbled badly. The wind was slammed from his body and a rock jammed into his kidney so hard he felt it must have punctured his back.

But Khyven had been in pain before. The key to survival was to keep moving. When you danced with death, you had to keep moving or death would catch you.

He rolled just as a curling wave of earth smashed down where he'd been, and he launched himself to his feet with a grunt. His sword was too far away, so he left it.

He still had the Mavric iron sword on his back. They weren't even an hour into this rescue and it looked like he would already have to draw it.

Blue wind gusted past him, showing him the path to the pedestal. He charged forward as a wave of blue wind rose to his left. He jumped away at the last second and a ton of rock and earth landed where he had been. He sprinted forward.

The blue wind formed into another wall, and he pulled up short just as a rock wall thrust up from the ground. Spikes of blue wind thrust up beneath him and everywhere around him. Khyven jumped straight up just as they became rock spikes. If he'd been a second slower, he'd have been impaled. The nearest spike grazed his shoulder, glancing off his shoulder plate, and he tumbled between the spikes.

The attack stopped, but he realized it was only because the wall that had blocked Khyven from reaching the pedestal obscured the Giant's vision. Perhaps he thought Khyven was dead.

He let out a quiet breath and looked at the jagged protrusions in the dirt-and-rock wall and saw a way up. Moving rapidly, he leapt onto the first tiny ledge and launched toward the second, grabbing it and pulling himself up the wall. He crested the top—

And stood face to face with the surprised Giant, who could now apparently move from the waist up, though his legs still seemed entirely made of stone.

Khyven pulled a dagger as three spears of blue wind stabbed up from the wall. He jumped toward the Giant, twisting as the spikes barely missed him. Khyven whipped his arm up and threw his dagger—

The Giant swatted him from the air.

It was like being hit with a pillar of stone. Pain exploded in Khyven's chest. He crashed to the ground and tumbled. Stars swirled in his vision. He couldn't breathe.

He had to get up. The Giant wouldn't hesitate. Spikes of earth would spear him if he didn't get up!

Khyven struggled, rising shakily to his hands and knees.

Flickers of blue shot up through him and all around him—

A raven's caw pierced the air so loudly it felt like someone had boxed Khyven's ears. The blue spikes vanished.

"Rauvelos!" the Giant growled. "I will gut you, bird. I will feast on your entrails!"

Enormous raven's wings blotted out the sky. A hurricane wind rolled past Khyven and slammed into the pedestal.

"Rauvelo—" the Giant's grinding voice cut off as the dirt of Slayter's spell scattered. The orange light burst apart like sparks from a fire.

Rauvelos's huge talon reached in, beneath the Giant's swinging fist, and its point shattered the clay coin. Blue light exploded into sparks, just like the orange light. The Giant screamed soundlessly, fists clenched in utter agony.

Then the stone took control again.

The Giant's flexed arms uncurled. His clenched fists opened and softened into relaxed hands. He stood straight and resumed the same haughty posture as before, staring off into the distance.

Heavy wings beat as Rauvelos landed before Khyven, settling himself on part of the cobblestone path that hadn't been uprooted. He folded his wings against his sides and the courtyard fell silent except for the hard breathing of Khyven and his friends.

The bird turned glittering black eyes upon them and Khyven felt the raven's anger emanating like a heat wave.

"I should eat you all," he said.

CHAPTER TWENTY

KHYVEN

Khyven struggled to get to his feet. Nothing seemed broken, but he felt like someone had taken a club to him. He shrugged his shoulders and tried to shake it off as he picked up his sword.

Vohn and Slayter slowly moved toward Khyven, their wide eyes fixed on Rauvelos.

The giant raven towered over them, and he truly looked like he was about to eat them. His gaze stabbed at Vohn and Slayter, then flicked to Khyven. The bird opened his beak, clicked it shut, then opened it again.

"Come with me." He turned and hopped once toward the castle.

"Where are we going?" Vohn asked.

Rauvelos stopped and his head swiveled on his body, facing backward to focus on Khyven. "Tell your friends to be quiet."

Khyven shot a fierce look at Vohn, who shut up.

"Rauvelos, we only came for information," Khyven said. "I wanted to ask—"

Rauvelos flicked his wing past Khyven's nose, cutting him off.

"This is not a parlor where we may engage in diverting conversation," the giant raven said. "Look." His extended wing was actually pointing at something toward the entrance to the courtyard.

Khyven spared a glance and almost jumped out of his skin. A horde of noktum monsters were clustered at the gate and all along the tumbled stone wall. The sky was filled with Sleeths, twisting and curling around each other like flying worms. Three enormous spiders, each at least three stories tall, loomed above the Sleeths on slender legs. Higher still, dozens of Gylarns flapped silently across the dark sky. On the ground, Kyolars and other creatures Khyven couldn't even describe paced and growled at the edge of the wrecked barrier.

"Senji's Teeth!" he swore.

"Now," Rauvelos said, "you can either quiet yourselves, follow me, and do as I say. Or you can go back home through that. They are eager to meet you, and they lack my willpower. Choose."

Slayter's mouth hung open, and Vohn looked like he was about to be sick.

"We'll go with you," Khyven said.

"So very wise," Rauvelos said, and he launched into the air. His heavy wings beat once, twice, three times, and he sailed in a perfect arc to the top of the steps a hundred yards away. He landed and settled his wings against his sides. "I suggest you hurry," he called, his voice carrying across the distance.

The three of them ran toward the giant stairway. The monsters behind them growled and wailed and shrieked. Khyven half expected them to leap over the wall and run them down, but they did not enter the courtyard. He suspected the only reason was because Rauvelos was standing on those steps.

Khyven and Vohn helped Slayter with the too-tall steps, and they finally arrived at the landing before the tall, broken doors. Without a word, Rauvelos pushed open one door and stepped inside.

He led them through the foyer, where the corpses of Giants—which Rhenn and her group had pilfered the last time they were here—lay. Rauvelos led them up the steps at the back of the room, which were shallower than the front steps, but still half again as tall as a normal stair.

They went up and up. Slayter began to struggle at the third flight.

"Where are we going?" Khyven said. "I don't know that Slayter can climb much more."

Rauvelos turned, his black eyes glinting. He nodded once and took a left at the top of the landing. With Khyven and Vohn's help Slayter made it, but he was limping heavily now. Rauvelos walked sedately, his backward crow legs carefully picking each step, until he reached a set of giant double doors on the left, opened them with a tap of his long beak, and disappeared within.

Khyven and his friends followed and entered a room unlike anything he'd ever seen. The walls were dark black and polished smooth, rising into a conical shape at the ceiling. Of course, everything in the noktum was some shade of gray or black, but Khyven got the impression that this room, if revealed in full sunlight, would still be jet-black, as though the very walls had been built from onyx.

Two tall, pointed-arch windows on the far side of the room opened out onto the courtyard far below. An enormous black cauldron sat on a circular dais to the left. The rest of wall space was covered in mirrors of all different sizes and shapes. Rauvelos stood before three identical dark mirrors as tall as he was. To the right of those was a diamond mirror and then a circular one, both huge. Mirrors of every conceivable shape dotted the onyx walls all the way to the conical ceiling. Through the magical sight of Khyven's Amulet of Noksonon, they all looked like flat pools of black water.

"Please close the door," Rauvelos said. Vohn, also spellbound by the strange room, glanced at Khyven, who nodded. The little Shadowvar pushed the thick, tall doors closed one at a time.

Rauvelos walked around the curved wall of the room and stopped in front of one of the looming windows.

"Do you know what you almost did?" he asked.

No one said anything at first.

"We are sorry," Khyven said. "We didn't mean to—"

"Ignorance is the hallmark your race, Human. But that does not excuse what you almost did. I should kill you all if for no other reason than to ensure you never have the chance to do such a stupid thing again. After seventeen hundred years, your kind has forgotten all of its hard-won lessons. Now you stumble around, touching your transient little spark of life to dry grass."

"But he is alive, right?" Slayter asked excitedly, his eyes gleaming. "I was right about that? His current state is a prison."

Rauvelos turned his beak toward Slayter, but he didn't say anything, as though he was contemplating if he should acknowledge Slayter's existence at all.

"I only wanted to question him, to know what he knew," Slayter persisted.

Rauvelos opened his beak half an inch and clicked it shut. "You wanted to interrogate Harkandos..." he said in a low, disgusted voice. "You are a child tottering on a ridge over a thousand-foot fall, and you have no idea how close you came to oblivion; how close you came to engulfing us all in war."

"I simply cast animation and speaking spells upon the stone," Slayter argued. "I did not transmute anything. I specifically didn't do that. I simply... wanted to give him a voice."

"Human..." Rauvelos shook his head gravely from side to side. "Harkandos *speaks* to stone. Stone is how my master trapped him. The spell that holds him uses his own power against him, and the spell is balanced—*perfectly* balanced. When Harkandos tries to break free, the spell increases commensurately. When he relaxes, the spell relaxes. You disrupted that balance. That was all the chance Harkandos needed."

"Fascinating," Slayter breathed, seemingly oblivious to the dire warning. "So Harkandos is actually imprisoning himself, a never-ending cycle of push and pull."

Rauvelos's eyes narrowed. "I will make a prediction for you, little mage. Your thirst for knowledge will kill you."

"Great Rauvelos," Slayter said, bowing deeply despite the fact that his leg must be in misery. "I beg your forgiveness. I have not properly demonstrated my gratitude to you. Not only did you save my life and the lives of my friends, but meeting you is the greatest honor I can imagine."

Rauvelos's round black eyes stared at Slayter so long a translucent eyelid flicked over them and back. The giant bird turned to Khyven, then back to Slayter. "I would eat you if not for Khyven."

Vohn moved closer to Khyven. Zeal lit Slayter's eyes as he stared at Rauvelos, like this was the most exciting and wonderful thing that had ever happened to him.

"So Harkandos is one of the Noksonoi who fought in the Human-Giant War?" Slayter pressed. "Was he a general? Did the Noksonoi have generals? So little is known about their organizational structure. Was there a king?"

Rauvelos turned to Khyven. "Khyven the Unkillable, tell your friend to stop talking now."

"Slayter, shut it," Khyven said. Surprisingly, Slayter did.

Silence fell over the room.

Rauvelos studied Khyven. Finally, the giant raven said, "The Helm of Darkness should have devoured you. That's twice you've surprised me, Khyven the Unkillable."

"It was actually fascinating," Slayter interjected. "We—"

Khyven drew a dagger and flipped it at Slayter. It flew past Slayter's ear and clanged into the wall behind him before clattering to the floor.

"Vohn, gag him if you have to," Khyven growled.

"Tell me," Rauvelos said. "How did you survive?"

Khyven didn't know how Rauvelos would react to Slayter's notion of putting the blood of a Giant into a Human's veins, so he said, "A Luminent soul-bond."

Rauvelos cocked his head. A heartbeat later, he said, "An interesting solution."

"Now that same Luminent—our friend—has been taken by a Nox, spirited away using some kind of magical cloak."

Rauvelos's head raised. "A noktum cloak?"

"I don't... I don't know. We think so. It was made of normal fabric on the outside—"

"But the darkness of a noktum inside," Rauvelos finished. "A noktum cloak."

Khyven nodded. "That's what Slayter guessed. What is that?"

"A magical item nearly as powerful as the Helm of Darkness." Rauvelos turned away, his giant talons clicking on the cobblestone. He gazed out the window. "You are refreshing, Khyven the Unkillable. But you are also a problem. I have made assumptions about you—that you have the protection of my master, that he wishes you to remain alive—but these may be incorrect assumptions. For instance, I now believe giving you the Helm of Darkness was a mistake. I thought any havoc you wreaked would be of little consequence to the world at large. I also thought it would kill you and I wouldn't have to consider your interesting presence any longer." He drew a breath, his huge body expanding and contracting. "But you survived. And now you want to fight a Giant."

Khyven's throat went dry. "The Nox is working for a Giant?"

Rauvelos swiveled his head and his profile cut the gray light of the window. "You insisted on stepping into a larger world, Khyven the Unkillable. Now you have."

"Why would a Giant want Lorelle?"

"Why would *Tovos* want her?" Rauvelos amended, looking out the window again. "That is the question. And a more important question I cannot fathom."

Rauvelos was silent for so long that Khyven opened his mouth.

"Your request, no doubt," Rauvelos cut him off before Khyven could speak, "is for me to assist you in entering the Great Noktum."

Khyven glanced over his shoulder at Slayter, surprised that the giant bird had said exactly what Slayter had. The mage's eyes gleamed as his guess was validated.

"How do you know they went to the Great Noktum?" Khyven asked.

"Mmmm," Rauvelos said. "Because Lord Tovos created the noktum cloaks. If this Nox is using one, then he is Tovos's creature. And if Tovos is anywhere on Noksonon, it is in the Great Noktum."

Khyven wasn't sure what that was supposed to mean. Where else could a person be except on Noksonon? In the ocean? On a ship maybe?

"If I were inclined to help you get to the Great Noktum, how do you propose to find her once you are there? Do you have an artifact that can track her?"

"We do." Slayter eagerly stepped forward, pulling a miniature metal house from within his robes. It was two inches square and the sloped roof opened at the top with a clever little hatch. Slayter demonstrated, clicking it open. "What I do is I set it on cleared ground. Not stone, mind you. Not grass, either, but dirt," he said. "Open the top and it reforms the dirt into the local terrain in miniature. She becomes a tiny figure on the map and we can see where she is."

Rauvelos did not seem impressed, though Khyven had thought the device... well... magical.

"What is its range?" Rauvelos asked.

"Ten miles."

Rauvelos peered at the item. "That's poor. Did you use a finger to calibrate the artifact to her presence?"

"Um," Slayter said. "No. A scrap of her clothing."

Rauvelos shook his head. "A finger would have been better. You could have attained a range of a hundred miles."

"I..." Slayter glanced at Khyven.

Vohn looked stricken. "A finger? Like a chopped-off finger?"

Khyven held his hand up to Vohn. "She was already gone."

"Ah. Well, without blood or tissue, a strand of hair would clearly be the way to go. You might have tripled your range," Rauvelos said.

"Her hairbrush was empty," Slayter said.

"But of course, Luminents don't shed hair like Humans," Rauvelos said. "Let this be a lesson for you, mage. You should cut a lock of hair from each of your companions. And your enemies, if you can. It's very useful to have."

That sounded ominous.

"So, can you help us?" Khyven asked. "Get there, I mean."

Rauvelos looked down at them all, then focused on Khyven. "Can I? Of course, I can. Should I?" He shook his head. "Tovos has kept his distance from my master's realm for centuries. And I have kept mine from him."

"Are you sure?" Slayter said.

Khyven shot a look at the mage, but Slayter ignored him and moved closer to Rauvelos.

Rauvelos swiveled his head and gave the mage a cold look.

"I locked two Helms of Darkness in my vault," Slayter persisted. "The one you loaned Khyven, and the other one."

"I took them, of course," Rauvelos said, as though daring Slayter to accuse him of stealing.

"Two Helms. The one you loaned Khyven, and the one Vamreth had."

The raven watched him.

"Well, where did the other one come from?" Slayter asked. "I imagine one cannot simply buy a Helm of Darkness at a traveling bazaar. It has to be given by someone inordinately powerful."

Rauvelos narrowed his eyes.

"My point is," Slayter continued, "maybe Tovos hasn't been respecting your boundaries as much as you think."

Rauvelos cocked his head. "You have an interesting mind, mageling."

Slayter gave a sweeping bow. "I am humbled you think so."

"I will help you," Rauvelos said abruptly.

Khyven had opened his mouth to attempt to convince Rauvelos to help in the wake of his inevitable refusal... Khyven closed his mouth and cleared his throat instead. "Thank you."

"I never liked Tovos. Neither does my master," Rauvelos said. "So yes, I can get you to the Great Noktum. Can I bring you back? No. The Great Noktum does not lie within my stewardship."

"Then how do we get back?"

"Since there is a noktum cloak in play, I suggest you steal it and learn how to use it."

"Steal it?"

"Or I suppose you could convince the Nox to give it to you."

"Would he?"

"No."

"What if we can't steal it?"

"Oh, you can't. Lord Tovos would have to be tied up in mystical chains, slathering and snapping before he'd let you take one of his cloaks. You're going to die."

Khyven exchanged a glance with Vohn.

"Don't look so surprised, Khyven the Unkillable. If your goal is to live, traveling to the Great Noktum is a terrible idea," Rauvelos said.

"Then why help us?"

Rauvelos shrugged, which was interesting to see on a giant bird. "You survived the Helm of Darkness. This is an equivalent bit of ridiculous nonsense. I'm curious to see if you survive this."

"Thanks," Khyven said drily.

The facile part of Rauvelos's mouth, just behind the beak, curved upward. That was what passed for a smile on the giant bird, Khyven supposed. "You could get out on the back of a dragon, I suppose. Is that how you will manage this impossible feat, Khyven the Unkillable? There is a dragon in the Great Noktum. His name is Jai'ketakos. I don't advise you wake him, though. He's been trapped in his cave for more than a thousand years."

"With a Dragon's Chain?" Slayter interrupted, so excited he'd taken another few steps toward Rauvelos. "Is he trapped with a Dragon's Chain?"

Rauvelos's round, black eyes shifted, flicked a glance at the mage, then looked back at Khyven without acknowledging Slayter's question.

"You could try to get out on foot, of course, but it's a weeks-long journey and your amulets will give out long before you make it a day. I could do something to extend the life of those amulets, I suppose, but if a servant of Tovos finds you, he's going to feel my touch in the spell. They'll instantly recognize what you are and kill you. And even if a servant of Tovos doesn't find you, the lands of the Great Noktum make my master's realm look like a fanciful garden. I predict you will last two days." Rauvelos cocked his head. "Do you still wish to go?"

"I have to."

"Of course. And the mage? You will take him? He is talented, and I imagine you could use those talents."

Khyven nodded.

"Of course. Then let us strike a bargain, Khyven the Unkillable. I will send you and your mage to the Great Noktum. You leave the Shadowborn morsel with me."

Khyven glanced at Vohn. "You want me to leave Vohn here?"

"As payment."

"So, you can eat him?" Khyven blurted. "No!"

"Khyven the Unkillable, you're being unreasonable. Basic politeness indicates you offer me something in return."

"I'm not going to let you eat Vohn!"

Rauvelos cocked his head.

Vohn's eyes were wide, but he didn't say anything.

"Vohn is my friend. I can't use him as a trade for favors."

"You most certainly can," Rauvelos said.

"I won't!"

"Is this how it works in Human society? You take and take favors and you give nothing in return?" Rauvelos said. "I begin to think you're slighting me, Khyven the Unkillable."

"I wasn't aware I needed to bring a Human sacrifice!"

Rauvelos sighed and lifted his beak toward the domed ceiling as though reminiscing. "Human sacrifice... Those were heady days," he said softly.

Khyven exchanged glances with Slayter and Vohn and wondered if they were in for a fight after all. While Rauvelos's attention was on his fond memories of Human sacrifices, Khyven beckoned Slayter and Vohn to back toward the door, though he didn't have much hope of outrunning the raven. But fighting would be worse. Rauvelos had contained Harkandos with relative ease, and the statue had nearly killed all three of them in seconds. Khyven didn't think much of their chances in a fight.

Rauvelos finally sighed and murmured to himself, "With one foot already in the mud, one might as well go swimming." He turned his gaze back to Khyven and seemed amused that they had backed away from him. "Very well, I will send you. If that is what you wish."

"All of us?"

"You may keep your little Shadowvar morsel."

"Thank you."

Rauvelos didn't acknowledge that. Instead, he walked across the stones toward the door, which swung open of its own accord as he neared.

"Come with me."

CHAPTER TWENTY-ONE

LORELLE

orelle fell back into the Nox's embrace and the cloak engulfed them both. It felt like the first time she'd stepped into the noktum. Cold flowed around her and through her like black tentacles of darkness, and those tentacles eased the burn inside her. It felt like the hellish sun had been covered over in cool shade. She gasped with relief. She'd forgotten what it was like to exist without that torturous pain.

Immediately after, she felt a squeezing sensation, like she was being forced through a tube. She tried to draw a breath but couldn't, and for a moment it felt like she was going to suffocate.

Then it eased, like her body was reconstructing itself in its normal proportions. The cool, covering darkness receded and she was suddenly standing on a meadow inside the noktum. She would have been blind except that her golden hair blazed in the dark, illuminating the charcoal grass with its purple outlines and the edge of a forest before them.

Her soul-burn flared back to life and she clenched her teeth to stifle a whimper. Lotura, she'd become so acclimated to the flames inside her that just a moment's respite showed her how horrible they really were.

She pushed a hand to her chest and looked over to find the Nox standing next to her, watching her. Lorelle and Rhenn had explored the noktum extensively, had created little stone trails to guide them safely through. She cast about for a landmark that would tell her where she was.

In the limited halo of her hair's light, she couldn't see far enough to catch a glimpse of any of their paths or to see which direction the old nuraghi loomed.

They stood at the edge of a forest, but it looked odd. It wasn't like the forest near Rhenn's camp. There were no pine trees or even aspens. Thick, gnarled oaks twisted their limbs toward the sky, full of charcoal leaves bordered in vanilla white.

Even under the magical light of her hair, which revealed objects in the noktum similarly to the way sunlight would, there was little color anywhere. The leaves had their yellowish borders. Hints of purple streaked the charcoal grass and the trunks of the trees. Strange, dark blue ferns grew between the trunks. It was as though the foliage had somehow adapted to a land that never saw daylight.

The Nox watched her, and she self-consciously removed her hand from her chest.

"That is our first order of business," he said softly. "I can only imagine the pain you must be experiencing."

"We're in the noktum?"

"Of course."

"You said you were taking me to a Plunnos."

"Which is in the noktum."

She swallowed that piece of information. Of course. She should have expected that anywhere they would go would be inside the noktum. She should have thought of that.

"We get the Plunnos first," she said tightly, wanting to push her hand into her chest again, but resisting.

"Lorelle," he said softly. "You are dying. The first thing you need is to cease dying. Don't you think?"

"You can... really fix this?" she asked.

"I haven't lied to you."

"Is it close to the Plunnos?"

He smiled sadly. "The Plunnos is close enough. It can wait. Now please, extinguish your hair and follow me."

"Which part of the noktum is this?" she asked. "I don't recognize it."

"Lorelle, please put out your hair."

She swallowed, and her hair only glowed brighter. "I can't."

He raised both eyebrows. "You *can't?*"

"I'm not... calm right now. I need some time to calm down—"

He cocked his head and compassion flickered in his eyes. "I didn't realize... My apologies." He strode toward her and held his hands out, palms up. "May I?"

"May you what?"

"Perform the *ak'tira* upon you."

"I don't know what that is."

"It is a technique by which I can help you extinguish your hair. We do it with our children before they learn control on their own. It will require that I touch you. May I?"

"I'm fine with my hair glowing."

That annoyed him. "Are you fine being eaten by a naguil?"

She had never heard of naguils, but the noktum was filled with monsters. "What's a naguil?"

He sighed. "Lorelle, I'm trying to help you—"

"You promised me a Plunnos, but here we are in a part of the noktum I do not recognize, and now you're threatening me with the attack of a creature I've never heard of."

"I would like to have this conversation," he said. "There are questions you have and there are many answers I can give. It is why I sought you out. But in my culture, stealth is paramount. We do not announce ourselves as we stride along like Lightlanders do. If we do not keep ourselves hidden, predators take an interest. Surely you know enough about the noktum to know this."

"I know."

"Right now, you are a shining beacon. We are both in danger." He held out his hands, palms up, and said, "Will you allow me to help you with your hair?"

She swallowed. "What are you going to do?"

"I'm going to touch you on the back of your head and…" He seemed at a loss for the word. "Calm you. That is the best I can describe it."

He approached her and stopped so close she flinched. She didn't let people touch her. No one except Rhenn.

When she was a child, Lorelle had loved contact of all kinds. Snuggling with her parents, sitting in Mother's lap, holding Father's hand on walks, hugging friends. But once the Change had come upon her, touch was the first thing to go. It too easily unlocked her emotions. She couldn't always control how she felt about things, but by Lotura she could keep from touching people. It had helped so much in the beginning.

"Are you ready?" Zaith asked.

"Fine," she said and her hair glowed brighter.

The Nox slid his slender fingers into her hair and cupped the back of her head. She stiffened, working against the painstaking control she'd forced upon herself years ago. But the touch was soft, gentle. Almost immediately, the burning of her soul eased like it had when they had teleported through the cloak.

It actually felt… good. Her hair glowed brighter. After she'd half-bonded with Khyven, she'd longed to wrap herself around him every time he was near. Now this touch, so unexpectedly intimate, sent a forbidden thrill through her.

His other hand slid over her belly just beneath her breastbone.

"Hey—"

A zing of lightning forked through her insides and a light *crack* sounded inside her head. Profound relief flooded through her like a dam had broken, letting water run throughout her insides. Her muscles suddenly relaxed. Her legs went limp, but the Nox held her upright.

Her hair's light winked out, plunging her into absolute darkness.

Her strength returned and she jerked upright, able to stand once more on her own. For a horrible moment, she thought she'd wet herself.

"Let go of me!" she demanded, and he released her.

Hastily, she fumbled with her pouches and found the one with her Amulet of Noksonon. Heart pounding, she looped the amulet over her head and traced the edge of it with her finger. Slowly, the darkness receded and she could see again in the gray tones the amulet provided. The terrain was no longer illuminated with the buttery light, showing the little color nuances around the leaves and the grass, but she was able to see everything and much farther than before. She saw the strange forest, the dark sky, the horizon, and a giant castle looming behind everything.

A shiver went up Lorelle's spine.

That wasn't the castle she knew. This one was taller, sharper, like the towers and the crenellations were designed to stab the sky. The entire structure was whole and unbroken, not a ruin like the one near Rhenn's camp.

"What are you doing?" the Nox asked. He squinted, noticing where her hand clutched the medallion. "Are you wearing a Lord's amulet?"

"What did you *do* to me?" she demanded, breathing hard. She checked herself, the back of her neck, the spot high on her belly where his hands had been.

"Where did you get a Lord's amulet?" he asked.

"What did you do to me?" she reiterated.

He raised an eyebrow.

"Answer me," she demanded. "Or I'm leaving."

A flicker of a smile indicated he found that amusing, but he answered her question. "I told you, it's the *ak'tira*, a trick that every Nox parent learns to keep their children alive. A Nox's hair—or a Luminent's—won't send the denizens of the noktum into a killing rage like natural light, but it does attract attention."

"I mean *how* did you do it?" She reached up and touched her hair.

"Here, every Nox is a master of her inherent abilities, Lorelle. We do not take pride in our limitations like Luminents do."

"There was a noise in my head. A... crack."

"I had hoped to have this conversation within the protection of the city—"

"Answer my question!"

He frowned. "Do you even know why Luminents glow, Lorelle?" he snapped back. "Do you even *know* why?"

"It's—The Luminents have always had it." Her parents had talked little about Luminent customs, but her mother had once said that the light in her hair, the lightness of their bodies, arose from the special relationship that Luminents shared with nature. "It's... the life force of the earth, because of the—"

"Nonsense." He shook his head. "That is nonsense. It is the doctrine the Luminents preach, but it isn't the truth; a lullaby sung to the ignorant. Luminents are not a spiritual strain of creatures who benefit from a harmonious connection to nature or whatever your parents told you. You, and all Luminents, are tools from a bygone age, nothing more."

"Tools?"

"You were engineered by the Lords. You and the Shadowvar, the Brightlings, the Delvers, the Taur-Els. My people as well. We were created and imbued with magic for a purpose. Our ancestors were hammered and shaped until we became something useful to the Lords."

A chill went through her. "When you say 'lords,' you're talking about the Giants."

"A crude name Humans use. In our culture, that descriptor is an affront. But yes. In Nox culture we honor the Lords," Zaith said.

"Lotura gave us life." She shook her head. "Luminents weren't created by Giants. That's not true."

"It *is* true. It's simply not romantic, so the Luminent High Council spun gossamer fictions instead. Fictions about being Lotura's Chosen. They also wove lies into your culture. For example—" he gestured at her chest where the burn seared her "—they told you what they wanted to tell you about your soul-bond. They created an aberration to confine you, trap you, to shackle you to their doctrines."

"What are you talking about?"

"Am I a slave to my soul-bond?" he asked. "No. It doesn't torture us because we know its true purpose, what the Lords intended. You have been taught that the soul-bond exists to bind you to another Luminent, to forge true love's connection." He shook his head. "That's a lie. The soul-bond doesn't have anything to do with love. The agony you feel isn't because you failed to find love, it's because you resist the call of the Dark."

That stunned her. She'd seen the effects of a successful soul-bond herself. Her parents had shared it, forged true love between them. She'd seen the soaring joy it had given them. She'd seen the soul-bond among many others, too, when she was young and lived in Lumyn.

"You're lying," she said.

"No. I'm challenging the lies you've already swallowed. I know it hurts but look at me." He held his hands out. "I am your age, yet I have chosen no mate. I have loved, but I am not bound. I have touched others, kissed others, and I remain unshackled. *I* may love as many as I wish and then move on. Can you?"

"That's... like Humans."

He made a sour face. "If you insist on being crude and comparing our elegant race to that chaotic mass of sweating, stinking, hairy creatures, fine. Yes, like Humans. And to answer your unspoken question, yes, if I decided bestiality was in my best interest, I could take a Human mate—like this Khyven of yours—and I wouldn't have to rip my soul to pieces to do it."

"How?" she asked in a ragged voice.

"Well, I *was* taking you there," he said. "But it seems you'd rather wait to see if a naguil flies by, or we run across an infestation of Zek Roaches."

"Taking me where?"

"To the Cairn. To break your addiction. To clear your thoughts. To fulfill the needs of that ragged soul of yours."

"What I need… is the Plunnos."

He sighed. "You cannot acquire, let alone use, a Plunnos if you are in this teeth-gnashing, breathless state. It's dangerous, where the Plunnos is. You cannot hope to succeed in taking it by tramping in there with your hair flaring and your soul burning. You'll die. Worse, you'll get me killed with you."

"I—This is—"

"Please Lorelle. Will you listen?"

She held up a hand, trying to marshal her thoughts over the excruciating pain and the challenges he was throwing at her. But if he wasn't lying, if all this was true, he was being exceedingly polite.

"I'm sorry," she finally managed to say.

"You are ignorant," he said. "It is not a crime in itself. We make allowances for the newly initiated. Still, it would behoove you to stop resisting me so much."

"I barely know you."

"And whose fault is that?"

"You never even told me your name!"

He raised an eyebrow. "The burden was upon you to ask, but you never did."

"You never properly introduced yourself."

"Oh, what foolish Human custom is this? You think I should have given you my name upon our meeting?"

"Of course, you should have."

The Nox drew a breath and let it out as though fighting for patience. "In my culture," he said calmly, "we prize stealth. If someone succeeds in sneaking up on someone else, as I clearly did with you back in Usara, the burden of introductions falls upon the surprised. When we first met, the burden was upon you to ask my name. You did not. I let your slight go by because I was there to help you understand. But even by Human standards, should you not have asked my name by now?"

Heat crept into her cheeks as she blushed. "I… I suppose. I'm sorry. Would you please… Will you do me the honor of telling me your name?"

He smiled. "Of course. I am Zaith D'Orphine, First Glimmerblade of the Arvak Nox." He inclined his head. "And I invite you to come with me." He extended his hand.

"To this Cairn?"

"Yes."

She nodded and started toward him, but she didn't take his hand. The thrill of his hand in her hair and along her belly still vibrated through her. She'd liked it far too much.

"If I may ask," he said, lowering his hand as they fell in stride together. "To which Lord does your amulet belong?"

"Which Lord?"

"Yes."

"It doesn't... We found them in the noktum. On... Well, on corpses."

He raised an eyebrow as though she'd said something ridiculous. "You don't *know* whose amulet you wear?"

"I just thought it was an Amulet of Noksonon."

"It *is* an Amulet of Noksonon. But *whose* amulet? It's important. The Lords didn't just go to war with Humans thousands of years ago. There were rivalries and bitter enemies amongst the Lords themselves. If you enter a noktum wearing another Lord's amulet, some creatures will know the difference, and they'll kill you for it."

"This amulet has always protected me from the monsters."

"I'm certain it did in your noktum. Is that where you think we are?"

Lorelle glanced again at the foreign castle towering behind the forest. There were hundreds of noktums all over Usara. This was not one of those. He'd taken her not just away from the city, but far away.

"We're not in the noktum near the city," she murmured. She suddenly realized how foolish this all was, how vulnerable she'd made herself. "Which—Where are we?"

"In the heart of the Great Noktum."

The Great Noktum!

The Great Noktum engulfed the center of the continent of Noksonon. Not only wasn't it in Usara, it was beyond the lands of Humans and Luminents both; south of Triada, south of the Rhaeg Mountains, south of Laria itself.

With one step into his cloak, she had traveled thousands of miles to the south.

She suddenly felt like the little girl who'd fled Vamreth that fateful night he'd killed her parents. Lost, uncertain, at the mercy of everything around her.

"Steady," Zaith said. He reached out as though to touch her, but she flinched away from him.

Her thoughts turned to Rhenn, stolen by Nhevaz, scared and alone, far from friends. She'd just done the same thing to herself. There was no way out of this noktum except by Zaith's hand. The thought paralyzed her.

No. She couldn't let fear have her. Her life didn't matter. She was here to save her friend. She would walk through a hundred noktums to get Rhenn back.

She took several deep breaths then looked defiantly at Zaith.

"Ready now?" he asked.

She nodded.

"Good." He reached out his hand again.

"I don't need your hand."

He smirked. "I wasn't offering it." He flexed his open hand once. "The amulet, if you please. You can't go prancing around the Great Noktum wearing another Lord's amulet."

"I can't give you the amulet."

"Why not?"

"I can't see without it."

"You..." He blinked. "You can't *see* without it?"

She clenched her teeth when she saw the compassion fill his eyes again.

"What?" she demanded tightly.

"Of course, you can," he said softly.

"You can see without your hair or a magical item to help you?" she asked.

"Of course I can. Would you like me to show you?"

She swallowed and it felt like the entirety of her pride was sliding down her throat. "Please."

He glanced around as though checking for threats and let out a breath. "Of course. You will probably need to sit."

"What are you going to do?"

"Something similar to what I did with your hair," he said. "I think."

"You think?"

"The Nox are born knowing how to see, Lorelle. It isn't something we have to teach our children. But I believe the principle is the same. Now please, sit."

She sat reluctantly and crossed her legs. He moved silently behind her and crouched.

"May I touch you again?" he asked softly.

She swallowed, then nodded.

His fingertips, light and deft, lifted the Amulet of Noksonon over her head. She stiffened but didn't resist.

The world went black and Zaith pushed his fingers into her hair just as before, cupping the back of her head. Tingles raced through her.

"Relax, Lorelle," he said softly. "You stand in your own way."

"I am... not used to relaxing. Every time I have relaxed in the past, my hair burst into light and my soul tries to latch on to those I love."

"Well, I don't want you to contain your power, I want you to *release* it. In this place, you need it. You've always needed it, in fact, and you've pushed it down and blocked it up because of what you've been taught. You are like a boat on a turbulent river that has been dammed. Your little craft rocks and slams against the dam as the water churns and spins you about. Release the dam, Lorelle. Release it, and let the boat do what it was made to do."

His other hand slid around her waist to press high on her belly. Her breathing came faster.

"It's there..." he murmured. "Let it go."

For as long as Lorelle could remember, she'd envisioned her mind like a room with a giant steel door. Every time she'd been in danger of opening a soul-bond to someone else, in danger of her hair flaring into light, she would shove her emotions behind that door and slam it shut. For the first time, she imagined herself taking hold of that steel handle and turning. She opened it and let everything out.

Another *crack* sounded inside her head, like someone breaking a twig.

She gasped as all the emotions she'd stuffed away for years—anguish at her parents' deaths, fear of the noktum, love for Rhenn, for her friends, for Khyven—churned through her like a river in flood.

Spun about on that tumbling surge, she forgot about Zaith, the noktum. She forgot about everything except that spinning and spinning…

She didn't realize she was slumped over, eyes squeezed shut, sobbing, until Zaith's voice brought her back.

"Come now, Lorelle," he coaxed. "Sit up. Sit up."

She did.

And opened her eyes to a whole new world.

CHAPTER TWENTY-TWO

LORELLE

Lorelle walked along the forest path behind Zaith, dazzled by the twisting, glimmering tree trunks, by the shimmering silver-lined leaves, by the purple-hued horizon. The grooves between the ridges of bark on the trees pulsed with dark purple lights. The lines on the leaves seemed to light up the dark with lemony-white. The sky itself was a deep indigo, lightening to lavender near the horizon.

Zaith himself looked different. In the light of Usara, he had looked like a midnight-skinned, raven-haired stranger. Here, while his skin remained the same color, his hair was dark indigo, and the irises of his eyes glowed a light purple.

After Zaith had opened her eyes to the wonders of the noktum, she had simply sat there, breathing in, looking around in wonder. It felt like her indrawn breath lasted an hour, one long gasp, as she saw things in a way she'd never seen before.

With the Amulet of Noksonon, she had only been able to see shades of gray. It was enough to distinguish ground from sky and trees from grass. Even the few times she'd looked upon the noktum with the light of her magical hair, she'd always thought the noktum was a gray half-world, blunted and ugly.

But it wasn't. By the five gods, it wasn't like that at all.

"It's beautiful," she murmured for the dozenth time as she followed Zaith. The stunning landscape had even, for a moment, distracted her from the fire inside her.

Zaith said nothing, but continued to lead her swiftly down the path, the edges of which sparkled with flickers of orange.

The forest gave way to a city Zaith had called Nox Arvak. Tall, thin houses with clay-shingled roofs lined the cobblestone street. House after house nestled in the leaves, and she realized Nox Arvak was possibly as big as the crown city of Usara itself, except that the artfully crafted houses blended with the trees. In Usara, trees were cleared to make way for stone structures. There were spaces where trees were allowed, but each was cultivated. Here, trees and houses co-existed. Some houses even had trees as part of their structure, like pillars before the entrance or a mighty oak built into the structure as a corner post. Some of the trees grew into houses. Some houses were perfectly symmetrical, some were intentionally asymmetrical.

Zaith led her further in, and soon she began to notice the people—all Nox like Zaith—in doorways or alleys between the houses. Once she began to see them, she was stunned she hadn't spotted them before. They were everywhere.

They all watched her, and their looks weren't kind. One of them, a tall wide-shouldered Nox with long purple hair, drew a dagger like he might attack, but he glanced at Zaith, sneered, and kept his weapon clenched in a fist.

"They don't want me here," she said.

"You're a Luminent."

"So, their stories about us are similar to our stories about you."

"Worse." He winked at her over his shoulder.

"Why bring me here?"

"Because you're not the only one who needs to learn."

"I saw a man draw a knife, but then he looked at you and didn't attack."

"That was Savenk."

"You know him?"

"I know most in Nox Arvak."

"He doesn't like you."

"He wanted to be a Glimmerblade, but he failed the test. I was one of his judges."

"Ah."

Rows of beautiful houses with purple wooden walls and canopies of lemon leaves gave way to a large open space, revealing the expanse of the indigo sky. Lorelle could barely speak for the beauty of it all.

The open space was centered around a large, circular fountain. Two figures intertwined as though locked in a dance: one female, one male. Wisps of diaphanous clothing spun off them in their twirling embrace. Each had an arm wrapped around the other with their free arms stretched wide. The woman held a large chalice in her free hand, reaching high as though offering it to the sky. Lavender water burbled from the chalice, creating a small waterfall where it caught on the folds of her diaphanous clothing. The water sluiced down the curving folds and flung water into the pool from dozens of places, some off the edges of their shoulders, some from where the cloth wrapped around their waists, and some from their knees.

The male thrust a giant sword aloft, straight up and down. He stretched, reached as though the sky would take the blade from him, looking earnestly at the point as though praying to it. The sword was enormous, at least as tall as the male figure who held it and wide as a hand. It looked similar to the Mavric iron blade Khyven had brought back from the nuraghi.

Concentric circles of purple and blue cobblestones radiated outward from the fountain to where the houses began.

"Lotura..." she whispered.

"Dear Zaith," someone said, an old and whispery voice, and Lorelle snapped her gaze away from the fountain to see a crowd forming at the edge of the concentric circles. Everyone hung back as though entering the circle around the fountain was somehow prohibited, all save one. An old woman approached, wearing white, purple, and lavender robes and bearing a staff that looked even older than she did, as though it was carved from the first tree that ever grew. The staff was bent and blackened and smoothed by the gripping of countless hands. The top curved like a question mark. The old Nox woman was also stooped from what must once have been a great height. Even with that, she stood eye-level with Lorelle.

Zaith descended ceremoniously to one knee, put his hand over his heart, and bowed his head.

"Aravelle," he said reverently.

"It makes this old Nox smile to see you again, Glimmerblade," Aravelle said.

Lorelle wasn't sure if she should bow, and she received no indication from Zaith. It was as though she suddenly didn't exist.

"The Dark takes our Glimmerblades out like the tide. Those who love you never know when, or if, it shall bring you back. We held you in our thoughts and are glad to see your return."

Zaith kept his head bowed.

"And you have brought something unexpected to us, I see," Aravelle said.

She approached Lorelle. The old Nox's bony hand reached forth from her voluminous sleeve and gently grasped Lorelle's chin. Normally, Lorelle would have shied away or reached up to stop Aravelle from touching her, but somehow she felt that would be wrong, perhaps even sacrilegious. The old Nox was clearly some kind of spiritual personage, and Lorelle was keenly aware of the seething anger from every person at the edge of the circle. She held her ground and let Aravelle clasp her chin.

The old woman's fingers were cool, her black skin paper thin and soft where it touched Lorelle's chin, but there was strength in the bony hand. The old Nox turned Lorelle's face gently one way and then the other as though inspecting her.

"My, but you are a pretty one, aren't you?" the old Nox said. "And in such pain. You twist in the fires of the Luminent curse. That you are still standing is testament to your strength.

Admirable girl. And this, I think, is why our dear Zaith has brought you to us."

Aside from reverently speaking this woman's name, Zaith hadn't said a word. His head was still bowed.

"It has been seventeen centuries since a Luminent walked the streets of Nox Arvak," Aravelle said. "This is… unexpected for us. I must apologize for the glares of my people. They do not understand why you are here." She turned her gaze to Zaith. "You have thrown a stone in the water, Glimmerblade." It sounded like a warning, but her voice and the twinkle in her eye suggested she liked a few stones thrown every now and then. "Rise and speak freely."

He rose gracefully to his feet. "I have come seeking help, Aravelle."

"Then you have come to the right place."

"I would…" he hesitated, but it was as though, with only the start of his sentence, Aravelle had heard his entire message in her mind.

"Ah…" Her gray eyebrows lifted. "I see." Her eyes narrowed to slits and she regarded Lorelle again. This time, it was more pointed, and clearly Lorelle came up short in the scrutiny.

Aravelle shook her head slowly. "Zaith… You reach for the stars like our beloved Uldantier." She indicated the sword-wielding figure in the statue. "I fear you shall be disappointed. This one is nearly dead from the Luminent curse. She will need more strength than she has left, I fear, for what you desire. And though her loyalty is strong, it is not toward you. Are you sure you would have her touch the Cairn?"

"It is… necessary," he said.

Lorelle didn't quite understand what they were talking about, but she knew it had to do with whatever magic was needed to mend her soul.

Aravelle drew a long breath and let it out. "I see." She shook her head regretfully. "You walk in lands that would blind the rest of us, Zaith. In these dangerous days, you must be our eyes. We will trust you."

A murmur of disapproval rippled through the crowd. There was a sharp clatter, steel on stone. Lorelle glanced to her left in time to see the Nox who'd drawn his knife earlier, Savenk. He'd thrown the knife to the cobblestones and stalked away, through the crowd until he disappeared.

Aravelle ignored the outburst. "I ask you again, Glimmerblade. You are certain this is what you would choose?"

"It is."

"Then come with me."

Aravelle turned and started away from the fountain. Zaith moved to take her arm. The crowd made a hole leading up the widest street, and Lorelle, Zaith, Aravelle, and her attendants moved through the rest of the seething Nox in silence. If glares were whips, Lorelle would have died of a thousand cuts.

Aravelle motioned with her free hand. "Come here, girl," she said. "Take my other arm. Help an old woman."

Lorelle moved to the her side and gently took hold of the thin, fragile arm. The old Nox glanced up from her stoop with an awkward bend of her neck. "You've shocked us by coming here, dear, but I can only imagine what a shock all of this is for you. Will you tell me what you know of the Nox?"

"I—That you live in the noktums. That you were once Luminents who had... fallen from grace." She felt heat in her cheeks as she said it aloud.

"And no doubt that we murder and steal and lie." The old Nox gave her a wizened smile. "And that we would boil your bones for our stew?"

"Something like that."

"Well, perhaps there is some truth to that."

Zaith raised an eyebrow.

"I am sure we would have fallen from grace, if we'd ever had any grace to start with." Aravelle winked.

Despite herself, Lorelle found that she liked Aravelle. She felt an easiness around the old Nox, an acceptance that stood in stark contrast to the hostile stares from all around them. Aravelle seemed like someone who had seen the turning of the world so many times that she was incapable of being surprised by swift turns of events.

Then something occurred to Lorelle, striking her like a bolt of lightning.

It was possible that this entire exchange, this seemingly innocuous chit chat, was Aravelle's polite way of waiting for Lorelle to introduce herself. Zaith's scolding about not giving her name to one who had snuck up on her—a Nox custom— came back in vivid detail. Though Lorelle had overheard Aravelle's name, the old Nox had not offered it. Zaith had not introduced her nor had Aravelle asked for Lorelle's name. That suddenly seemed conspicuous. If giving one's name was a form of deference in Nox culture—given to a stranger whose abilities and experience outstripped one's own—it made sense that this would also extend to an elder.

Lorelle stopped and inclined her head. "My apologies, venerated one. My name is Lorelle Miere."

Lorelle raised her head and saw a merry twinkle in Aravelle's eyes again, and she nodded her head as though Lorelle had passed some test.

"My thanks, Lorelle Miere. I am Aravelle L'orntia, elder of Nox Arvak and Voice of the Dark."

Lorelle inclined her head in an imitation of Aravelle's gesture. "I am most pleased to meet you," she said in the courtly manner her parents had taught her when she'd first come to Usara.

"The similarities in our names is a curiosity to me," Aravelle said. "Aravelle and Lorelle. We could be sisters by the sound of it. I wonder if we share a branch somewhere far down the tree."

"That we are related, you mean?" Lorelle asked.

"Sometimes the Dark speaks in such ways. It appears, perhaps, that you *are* meant to be here." She glanced sidelong at Zaith. "Tell me, has our Glimmerblade already begun educating you?"

Lorelle thought of the whirlwind of the last day. By Lotura, had it only been a day? She felt like she'd lived an entire lifetime.

"Yes… Aravelle." Lorelle felt like she should be giving the woman an honorific, calling her "Your Majesty or "Your Grace" or something of that nature, but she had no idea what that honorific should be.

"She is lacking in knowledge, Aravelle," Zaith said. "Even of Luminent culture."

"Hmmm," Aravelle said.

The crowd slowly dispersed as they walked up the cobblestone street, which Lorelle had deduced was a main road through the city. By the time they reached an open-air rotunda at the end of the street, only Zaith, Lorelle, and Aravelle remained. The crowd had completely gone.

The rotunda was made up of purple pillars and lintels of marble with glowing white veins. In the center was a craggy black stone over ten feet tall. The jagged monolith jutted left and right as it reached toward the indigo sky. Dark, pulsing purple light glowed deep in cracks running the length of the stone.

"The Cairn," Zaith said.

"I will leave you now, Glimmerblade. Proceed with my blessing. Please the Lords." She gave the barest gesture with two fingers and he bent before her. She kissed him lightly on the cheek. *"The Dark keeps all secrets."* She whispered the words like a prayer.

"So we listen close," he murmured back with the same reverence.

The old Nox turned. Three young Nox in black robes materialized from the irregular shadows that seemed everywhere in this place, came to her side, took her arms, and helped her walk away.

When they were alone, she turned to face Zaith.

"This is where you will mend your soul," he said.

CHAPTER TWENTY-THREE

LORELLE

Lorelle gazed at the monolith. Just looking at it eased the burn in her chest like traveling through Zaith's cloak had done. She glanced back to where Aravelle had retreated.

"Who is she?" Lorelle asked. "The Nox queen?"

"We don't have queens in Nox Arvak," he said.

"I just… She is obviously a person of great importance."

He smiled softly, as though her comment was an understatement.

"That mob wanted to kill me, but they didn't because of her. How should I call her? Does she have some honorific?"

"Aravelle is the Voice of the Dark."

"So, she *is* your leader."

"She is the one for whom we still our hearts to listen to her words. Of us all, she best understands the whispers of the Dark. And so she speaks for it."

The Dark keeps all secrets, so we listen close…

"She said a phrase to you," Lorelle said. "What was that?"

"A reminder. We learn the words when we are children. We spend our lives living up to it."

"Secrets and listening?"

"Simply one line from the Nox Decrete."

"Decrete?"

"A mantra, if you will."

"That one line is your mantra?"

"It is the first line meant to indicate the rest."

"How much more is there?"

"Would you like to hear it?"

"Please."

He spoke the words softly, with reverence:

> *The Dark keeps all secrets, so we listen close*
> *The Dark lives in silence, so we are its voice*
> *The Dark swells with power, so we may know strength*
> *The Dark holds our future, to give us at length*

"So, everything comes from the Dark," she said.

"Is it really so different from how Lightlanders feel about the sun?"

She looked around. Her new eyes brought the noktum into brilliant, colorful clarity. It was as though, because there was no light overhead, everything glowed with its own inner vibrancy. There were still shadows everywhere, but they weren't the same as shadows in a world lit by sunlight. The patches of darkness weren't—couldn't be—a function of light because there was no light. Shadows existed as their own entities, like the buildings and the trees. Some didn't even make sense, they just grew out as incongruous formations from walls or pillars or trees, like animals lying in wait.

"We have crossed the first threshold," Zaith said. "Aravelle's blessing. You have permission to approach the Cairn." He tipped his chin at the craggy, cracked monolith.

"She calls you Glimmerblade sometimes. Don't you have an honorific for her?"

"I'll tell you all, Lorelle. But would you not rather have this discussion once you've mended your soul?"

The moment he mentioned her pain, the searing burn seemed to increase.

"How does it work?"

"Put your hands upon the Cairn," he said.

"And then what?"

"That is all. It will do the rest. The pain you feel will be replaced by a calm you have never before experienced."

"Just put my hands on it," she repeated.

He gestured with his hand for her to proceed.

"What's going to happen?" she asked. "Beyond what you're saying."

"It will unravel the need you have developed."

"How is it going to do that?"

"If you do not do this first, we cannot go hunting for the Plunnos," he said.

Already Zaith seemed to understand her. He was right. That was really the only question that mattered.

She faced the Cairn, reached out, and put her hands on it.

CHAPTER TWENTY-FOUR

LORELLE

The moment Lorelle touched the Cairn, darkness dropped on her like a shroud and she went blind. She gasped and tried to let go, but she wasn't in her body anymore. It was as though her heart and soul had tumbled into a free fall inside the darkness of the stone.

She was vaguely aware of her body somewhere far behind her. She could feel her fingers clutching the stone, her eyes staring sightlessly ahead, but it was all so far away. She was barely connected to her hands or legs anymore, though she could feel her fingers clenching the stone hard; she simply couldn't make them let go.

But the soul-burn in her chest was as fierce as ever.

"Lorelle…" A whispering voice slithered past her, next to her ear. Except she had no ears.

"Where am I?" she screamed, but she had no voice. Instead, the intent of her message moved away from her like ripples on a pond.

"Lorelle…" the darkness said again, and the voice became clearer. *"Why have you come?"*

"To mend my soul," she said into the darkness.

She couldn't see anything, couldn't make out the littlest detail, let alone any kind of distance, but she felt like she was being pulled forward.

"This… is your soul," the darkness said.

Her soul-burn flared. The blackness shifted and a tapestry floated forward. The glowing threads made beautiful pictures, one after the other, shifting images. There were too many pictures to conceivably fit, but somehow, they did, each growing larger when she focused on it, then shrinking back when her gaze moved on, as though her gaze alone was a magnifying glass. The pictures were moments in her life, each one framed in golden thread the color of her hair.

In one picture she walked by the Iridescent Canal in Lumyn, seven years old.

In another, a vicious tangle of black threads showed her and Rhenn standing before the noktum at ten years old, Vamreth aiming a crossbow at them.

Another showed black threads mixed with shining white as she and Rhenn discovered their first Amulet of Noksonon.

Yet another wove together vibrant reds, creating the moment when she sat on the slope in Rhenn's camp, her knees bent and her feet bare, wearing her red dress for Khyven.

But the blanket was not whole. One entire side had been ripped away, exposing angry, agonized tendrils burning like glowing coals, squirming like worms. These threads sought the missing half, the half of her soul that now resided inside Khyven. The pictures that moved across the tapestry approached the rip, then recoiled and shrank as though the raw edge was painful to them.

"Mend it…" the darkness said.

"How?" she cried.

"Mend it…" the darkness repeated.

"How!"

She desperately studied the questing threads. There was nothing for them to latch onto, nothing except the darkness.

The darkness...

The writhing tendrils flailed in the black, but Lorelle suddenly imagined the darkness as a vast tapestry of its own with threads just waiting to tie into hers.

The moment she thought this, the reaction was immediate.

One writhing, burning thread burrowed into the darkness. It turned black and the darkness seeped into the tapestry along that single thread, weaving into the pictures.

She felt a slight ease in the burn. She imagined a second thread doing the same. It turned black, another thin stripe raced across the tapestry of her soul. Then another. And another.

With each thread that turned black, the tapestry not only became darker, but the wriggling threads eased, linking to the darkness and going quiet.

Her pain began to fade, as did her craving for Khyven.

She gasped in relief as she changed thread after thread. The pictures remained the colors they had been, depicting the same moments from her life, but the frames changed, one by one, from gold to black. The remaining threads responded, connecting to the darkness without her asking, without her envisioning it. Thread after thread after thread changed, racing through the tapestry.

"*Wait!*" she cried, feeling a sudden, profound remorse. The pain was receding, but so was her bond to Khyven. Was that what she wanted?

"*Stop!*" she shouted.

The transformation ceased immediately, but it was almost too late. Only eight threads had not connected to the darkness.

"*Finish...*" the darkness urged, and the compulsion was so strong she almost gave in. It was just eight little threads. What did she care about eight little threads?

Another thread slowly changed, racing across the tapestry. Then another. Then another—

"*Stop!*" she insisted, panicked.

"*You must finish...*"

"*No!*"

The will of the darkness set itself against her, pushing, and she felt the walls of her mind collapse. The darkness oozed inside her, tried to steal her resistance. It was in her soul; throughout everything she was or had been.

"*No!*" she screamed in that place where no voice carried. She fought with everything she had.

"*No!*"

The darkness crashed in on her from all sides, drowning her. And she knew no more.

CHAPTER TWENTY-FIVE

LORELLE

Lorelle's eyelids fluttered open. Zaith was leaning over her. She lay in his lap while he held the back of her head like he'd done before, fingers intertwined in her hair. Her mind felt thick and cloudy. She remembered putting her hands on the Cairn, falling into darkness and then…

Nothing. She remembered nothing after that.

"What happened to me?" she asked.

"How do you feel?" He pushed tendrils of black hair away from her face.

Black hair!

Lorelle sat bolt upright and pulled away from him. She yanked her hair in front of her eyes. It was midnight black with a purple sheen, just like Zaith's.

Her arms were midnight black like Zaith's and Aravelle's!

"Lotura!" she gasped. She strained to remember what had happened. She felt like she should know. Something momentous. Something… hard. A fight?

She couldn't remember.

Zaith was calm. "Tell me how you feel."

"Like someone… twisted my body into the shape of a new one…" She trailed off.

Then it hit her. Her soul-burn was gone. The searing pain was just… gone. Nothing at all.

"The burn…" she whispered.

"Yes," Zaith said.

She felt giddy. She felt like she could jump straight up into the sky. Lotura, the pain was gone! She had forgotten what it felt like to be free of the tearing, searing agony.

"As I promised, you are free."

"But I don't… I don't remember what happened. Why did my hair… my skin…?"

A flicker of a memory flashed through her, quick and elusive like a glimmer of light. Pain. Anguish. A fight…

But then the memory was gone.

"The Cairn unlocks your potential," he said. "It strips the Luminent curse laid upon you at birth."

"It was… I think it was painful," she murmured. But no, that wasn't the right word. Why couldn't she remember?

"Is it painful now?"

"No…" She didn't feel the burning of the incomplete soul-bond anymore, but there was something different inside her replacing it, a coolness like the air that comes off a lake. She looked around at the strange noktum with its indigos and purples and she suddenly felt like she belonged here. Here felt… safe, not dangerous.

"Will this… Is it going to stay this way?" She held out her hair.

He hesitated, then said, "For now."

"You mean I'll change back?"

"It will stay as long as you need it, as long as you are in the noktum and using the Dark to aid you."

"You mean this—" she indicated herself "—will change back when I step out of the noktum?"

"Unless you choose to make the transformation permanent."

"What?"

"You joined with the Dark. You bonded those ragged ends of your soul to the great tapestry of the noktum itself. That is what is assuaging your soul-bond. But you stopped just before a complete connection."

Now it returned to her. She had fought the final merging of the threads. There were only five left. Five that still longed to complete the bond with Khyven. And she'd left them like that. Now that she remembered, now that she concentrated on that small part of her soul, she could feel it, tiny and still burning. But it wasn't overwhelming. It felt, instead, like a warmth in her chest.

"To make the transform permanent, you will need to complete the bonding of—"

"I'm not going to do that."

He hesitated, and for the first time he seemed not to know what to say.

"I'm not here to join you. I'm here—"

"To save Rhenn," Zaith finished softly. "Yes. I understand."

"Yes," she said. "The Plunnos. Are we going there now?"

"Tomorrow. Tonight, we rest."

The moment he said it, Lorelle felt the weight of her exhaustion. She hadn't slept in days. The only thing keeping her awake had been the pain and now, with the pain gone, she did want to sleep.

She looked overhead. Nothing in the sky indicated what time it was. "Is it still night? I mean, in the other world. In the daylight world. How do you tell one day from the other in this place?"

"The surge is nearly upon us. We will take shelter, sleep, and go after."

"What's the surge?"

"It is the apex of what we call the shadow cycle the Great Noktum. There is a surge and an ebb."

"Of shadows?"

"Yes. And when the surge is upon us, it is possible to be swept away south."

"Why? How?"

"There is much to learn, Lorelle, and I will tell you all. For now, though, sleep."

"I am tired," she finally admitted. "Where do we sleep?"

"I was planning for you to sleep in Aravelle's guest house. I'm sure you will find it to your liking."

"Very well."

He inclined his head up the street. "Peaceful dreams, Lorelle." He turned and began walking away.

"Where are you going?"

"They will care for you." He turned back and nodded past her shoulder.

She looked, searched, but couldn't see anyone. The empty rotunda and the twisted shadows around the pillars seemed to mock her.

There seemed only darkness and the silent street until three Nox emerged, seemingly growing from the shadows. They approached her, wearing impassive expressions, and the first of them inclined her head and gave a quick curtsey.

"I am Lorelle," Lorelle introduced herself first, remembering her Nox etiquette at the last second. She suddenly felt cut adrift without Zaith. He'd been her sole guide since she'd stepped into the Great Noktum.

"I am Maid Hoxa," the Nox replied. "Will you follow me?"

"Yes," Lorelle said.

Maid Hoxa led the way with Lorelle right behind and the two other Nox trailing. Hoxa led her through the streets to a palatial structure. It sprawled on a small rise, taking up the same space as a dozen of the houses she'd seen entering the city, and it was made of the same white-veined purple marble as the rotunda of the Cairn. Her guides led her up a path to a side building. There were several of them, round structures like the rotunda of the Cairn, except with roofs, walls and doors.

"If you please, these are the Maiden Houses. You may stay here, alone. If you would rather have company, I have been authorized to take you in the Sensual Houses—"

"This is fine. Thank you, Maid Hoxa." Her three guides bowed at the same time and backed away.

Lorelle entered the little house, peering into the oddly shaped shadows within. There was a bed with a soft coverlet, a dresser, a freestanding cloak rack, and a mirror. Everything, including the border of the mirror, was made of a lemon-colored wood.

She turned and locked the door. Suddenly, the thought of sleeping in that comfortable bed seemed like a wonderful idea.

"You and me," she murmured to the bed. She approached it, pushed at it. It was as soft as any bed in Usara. She fell face first upon it with a sigh and felt her exhaustion pull down on her.

That's when the assassin attacked.

CHAPTER TWENTY-SIX

LORELLE

Needles of ice jabbed her soul, warning her of the attack. She felt the assassin cutting through the shadows behind her. She felt the point of the knife on its way toward her.

It was as though she *was* the Dark, like the shadows were somehow an extension of her own body.

She spun off the bed. Her feet hit the floor and she arched backward as the blade sliced the air over her belly. Her fingertips touched the wall and she rebounded, drawing a dagger.

The Dark flowed through her, and she moved with it. The assassin, wearing a black mask from nose to neck, leaving only his hate-filled eyes visible, tried to slash backward as he stumbled over her, aiming for her neck, but he missed. She flipped her dagger and jammed the pommel into his chest just below his ribcage.

The air blasted from his body and he doubled over, staggering past her. She spun and pursued, bringing her knee up into his nose. His head snapped up and she whacked the pommel of her dagger across his temple.

The man thudded to the floor, unconscious.

Euphoria raced through her entire body, more pleasurable than anything she'd ever felt. The darkness felt like a tongue sliding across the man's defeat, and she tasted every delicious bit of it.

"Lotura!" she gasped, crouching. The tingling sensation went on and on. She crouched there, shuddering, trying to assimilate the rush. The dark amplified her victory into pure sensation.

Only when it began to recede did the guilt follow. She approached her fallen foe and touched his neck. His pulse beat strongly. She hadn't killed him, thank the gods. She turned him over and pulled down his mask. It was the man from the crowd—Zaith had called him Savenk—who had drawn his dagger and snarled at her.

The darkness warned her that someone was near. This time is wasn't needles of ice, but more of a cool whisper.

She crouched, gripping her dagger, ready to leap again. She scanned the irregular shadows of the room.

Zaith crouched in one of the thin windows, his hand on the windowsill next to his boots. His silhouette cut into the purple sky behind him. He watched her; his dark face thoughtful.

The door opened and Lorelle whirled. Maid Hoxa and two attendants entered.

Was this an all-out assault? Had they brought her here just to kill her? Lorelle drew a second dagger and backed away from them.

"They're not here for you," Zaith said. "They're here for Savenk."

Without a word, Maid Hoxa and her attendants lifted Savenk and carried him from the room, closing the door silently behind them.

Lorelle blinked and slowly stood. She kept her connection to the Dark, though, feeling through the shadows for any possible threat.

There was only Zaith. She looked at him and his eyes glittered as they watched her.

"Did you know he was going to attack me?" she demanded.

"It was likely since he was hiding in your room."

"He was here when you left?"

He nodded.

"You could have warned me!"

"Hmmm," he said, as though contemplating that.

"Zaith—"

"I wanted to know if the noktum would speak to you."

"And you were willing to risk my life? He could have killed me!"

"No," he said. "I was here."

She held up her thumb and forefinger, an inch apart. "His dagger came this close to my stomach."

His eyes narrowed and a small smile curled the corners of his mouth. "And yet, here you stand."

She wanted to strike him. She almost did.

"Some lessons can only be learned a certain way. You trusted the noktum. That is what matters."

Lorelle remembered the wash of pleasure at her victory, how good it had felt. Suddenly, it made her feel sick to her stomach. She'd never reveled in violence before.

"What did you do to me?" she breathed.

"Given what I promised: freedom. The ability to feel what you feel, not lock it away. The ability to throw off the Luminent curse."

"I hurt him," she murmured.

"*He* would have killed you. But he could not because the Dark is with you."

"You sent him here?"

Zaith shook his head. "He acted on his own. I needed to see if your sense of the Dark outstripped his own. I merely did not stop him."

"Outstripped his own? You mean what I felt... it's more than what he can do?"

"He has not bonded through the Cairn."

"I thought all Nox did."

He smirked. "No. Only Glimmerblades."

"I don't want to become a Nox or a Glimmerblade. I just want to get Rhenn back."

"Bonding with the Dark is essential to achieve your goal," Zaith said.

"I don't want your powers!"

"Lorelle, you don't need to lie to yourself anymore. It is all right to revel in your abilities and in your emotions. I saw you when the Dark rewarded your victory. In Nox Arvak, there's no need to hide how you feel. You don't need to craft the Luminent illusion of control. It doesn't serve you."

"I…" She remembered the glorious freedom of moving with the Dark, the shuddering euphoria of her victory.

"We have come a long way in a short time," Zaith said, "but that is because you have time constraints. If it will comfort you, remember this: without your connection to the Dark, without these new abilities, you cannot obtain the Plunnos. You'd simply die in the attempt."

Lorelle's cheeks grew hot. "Where are we going? Why do I need all of this?"

"Tomorrow," Zaith said. "You've done enough for today. And even those of us who are one with the Dark need rest."

"You must be mad. I won't sleep knowing assassins will be creeping into my room."

"No more tests," he said. "I have instructed Maid Hoxa and her attendants to ensure no one disturbs you again."

Zaith glanced over his shoulder at her, then dropped into the shadows.

Lorelle paced the little round room for an hour, waiting. Just because Zaith said there were no more tests didn't mean there weren't. But after an hour, she laid down on the bed and explored her new sense of the Dark, searching for anyone creeping through the shadows to attack her.

No one did.

After an hour of the soft bed, waiting for danger that wasn't there, her exhaustion finally had its way.

She slept.

CHAPTER TWENTY-SEVEN

ZAITH

Zaith materialized in his room at Lord Tovos's castle. He had been directed not to use the noktum cloak within the castle, to teleport outside and use the servants' entrance. He suspected this was to remind him of his place, and Zaith wasn't interested in ingratiating himself to the Lord right now.

Zaith felt conflicted and it inspired a recklessness in him. He wanted to sabotage his victory. He'd done his duty, yes. He'd brought Lorelle into the Great Noktum, and she'd bonded with the Dark—almost entirely—in just a few short hours. That was even faster than Lord Tovos's unrealistic demand.

Yet his victory felt hollow.

He'd lied to her to bring her here. The trap was about to be sprung on her, making her a slave to Lord Tovos for the rest of her life. That was fine. It should be fine. It was going to save Zaith's family. He was serving the whole of Nox Arvak, which was his sworn duty as a Glimmerblade. He shouldn't care about one Luminent. She was a means to an end. Delivering her to the Lord was his duty. He shouldn't care.

Except he did.

Lorelle wasn't what he thought she'd be. Arrogant. Ignorant. Secure in her superiority just like every other Luminent. She wasn't like that at all. She cared only for her friends. She was loyal. She served her tribe. She was driven, determined, and as tough as anyone he'd ever met. By Grina's sharp nails, Lorelle shouldn't even be alive, let alone standing and fending off assassins. That she'd managed to survive weeks with half a soul was unthinkable. Zaith had never even heard of such a thing.

The more he tried to turn away from it, the more obvious it became. She was just trying to save her family like he was trying to save his. They were the same.

It was dangerous thinking. He'd delivered her to the Lord. There was no going back. He was serving his people. His family. This was what he must do, his purpose as a Glimmerblade.

So why did it feel so wrong?

He'd promised her freedom, and he'd delivered her into slavery. Amidst all the truths he'd told her, the grand lie stayed hidden. Bonding with the noktum bound her to Lord Tovos. Zaith had fastened a collar around her neck, clipped a chain to it, and handed that chain over to Lord Tovos.

Doubt and self-recrimination grew within Zaith, transforming into a sickening foreboding.

The truth was he hated Lord Tovos. And he liked Lorelle.

And that was a truth he could never reveal.

He shook his head. Liking a Luminent... It was ridiculous. Zaith killed Luminents. That was what Glimmerblades did.

Humans... Luminents... They were supposed to be the enemy. The Lords were gods. He'd believed that his whole life. He'd believed it having never met a Lord before.

They'd been absent for almost two thousand years, and Zaith's people revered them, taught that it was a spiritual mandate to serve them. But now that a Lord had actually returned, all of Zaith's thoughts were sacrilegious.

He twitched his head. Even thinking such things in this place could cost Zaith his entire family. Lord Tovos could use his magic to read Zaith's mind if he wanted.

"You may find your temerity bracing, Nox," Lord Tovos's voice slithered into the chamber, stopping Zaith's heart.

Lord Tovos materialized in the corner of the room. Normally, the noktum would have warned Zaith if someone tried to sneak up on him using the shadows, but the Dark obeyed Lord Tovos first, all others after. If the Lord wished to remain invisible to his servants, he would.

For a moment, Zaith thought the Lord had actually read his mind.

"But I find it tedious," Lord Tovos continued. "Break one of my rules again and your family will suffer."

Cold relief flooded through Zaith. No. He hadn't read Zaith's mind. The Lord was referring to Zaith's ill-conceived teleport directly to his room.

"I have brought Lorelle," Zaith said. Best to get to business. Best to get to the point.

"I know. I am watching, Zaith. I knew the moment the girl touched the Cairn. The question is why you felt the need to flaunt my rules by teleporting here?"

Zaith raised his chin, but once again he couldn't match the Lord's stare for more than a second, and he looked to the side. "I have done as I promised, Lord, and sooner than you—"

"Have you? Were you simply going to gloss over the fact that Lorelle did not fully bond with the noktum? Your task was to sever her soul-bond to the Human and bring her into the Dark. Are you trying to convince me that the task is complete?"

So, the Lord knew. It was such a subtle thing that if Zaith hadn't been standing right there, his hand on the Cairn as well, he would not have noticed those five tiny threads Lorelle had protected.

But of course, he knew. The Lords were the absolute masters of the noktum.

"How do you think I should respond to this?" Lord Tovos continued.

"I only live to serve you, Lord Tovos," Zaith said.

"Do you?"

"I wasn't sure it mattered. Those five threads."

Lord Tovos narrowed his eyes. "You like her."

"She's a Luminent," Zaith said derisively.

"Let me make myself perfectly clear to you, Glimmerblade, in case there is any doubt. If you interfere in my plans for her, your family will die, Lorelle will die, and you will die. In that order. You will get to watch each of them depart before I give you permission to die."

"Yes, Lord Tovos."

"Must I make an example of another of your loved ones?"

"No, Lord Tovos."

"You stand for your entire people, Zaith. If the Nox are of no use to me, then they may as well not exist at all. Do you understand?"

"I understand, my Lord," Zaith said, frightened and yet still seething inside.

"Deliver what you promised. You have one more day."

"I—yes, Lord Tovos."

"Well?"

"When she wakes, she will wish to search for the Plunnos…" Originally, Lord Tovos had said to bring her to the castle. But Lorelle was supposed to be fully bonded to the Dark by then. Zaith wasn't even sure if Lord Tovos possessed a Plunnos. Surely, he did, but…

"Manufacture an adventure for her. Take her into the wilds and convince her to complete the bond."

"Of course, My Lord."

"Wait…" Lord Tovos looked over Zaith's head, contemplating, then turned his focus back on Zaith. "Jai'ketakos."

Zaith's eyes widened. "My Lord——"

"That is your path. Jai'ketakos. He has a Plunnos. Perhaps several. Take her there. To slip by him, she will need a full connection to the noktum. It gives you the perfect reason to convince her."

Zaith opened his mouth but had difficulty closing it. "My Lord, the dragon… He has not been disturbed for thousands of years."

"Then you must be stealthy, hadn't you?"

"It will kill us both."

"Let death be your reward," Lord Tovos said, his black eyes flashing. "If you are not equal to this mission."

"Lorelle will also be dead."

"If she is not entirely bonded to the noktum, what use is she to me? I can as easily use another of her friends. For now, your hope—your quest—lies in that cave, in the dragon's lair. Take Lorelle's soul in hand. Bond her to the noktum forever."

"My Lord, I believe I can get her to trust me, to complete the bond, without taking her to the dragon—"

"I did not ask you for what you believe. Go now. And be grateful."

The noktum cloak flew from the bed toward Zaith. Before he could protest, it enveloped him.

Zaith's room in the palace vanished and he suddenly stood a stone's throw from the guest house where Lorelle slept.

He paused for a long, hateful moment, then spoke to the quiet.

"Yes, My Lord."

CHAPTER TWENTY-EIGHT

LORELLE

Lorelle sat up, blinked, and looked around. No sun rose outside, turning the sky blue and throwing yellow light across the land. There was nothing she knew that showed time had passed, but she felt rested, like she'd slept an entire night.

The noktum's sky remained dark indigo. All the shadows within her room, haphazardly placed with no definitive light source, had all moved. She felt there was some kind of sense to it, even though she couldn't figure what it was. Somehow, in this place, the movement of the shadows, not the sun, defined the passage of time.

She felt refreshed and rejuvenated in a way she couldn't ever remember feeling. So many things felt different now. Before her transformation at the Cairn, she had always been able to feel Khyven within her. In Usara, even if she'd managed to fall into a fitful sleep for half an hour, when she awoke she was always thinking about him: his half-charming, half-feral smile; his wide-shoulders and large, capable hands; his bold decisiveness and speed of action.

She'd even been able to feel him at a distance, like a lodestone within her chest, pointing in his direction.

Now, all that had vanished, covered over with the cool confidence of her new connection to the Dark. For the first time in weeks, she couldn't point out which direction Khyven lay. She wasn't thinking about him constantly. It was as though something she'd been holding in her hand suddenly wasn't there anymore.

She closed her eyes and searched inside herself for the burn that had been all-consuming mere hours ago. At first, all she felt was that cool darkness, but then...

There it was.

Buried deep, those five fiery threads still writhed, and when she concentrated on them, she felt that familiar yearning for Khyven. His face rose in her mind. Her desire for him was now an enjoyable thought. It was easily controllable, a warmth in her heart instead of a searing agony. She could think of him, even *want* him, without having to suffer.

The freedom of that intoxicated her. She could choose—or not choose—and there was no punishment. If she decided to love Khyven, it would be just that, *her* decision.

Lotura's wisdom, Zaith had been right. Her life before had been so different, and if the only change was the painful rules of the Luminent soul-bond, then perhaps it was a curse.

She rose and stretched, reaching toward the ceiling and feeling her muscles, feeling the healthy vigor of them without the constant presence of the soul-bond's saw dragging back and forth across her innards.

She looked down at herself and wrinkled her nose. She'd fallen asleep in her clothes and she felt the dry sweat of the previous day's exertions.

A nightgown and nighttime amenities had been provided for her, laid neatly across the back of a cushioned chair by the door, but she'd left them alone. She hadn't wanted to risk divesting herself of her clothes and weapons should she need to wake and move quickly.

But now she desperately wanted a bath——

She felt something move. She didn't hear it with her ears, didn't glimpse it with her eyes, but she *felt* it inside herself. Inside the Dark. Something was moving through the shadows close to her.

She closed her eyes and turned.

An incongruous shadow draped over the window to the right of the door, as though someone had painted it there. She still wasn't used to the odd manner that shadows positioned themselves in this place but she could feel what was inside it.

Nothing. The shadow was empty.

She kept turning, feeling the other shadows inside the room, and this time she did sense someone. They were approaching her guest house, approaching the window by her bed.

Quiet as a breeze, she drew her dagger, slid into the empty shadow next to the window, and pressed herself against the wall.

The window opened silently. She suddenly realized that the door to her room had been equally silent. Come to think of it, she hadn't heard one squeak of a doorjamb or rattling of a cart since she'd entered Nox Arvak. Everything here seemed meticulously maintained, designed to remain quiet.

She held her breath and the intruder appeared. In the depths of the crooked shadow by the window, she couldn't quite make out his silhouette, but something about the way the figure slid through the dark evoked familiarity.

Zaith.

He leapt lightly to the windowsill and crouched, scanning the room, looking for her. He didn't see her. He didn't know she was right next to him, that she could reach out and touch him if she wanted. The thought made her giddy.

She silently lifted her dagger and tucked it under his chin.

"And you are?" she whispered playfully.

Zaith's eyebrows lifted and he glanced sidelong at her without so much as a twitch. He squinted as though she was difficult to see.

"Well, well, well…" He carefully pinched the tip of her dagger and tried to move it away from his throat, but she held it firm.

"An introduction, if you please," she said.

"An introduction?"

"I snuck up on you. Where are your manners?"

"That is only for two people who do not know each other."

"I want one anyway."

He smiled, then carefully inclined his head. "Very well." He looked significantly at the dagger. She withdrew it.

"If I may present myself," he said formally. "I am Zaith D'Orphine, First Glimmerblade of Nox Arvak."

She made the dagger vanish into its sheath. "Pleased to meet you, I'm Lorelle, and I need a bath."

"A bath."

"A quick bath."

"Well… I wouldn't want you to think we're uncivilized in Nox Arvak. Aravelle's bath house is the finest on Noksonon. I will take you."

"A bath first, then the Plunnos," she said.

"Of course, my lady." Zaith bowed gracefully. "If you will follow me."

CHAPTER TWENTY-NINE

LORELLE

er bath was absolutely decadent. Zaith hadn't been lying about the bath house. It was every bit as impressive as he'd said. There were ten tubs of hot water set in the floor of a huge, marble room with open windows. At least two dozen Nox had been bathing in the large, high-ceilinged room, but Lorelle's attendants took her to a private bath through a door off to the side.

After she finished, they provided her with Nox traveling clothes, all of which fit as snugly as a glove. She'd never worn clothing so tight that wasn't restrictive. The fabric was unlike anything she'd ever felt before. Smooth like silk, but it didn't bind. It... stretched. It was as though the clothing was partly *made* of shadow. Not only did it give her freedom of movement, but it blended with the Dark.

The attendants took her to a stable. There were no horses, but rather vicious-looking Pamants. She'd ridden plenty of Pamants, but none had looked like these. These fierce-looking creatures had raptor-beaks, curved and sharp for tearing meat, unlike the straight, spear-like beaks of the Pamants. Pamants looked like giant, beige woodpeckers, while these resembled giant black eagles.

"What are those?" she asked of Maid Hoxa.

"Talyns, my lady," Maid Hoxa said. "Have you not seen one before?"

"Never."

"They are fine mounts. All have been well trained. They will not hurt you."

"They'll even protect you, come to that," Zaith said, and she turned to see him walking toward her holding the reins of two Talyns. Their fierce, angry eyes made them look like they were ready to attack, but they didn't.

"You look good in shadow," he said, looking her up and down and nodding at her new attire.

The compliment warmed her, and she allowed herself to feel it, and his gaze, without worry. She was warming to her newfound freedom, and she had to admit it felt glorious. Any time a man had taken notice of her before, Lorelle's first response had always been to stay on high alert, lock away any desires she might have, and concentrate on rebuffing their advances.

But now there was no danger. She didn't have to worry about accidentally starting a bond with Zaith. She was already bound to the Dark. As he had promised, she was free to experience whatever new sensations came her way. The euphoria of her victory over Savenk. The luxurious decadence of the bath. The tingling pleasure of Zaith's flirtation. She could even flirt back if she wanted.

"I *am* the shadow." She winked.

He chuckled. "So you are."

Reluctantly, she turned her attention back to the task at had. Rhenn. All this freedom was well and good, but her friend wasn't free yet. She wasn't about to forget that.

"The Plunnos," she said.

"Yes." He nodded gravely.

"Where is it."

"A two hours' ride distant. But first, I need to give you some information."

"Let me guess," she said. She thought about the Readers and how they'd killed the thieves who'd had the temerity to steal from them, about the Reader who had developed such an intricate plan to keep Lorelle from taking it. "The Plunnos isn't just lying on the ground, waiting to be snatched up."

He smiled. "Not exactly, no."

"Who's guarding it?"

"A dragon."

"A dragon?" That stunned her. Dragons were myths.

"What do you know about dragons?" he asked.

"About as much as I know about Giants."

"Well, there are two kinds of dragons: lesser and elder dragons. Lesser dragons are similar to Jaelderons."

"Jaelderons?"

He glanced at her, made a gesture with both hands. "Huge? Scaly? Big antlers?"

She gave him a blank look.

"You don't have those?"

"I don't think so."

Zaith snapped his fingers. "Moose!"

"Moose?"

"Certainly, you have moose."

"Yes, we have moose. What do moose have to do with dragons?"

"Lesser dragons are like moose. But rather than a big, dumb, dominating beast that will stomp you if annoy it, you have a big, dumb, dominating beast that will actively hunt you and eat you. That's a lesser dragon."

"And that's what we're facing?"

"No. We are going to rob an elder dragon."

"And elder dragons are sweet and lovable, right?"

"Hmmm." He pointed a finger at her. "Imagine, if you will, the opposite. Elder dragons make lesser dragons look like rats.

You mentioned Giants before, and that's what elder dragons are. They are Lords who transformed themselves into those majestic, deadly monsters. They are enormous."

"And this dragon has the Plunnos."

"Jai'ketakos."

"That's the name of the dragon?"

Zaith nodded. "And he is only a monster in size and deadliness. Don't make the mistake of thinking he is a lesser dragon, with the intelligence of a moose, simply because he looks similar. Jai'ketakos is every bit as smart as you are and a thousand times more knowledgeable. If we wake him—if he catches us—we die. Only with the full blessing of the Dark can we hope to sneak up on this creature."

A thrill went through her. She felt the darkness within herself, and she longed to use it, to test her abilities, to slide from shadow to shadow.

"But first, we have to get there," he said. He handed her the reins of one of the Talyns, one with a golden, glowing stripe across his head from his nose to halfway down his mane of feathers.

She cautiously mounted the Talyn just like she would have mounted a Pamant, all the while expecting the angry-looking bird to turn and take a chunk out of her leg with its razor-sharp beak. It did not. In fact, it seemed far better trained than most of the Pamants she had ridden.

"Ready?" Zaith asked. She nodded.

Over the course of the next two hours, Lorelle and Zaith galloped through the forest, and then across a wide, flat field toward a sharp slope that curved upward to a ridge. Behind the ridge emanated a glowing, pale yellow light.

When they reached the base of the slope, Zaith pulled on the reins of his Talyn. The giant bird squawked, halted, and Zaith dismounted.

She did the same, swung a leg over, and dropped to the craggy ground. Her Talyn tossed its head and glanced arrogantly down at her. The queer glow behind the ridge fascinated her.

She'd seen nothing like it anywhere in Nox Arvak. The glow was bright in the same way daylight was bright.

Zaith let the reins of his Talyn hang loose and he came toward her. She brushed off her skin-tight black pants and flung her midnight black braid over one shoulder.

"Now," he said. "Let's take a look, then come back here."

"We don't take the Talyns?"

"We stay as quiet as we can from here on," he said in a low voice.

She nodded.

Together, they crept up the slope to the top of the ridge where the unnatural glow emanated from. As they crested the rise and cautiously peeked over, the sight took Lorelle's breath away.

Below them lay a deep, craggy valley. There were no trees, there was no vegetation of any kind, only volcanic stone and an entrance to an enormous, silent cavern. The sky over the far ridge of the valley looked cracked, like the deep indigo to which she'd become accustomed was nothing more than a fragile dome of glass and someone had smashed it with a hammer. It was shot through with streaks of stark white light that crackled like lightning.

It was the first place inside the noktum she'd ever seen that actually *had* light.

She must have stared at it for longer than she'd thought, because she snapped from her reverie when Zaith patted her on the arm. He gave a tilt of his head while he held a finger to his lips, indicating they should retreat down the slope. They crawled down the rise until the valley, and that odd, broken sky, vanished from view.

"That is his cave. Jai'ketakos is in there," he whispered, as though now afraid that the dragon could hear them all the way up and over the ridge. "I wanted you to see it and absorb it before we head down."

"Why is there light in the sky?" she asked. The blinding streaks were so bright she couldn't look directly at them.

He nodded. "That is the Lux."

That name rang a bell of recognition. She'd heard of the Lux during her history lessons with Rhenn when they were children.

"It's a spell of some kind, right?" she asked.

"A master spell of the Lords from millennia ago. Do you know why there are noktums on Noksonon?"

"The... Human-Giant War," she said. "An attack of the Giants."

He shook his head. "No. The noktums were created long before you Lightlanders rose up against the Lords, back before Humans even recorded time. Once, the entire continent of Noksonon was covered in darkness. There were no patches of daylight where you Lightlanders now live. The noktum we are in—the entirety of all noktums on the continent—are the result of a master defensive spell."

"I thought you said it was before the Human-Giant War?"

"There were other wars, Lorelle. The Lords once fought each other."

"Other wars?"

"Lords from other lands, yes."

"There are lands besides Noksonon?"

"Five, in fact, that I know of. Noksonon, Lathranon, Drakanon, Daemanon, and Pyranon. They are connected by the Thuroi. And while all Thuroi are the same, each Plunnos is different. Some will teleport you to another Thuros on Noksonon. Some will teleport you to one of these other lands, far away. I would guess *that* is where the Betrayer took your sister."

"The Betrayer? You mean Nhevaz?"

"The Betrayer is our name for the rogue Lord called Nhevalos."

Nhevalos! That pulled Lorelle up short. "So Nhevaz *was* a Giant?"

"Of course, he was. Only the Lords may use the magical portals. I surmise the Betrayer took the name Nhevaz to better hide among your kind, but yes. I am nearly sure that was him."

"But he wasn't... large. I mean, he was large for a Human but not anywhere close to the size Giants are supposed to be."

"The Lords possess vast magic. If he wanted to appear as someone your size, I imagine he could."

"Where did he take Rhenn?"

"I do not know. He could have taken her anywhere."

Lorelle turned her attention back to the glow on the horizon. "So, the noktum is a spell, and the Lux?"

"A counter spell," he murmured. "Back during the wars between the Lords, they vied for territory against each other. The Lords of Noksonon created artifacts to help them see and move in the dark—like noktum cloaks—and then they created the noktum itself to give themselves an advantage. When the Lords from other continents attacked, they found themselves lost in the Dark. Later, of course, The Lords created races to serve them in the noktum, the Nox and the Shadowvar, races who could thrive in the Dark."

"And the Lux was meant to destroy it all, to return the continent to normal," she said.

"To a land of daylight, yes." He nodded. "At first, the Lux broke the noktum into a thousand pieces, opening the spaces for daylight to once again bake the lands of Noksonon. That is why you Lightlanders have a place to live. Naturally, the noktum fought back. What you see now is the ongoing battle between those two great spells." He pointed at the white streaks in the sky. "The noktum eternally tries to devour the Lux, and the Lux eternally tries to shatter the noktum. It has been this way for millennia."

"Can you... travel through the Lux? If we crossed over from here to there, what is it like?"

"Mortal eyes cannot withstand its light. Even Lightlanders. You'll go blind."

"So, into the dragon's cave."

"Yes," he said "Jai'ketakos has slept for millennia. If we do our jobs correctly, he will sleep for many more. All we must do is dance with the Dark and not make a sound. We find the Plunnos, we take it, we leave."

"And if the dragon wakes?" she asked.

"Then we die."

"We can't fight it?"

"Not even with an army of Glimmerblades and Darkweavers."

"Darkweavers?"

"Aravelle is a Darkweaver. The Nox equivalent of your friend Slayter. A mage."

She nodded.

He started up the ridge again, but she touched his arm.

He glanced back at her.

"Zaith, I have to ask you something before we go in there. I... have to know."

He turned, coming a little closer.

"Why are you helping me?" she asked. "Why do this? You could die. So why are you doing it?"

"It is my duty, as a Glimmerblade."

"To guide Luminents to the truth, yes. To bring them into the noktum, yes. But not to fight a dragon."

He hesitated. "You needed help."

She shook her head. He was definitely keeping something from her. She was sure of it now. "There are thousands of Luminents. Why me? Why not them? Tell me, Zaith. Please."

He glanced up at the ridge. Finally, he shook his head.

"Zaith..."

"I don't want to tell you." He looked at her, his eyes haunted.

"I know you don't, but please."

He watched her, his brow furrowed. "I was sent. Glimmerblades, we... We kill Luminents, Lorelle. Usually. We're assassins."

Her heart beat faster.

"That's what I was *sent* to do," he said. "That's why everyone in Nox Arvak was stunned when I walked into the city with you. That wasn't supposed to happen. That's why they were angry."

"Why didn't you kill me?"

"I don't know. I—When I got to Usara, you were already dying, and yet you refused to give up on your friend. I've never seen anyone hold off the soul-bond like that before; endure such pain for her convictions. You weren't like any Luminent I'd ever been sent to kill. So, when the time came I hesitated. Instead, I followed you. I watched you in your pain. I came to admire your dedication to your friend, Rhenn. I made a different choice."

He moved closer to her. She felt she should let go of his arm, but she didn't.

"I thought you could be..." he breathed. "I thought maybe you would... join us. The Nox. We do that sometimes, too. Bring Luminents into the Dark. I wanted you to."

"Why?"

Again, he hesitated. "Do you really not know?"

He leaned into her and she didn't back away. His lips brushed against her cheek, then her lips. She stiffened. Her instincts told her to draw away, but...

Zaith had shown her a whole new world. She believed him, that the Luminents had somehow cursed their people. The freedom she'd known in the short time she'd spent here, it was a revelation. She wasn't bound by those rules anymore, the rules of her parents, the demands of control.

She turned into the kiss and pressed her lips to Zaith's. The kiss went on and on. Little jolts of lightning forked through her, promising something even better than the kiss, something more, something so deliciously pleasurable she hungered for it.

She pushed her fingers into his hair, cupping the back of his head like he'd done to her. His arm encircled her waist, pulling her to him. She felt the heat of his strong body against her, smelled his hair, and her fingers gripped him...

She wanted this. She wanted to lose herself inside him, give herself to him with reckless abandon.

Zaith suddenly pulled away, breathless, leaving her breathless as well. She blinked.

"Don't..." she murmured, pulling him back until his forehead touched hers. "Don't stop."

"I…" he breathed. "This is probably the most dangerous place in the whole world to do this."

"Yes," she murmured, holding on to him. For this wild moment, she didn't care. She'd been cautious her whole life, and she simply didn't care about anything but the kiss. "Yes, it is."

"You are something," he breathed.

She brought her lips closer to his, but he gripped her shoulders tighter, stopping her.

"If I were to choose my death," he said, "this would be a good one. But, Lorelle, you came with a purpose and I would see that through. Perhaps…" He swallowed hard, like there was something more, like he wanted to say something and yet at the same time didn't. "Perhaps we can save this moment as a celebration. When we return with the Plunnos."

Disappointment fluttered in her stomach like a broken butterfly.

"Yes." She swallowed, nodded. "You're right, of course." She suddenly felt dizzy, lost. She took half a step away from him, fighting to come to her senses, fighting down her disappointment.

He was right, though. She wasn't here to kiss him. She was here to help Rhenn. Lotura, had she forgotten that?

"I think my bond with the noktum has made me a bit reckless," she joked, and it sounded feeble. Not a joke at all. A statement of fact.

"There is something we *could* do, though," he said. "Something that would aid us in our endeavor."

"Yes?" Excitement fluttered in her belly.

"The bonding? Your bonding with the Dark, when you laid hands on the Cairn? You held back, yet there are still advantages to be had. Advantages that would be useful as we sneak into the dragon's lair."

She remembered those last moments in the Cairn. The threads of her soul connecting to the noktum, faster and faster, until she'd shouted—

"Some of the… threads," she murmured. "I kept them. I kept them the same. Five threads." Five threads that still belonged to Khyven.

She didn't want to give them up. She'd given him half her soul for a reason. She had *wanted* him to bond with her. It just became so complicated when Rhenn was stolen.

But that was before she'd experienced her bonding with the Dark. By Lotura, Zaith had been right. She'd stepped into the freedom she'd always wanted. But she did love Khyven. That hadn't been a mistake, hadn't been a rash decision. She'd been prepared to die for him, and during those months he'd lain comatose, she'd harbored the forbidden hope that he would wake, that he would choose to bond with her.

That he would be that one-in-a-hundred Human who could successfully make the bond.

"To be truly one with the Dark, you must completely release the half-bond you created. You must release that failed connection." He leaned toward her, brought his lips to hers again, brushed them lightly. "We can do that now. I will show you. We don't need the Cairn anymore."

He was so close. She wanted him there, wanted to kiss him again, but she put a hand on his chest. "But I already feel the Dark within me. Why must I do more?"

"Your skill with the shadows is powerful. You proved that with Savenk. With me, for that matter. But it is only a fraction of what it can be," he murmured. "If you can do this much with just a partial bond, imagine what you could do with a full bond."

She turned her head away. "I don't know."

"Is it him? Do you actually wish to soul-bond with Khyven?"

Was that pain she heard in Zaith's voice?

Her heart constricted, and the worry she'd known all her life returned with a vengeance. Decisions with no going back. Actions constrained. Responses so carefully chosen. In her rush to enjoy her freedom, to simply pluck fruit from the vine and not care about consequences, she hadn't thought about how Zaith might feel.

"Just a little more and you'll be one of us," Zaith said.

"Zaith... I don't know if I want that."

"You've experienced freedom for the first time in your life, and you want to go back?"

"N-No, but—"

"We are your kind, Lorelle. *That's* what I sensed when I followed you. That's what I felt when I disobeyed the order to kill you."

She shook her head. It was all so confused and jumbled. She wanted him, but not what he offered. And there was no proscribed behavior for this; no parental wisdom or Luminent law. She was well beyond those boundaries. Lotura! Was this what freedom was like?

"We should go," she said. "This isn't the time for—"

"It *is* the time," he said. "Commit to us, Lorelle." His hand slid up the back of her head, fingers in her hair, and she drew a deep breath, leaning back into it.

"I... I came here for Rhenn," she said.

"And this will help her. We'll get the Plunnos and then, I swear to you, I will go to the ends of the earth and beyond with you until we track her down."

Every word he spoke vibrated with passion, and she believed him. But it felt like she had to give up one life for the other. Becoming a Nox meant staying here.

She'd sworn she'd do anything to save Rhenn, but could she give up the rest of her family? Could she release Khyven and Vohn and Slayter?

"Give up one life for another..." she murmured aloud.

"It's what you want."

"How do you know?"

"Because I know you. I've watched you transform, and it has been... beautiful."

She turned her head away and her black hair fell in her face, shielding her. She'd come so far so fast, and it *was* glorious, but when she looked in the mirror, even when she simply looked at her own hands...

They were the hands of a stranger. Everything here seemed dreamlike. It was so easy to flow along because what does it matter what you do in a dream?

"I can't decide this right now," she said.

"Lorelle—"

"I can't. Don't ask me again."

His hands slowly released her, and she felt their loss. She drew a shuddering breath and almost broke. She almost told him to envelope her again, to hold her and kiss her. She almost cast her line away from the shore forever.

He paused for a moment, then whispered, "Of course."

"I'm sorry, Zaith. I just... I need more time."

"You have come so far so fast." He nodded, perhaps shaking off his disappointment. "I understand. We will face the dragon without the final bond. Together. Are you ready?"

She nodded.

He drew a breath and glanced up at the ridge. "Then stay close to me." He started back up the slope.

CHAPTER THIRTY

LORELLE

The white streaks looked angry vibrating against the indigo sky as they crept down into the valley. Zaith led her around to the edge of the far ridge, approaching the mouth of the cavern like it was the mouth of the dragon itself. It was the first time she'd seen him so cautious. Zaith had always been confident before, but now he slid carefully into every shadow.

Lorelle flowed from shadow to shadow behind him and followed him into the cave.

Stalactites pointed down and enormous stalagmites jutted up like teeth. They clung to and slid through the irregular shadows with Zaith always in the lead. Every twenty feet or so smaller passages, that looked like they had been created specifically for Human-sized visitors, branched off left or right from the main tunnel.

The light from the Lux faded behind them until it was just the glowing circle of the cavern's mouth, and her night vision returned without the blinding distractions of the angry white streaks. The stalactites and stalagmites became purple again, with just a hint of orange running through them.

Zaith stopped and seemed to think, like he was consulting a mental map. He finally nodded toward a smaller passage on the right-hand side, and they crept silently into it. He led, blending with the shadows until she couldn't actually see him with her eyes anymore.

But she felt him through the Dark, his body flowing gracefully like water from one crooked shadow to the next. She followed, the Dark guiding her footsteps.

A yellow glow swelled ahead, and they approached even more cautiously, slowing to almost a crawl.

They stopped at the end of the tunnel, which opened into an enormous cavern, larger even than the main tunnel. Piles of gold and silver, gemstones and overflowing caskets of jewels created a mountain of treasure so high it touched the stalactites along the ceiling. At the base of the treasure pile, coins and diamonds littered the ground. Just a handful of that mountain was more wealth than most subjects of Usara would ever see.

Five towering torches—twenty-foot-tall steel cylinders—supported dishes burning with natural firelight. It drove back the irregular shadows of the noktum and illuminated the cavern with bright yellows and oranges, creating the harsh, predictable shadows of a daylight land. She had never seen natural light in the noktum before. Even the Lux was a supernatural light that seemed to attack the sky, but it still didn't create normal shadows like this.

Seeing the natural light chilled her. In any other place, light like that would bring a horde of monsters, crazed with the need to extinguish the fire, killing themselves in their desperation to do it.

But apparently even the monsters of the Dark feared to come to this place.

Together she and Zaith slunk up to the edge of the passageway so they could survey the entire room.

And there it was.

The vast, glimmering black body of the dragon lay at the base of the mountain of treasure, coiling around it. Lotura! The thing was easily as large as Aravelle's entire palace. Its long, smooth head came to a beak-like point beneath two huge nostrils. Thick, black horns poked out from its neck, and two more sloped backward from its head just above its ears. A deep groove, almost a cleft, ran down the center of its scale-covered skull between the closed, bulbous eyes, then rose, forming a ridge. The ridge became more pronounced near the back of its head, before it swirled into another single horn, angled up and back. Curls of smoke rose from the dragon's nostrils as it slumbered.

Lorelle stared, frozen. It was one thing to have a dragon described to her. It was entirely another to stand before its staggering majesty. From the base of its belly to its ridged back, it had to be at least two stories tall. Its folded wings were a hundred feet long, and she could only imagine how huge they would be when fully opened.

Its scaled arms, tucked under its immense body, were wider around than the thickest tree. Just one of its claws was as thick as her thigh, curved like a wagon wheel to a wicked point.

She glanced away, trying to focus on her purpose, but she quailed as she looked at all those coins. The Plunnos was a coin. How were they going to find one coin in that pile? And even if they did find it, how were they going to remove it without the other coins clinking and waking the thing?

Deep in the shadows, she still couldn't see Zaith, but she knew where he was and touched his arm. She didn't dare speak, but she felt that he understood her meaning. He had to be thinking the same thing.

What do we do now?

Zaith's hand emerged from the edge of the crooked shadow, barely showing, but it was enough to point.

She followed the angle of his finger with her gaze. At the top of the pile sat a small chest. Was he implying the Plunnos was there? Inside that chest?

She examined the cavern and tried to figure out a way they could get to the top of the pile without causing an avalanche of coins. Perhaps they could find a higher spot and rig a line of some kind from one of the stalactites.

Then she noticed steps had been carved into the rock wall on the far side of the room. They went up and up along the wall, higher than the apex of the treasure pile. Her thoughts trailed off as her gaze reached the landing at the top.

A Thuros!

It looked exactly like the one in Rhenn's palace. It was the same height. It bore the same symbols on the pillars. The inside of the archway swirled with the same colored lights.

Her imagination went wild. Rhenn might be just beyond that door. If they could get the Plunnos now, she wouldn't have to return to Usara to go after Rhenn. Lorelle could follow her straight from this room.

The five remaining threads of her soul grew warmer, glowing in the dark tapestry of her soul. Just the thought of reuniting with Rhenn made her think of Usara, of Khyven, of course, but also of Vohn and Slayter.

Those five threads glowed brightly, reminding her of the world she had left behind. Zaith wanted her to give those threads up. But just the thought of Rhenn made them glow brighter, made her remember why she had come here in the first place, and she now knew she could never give up those threads to the Dark. No matter how much Zaith wanted her to become one with the Nox. No matter how free he made her feel or how enticing it had been to have his hands on her body, his lips on her lips. She could never stay in the noktum forever. And not just because of Rhenn. But because of brilliant, quirky Slayter. Because of earnest Vohn. And because of Khyven.

Lorelle had a family, and now more than ever she knew she had to get back to them.

The glow burned brightly within her and she longed for them all. It even seemed she could feel them—each one of them—through those threads, that connection to her true life.

Zaith's urgent hand gripped her arm and she started from her revelation.

Horrified, she realized the warm glow inside her hadn't stayed on the inside. A single lock of her hair glowed, pushing back the shadows with the rich, buttery light of her original golden hair.

She drew a sharp breath and shot a look at the sleeping monster.

The dragon opened his burning yellow eyes.

CHAPTER THIRTY-ONE

LORELLE

aith clenched her arm so hard it hurt and she immediately controlled the glow of her hair. The light winked out.

But it was too late.

"Visitors," the dragon said in a deep voice that shook the entire cavern. "I haven't had visitors in a long time. A long time. And I do love them so."

The dragon's tail vanished from its side of the treasure trove and whipped around toward them. The tip snaked into the tunnel and caressed Lorelle on the cheek, so soft, like the touch of a friend.

"Oh… yes…" the dragon breathed and its vast bulk shivered. Coins clinked and slid down the pile.

"Run!" Zaith shouted. They sprinted away from the tail's quivering tip and rushed up the corridor, leaping from shadow to shadow. The dragon vanished from view.

"Oh please," the dragon thundered, his voice echoing down the tunnel. "Don't be rude."

Booms shook the corridor and rock dust sifted downward. They flew like the wind and reached the entrance of the small corridor in moments—

—to find the dragon's snout waiting for them, his smoking nostrils filling the entire opening.

They skidded to a stop. Zaith bared his teeth, glancing desperately back the way they'd come, back toward the treasure pile.

"The cloak," she said. "Use the cloak!"

He hesitated.

"Ah!" the voice boomed from the entrance of the tunnel. "There are two of you. I only saw the one. Do you know what this means?"

"Use the cloak—"

The entire left wall of the corridor turned to sand and fell to the ground, opening into the main hallway where the dragon crouched. His huge claw lashed out, faster than either of them could react, and one of those wickedly curved nails slammed down right between them, knocking them to the ground on either side of it.

"It means a choice," the dragon rumbled. "A delicious choice. I see you have a treasure of your own, a noktum cloak. Old Tovos doesn't give those to just anyone. And now the choice comes together, the glorious edge of the knife where fate bows to mortals." It lowered its head, and Lorelle looked for a way around the claw. Zaith stood just beyond, but she hesitated to go to him. The dragon's claw had moved so fast it had been a blur. She couldn't just leap over it and expect to reach Zaith, and she didn't want to run back toward the treasure trove.

"The choice... the choice... the choice... I shall state it, then I will leave it in your hands. Here it is: One of you shall die a horrible death. The other shall return to the life they knew. Which will it be? Choose."

Zaith leapt over the claw toward Lorelle, taking the decision out of her hands. His cloak unfurled to wrap around her—

The cloak stopped as though some force had pinned it to the air. It held Zaith by the neck as he dangled. The cloak came to life and wound about Zaith, binding him, holding him a foot above the dragon's claw.

"Lorelle!" Zaith cried. The cloak engulfed his face, balled up, shrank, wound smaller and smaller into a little black knot—

And it was gone. Zaith was gone.

Lorelle stood stunned.

"Well chosen. Well chosen," the dragon said. It removed its claw from the dusty opening and lowered its snout to the ground, its burning yellow eyes focused on her. "As promised. One happy life..."

It grinned.

"And one horrible death."

CHAPTER THIRTY-TWO

LORELLE

Lorelle's heart beat so fast she thought it would burst out of her chest. She felt helpless, that same cold, trickling feeling she'd felt the moment Vamreth had lowered the crossbow at Rhenn's heart when they were children.

But this time there was no noktum behind her. No escape. The dragon seemed to fill the entire cavern and the thought of running seemed useless. Zaith had moved as fast as Lorelle had ever seen anyone move—Human or Luminent or Nox—and still the dragon had been faster.

And the dragon clearly had magic.

"You're a Luminent," the dragon said, cocking its head, "dressed up to look like a Nox. How… interesting. One doesn't see that every day."

Lorelle looked left and right. She had to try something!

The dragon's yellow eyes narrowed. "Ah…" it said, as though it had just figured something out. "So, it's happening at long last."

She could barely breathe through her panic, but she seized on the curiosity in the monster's voice. "Happening? W-what's happening?" she stammered.

"Ah, she has found her tongue. I remember, long ago, another young Luminent. She never did find her tongue. I waited oh so long for her to say something, but she just stared at me." The dragon sighed. "So, I ate her."

Lorelle swallowed. "W-when you said something was happening, you sounded... like it surprised you."

"Oh, it does," the dragon said. "A Luminent in my domain. The last time Luminents came here, they came to kill me. A whole army of them. I splattered them across the walls, one after the other until that last one I mentioned. But she wouldn't speak to me. Just couldn't speak at that point. I pray you'll do better."

"That was... during the Human-Giant War?" she asked.

"Oh, well done," it said. "Yes, it was. I was ordered to protect this Thuros. Ordered... Me! Do you know how many years I've been here?"

"Thousands," she said.

"One thousand nine hundred and eighty-four," it said. "Do you know how long it's been since anyone has visited me?"

She opened her mouth, but nothing came out.

"The army of Luminents, that bloody, tasty day so long ago. Do you know how long ago? Do you know how long I have been here, little Luminent? How hungry I am?"

"They came... to fight you?" she finally managed to say.

The dragon smiled. "Oh, I like you. You think that if you can keep me talking I will not devour you."

Her heart hurt, like she'd swallowed a stone and it was stuck in her chest. She prepared to leap away, to do something—anything—to escape.

"But I have no intention of eating you. Hungry as I am, your presence here means something far more than the appearance of a tasty tidbit. One does not gobble up omens. Do you know what you represent? Do you have any clue?"

Lorelle tried to answer, but the dragon's suddenly feral gaze seemed to paralyze her.

The dragon poked his nose a little closer, until it was in the wrecked corridor. The smoke from its nostrils curled around her like hot steam.

"Change," he whispered.

Its lips pulled back, exposing rows and rows of tall, sharp, white teeth behind its horned beak of a snout.

"I have slept," the dragon continued. "I have dreamed of this moment. Your touch. My chain going slack at long last. You, little Luminent, are a glittering jewel. More valuable than anything in my hoard, and I will not waste you. So, fear not. You get to live."

Breathing hard from her pounding heart, she tried to think of what to say. "Thank you."

"Tell me, what is a Luminent doing in the Great Noktum? Why does she have a Nox chaperone? How and why did she bind herself to the Dark? A Luminent? Binding herself to the Great Noktum? Incongruities. Impossibilities. The wheel has turned. Do the winds of change blow in the lands of daylight? Are the Noksonoi on the move at last?"

Noksonoi... She knew that word. Slayter had mentioned it. That was what the Giants had called themselves.

"One, at least," Lorelle said. "Nhevalos."

"Nhevalos!" the dragon roared, and the heat of his breath washed over her.

"You know him," she said.

The dragon's eyes burned brighter. "Oh, we all know *that* name. Did he send you here?"

"No. He stole my sister."

"Which is the reason you are here?"

"Yes."

"Then he did send you."

"Why do you say that?"

"Because that is Nhevalos's way. He tinkers here and something happens there. He whispers in Demaijos and it becomes a shout in Usara. He steals a sister and a lost little Luminent wakes a dragon. The Noksonoi *have* returned, and Nhevalos's clever whip goads them, as ever." The dragon narrowed his eyes. "So, the Betrayer hints that your sister is here and you fling yourself after her. Well, I am sorry to tell you, my delectable morsel, but she is not here."

"I didn't come here to find her."

"Oh?"

"I came to get a Plunnos. To follow Nhevalos."

"Ah, he took her through a Thuros," the dragon said, and his eyes glanced briefly at the swirling Thuros perched above his hoard.

"Yes."

"The question then is, as it ever is with Nhevalos: has he ensured you won't ever follow him, or he has he ensured that you will? Which do you suppose it is?"

"There are no—I haven't been able to find a Plunnos. Zaith said you have one."

"Oh, I do. And Zaith led you here, you say? The Nox with the noktum cloak?"

"Yes."

"So, it was not Nhevalos who sent you, but Tovos?"

"I—Who?"

"Mmmm," the dragon rumbled. "You don't know who Tovos is."

"No."

"I would bet Zaith does. Have you known him long?"

It seemed she'd known Zaith for a lifetime.

"No."

"But he is your friend, yes? Your *good* friend. Your trusted friend who would never do anything to harm you…"

Lorelle narrowed her eyes.

The dragon sighed contentedly. "Very well. I think I understand." He glanced sideways at his treasure pile. "It's time to play the game. It's time to pay Nhevalos back."

"Pay him back?"

"Who do you think trapped me here after I laid waste to his Luminent army?" He indicated a giant, glowing golden chain lying at the base of his hoard. There was an open manacle attached to it, but the glowing chain seemed to go nowhere. A six-foot length of it hovered in the air. "And now Tovos has sent me a lifeline. My thanks, Little Luminent."

"Y-you're welcome."

"You have given me my freedom, so I will give it back to you in return." The dragon laughed and the sound shook the walls. Dirt sifted down. A stalactite broke free from the ceiling and crashed into the gold, causing a small landslide of coins. "You came to the heart of the Great Noktum, to my lair, to find a Plunnos." The dragon's flaming eyes blazed at her as it raised its head. "And you shall have it."

The horde of coins shivered and several thin avalanches of gold slid down as it rumbled. The box at the top of the pile flew into the air. It flipped open and a Plunnos floated across the distance to land atop the dragon's claw, where it spun and danced on the creature's knuckle.

"You've invigorated me with your incomplete bond to the noktum and your Nox disguise. The wheel turns and I will do my part. Take it." He twitched a knuckle and flipped the coin toward Lorelle. She caught it with both hands.

Her fingers closed around it and she felt its power. The fake Plunnos had been nothing but a coin with a convincing weight and arcane symbols engraved upon it. This was warm with an inner heat, inordinately light, and yet she sensed it would survive being smashed between two boulders without bearing a scratch.

A long, insidious smile spread across the dragon's face. "Open the Thuros, little Luminent. Chase your sister."

"Thank you. Do you…" she began to ask, but hesitated.

The dragon raised a scaly ridge above one eye. "Yes?"

"You say Nhevalos took Rhenn for a reason. Why? Why would he take her?"

The dragon let out a *whuff* that shook its long neck. Was that a dragon laugh?

"Which brings us to our crossroads, little Luminent. We cannot part company without a crossroads. I will give you a choice. Your first path is this: I will tell you everything you wish to know. Everything your curious heart desires. I will answer every question you can think of about Nhevalos, about his methods, about why he would want your sister. About Tovos and your good friend, the

Nox. Then, when we are done, I will devour you. But—" the dragon raised a claw as though to emphasize his point "—once you are dead, I will put the Dragon's Chain back around my ankle and my confinement will begin anew until another traveler comes to free me. I will stay here in my cave and sleep for another thousand years." It lowered its chin.

"Here is your second path: You can take the Plunnos you came for. Abscond with your prize and with my blessing. The Plunnos will be yours and you will be free to seek your sister."

"You'll just let me go?"

"With the Plunnos. With the Thuroi at your command and your sister in reach."

Lorelle's heart thumped. Was this some cruel kind of torture to get her hopes up and then dash them?

"I will take the Plunnos," she said.

"Of course, you will," the dragon said, and that frightening smile spread across his face. "Be free then, little Luminent. Dance to Nhevalos's tune, or to Tovos's—whomever is playing the harp. But remember, I gave you the choice. Remember you stood on the knife's edge, and you bent fate to your will." The dragon rose and turned its head toward the exit of its cave. It drew a deep breath. "Yeeesss..." it sighed; the word stretched, like the dragon was luxuriating in it. "It is time for me to see what has become of Noksonon."

The dragon started up the main corridor, toward the exit, each heavy footfall shaking the walls.

Lorelle ran after the creature. She didn't know why, but she chased it, clutching the Plunnos in both hands, feeling a deep foreboding that somehow, she had made the wrong choice.

It launched into the sky when it passed the mouth of the cave. She ran into the open air and squinted up at the painfully bright streaks of white as the dragon pumped its mighty wings, buffeting the crevice with a hurricane wind.

She squinted as dust and rock swirled around her. The dragon let out a thunderous scream, so loud she gasped and pressed her hands to her ears.

Clenching her teeth, she craned her neck and saw the dragon winging higher and higher. It blew yellow fire all around, filling the indigo sky with natural light. Even at this distance, Lorelle felt the heat of it.

In moments, the dragon was nothing more than a speck of black against the purple. The yellow fire around it died, and then she could no longer see it.

The dragon's ominous words rang in her mind. *Remember, I gave you the choice. You stood on the knife's edge...*

And you bent fate to your will.

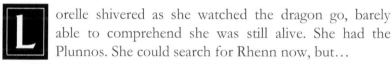

CHAPTER THIRTY-THREE

LORELLE

Lorelle shivered as she watched the dragon go, barely able to comprehend she was still alive. She had the Plunnos. She could search for Rhenn now, but…

Guilt and hope warred within her. She had what she needed, what she'd come for, but at what cost? Zaith was dead. He'd screamed her name as his own cloak devoured him at the dragon's command. The dragon had promised one of them would live and one would die.

But the dragon had also spoken in riddles. Zaith had screamed, but was he really dead? The cloak had balled itself up just like the first time she'd seen him teleport on the dock in Usara.

Was that the horrible death the dragon had promised? Or had the dragon simply taken hold of the cloak's magic and teleported Zaith elsewhere? Could he still be alive?

If he was, she had to look for him, didn't she? To find out if he was all right?

She looked back into the yellow glow of the cave. The Thuros was there. Rhenn was there.

She sprinted back inside, her feet flying over the rough rock. She skidded to a stop before the mountain of treasure surrounded by its giant braziers of natural light. To her left, the long, rough-hewn staircase leading up the cavern wall stretched into the flickering shadows.

She ran up the stairs, taking them three at a time until she stood breathless before the Thuros. Blue, brown, green, red, and black swirled in the archway…

"Take me to Rhenn," she whispered, clenching the Plunnos in her fist. She squeezed her eyes shut and envisioned her friend in that last second before she had vanished into the swirling colors.

Take me to Rhenn…

She opened her eyes and lobbed the coin at the swirling colors just as she'd seen Nhevaz do. It clinked, rebounded unerringly back into Lorelle's hand.

No portal opened. The colors simply continued swirling. Her heart sank.

She clenched her teeth, walked forward, and slammed her fist against the solid colors—

Her hand passed through like it was water, just as Nhevaz's body had passed through.

She cried out in joy and charged into the colors.

The swirling lights slithered over her and she felt like she was being dipped in a vat of oil. It saturated her hair, slid around her neck, arms, breasts, belly, and legs like she was suddenly naked.

Then she was through. She fell to her knees, gasping. She looked down at herself, expecting to find herself stripped and dripping in oil—

But she was dry. Her black Nox clothes were exactly as they had been.

She shivered, then looked up to see where she was. The swirling colors of the Thuros illuminated nothing, but the room was shrouded in darkness. A natural darkness, not the deep dark of the noktum. But normal darkness now seemed like twilight to her noktum-enhanced eyes.

She stood atop a dais with shallow steps leading down to a circular room with stone walls. In the center was a giant pillar with a door on it, and she recognized it all. This was the basement room of the Usaran palace, right back where she'd started.

"No..." She looked around helplessly. For a moment, she had hoped this was simply a similar basement, perhaps in another kingdom, built in exactly the same fashion.

But she knew this room too well. The two gates barred the tunnel to the noktum where she and Rhenn had fled a decade ago, where Rhenn, Khyven, Vohn, and she had emerged mere months ago to take back the kingdom.

Lorelle spun about and faced the swirling colors again. She imagined her friend, but this time she pictured only Rhenn. Not Nhevaz, and not this room. Just Rhenn, surrounded by a golden light.

"Take me to Rhenn!"

She threw the coin, it bounced back to her hand, and she charged into the Thuros. Oil slithered over her body, through her hair, around every inch of her—

She gasped and stumbled through, once more dry and clothed and—

"No!"

She was on the landing overlooking the dragon's horde of gold. She spun about, desperately threw the coin, and leapt into the Thuros again while shouting Rhenn's name.

It took her back to the room in Usara.

Lorelle hurled the Plunnos away. It clinked off the center wall and fell to the ground, rolling noisily around and around until it settled.

She collapsed to her knees at the base of the dais.

"Rhenn..." she murmured, heartbroken.

After everything she had still failed. She'd *found* the Plunnos. She had used the Thuros, but she couldn't get to Rhenn.

She glanced at the door to the stairway. Her heart ached as she thought about climbing those steps and returning to the queen's meeting chamber to find Vohn, Slayter, and Khyven arguing about how to run the kingdom.

She couldn't go up there. She might have lost control of her quest for Rhenn, but her other friends—her family—were still safe here in Usara. That's where they had to remain. The moment she told them she had a Plunnos, they would insist on helping her, going with her, and she wouldn't risk them coming to the noktum. Zaith's interest in her had protected her, and now her bond to the Dark protected her. But her friends were still just Lightlanders. They didn't belong in the noktum.

She glanced back at the Thuros. Zaith knew about the other continents. He knew about the Plunnos.

And he might still be alive.

She retrieved the giant coin and, as she had expected, there were no marks on it from where she'd hurled it against the wall. As Zaith had promised when they'd first met, the Plunnos appeared to be unaffected by anything she or the mortal world could do to it.

She ascended the dais, flicked the coin at the swirling colors, and, once more, stepped into the swirling lights.

CHAPTER THIRTY-FOUR

ZAITH

Lorelle!" Zaith shouted as the cloak bound him up and forced him through the noktum.

His scream of frustration turned to pain as he was squeezed through the portal of darkness. This time, the thin tube felt like it was lined with razors. Flashes of white-hot light slashed him again and again. It felt like he was being cut to quivering ribbons.

Then he was sobbing, crying for death, his body ringing with the sudden absence of the pain…

He shuddered, his knees pulled against his belly, fists clenched. He was alive. Against all odds, he lived.

He distantly sensed someone was calling to him, and he began to feel sensations aside from the horrible slicing. He lay on a soft bed.

Through tear-drenched eyes, he saw Aravelle leaning over him with a grave expression. A healer and three of her attendants stood behind her.

"Zaith?" Aravelle asked in her whispery voice.

"Where… Where am I?"

"Dear boy," she said, and he could hear her relief, "you are in my apartments. They found you at the edge of the city and brought you here."

He had no recollection of that.

"How… How long?" he asked.

"They found you more than an hour ago. I thought we'd lost you. You've been screaming and shaking like your mind had gone. Only in the last few minutes did you go quiet."

He sat up and looked around.

"Move slowly," the healer said. "We don't know exactly what was done to you."

"The cloak. It was used against me, triggered too close to the Lux," he said. "The light tried to devour me. It… cut me." He looked down at himself, expecting to see bloody slashes. "Was I…? Was I wounded?"

Aravelle motioned to her retinue. The attendants left without a word, but the healer hesitated. "He will be fine now," Aravelle assured her. Reluctantly, the healer joined the others and closed the door. "Tell me, Glimmerblade. Did you succeed? Will the Lord be pleased?"

Zaith clenched his teeth and shook his head. "Lorelle is dead."

"No…"

"Lord Tovos will come now," he said. "He will kill my family." Zaith's head pounded. "He will punish all of Nox Arvak." The weight of his failure pressed down on him. He tried to think his way clear, but he couldn't see an answer.

"I think it is time for you tell me of your mission," she said.

Zaith thought about it. Lord Tovos had told him to remain silent about his purpose, even to Aravelle. But she was right. It could hardly matter now that he had failed. The more the old Darkweaver knew, the better she'd be able to protect their people.

"I was to seduce her," he said. "To… to turn her."

"To complete her bond with the Dark," Aravelle said.

He nodded. "So Lord Tovos could… take control of her. As he can with us."

"How many threads remained?" Aravelle asked.

"Five. But even with those remaining, still connected to this Human she loves, her connection to the Dark was uncanny. It was as if she was truly meant to be one of us. It rivaled my own connection, perhaps even yours. But it wasn't enough, apparently. Lord Tovos demanded the bond be completed. I had planned, in the flush of our victory, to finish the job. A celebration here. I was going to… convince her to stay, to take the next step."

At his stumbling speech, Aravelle raised an eyebrow. "I have never seen you like this, Zaith. Are you certain you were doing the seducing, and not the other way around?"

"She was unlike any maid I have ever known," he murmured, "I will confess to that. But I knew my mission. I would never compromise the lives of my family. Your life. The lives of everyone in Nox Arvak, perhaps. I stayed true to my purpose, Aravelle. I stayed true. But we woke the dragon."

Aravelle's old eyes went wide. "Oh, my child. You went to steal from Jai'ketakos?"

"I was ordered to."

Aravelle put a hand to her mouth. "Grina have mercy…"

"I have to leave," Zaith said. "I have to get as far away from here as possible. It is the only way now." It was a poor plan, but he could think of no other.

"Dear Zaith—"

"You must say you never saw me," he said. "That I never returned. Let him believe both Lorelle and I died."

"And where will you go, child?"

"Into the wild."

"Alone, you will die."

"I will receive what I deserve."

"He will chase you, child."

"Then I will hide."

"From a Lord of the Dark?"

Zaith levered himself to his feet. Every part of him hurt. "You should never have brought me here—"

"Perhaps there is another path. Perhaps she lived and all is not lost."

"A dragon, Aravelle. Jai'ketakos."

"Did you actually *see* her die? Perhaps—"

"He said one of us would live and the other would die a horrible death. I lived."

Aravelle raised her head and closed her eyes, like she was sniffing something on the breeze. Zaith recognized she was using her senses in the Dark. Someone approached.

Aravelle turned toward the doorway and Zaith followed her gaze.

Lorelle emerged from the crooked shadows behind the arch.

"Perhaps it is not quite so simple," she said.

CHAPTER THIRTY-FIVE

LORELLE

Returning to the Great Noktum filled Lorelle with the power of the Dark once more. It was like stepping out of a warm bath then back in again. She felt welcomed and powerful. She felt… like this was where she belonged.

She half thought the dragon would have returned during her absence and lay coiled around its treasure trove once more.

But Jai'ketakos was gone.

She left the cavern, climbed the ridge, and found that, miraculously, the well-trained Talyns were still there.

She vaulted into the saddle and rode her Talyn back to Nox Arvak while leading the other.

As she approached, two Nox sentries approached her. She gave them the Talyns and said that she had to report to Zaith. They didn't like that, and when they came forward to bind her hands, Lorelle let the darkness flow through her and stepped back into a shadow. She thought they would follow, but as she slipped from patch of moving darkness to patch of moving darkness, she escaped. They shouted and chased, but they couldn't see her, couldn't sense her like she sensed them.

Ever before, she had compared herself to Zaith. His facility with the Dark far outstripped her own, and she had assumed all other Nox were like him. But she suddenly realized she had greater facility with the Dark than even these Nox sentries.

She made her way to Aravelle's palace. By the time she sneaked past the palace guards, she could feel Zaith—thank Lotura he was still alive!—and Aravelle within. They were like little bits of warmth within her mind, growing warmer as she drew nearer.

She even slipped past Aravelle's attendants and made it all the way to the room where both Zaith and Aravelle talked. They were clearly discussing her. She paused in the crooked shadow by the archway and hid like the assassin they'd allowed in her room. She had no desire to hurt them, but the thought of escaping their notice gave her a thrill.

"Perhaps there is another path. Perhaps she lived and all is not lost."

Lorelle imagined herself melting together with the Dark, sliding into the room.

"A dragon, Aravelle. Jai'ketakos."

"Did you actually *see* her die? Perhaps—"

"He said one of us would live and the other would die a horrible death. I lived."

Aravelle raised her head and turned toward the doorway.

What the sentries—and neither Aravelle's guards nor attendants—could not sense, Aravelle seemed to feel instantly.

"Perhaps it's not quite so simple," Lorelle said, emerging from the shadows.

Zaith stood. The old woman smiled from ear to ear.

"Lorelle!" He leapt to her. He looked like a man condemned to death who'd been given a sudden stay of execution. He grabbed her arms then hugged her, and she hugged him back. "I thought you were dead," he murmured.

"I thought *you* were dead," she said. His hands on her, the warmth of his body against hers felt so good.

"This is an unexpected joy," Aravelle said. "Meant for two, I think, and not three." She stood, hobbled slowly to the door, and left without another word.

Heat climbed Lorelle's neck to her cheeks.

Zaith led her to the bed where they both sat. He clasped her hands and said, "By Grina's sweet smile, Lorelle. How did you escape?"

She told him the entire story.

"The dragon *changed* his mind?" Zaith asked.

"It was... a bit of a whirlwind. I think he intended to kill me, and then he came up with an alternate choice. He seemed to like the idea of giving choices."

"So, you have the Plunnos?"

She pulled the giant coin from her pocket and handed it to him. He turned it over, marveling.

"Except I can't make it work," she said. "I was hoping..." She let the sentence hang.

"Ah," he said. "That I would know how to work it?"

"Yes."

He nodded solemnly. "Yes. Or more to the point, *we* can tell you how it works."

"We?"

"I do not know the secrets of the Thuros. Not like some of us. Even Aravelle may not know the specifics, but we have such knowledge in the great library and academics who will be able to tell you everything you need. I will ask Aravelle to put them to work."

A wash of hope flooded through her. "Thank you!"

"Of course." He stood and she stood with him. He looked relieved and happier than she'd ever seen him. "You cannot know how good it is to see you alive." He led her to the doors. "I know how much you enjoyed your bath this morning. Why don't you indulge yourself again while Aravelle puts the academics to work?"

She hesitated.

"It will take time, Lorelle."

She relaxed and let out a breath. "Of course. I'm sorry. I don't mean to seem ungrateful."

He chuckled. "I'm still overwhelmed that you're alive. We both need to calm down a bit and then we'll gather the last piece you need to complete your mission."

She hesitated again, then nodded. "Very well. Another bath."

"Come."

CHAPTER THIRTY-SIX

KHYVEN

Khyven gasped and fell to his hands and knees. The pain was unbearable. He'd been cut before. He'd had broken bones. He'd once been run through in the Night Ring. He'd even almost melted his entire body to sludge by donning the Helm of Darkness.

He'd never felt pain like this.

It was as though his entire body had been squeezed through a pipe, despite the fact it didn't fit. His organs mashed together. His spine twisted. His legs and arms bent past the breaking point, and yet they did not break.

And it all happened in one, excruciating instant.

Saliva dripped from his open mouth. He panted and panted, staring down at the charcoal-colored grass in the grayscale world of the noktum.

If a hungry Kyolar had happened upon him in that instant, Khyven would have rolled onto his back and welcomed the killer claws. All he wanted to do was die.

But slowly the pain receded and a desire to live flickered within him again.

He coughed and vomited upon the grass, sucked in a deep breath, and vomited again. To his amazement, his crushed lungs still expanded. His squashed organs seemed to have returned to their normal size. His arms and back weren't broken, though they shook from their recent trauma.

He was going to live.

Vaguely, he became aware of Slayter on one side of him and Vohn on the other. They were both vomiting as well, except Slayter was trying to talk while it was happening.

"Amazing—" Slayter vomited, cutting himself off, but he continued talking as soon as his body stopped spasming. "I wonder if our bodies are actually—" he vomited "—c-compressing and expanding—" vomit "—or if it's just something we imagine." Vomit.

"Shut up, Slayter!" Vohn growled, wiping his mouth with his hand, and then wiping it on the grass. He threw up again.

"Let's…" Khyven said, levering himself to his feet, this time managing to control his urge to throw up, "never do that again."

He couldn't afford to spend time on his hands and knees. Rauvelos had confessed that they might be heading straight into danger. It was the noktum, after all. Khyven had to start paying attention to their surroundings.

In the noktum by Usara, a person only had a few seconds before the native creatures began to arrive. He had no reason to think the Great Noktum would be any different.

He drew his steel sword, leaving the giant Mavric iron blade safely in its magic sheath, and scanned the clearing. A giant forest of charcoal-colored oak trees rose up to his left and behind it another of those creepy castles like in their home noktum. To the right and behind them were grasslands, with another forest far way, and mountains behind it.

"I wonder if…" Slayter began, then he vomited, "…if I could replicate that spell with—"

"Slayter, do the math another time," Khyven said. "I need you to create the spell to find Lorelle. Do it now. We don't know how long we'll be safe in this spot."

"Of course, of course." Slayter doubled over and held his stomach, but he paused and managed not to vomit this time. After a moment, he nodded and crawled on all fours away from his splatter of regurgitation. He stopped before a little dirt patch mostly free of the ever-present charcoal grass.

He pulled out the little house and planted it squarely in the middle of the dirt. With practiced speed, he pulled his metal scratcher from a pouch, smoothed the dirt, and expertly sketched a symbol next to the little artifact. It began to glow.

The dirt jumped, like an earthquake had occurred only in that area, then a miniature forest, a flat plain, and the exact same castle in miniature, all formed out of the dirt, spreading past the original spot Slayter had chosen, through the tufts of grass, spreading out to an eight-foot radius with Slayter in the middle. Everything was rendered in exquisite detail. At the far end of the dirt model, on the edge of the forest just before the miniature castle, glowed a little orange dot.

"Well!" Slayter said. "Rauvelos knows his business."

"What? What is it?"

"Oh, she's there." He pointed at the distant forest. "See that? She's beyond that. About four miles away. Brilliant. He put us well within the ten-mile range."

"That's great news!" Khyven said. "She's in the forest?"

"There's a city inside. You can't really see it, but it's there, past the trees."

"The Nox," Khyven said, then glanced at Vohn, who was holding his belly and looking very unhappy. "It's one of those words that's singular and plural, right? One Nox? Many Nox?"

Vohn nodded and grumbled something.

"What?"

"I said yes. I also said I find words like that annoying," Vohn barked.

Khyven got the impression that Vohn found everything annoying at the moment.

"Let's take a breath," Khyven said. "We seem to be safe for the moment, and we probably shouldn't just go storming into the woods. She's close right now, but according to Rauvelos that Nox has a teleportation cloak. He could just up and take her somewhere else if we're not quick enough. We need to find her and get her home."

"Unless she actually is on the trail of a Plunnos," Slayter said.

"Unless that," Khyven said. "Then we get the Plunnos and then get her home."

Slayter looked like he had fully recovered from the gut-churning nausea and he looked at Vohn, who clearly had not. He was still holding his belly and squeezing his eyes shut like he wished he was anywhere but here. The mage looked down at his waist, flicked open the little cylinder where he kept all his clay disks, and quickly clicked through them with his slender fingers. He selected one, pulled it out, and used the metal scratcher to finish the line.

Orange light flared and he tossed the coin to Vohn. "Put it against your belly," he said.

Vohn looked at him suspiciously.

"Quickly," Slayter said. "While it's glowing."

Vohn scooped up the coin and put it against the front of his tunic.

Slayter rolled his eyes. "Underneath."

Vohn snarled but did as he was asked. His eyes flew open, he straightened, and he drew an easy breath. He glanced at Slayter in surprise.

Slayter winked. "Now snap it or I'm going to have your roiling belly in my mind for hours."

Vohn snapped the clay coin in two. The orange light flared, then vanished. Both he and Slayter sighed.

"Better?" Slayter asked.

"Annoying as you are, you are useful," Vohn said.

"You're welcome," Slayter said.

Khyven scanned the tree line again. Rauvelos had been true to his word. Once the giant raven had committed to helping them, he hadn't held anything back. He'd given them a map of the area and teleported them directly here.

Granted, the teleport had made them all vomit their guts out, but the city of Nox Arvak was right where Rauvelos had said it would be.

"If you manage to not die in the transition," Rauvelos had said, "and if you manage to avoid getting eaten in the first couple of seconds of your arrival, then you'll only have to fight off whatever creatures you run across. If those creatures are agents of Lord Tovos, you'll die. If they're *not* agents for Lord Tovos, you'll just have to fight them. Which will probably kill you."

Rauvelos hadn't been encouraging, but he *had* extended the life of their Amulets of Noksonon. Which had turned their mission from flat-out impossible into only foolhardy.

"I've increased the potency of the amulets," Rauvelos had told them. "This lot hasn't been imbued with magic for almost two thousand years. Instead of one hour, you should be able to get two entire days out of them. After that, they're going to need to be recharged again. Mage, I give you these." He handed Slayter three items that looked like small, shallow glass bowls with just enough room for an amulet to click inside them. "These are fragile. Break them, and they won't work. Place the amulets securely in the indentation and submerge them in water—you'll have to find a stream every two days—for an hour. It will reinvigorate the amulets. You'll have another two days without having to leave the noktum."

"Thank you," Khyven had said.

"There is a downside," Rauvelos had continued. "These amulets belong to Lord Nhevalos. They have been restored to full strength, so... if you get within a dozen yards of Lord Tovos's agents, they're going to sense you, and they'll come after you. This will limit your ability to sneak about where Lord Tovos's agents might be. Pray your friend hasn't gone there. As to the rest of the denizens, they won't care one way or another. They'll treat you like the Kyolars do here, pace you and look for an opening but they'll be reluctant to burn themselves."

Khyven came out of his reverie and found his friends ready to hike. He reflexively touched the amulet at his neck.

"Ready?"

Vohn nodded.

"Ready, Sir Knight," Slayter said.

They began their hike. Slayter barely limped; Rauvelos had given him a salve that had worked wonders. The three kept a steady pace, and Khyven began to feel optimistic. They knew where Lorelle was. Now they just had to reach her.

A soft, almost inaudible whir behind Khyven brought him around.

"Well, that was nice while it lasted," he said softly, slipping a dagger from his belt to join the ready sword. He peered into the long grass. Vohn and Slayter turned, saw his expression, and searched intently in the direction Khyven was looking.

A trio of shapes crept toward them.

CHAPTER THIRTY-SEVEN

KHYVEN

Thirty paces away, a giant cockroach emerged from the tall grass. Easily six feet long, its body scuttled low to the ground—just below the top of the grass—held aloft by short, angular legs. Two long feelers, the thickness of Khyven's arm, extended several feet into the air. Each feeler was topped with a vaguely Human head. Each had pale skin, Human noses, Human lips, cheekbones, and straight, black hair, but that was where the resemblance ended. The jaw was long, with pointed, carnivorous teeth, and the eyes were the multi-faceted orbs of a fly.

The whirring came from its wings as they fluttered excitedly against its back. The clicking came from the jaws as they opened a quarter of an inch and snapped shut, over and over again.

Another cockroach emerged from the grass behind the first, and another to the left.

A thrill of fear rushed through Khyven and the blue wind leapt to life, swirling through the tall grass and around the cockroach monsters.

"Grina's Breath…" Vohn said. "Is this for real?"

"They look real to me," Khyven murmured, moving to stand between his friends and the monsters. The blue wind swirled through the grass, weaving between the blades without disturbing them.

"I have something for this. I have something for this," Slayter murmured.

The mage fumbled with his coin cylinder, but the nearest cockroach hissed and charged. Khyven was astonished at how fast it moved.

The others followed right behind it.

He surged forward, closing the distance between himself and the first cockroach. A lance of blue shot out at him and he spun just as one of the heads snapped its needle teeth next to his neck.

A forest of blue funnels sprouted on the cockroach, mostly on the vulnerable neck stalks, but some in the cracks of its shell. Khyven went for the easiest.

His sword whistled briefly then sliced through both neck stalks at once. The heads thumped onto the ground, the necks writhing. The cockroach went crazy, flailing its legs as it ran awkwardly to the left, missing Slayter by half a dozen feet.

"Well, they're not smart," Khyven said as he spun to brace the second. The other two swarmed him.

"I've got this. I've got this," Slayter said, his clay coins clicking.

"Get it faster!" Vohn barked.

Blue spears of wind launched at Khyven from left and right. He leapt into the air, avoiding two as one lanced right where he'd been standing. As he did, he slashed at the blue funnels all around him. The cockroaches were fast. They were deadly, but those necks were right out in the open.

He got two stalks before he landed, spun, ducked another attack, and sliced another head. One cockroach had lost both its heads, and it went crazy like the first, running off blind, its sharp legs scuttling like mad.

Slayter held a coin aloft, and it was already glowing orange. He snapped it, and an orange glow suddenly emanated from the teeth of the remaining cockroach's head...

... and from the teeth of fifty heads in the darkness of the grass behind them.

"What? What did that do?" Vohn demanded.

"Uh," Slayter said. "Wrong coin. But that is interesting. There are an awful lot of them, aren't there—"

"Slayter!"

Khyven dove over the nearest cockroach, the one that still had one head. It caught his boot with its teeth and he went down, but the thing couldn't hold on. Khyven rolled awkwardly to his feet, dodged, and lopped off the final head. The last cockroach from the original three ran off.

The rest charged.

Slayter frantically clicked through his coins.

"Slayter!"

"I think we're going to need a plan of escape," Khyven said, looking at the horde scuttling toward them across the field. They were still fifty feet away but closing fast. He braced himself.

"Oh!" Slayter glanced up. "And don't let them bite you."

"That's the plan," Khyven said.

"No, I mean their teeth are venomous. That's what that last spell showed."

Khyven glanced down at the three tiny holes in his boot where the teeth had almost got him. "All right. Good information. Thanks."

The cockroaches approached fast, all intent on Khyven. Their heads had retracted right up against their carapaces, and Khyven doubted the thick shell was going to fall to his sword as easily as the thin necks.

The Mavric iron whined in his mind. It vibrated like it longed to be taken out of the sheath.

Khyven didn't want to draw the thing if he didn't need to, but taking on three cockroaches at once had just about been the end of him. He sheathed his steel sword, reached up and gripped the hilt of the Daelakos's Blade.

The whine stretched out, almost like it was trying to form a word. If it was a word, Khyven didn't understand it, but he didn't need to. He felt its excitement. The sword wanted to kill. Khyven pulled it from its magic sheath.

The cockroaches charged. Blue spears shot toward Khyven. The Mavric iron sword grew warm in his hand, lighter than a feather.

"This!" Slayter exclaimed, pulling a coin.

Khyven dodged the first attack, spinning through the throng as toothy head after toothy head snapped at him, missing by inches. The Mavric iron sword slashed and cut, moving in response to the blue spears and funnels as though the sword itself could sense them. Heads flew. Black ichor splashed the ground. Cockroaches fled in crazy, zigzagging patterns as they lost their heads, but more replaced them, converging on Khyven.

Slayter yelled, his voice growing louder as he held the coin high. Fierce orange light blazed from it and from Slayter's mouth.

A single bolt of orange lightning shot from the coin into the air over the horde of cockroaches, forming a crackling ball of light, then a hundred jagged spikes of orange light lanced down. Every one of the fifty-some creatures shuddered as the lightning speared them. Every head sprang up to full extension, mouths open in silent screams that seemed to mimic Slayter's scream.

Khyven flinched as orange lightning struck all around him. Every single cockroach slumped forward in the grass, dead and smoking, heads dropping to the ground on limp stalks. Every carapace had a glowing hole the size of a fist.

A haze of smoke drifted above the field of corpses, and the smell was horrendous.

Khyven gagged and staggered back from the carnage, an arm over his nose and mouth. "Senji's Teeth!" he murmured. The Mavric iron sword whined in his head, disappointed.

"See?" Slayter said brightly, clutching the broken clay coin, his grin wide. The grin faded, his eyes rolled up into his head, and he collapsed.

CHAPTER THIRTY-EIGHT
KHYVEN

Slayter!"

Khyven sheathed the Giant sword and ran to the collapsed mage. The stench of burning insect wafted over the field in a haze.

"That is unpleasant," Vohn said, who was already at Slayter's side.

Khyven stood guard, scanning the field, looking for more cockroaches. But if there were any that hadn't been taken by Slayter's orange lightning spell, they had fled.

Perhaps they were smarter than they seemed.

"Well, this is exactly the sort of thing we didn't want to do," Khyven said, putting his elbow over his face again. It smelled like rotten fish that had been charred on a bonfire. "Rauvelos said not to use strong magic at the spot where we arrive because it might attract attention."

Vohn nodded, his brow furrowed as he lightly touched Slayter's neck and cheek. "He's unconscious, but breathing," Vohn said.

"Anyone—or thing—who was looking is going to see Slayter's magic show for miles." Khyven paused.

"I think he just overexerted himself," Vohn said. "Lorelle has an herb that—" The Shadowvar cut himself off and glanced at Khyven as though he was just realizing where he was. "Sorry. Habit."

"We're getting her back," he said.

"You realize how crazy this is," Vohn said, finally raising his head and looking at the field of charred cockroaches. "We're taking on an entirely unknown noktum thousands of miles from home. We've barely just arrived and already we've done all the things we shouldn't."

"Let's just get clear of this spot." Khyven picked up the mage, who weighed practically nothing, and slung him across his shoulders. Vohn checked the ground to ensure that Slayter hadn't dropped anything when he fainted. Satisfied, Vohn rose and nodded.

"Come on." Khyven strode away from the stench. "Quickly."

With the mage on his shoulders and the map Slayter had created firmly in mind, Khyven continued toward the distant trees. It took them the better part of an hour to reach them, but no other creatures attacked them in that time. Either any interested creatures had seen their magic and decided they were too dangerous to stalk, or they'd been ridiculously lucky and no other creatures had actually seen the fight.

Just as they reached the charcoal canopy of the wide, fat leaves, Slayter stirred.

"Mmmm," he murmured.

Khyven stopped just inside the trees and quickly looked around to make sure they weren't stepping from one horror into another. But the woods appeared to be quiet, and he felt safer off the wide-open field. He put Slayter down and propped him against a tree.

Slayter blinked. "It worked. We're alive. That's nice."

"It just about killed *you*." Vohn squatted next to the mage, a stern expression his face.

"Well, it's a big spell. My biggest ever, actually," Slayter said. He blinked each eye, one at a time, patted his pouches, then reached into his robe and withdrew a small steel vial. He uncorked it and downed the entire thing.

He sat bolt upright and jumped halfway to his feet. He stumbled, knees bent, and leaned against the tree.

Khyven leapt forward to catch him. "What was that?" he demanded.

Slayter shook his head, then grinned like he'd just slammed two shots of Triadan Whiskey. He coughed and a tendril of blue smoke wafted out of his nose. "Just something to... shock the soul back into action. If I'm going to be any good to you in this adventure, I'll need my magic. This'll get me through a day or two."

"A day or two?" Vohn asked.

"Yes."

"And then what?"

"Let's face it," Slayter said. "We've just plunged into the Great Noktum with three limited amulets, minimal weapons, and no idea what to expect. If I'm going to die, I'd rather die saving one of you."

"After a day or two, you're going to *die?*" Vohn asked.

"No." Slayter shook his head. "No." He waved a negligent hand. "I mean, probably not. If we make it back. If I have enough time to work on an antidote. If I'm still awake. Then I can reverse the effects." He held up a finger like he'd had a brilliant idea. "And it's even more likely if we bring Lorelle back. She could definitely do it."

"You're an idiot," Vohn said. He looked at Khyven. "Are we all expecting to die, then?"

"No," Khyven said. "We're getting Lorelle back." He peered into the woods. When they'd first entered, he'd liked that the forest was quiet. There were no giant cockroaches. No Kyolars slinking between the trees. No Sleeths diving at them. But Khyven was beginning to get suspicious. The woods were deadly silent, like the creatures that might make noise were holding their collective breath.

"I don't like this," Khyven said. Vohn and Slayter stopped arguing and also looked into the silent woods. They all stepped back to the tree line of the forest, back to the edge of the field.

Slayter reached down to touch his coin cylinder—

A black arrow shot from the shadows and pinned the bottom of his dagged sleeve to the tree next to him.

"Erp!" Slayter said.

The blue wind leapt to life and Khyven drew his steel sword... but no spears of light launched at him. Instead, he saw wafts of blue wind hovering in the trees ahead of him. Points of blue light were everywhere, directed toward him, but they didn't launch at him. They stayed silent, glowing indications that death stood ready all around them... but wasn't yet attacking.

The Mavric iron sword whined. Khyven didn't draw it, but he had the sense that he should look behind himself.

He did.

A tall Nox stood there, between them and the field they'd left. He had black hair, midnight black skin, and he wore all black, just like the Nox who'd taken Lorelle.

"Drop your weapons and come with us," the Nox said, "and we won't kill you."

CHAPTER THIRTY-NINE
LORELLE

Lorelle soaked in the steaming bath for more than an hour. Twists of orange coiled along the bathhouse ceiling and she let her mind drift as she looked up at them. There was an order to the twists, but she couldn't figure what it was. They looked like constellations linked together with strings of orange light, but there were no stars within the noktum. She couldn't imagine why the Nox would paint stars upon their ceiling if they never saw them. There was still so much she didn't know about Nox culture.

Letting out one last, satisfied breath, Lorelle rose from the bath. A young Nox girl sitting on an obsidian bench by the wall jumped up and ran forward with a towel. She wrapped it around Lorelle.

"Thank you," Lorelle said. The Nox girl ran back to the bench and sat, presumably waiting for anything else Lorelle might need. She toweled herself off, still not used to the fact that her skin was midnight black and that her hair glowed purple except for the one lock of gold that had flared to life in the dragon's lair.

Once Lorelle finished drying, the girl rose and came forward again. Lorelle looked for the clothes she'd worn to the dragon's lair, but they were gone.

"Where are my clothes?"

"They are being laundered, Maid Lorelle," the girl said.

"And my pouches? My weapons?"

The girl brought out a wooden box and opened it. All of Lorelle's effects lay inside: her daggers, her pouches and herbal kit, the sheath for her blowgun, and the slim, flat pouch that contained the Plunnos; she checked it, the Plunnos was still safely inside. She let out a breath of relief. Only then did she realize that there were no alternate clothes.

"What am I supposed to wear?" she asked.

"Your dress, Maid Lorelle." The girl held up a slinky, shadowy dress. It had thin straps at the top and a hemline that might optimistically reach halfway down Lorelle's thighs.

"I'm to wear this?"

"For the celebration."

"What celebration?"

For the first time, the Nox girl hesitated, like she had been prepared to answer all questions except that one.

"Ah, for your return?" she said, making it sound more like a question than an answer. "Aravelle announced it while you were bathing."

Lorelle hesitated, then took the dress. The fabric slithered through her fingers like liquid. She slipped it over her head and pulled it into place. It was every bit as short as she'd suspected, but it felt divine, like a piece of liquid shadow. A pair of black slippers with a modest heel sat next to the bench and she slipped them on.

Between the residual glow from the bath and the sheer fabric of the dress, she felt like she was half floating.

She paused and looked down at the rest of her effects. She felt naked without her weapons and her herbal knapsack, but...

Relax, she thought and judiciously decided to take only the pouch with the Plunnos. How would it look after everything

Zaith and Aravelle had done for her to show up in a party dress with her weapons strapped on?

After a momentary misgiving, she left the rest of her pouches and weapons in the box.

"Will you see that this gets to my room?"

"Of course, Maid Lorelle," she said.

"And take me to Zaith?" she asked.

"Yes, Maid Lorelle," the girl flowed to the door, held it open, then led her through the tall, arched hallways of the palace with its multicolored, glowing art on the walls. There were no canvas paintings in Nox Arvak like there were in the Usaran palace. Instead, frescoes had been painted directly on the wall with some kind of luminescent paint. At least, that's what it looked like.

As they neared the front of the palace, Lorelle heard music, a haunting melody rising from stringed instruments. The Nox girl led her through the front doors of the palace onto a wide circular veranda, open to the indigo night.

Tables of food lined the edge and dozens of Nox were holding plates and picked morsels from the trays. A dozen people spun gracefully through a synchronized dance in the center of the veranda. Three shallow steps led down to a cobblestone courtyard, and a half dozen musicians sat to the left of the stairs, playing strangely shaped stringed instruments that produced the haunting song.

Orbs hung from open-air archways over the veranda, casting everything in a magical blue glow. Lorelle stood at the entrance to the palace, taking in the sheer beauty of it.

"In Nox Arvak, we believe in celebrating our victories," Zaith murmured from beside her.

She turned and smiled. She'd been so taken with the decorations she hadn't thought to feel through the Dark to see if anyone was sneaking up on her.

"Lotura, I wasn't in the bath that long, was I?"

"We can be quick when we need to be," he said.

"I should say so. This… is enough to take my breath away."

"This—" he gestured at her dress "—is enough to take *my* breath away."

That familiar heat climbed her cheeks as she blushed. In the past, she might have run from that feeling, but she wasn't going to tonight. Tonight, she was going to luxuriate in it.

"Thank you, sir," she said. "You look quite dashing yourself." He had shiny black boots, tight breeches, and a jacket that flared at the shoulders. She gestured at the dancers. "They are wonderful," she said.

"Our best."

"I can tell."

"Ah, you like to dance?"

She let out a sigh. "I used to. More than just about anything."

He extended his hand. "Then we must join them."

"I don't know this dance," she said, though she wanted to learn it. She put her hand in his.

"You will pick it up quickly, as you do everything else," he said. "I will lead you through it."

"I've noticed."

He grinned at her double-entendre, then pulled her onto the dance floor. The musicians played a quick-paced, yet still haunting, song and the Nox on the veranda spun and twisted. Lorelle had always enjoyed watching the Humans dance at Rhenn's camp.

But the Nox were a completely different level of grace and ability. They swooped like dark ravens, sprang like shadowy deer, they spun and touched and then spun away again. It was like a beautiful painting in motion and Lorelle flung herself into the center of it with abandon. She danced like she'd always longed to dance at Rhenn's camp. The Dark filled her. The music filled her, and she soared through the air. She reveled in the weight of her body as she landed, luxuriated in the brief touches of hands on hands as she and Zaith came together, then spun apart again.

The unfettered freedom coursed through her.

All too soon, the music ended and Lorelle finished her dance with a slow spiral to the ground, her free leg sweeping as she descended, sitting and then curling her leg around herself as she bowed her head.

Silence fell as the last chords of the song faded and a respectful applause arose. She blinked and looked up to find all the other dancers surrounding her, clapping. Zaith stood next to her, looking down with hungry eyes.

"Stunning," he murmured. Just one word, but with the heat in his eyes, it told volumes. He extended his hand just as the musicians began again, this time with a slower melody.

She rose and his arms encircled her, drawing her close as they moved to the new tune. Sweat beaded on her forehead and her breath came fast.

"You are exquisite," Zaith said.

"I haven't danced like that in…" She trailed off. "I have *never* danced like that, but I have imagined it in my dreams."

"Then let's not wake."

They danced. Slow, sensuous dances where Zaith's hands rested on the small of her back or the nape of her neck, and she was acutely aware of his touch. Fast, acrobatic dances where Lorelle pit her athleticism against Zaith's, and they matched each other move for move.

The night became a glorious blur. Yet when the musicians paused and put their instruments on curved wooden racks beside their chairs, she only felt like they'd been dancing for a handful of minutes.

Breathing hard, she glanced at them, then back at Zaith. "That's all?" she asked.

"An hour is a good start."

"Has it been an hour? Lotura, it seems barely half that."

He grinned. "A full heart pays no attention to the minutes, they say."

She glanced wistfully at the resting instruments.

He chuckled. "Even musicians must rest. Don't worry; they will begin again. Are you not thirsty?" He indicated the food tables. Two of Aravelle's attendants stood with glasses of wine in their hands, ready for them. Zaith took them and handed one to Lorelle.

"Shall we walk?" He led her down the steps of the veranda onto the courtyard, then off the paved street and into the dark forest. A soft path paved with glowing amber moss led through the trees. Zaith removed his slippers at the threshold and stood barefoot on the spongy moss. Eager for the new experience, Lorelle did likewise. The soft moss shaped to her feet, like a thousand tiny fingers were holding her up. It was glorious. She followed Zaith, reveling in the soft prickles beneath her feet. They left the crowd behind, and the noktum wrapped them in its quiet, peaceful embrace.

"Such a beautiful night," she said, breathing it in.

"You are the one who makes it exceptional. My people were spellbound watching you. Where did you learn to dance like that?"

"In my dreams," she murmured.

"You never danced like that with the Humans?"

"No."

He sighed. "It is… a shame you spent so much time with your true self locked away. But I am glad you have finally had a chance to explore what you truly love."

She glanced at him but didn't respond.

"You belong here with us, Lorelle," he said softly, a half-smile on his lips. He pulled her to him and she went. She wanted his arms around her. His hand cupped her head, fingers sliding into their regular spot. Gods of Dark and Light…

She drew a breath and closed her eyes.

His lips touched hers and she kissed him. She pushed herself into him. Zaith finished the kiss and withdrew enough to look in her eyes. His palms remained warm against her cheeks, his lips only inches from hers.

"When I first met you," he murmured, "I thought you were a lost, blind Luminent shaped by the crude hands of Humans. I could not have imagined how thoroughly the Dark would fill you, would lift you up. Your grace with the shadows puts my people to shame. You've only been here two days and yet you are as talented a Glimmerblade as I am."

This was what she'd wanted a dozen times in her life, this closeness. This flirty abandon. It was what she'd wanted to do with Khyven, but she had always denied herself. Every time.

"You were born to be a Nox," he murmured.

She couldn't deny the power of his statement. Here in Nox Arvak, she was free in a way she'd never been free. Everything here was straightforward. There were no complications. No consequences. Yet her world in Usara was *only* complications and consequences. It would be so much easier to stay here, in this place. It was like a waking dream.

A dream...

She hooked a finger around her single lock of golden hair, pulled it out and let it fall in front of her. The last remnant of her old self. The last remnant of the person she had once been.

It had only been two days. Lotura's wisdom... two days?

"But I'm not," she whispered. "I'm not a Nox."

She closed her eyes, feeling the exquisite loss as she put her hands on Zaith's, took them away from her face and held them. "I'm not a Nox, Zaith. I have friends. I have a family. I have... someone I may be in love with. I have a life."

Confusion flickered in his eyes. "Khyven?"

"It would be so easy to get lost here, in your culture, in your hands. In the Dark. It all seems like a dream to me, but the only reason I can dance with you, the only reason I can be here now, in your arms, is because it's a stolen moment while I wait upon your academics to help me with my true purpose. The dream is lovely, but I must wake at some point."

"Why?"

"Shall I just leave my family behind? I came here alone to keep them safe. And when I retrieve Rhenn, what then? Do I drop her off in Usara and come back here? My heart would shrivel."

"There is more I have yet to show you. The bonding is not yet complete—"

"It is for me. Throwing myself further into the Dark is tempting. To let things be simple and uncomplicated is tempting.

To dance with you, to lose myself in sensations that I…" She shook her head. "But I can't stay. You know that. You've known that from the start."

He turned away, emotions warring his face. "So… you will not complete your bond with the Dark."

"My connection to Khyven… It wasn't an accident. It wasn't… a mistake."

"He's a Human. You can't possibly hope to have a life with him."

"I don't know," she said. "Maybe I can't. But I love him, Zaith. That part is true. And I didn't know then what I know now. I never broke the dam with him, lost control with him like I have with you. Who knows what could happen if I didn't hold myself back."

Zaith shook his head.

"Until you came along, I didn't think I had a choice," she said. "*You* gave me that choice, but I must still choose."

"And you would not choose me?" His voice cracked.

"After Rhenn is safe. After I've… settled things with Khyven… I don't know. All I know is that I can't make that decision until I know Rhenn is safe. Until I return home."

"I think you do know," he said, trying to keep the bitterness out of his voice. "I think you've already made your choice."

"Zaith… I'm sorry," she said. "I didn't come here to dance, to kiss you… They have been wonderful distractions, but that's all I can let them be. I need to make my family safe first. Can't you understand that?"

He let out a breath and bowed his head. "Yes. I can understand that."

"Zaith…"

"I… I wish I'd never met you," he said softly.

Her stomach churned. "Don't say that. Please don't say that."

"I was not conflicted, about anything," he said softly. "And then you came. And I…"

Lorelle had reveled in losing control because Zaith had said she could, because he'd shown her how to slip the noose of the soul-bond. For as long as she'd been alive, she'd feared her loss of control because it could hurt her and those around her.

"This is my fault," she said. "I've been so intoxicated with what you've shown me, I wasn't... cautious. I didn't mean to hurt you."

"You were supposed to be simple," he murmured, and it seemed he was talking to himself.

It sounded like he'd had a plan for her, a plan that hadn't worked. Lorelle tilted her head. "What do you mean?"

He glanced over his shoulder at her, his eyes haunted.

A tingle of foreboding ran up her spine as she remembered some of the dragon's words.

"But he is your friend, yes? Your good friend. Your trusted friend who would never do anything to harm you?"

"Zaith... Is there another reason you want me to bond completely with the noktum, aside from what you said?"

She saw the struggle in his eyes, and she'd never been more sure of anything. Bonding with the Dark... He had an agenda there.

"You don't know who Tovos is. I would bet Zaith does..."

"Zaith," she said. "Who is Tovos?"

Zaith's head came up, surprised.

"Lorelle..." He reached out to touch her but quickly lowered his hands. He drew a slow breath, preparing... whatever he was going to say.

"Tovos is—"

Far to the north, above the treetops, red-orange fire mushroomed into the indigo sky. Natural light, just like the braziers in the dragon's lair.

Zaith and Lorelle spun, staring north.

The *boom* of the explosion reached them a split second later.

"Grina's nails..." Zaith murmured, wincing at the horrible sound.

"No," Lorelle murmured.

Remember, I gave you the choice. You stood on the knife's edge, and you bent fate to your will.

"Zaith, we have to get to Aravelle." She grabbed his hand and sprinted toward the palace, running fast over the orange moss path. He ran smoothly with her.

"What is it?"

"You have to tell everyone to get out of the city!" she shouted.

"Lorelle, what—"

"The dragon! The dragon is here! And he—"

Nox Arvak exploded in flames.

CHAPTER FORTY

VOHN

Vohn sneered at the three Nox who slithered out of the darkness with their weapons raised. The Nox loved deception. If they had revealed three fighters, there were at least five times that in the shadows behind them.

He put on a bold face, but he couldn't recall the last time he'd been so scared. He'd fled Nokte Shaddark, his hometown, because he hadn't wanted to face this reckoning. He'd chosen to live in the light among Humans rather than face the price extracted by the Dark.

Vohn had to allow that, perhaps, not all the Nox were fiends. But if there were good people among them, they were unlikely to take the side of trespassers in their domain.

"Drop your weapons and come with us," the lead Nox said. "And we won't kill you."

Which meant this was going to erupt into mayhem.

This Nox didn't know Khyven. The Ringer hadn't come here to surrender. The man was all-or-nothing, and he seemed to have no fear when it came to combat, no matter the odds.

Violence seemed a comfort to him. Khyven would rather leap into a brawl, even horribly outnumbered, than back down.

"And who's going to kill us? You and your friends?" Khyven asked predictably.

The Nox gave a cruel smile. "Just me."

"I doubt that," Khyven said.

"Your arrogance doesn't impress us, Human."

"Well, my arrogance takes a while to warm up," he said conversationally. Khyven was like a cobra that way, mesmerizing his opponents with casual banter until he struck.

Vohn had never seen a Human as fast as Khyven, and he was certain this Nox never had. Vohn had once thought Rhenn the fastest Human he'd ever met. The queen was as talented a swordsman as anyone, but Khyven had bested her. With a wooden sword.

"Are you trying to say you want a one-on-one duel with me?" Khyven let his sword point dip and aimlessly waggle back and forth like he wasn't taking this exchange seriously, like he didn't really think the Nox would attack. "Because I don't think that's a good idea. For you, I mean. You'll want at least two or three of your friends to assist." His casual tone was an act, as was the seemingly innocuous way he rubbed his neck with his free hand.

The Nox, however, saw the gesture for what it really was.

"Keep your fingers away from that Mavric iron, Human. And tell your mage to keep his hand away from the metal cylinder. Our orders, strange as they are, are to bring you back unharmed. But if you touch that magic blade, or if we see the mage touch that cylinder, or do anything indicating a spell, we *will* feather you with arrows before you can blink." Khyven and the Nox matched stares, Khyven with a roguish smile, the Nox with his cruel, thin one.

"Shall I take their weapons, Shadowmaster?" another Nox asked.

"Let's talk instead," Khyven said. "Perhaps you can help us."

The Shadowmaster's eyes became flinty and Vohn's stomach clenched.

The Nox subordinate looked from his superior to Khyven and back, but the staring war continued. Finally, with no clear winner, the Shadowmaster said, "No."

"No?" the Nox asked incredulously.

"This one wants to die with his sword in hand, and if he demands it, I'll oblige him. Let's talk about your choices, Human," the Shadowmaster said.

"I love choices," Khyven replied.

"You can die here or you can surrender, give us your weapons, keep your dignity, and, as long as you behave yourselves, your lives. Those are your two choices. That is all. Personally, I wouldn't give you the second, but I have been ordered to extend that courtesy to any Humans we found wandering our perimeter. I assume you are friends of the Luminent Lorelle."

Khyven glanced sharply at Slayter. The mage grinned like he'd somehow expected this. Vohn would swear Slayter looked like he was having the time of his life, as if witnessing a horde of Nox was absolutely worth the fact that he might, in a moment, die.

"You know Lorelle?" Khyven asked.

"No Luminent has set foot in Nox Arvak in centuries. Everyone knows the name Lorelle."

"Is she safe?"

The Shadowmaster smiled cruelly again. "I will repeat your choices: you can die here, or you can be brought to a place and time where Aravelle will decide what is to be done with you. Have I somewhere mentioned a third choice that involves me answering your questions?"

"You remind me of a king I used to know," Khyven said. "He thought he had everything in hand, too."

"A threat," the Shadowmaster said. "Amusing." He held out his hand. "Last chance, Human. Death or capture?"

Vohn felt a grudging respect for this Nox. He wasn't stupid. He didn't have to phrase it like that. Apparently, he knew Khyven better than Vohn assumed, knew how the Ringer would respond to the word "capture," and was spoiling for a fight. Khyven wasn't going to give up his sword. To Khyven, letting go of his weapon and trusting an enemy was lunacy.

"Khyven," Vohn warned. "Maybe Lorelle sent them. Maybe she's made friends here. Maybe they're here to escort us. Just—"

"I understand my choices," Khyven said. "I don't think he understands his."

"Khyven!"

"Is that a dragon?" Slayter blurted, pointing up at the sky with his free hand.

It was such a bizarre statement that the Shadowmaster actually glanced in the indicated direction.

His eyes widened. He sucked in a breath to shout orders—

Khyven attacked like a bolt of lightning.

Everything seemed to happen at once. The Shadowmaster flew backward into the darkness. Something punched Vohn in the chest so hard he sat down.

And the forest exploded into flame.

CHAPTER FORTY-ONE

LORELLE

T he mushroom of natural fire was like a sunburst in the sky, and both Lorelle and Zaith shielded their eyes.

"What was that?" she asked. There were so many natural phenomena in the noktum that she wondered if this was something expected, something she simply hadn't seen before. But one look at the alarm on Zaith's face told her this was nothing he'd ever seen before.

"The dragon," she murmured.

"Grina..." he whispered. "What did we do?" Zaith threw his wine glass to the ground and sprinted back up the path, moving with more speed than she'd ever seen. Lorelle hurried after him, but fell quickly behind. She'd never seen Zaith run at full speed with no care whether she could keep up or not.

Lorelle burst into the courtyard before Aravelle's palace seconds after Zaith and skidded to a stop next to him. All the partygoers were frozen, looking to the north where the fire was fading, leaving a silhouette of smoke behind. The onlookers were fixed on where the fire had been, but Lorelle searched the skies around it...

And spotted the dragon. Its lithe, black silhouette moved against the indigo sky. It seemed like a bat at first, but it soon got bigger and bigger, and it was coming their way.

A scream rose from the group as the dragon's shape became clear, far too large to be any normal animal.

Zaith stood with his mouth open, as if his mind couldn't comprehend what he should do next to protect his people from the dragon.

"Aravelle," Lorelle said, and that snapped Zaith out of it. He launched himself forward, leaping over the heads of the stunned Nox to land on the veranda. Lorelle leapt after him, barely clearing the crowd and almost kicking one of the former dancers in the head.

"Where is she?" Zaith demanded of the stunned attendant who had given them wine. The young man just stared at him. Zaith grabbed him, showing teeth. "Where is she?"

"Th-The library," the attendant stuttered.

Zaith spun on Lorelle, a snarl on his face, his eyes flashing. For a breathless instant, she thought he would attack her.

"Get Aravelle," he growled. "Find her. Get her into the shadows. If you ever had any care for us at all, get her out of here!"

Zaith jumped off the veranda, clearing the wall and landing on the courtyard below, before heading into the city.

"Where are you going?" she shouted.

"Get her! Protect her!" he yelled back, and then he was gone, vanished around the edge of a house.

She shot a glance to her right. The dragon was so close he seemed to swallow the horizon. She spun and sprinted up the steps into the palace. The screams rose behind them as the partygoers scattered.

"Aravelle!" she shouted. Doorways and windows flashed by as she ran for the library. She sprang onto the wall and ran across it in an arc before regaining the floor to keep her speed up. Her legs burned as she pounded down the hall toward the library.

"Aravelle!" she called again. The old Nox was just exiting the giant double doors on the right and she looked up when she heard her name. One of the old Nox's attendants was further down the hall, as if Aravelle was about to go from the library deeper into the palace, probably to her rooms.

The Nox attendant's eyes widened when he saw Lorelle bearing down on them. The attendant snarled as he drew a dagger. From the very beginning, most of the Nox had thought Lorelle was an assassin. She'd started to gain their trust, she'd thought, but no doubt the attendant was sure this was his worst nightmare coming true, that Lorelle was finally showing her true colors. Lorelle didn't have time to explain, nor to tell the attendant that a far worse nightmare was almost upon them.

There was a window directly across from the library's great double doors, and Lorelle's plan came together in a second. Crooked, nonsensical shadows hovered on either side of the window and just beyond.

The attendant moved fast, drawing and flipping the dagger at Lorelle. Aravelle simply stood there, unafraid, a look of concentration on her face, as though she might understand why Lorelle was running at her, full tilt.

Lorelle let go of her control, let the darkness flow through her. She saw the dagger coming her way, but more than that, she felt it pass through the two irregular shadows near the wall.

She swayed, her left shoulder leaning back even as she reached for Aravelle. The dagger missed her by a hair as she caught hold of the old Nox.

"Lorelle—"

But Lorelle didn't answer, didn't say anything.

Get her into the shadows...

Aravelle's mouth turned into an "O" as Lorelle spun, using the old Nox for a counterlever as she propelled them both in a tight three-quarter circle toward the shadows, toward the window. The attendant cursed and gave chase.

Lorelle felt the cool strength of the shadow envelope her. She felt the glass of the window shatter as her back hit it, her arms protectively around Aravelle.

The palace exploded in fire.

CHAPTER FORTY-TWO

KHYVEN

Khyven saw the dragon half an instant after Slayter, and he knew what it meant. Not in terms of the dangers of dragons or what he might expect in the next few seconds from that quarter. He didn't know anything about dragons. He knew even less about Nox.

But Khyven knew combat.

The dragon had grabbed everyone's attention, which had been focused on Khyven up to that point, and that was an opportunity not to be missed.

He twisted, bringing all the speed of his pivot into the muscle of his shoulder and planted a palm in the center of the Shadowmaster's chest. The man vanished into the foliage like Khyven had shot him from a catapult. That surprised even Khyven. The man was as light as a paper cutout!

He didn't spend time thinking about his luck, though. He spun, drew a dagger, and slashed through Slayter's sleeve, freeing him from the arrow pinning his arm to the tree.

He kept spinning, staying in motion. A moving fighter was far more difficult to hit, and already two lines of blue wind shot from the darkness. They'd loosed arrows: one for Slayter, one for Khyven. With a grunt, Khyven thrust his dagger precisely into the path of the blue line headed for Slayter even as he twisted his torso to avoid the one that would have punched into his belly.

The first arrow sparked on Khyven's dagger as it was deflected. The second whistled past Khyven, the arrow's feathers humming against his armor, and hit something behind him.

Khyven, still moving, drew his sword and spun toward the archers. Archers loved distance. It was easy to pick people off when they were twenty feet away. But they liked it a lot less when a swordsman leapt among them. Arrows made for horrible shields.

He charged—

—and the forest exploded in fire. The flames engulfed Khyven, blasting him backward. He tumbled through the tall grass and came to his feet, expecting to be charred and bloody.

He wasn't.

Stunned, he looked back at the forest. The trees where they'd all been standing flared like an enormous torch. Nox screamed. Shadowy figures thrashed in the flames, trying to escape as their bodies burned.

Blinking, he looked down at himself again. He should be incinerated…

"Ha!" Slayter hopped toward Khyven on one leg, looking triumphant. Orange light surrounded his fist as bits of clay fell away.

Only then did Khyven see the nimbus of orange light around himself. It slowly faded, and he flinched, bringing up a hand to shield his eyes as he suddenly felt the heat of the flames.

"Slayter!" he exclaimed.

"Right? I knew I'd have reason for that spell some day!" the mage exclaimed. "They laughed at me, but I made it anyway. 'When are you going to ever face dragon fire?' they said. 'You're wasting your time' they said. Who's laughing now?"

Khyven shook his head. "Where's Vohn?"

"I got him." Slayter pointed into the tall grass. "He tripped over his feet in there, but I got him."

Khyven spotted the white horns of the Shadowvar as he raised his head, looking dazed.

"What about the rest of them?"

"I was supposed to save them, too?" Slayter asked.

"Are they dead?"

"It's dragon fire!" Slayter replied, as though that explained it all. He was still hopping on one leg.

"What's wrong with your leg?"

"I'm not very graceful, is all."

"Your prosthetic?"

"It got hung up. It's sort of backward now. Stupid roots are everywhere in there. I'm sure you didn't notice. Your feet seem to have eyes of their own, but not all of us can be Ringers. Although I have wondered what it would be like—"

"Slayter!"

Slayter's eyes widened, as though he honestly didn't realize that talking about his idle fantasies about being a Ringer while surrounded by dragon fire was out of place.

"Check on Vohn. I'm going to see if anyone survived," Khyven said.

"Oh, right. Of course."

"And tell me one thing, is that dragon coming back?" Khyven scanned the sky, but he couldn't see anything.

"Uh," Slayter said. "I don't know. That's not... How do I predict a dragon? I'm not a Lore Mage."

"Fine. Don't trip on anything else."

"Don't trip on anything else, he says," Slayter murmured to himself. "Just be like me, he says. It's easy, he says." Slayter hobbled toward Vohn lying in the high grass.

Khyven approached the burning forest, squinting at the heat, and he tried to see if anyone had survived. It didn't seem likely. It looked like the flames had struck exactly where the archers had been.

He spotted someone. To the right of the fire, a figure staggered at the edge of the woods. Khyven sprinted toward it, wincing at the heat, and reached the Nox.

It was the Shadowmaster. His right arm and the right side of his face were burned and bubbling. He stumbled, a surprised look on his face, like he wasn't sure where he was.

"Come on," Khyven said, putting the Nox's good arm over his shoulder and half-carrying him away from the blaze.

The Nox slumped against him, his feet barely moving as Khyven took his entire weight and got them to the grass. He laid the man down.

The Nox's right eye was burned blind, his teeth were exposed on the right side of his face, but still he tried to talk. "Nox..."

"They're... They're gone, I think," Khyven said. He'd been prepared to kill this man, to fight to the death, but no one should have to suffer this.

"Nox... Arvak..." the Shadowmaster said. He reached awkwardly with his good arm across his body, toward the forest.

No, not toward the forest, toward the city beyond the forest.

"Nox Arvak is your city," Khyven said.

"Family..." he said.

Something dark and immense blotted out the charcoal sky for an instant, and Khyven flinched. The dragon!

Its massive bulk flew low to the ground, flashing past them, circling the forest then straightening, heading for the city.

"Please..." the Shadowmaster said.

A piercing roar shook the air and another blast of fire erupted on the other side of the forest, where Slayter's map had shown the city to be.

"Is that where Lorelle is?" Khyven shouted at the Shadowmaster over the continuing roar of the dragon. "Is Lorelle in the city?" he demanded.

The man let out a long sigh, his eyes went glassy, and he stopped breathing. He was gone.

The dragon's roar finally stopped, only then did Khyven realize Slayter had been shouting for him.

"Khyven!" he called. "Khyven get over here." He sounded panicked. Slayter was never panicked.

Khyven leapt from his crouch to a full sprint and made it to them in a heartbeat, sliding to his knees next to Vohn.

Vohn stared up at them, his eyes watering. "I knew... I knew if I... was friends with you long enough, Khyven... it would be the death of me."

A black-feathered arrow was sticking up from the little Shadowvar's chest.

CHAPTER FORTY-THREE

KHYVEN

Khyven ran through the forest, carrying the unconscious Vohn in his arms. The little Shadowvar weighed practically nothing, but Khyven's guilt dragged at him like an anchor.

The arrow stuck in Vohn's chest had been meant for Khyven. He remembered dodging it, remembered hearing it strike something behind him. That something had been Vohn.

Khyven wanted to fight someone, wanted to kill an enemy, but all he could do was run pell-mell through these damned trees toward a burning city, hoping against hope that Lorelle would be there and, if she was, that she'd be able to help Vohn.

Every bit of this was Khyven's fault.

The conversation he'd had with Vohn just before they'd gone to search for Rauvelos had been heated. Khyven hadn't wanted Vohn on the trip. The mage, yes. Going deep into the Great Noktum, it made every kind of sense to take a Line Mage with him. For one thing, he knew every damned thing, and he could do things Khyven didn't understand. Most importantly, he could find Lorelle with the little gadget he and Vohn had created.

But Vohn wasn't a mage, and he sure as hell wasn't a fighter. He was a scholar. He made trinkets. He was a voice of reason in the council meetings, a mediator between Slayter's esoteric ramblings and Khyven's emotional outbursts. That final moment, when Khyven had finally relented, played over and over in his mind:

● ● ●

"The last person who should go adventuring into the wild, into the uncharted noktum, into jaws of certain death, is you," Khyven pointed out.

"Really?"

"Vohn, you could barely run five hundred yards through the noktum." Khyven recalled his first trip into the noktum through the Night Ring. "I had to carry you."

"I would say I have far more experience rescuing a friend than you," Vohn replied calmly, referring to the time when he'd snuck into the Night Ring and freed Khyven and Shalure from Vamreth's cages.

"That was different—"

"Who carried whom that time?" Vohn cut him off.

"Vohn…" Khyven said, but he could think of no rejoinder. Khyven would be dead if not for the little Shadowvar.

Vohn continued packing.

"This isn't the same," Khyven said. "This is likely the Great Noktum we're talking about."

"And for some reason you think this means you are better suited?"

"You're not a fighter, Vohn."

"Certainly not," Vohn agreed.

"We're going to need to fight."

"Of course. And for that we have you. Who better to handle combat than Khyven the Unkillable? And what if you need information? Shall we rely on the giant hole in your education to sustain you?"

"I'll have Slayter."

"Who will undoubtedly abandon you the moment a glowing noktum frog catches his attention."

"Vohn—"

"I am going."

Khyven clenched his jaw. "Well, I'm not taking you."

"Aren't you?" Vohn continued packing like a tolerant parent listening to the tirade of a child.

"I'm not going to risk you!"

The passion in Khyven's voice actually made the Shadowvar pause and look up. A small smile crossed his face. "Khyven..." he said softly. "Well, well, you're genuinely concerned. I'm... honored."

"What?"

"You actually mean that. You're afraid for me."

"Well of course I am! That's what I'm trying to tell you, you stubborn little—"

"I remember a time when you didn't care about anything except yourself."

"Don't change the subject."

"I care about you, too, Khyven. We're... family now. You and me, Slayter and Lorelle and Rhenn."

"Then you'll stay?" Khyven said, hoping for a moment.

"Don't be silly. I'm going."

"No!"

He chuckled. "It's sweet. Really. I think you would stand as a shield between everyone you love and a horde of Giants if you had to, but you sometimes miss the obvious."

"What's the obvious?"

Vohn turned and looked up at Khyven. He felt like he was supposed to get something from the gesture, but he didn't know what.

Khyven frowned. He hated it when Vohn did this. The Shadowvar would sometimes just stand there like the answer was obvious and wait for Khyven to put it together. All it usually did was make Khyven angry. Like now.

"What?" Khyven growled.

"Look at me."

Khyven glanced up and down at the Shadowvar. He stood about five feet tall with midnight black skin and milk white horns.

"What am I supposed to be getting from this?"

"I'm Shadowborn."

That was the first time Khyven had heard that term.

"I thought you were a Shadowvar," he said.

"Of course I am."

Khyven sighed in frustration. "Then what does that mean? Shadowborn versus Shadowvar?" he chewed the words out.

"It means my race was created to live in the shadows. When the Giants altered the races, they altered some to specifically live in the noktum. These were called Shadowborn. I can vanish in shadows, provided my horns are covered. My skin is as black as jet. Did you think that was coincidence?"

"I don't know. I assumed you were just a different race, like Lorelle. You both have powers."

"Lorelle is a Luminent. She is not Shadowborn. But the Nox are. Like me. You talk of entering this wild noktum where we won't know anything. There are… things that only Shadowborn can feel in the noktum. Who do you think helped Rhenn chart our noktum?"

Khyven cocked his head.

"My point is that I can certainly help you. You see me as a liability, but I'm an asset you desperately need."

❧ ❧ ❧

Khyven hadn't had a response for that. On the surface, it made sense, so he had reluctantly acquiesced and brought Vohn along. But even then he'd felt, deep down, as certainly as he knew danger was coming when a spear of blue wind flew at him, that it was a bad idea to bring Vohn.

Now he sprinted along the edge of the trees, trying to outrace the fire that was consuming the forest, heading toward a place where there was barely a sliver of hope to find help. Most likely he'd find more danger and another opportunity to fight for his life, in the hopes that he might somehow save the little Shadowvar's life.

Slayter limped behind him, barely keeping up. "I've made sure—" he huffed "—the blood won't... leave his body..."

The mage had cast a spell upon Vohn the moment they'd realized the wound was mortal. Slayter had maintained over and over that he was not a healer. Magic and healing didn't go hand in hand unless that was the specific type of magic a person learned, called Life Magic. But Line Magic, the kind of magic Slayter practiced, could do a little bit of everything, just weaker than other types.

In essence, Slayter was a magical jack-of-all-trades.

"It won't... heal him...—"Slayter huffed "—it'll just... keep his blood... in his body... for a while."

The fire roared to their left, spreading across the leaves like it was chasing them. One of the trees exploded and Khyven turned his body, shielding Vohn. That was the second one he'd seen do that. He wondered what these trees of the Great Noktum were made of that caused them to explode when exposed to fire.

"That's...—" Slayter huffed "—fascinating... Why... do you think... they do that?"

"Run, Slayter," Khyven growled. Vohn had gone completely limp.

They cleared the edge of the woods and it opened into a city at least as large as the crown city of Usara.

It was destroyed.

Everything was burned. Some of the houses had already been reduced to smoldering bits of char, while some still flamed like giant torches.

"No..." Khyven murmured. If Lorelle was here, odds were she was as charred as these buildings. He slowed to a walk, looking for something, anything, that might give him hope.

Slayter finally caught up. "Senji's Boots—" he huffed "—the city... That was fast. But then... dragon fire burns hotter... than other fire."

Khyven looked at the fire and smoldering ruins. Charred corpses lay everywhere. He searched for a single soul who had survived, but they all seemed dead.

A flicker of movement caught his eye, and he squinted. At first glance, he didn't see anything, but then it moved again. It was... someone... moving over the remains of a small house. Only charred spears of wood and smoking ash remained where the building had once been. Khyven could see the skeletal remains of several figures in the fire.

The man was cloaked... a cloak that seemed part of the darkness. Only the man's head and boots were visible, but Khyven recognized him.

He was the Nox. Lorelle's Nox.

"You!" Khyven handed Vohn over to Slayter, who grunted under the weight.

"Khyven, what's happening?" Slayter asked.

"That's the one," Khyven said. "The Nox who stole Lorelle. The one who started this entire thing."

"Khyven the Unkillable," the dead-eyed Nox said, seeming to notice them for the first time. "You have surprised me. Well done." His voice lacked all emotion, as though his soul had been leached from him. "I am Zaith D'Orphine, First Glimmerblade of the Nox of Arvak."

"I don't care," Khyven growled. "Where is Lorelle?"

Zaith looked back at the charred corpses, then into the distance toward some other part of the city. "In our culture—" he seemed to be talking to himself "—when someone sneaks up on you, it is the responsibility of the surprised to introduce themselves..." He glanced at Khyven.

"Where is Lorelle!"

"She loosed a dragon," Zaith continued as though he wasn't listening to Khyven. "We both did. And now everyone I love is dead."

"Where *is* she?"

"*Everyone* I love is dead," he said with emphasis, turning his dull gaze on Khyven. "She was in the palace," Zaith said, "with Aravelle. It was the first place the dragon attacked."

It felt like a spear had plunged into Khyven's heart. He couldn't breathe.

"What... did you do?" Khyven said through his teeth.

"Everything. I did everything. I served my people. I followed the will of the Lords. I took Lorelle to the dragon's lair as I was commanded. And I failed."

"You brought her here to die..." Khyven put his hand on his steel sword.

"Khyven wait," Slayter said.

Zaith turned, and his dead eyes flickered with life. "I brought her here to *live*, Khyven the Unkillable. You had yet to see her alive, but I did. She was never yours. She was a Nox, body and soul. She was dying under your seemingly well-meaning demands, your constructions, your ignorance. You were killing her because you had no idea what she needed. Because you're only... Human." He bared his white teeth. "Blind, uncomprehending, and stupid."

Khyven drew his sword.

"Yes," Zaith breathed, and a blade appeared in his hand, the same blade that had tasted Khyven's blood in the Usaran palace. It glowed like a shaft of moonlight. "Come, Khyven the Unkillable. Let me show you just how ignorant you are. Let me strip that ridiculous nickname from you at long last."

Khyven's heart began to pound, and the blue wind swirled around him and Zaith. It had only begun to form when three spears launched at him. Khyven spun as he dodged the first two and put his sword in front of the third.

Zaith's hidden dagger tore through Khyven's shirt, missing his flesh by an inch, and his moonlight sword clanged against Khyven's, deflected.

Khyven roared, grabbed Zaith's head, and brought his knee up—

The man vanished, and Khyven's knee swept through empty shadows.

Khyven's lesson from his fight with Txomin rose in his mind. The Nox was a master of the shadows, could disappear and reappear at will. Khyven would never see him coming.

But Khyven didn't need to see.

He closed his eyes and focused on the blue wind.

A single spear lanced at his back from the shadows, so fast that if Khyven hadn't closed his eyes instantly he would have died.

He twisted, bringing his sword around in the same motion and slamming into the lance of blue, even as he opened his eyes again. Steel clanged and the Nox grunted. Khyven's block, delivered with every ounce of his strength, sent the Nox flying a dozen paces away. The agile Nox tumbled and came to his feet, but Khyven leapt after, not giving him time to recover.

Zaith threw up a hasty parry as Khyven struck. A spear of blue came at him, which he dodged, and two blue funnels appeared on Zaith, a light one at his shoulder, and a dark one in the center of his chest.

Khyven struck—

Zaith vanished.

Khyven closed his eyes and "saw" a big blue funnel ten feet behind him. He spun, drew, and threw his dagger with unerring accuracy.

Zaith grunted. Khyven opened his eyes to see his dagger in the meat of Zaith's thigh. The Nox fell to the grass, clutching his leg.

"How…?" Zaith murmured. "It's not possible. No Human could…" he trailed off, and his eyes widened. "That wasn't luck," he whispered. "Not twice. You're doing that on purpose. You… have control of it." The Nox glanced at Slayter, as though the mage might be the reason. Slayter, who had finally laid Vohn in the grass, was hastily clicking through his clay coins, obviously looking for the right spell.

Khyven stalked Zaith and drew another dagger.

"Tell me Lorelle is alive," Khyven growled.

Zaith stared at Khyven in wonder, not fear. "*You're* the one," the Nox whispered. "*You're* the Greatblood…"

"I'm the what?"

"It's not the queen. He's looking for the wrong Human. The Betrayer fooled Him... by taking the queen. *You're* the one he wants... And you're right *here!*"

If this fight had been in the Night Ring just six months ago, Khyven would have cut the man's soliloquy short by lopping off his head, but Khyven hesitated. Something warned him that this Nox was saying something important, even if Khyven didn't understand it.

"What are you talking about?"

Zaith glanced at his ruined city, at the rubble of the house that, Khyven guessed, had contained his family. The Nox's gaze hardened and he looked back at Khyven.

"Don't tell Him," Zaith said in a hoarse voice.

"Tell who what?"

"Lord Tovos. It's you He wants, but He doesn't know it. If you show Him, he'll kill you. He only wanted Lorelle because he thought the *queen* was a Greatblood."

Khyven stuck the point of his sword into the clasp that held the Nox's cloak and twisted. The catch snapped and the cloak slid to the ground like falling water.

Let's see the nimble jackrabbit hop around without his favorite toy, Khyven thought.

"Make. Sense," Khyven commanded. Lord Tovos. That was the Giant Rauvelos had said had most likely sent this Nox to grab Lorelle. But here the Nox was telling Khyven to keep something hidden from his master.

Zaith glanced at the cloak on the ground, then back up. The tough bastard still didn't look afraid. "Well played, Khyven the Unkillable," he said. He let his sword fall on top of the cloak and held up his hands. "Strike quick but remember what I told you. If you value your life and the lives of all those you love, don't use your magic on the Lord."

Khyven let the point of his sword linger at Zaith's throat. No spears of blue came at Khyven, and the man's body was a forest of blue funnels.

"What is a Greatblood?" Khyven pushed the point gently into the skin below Zaith's throat. A dot of blood welled up. Zaith stared at Khyven with the eyes of a man ready to die. Still no fear.

"Khyven!" A familiar voice broke the silence. He jerked his head up.

A slender Nox woman in a short dress stood on the rise behind Zaith, a single lock of golden hair blazing at her brow.

CHAPTER FORTY-FOUR

LORELLE

Lorelle woke, disoriented. Her ears rang. Her cheek pressed against the warm marble floor. With a groan, she blinked and raised her head. Smoke hung in wisps amongst the shadows just outside the palace. Flames raged around her, but miraculously, she lay in a spot that wasn't burning.

She shook her head, trying to remember where she was and what had happened.

She was in the Great Noktum. In Nox Arvak, in the palace. The dragon had attacked. Zaith... He'd sent her to protect...

"Aravelle!" Lorelle shouted and cast about. It all came back to her now. She'd sprinted into the palace when the dragon attacked. Miraculously, amidst the chaos, she'd actually found Aravelle in her library. She'd flung herself and Aravelle out the window just before an explosion of fire.

She sat up, blinking. Smoke stung her eyes. She couldn't see clearly, and she could barely breathe.

She crawled about in the smoke, hands groping. Her hand fell on warm flesh. Lorelle scrambled over, coughing as she looked down at the half-burned form of Aravelle. The old Nox had sustained burns on the right side of her body, all along her right arm and leg, and on her right cheek.

"No…" Lorelle murmured. "Please no."

The old Nox moved. She was still breathing!

"Just stay still, Aravelle." Lorelle reached for her healing satchel—

Only to remember she didn't have it. She was wearing only the short black dress given to her for the celebration. All she had was the slim pouch with the Plunnos. She'd even left her slippers back in the woods.

She had to get back to her room, to the box that held her healer's kit.

"I have—" she coughed "—something that will help you." Stars appeared in her vision as the thick smoke choked her. She and Aravelle couldn't stay here much longer. She had to get the old Nox to safety.

She slipped her arms carefully beneath Aravelle's knees and her frail shoulders—

Aravelle's unburned hand grasped Lorelle's arm like a claw. The old woman's gummy eyes struggled open.

"Dear child…" she whispered. "I'm sorry… So sorry…"

"It's all right," Lorelle said. "I'll get you to safety. Just hold on." She braced herself to lift the old Nox, but Aravelle let go of her arm and placed her hand alongside Lorelle's temple. Her thumb swiped gently across the center of Lorelle's forehead. A tingle swept through Lorelle and the golden lock of hair at her brow glowed.

"The Lord comes…" she said weakly. "Run, child… I think… maybe we were wrong to bring you here. Perhaps we were wrong… But perhaps… you could escape… if you run…"

"We're both getting out of here."

"Run, child… Run now…" Aravelle let out a long breath and closed her eyes.

"Aravelle?" Lorelle said.

The old Nox stopped breathing.

"Aravelle!"

The tingle the old woman had infused into her slowly changed to a warm, intimate knowing. Lorelle felt the rush of the Dark inside her and all around her, the shadows intermingling with the smoke.

And someone was moving through those shadows.

The Lord comes...

She coughed, covering her mouth with her arm and reaching for her dagger—

Except she didn't have that, either.

Run, child... Run now...

She belatedly took Aravelle's advice and leapt to her feet—

The smoke fell to the ground like black sand.

An enormous man towered over her.

"Lotura..." she murmured. The man stood well over ten feet tall. A Giant! Gods, he was a Giant!

He had angry, slanted eyes beneath angry, slanted eyebrows. His skin was pale like a Usaran. His black clothes fitted tightly to his body, a black scale mail shirt ending in a thick black belt and black pants tucked into knee-high black boots.

"Well, it appears they were all traitors." The Giant stepped forward and stamped hard on Aravelle's chest, crushing the woman beneath his enormous foot, which was nearly as large as she was.

"Aravelle!" Lorelle screamed.

"I was hoping to do this in secret, but I am done waiting. The Glimmerblade failed me, and this will have to do," the Giant said, looking over her head as though he could see something far away.

Lorelle cursed herself for leaving all her weapons behind. Couldn't she have at least strapped a dagger to her waist?

She flicked a glance at Aravelle's body. Did the old Nox have any weapons? No. There were only pouches.

Lorelle's gaze came to rest on the belt of the Giant. There were plenty of weapons there. The Giant wore a sword across his back that no Luminent or Human could even lift, but he also had a short sword on his left hip that looked the same size as

Khyven's longsword and a dagger on his right hip that was almost as long as Lorelle's arm. *That* she could use.

She let the Dark flow into her, imagined herself floating on it like a boat on a river. She vanished into the crooked shadow behind her, flitted quickly and fluidly to another shadow, then to another, circling the Giant and emerging behind him. Quick as a thought, she yanked the sword-sized dagger from his belt and slashed around to the other side, intending to cut into the Giant's hamstring, bring him down to her level—

The Dark, intertwined with Lorelle's soul, suddenly clenched, freezing her. Her dagger stopped an inch from the Giant's flesh.

She screamed and crashed to her knees on the marble floor next to Aravelle's crushed body.

The Dark hauled her upright.

"Rrnnnngggrgh!" she shouted, and that was the last sound to come out of her mouth. She tried to fight the force that had taken control of her body, but she couldn't.

"I am Lord Tovos," the Giant said, turning around and looking down at her. "That was a nice bit of shadow-shifting. Zaith was right about your talent."

Her body turned and began walking awkwardly toward the shattered window. Lorelle's body marched like a marionette on strings.

"But he was wrong about everything else. When put to the test, he failed. I will put *you* to the test very soon, Lorelle friend of Rhennaria Laochodon. Pray you do not fail me. Pray you never know what it is like to fail me, for you are about to see what happens to one who has."

Her body awkwardly ducked through the shattered window and started up the smoky hallway, and Lorelle watched from within herself with growing horror.

At a gesture from Tovos, the smoke cleared like it had before, falling to the ground. He walked sedately behind her.

"Your connection is exquisite. And once we have you fully bonded, this won't be such a struggle for either of us. But time enough for that later," Tovos said.

Fully bonded… With the Dark.

The dragon's words returned to her.

You don't know who Tovos is. I would bet Zaith does. But he is your friend, yes? Your good friend. Your trusted friend who would never do anything to harm you?

Despair flooded through her.

"Zzzaith!" she managed to say despite the fact that the Dark tried to keep her jaw clenched tight. The golden lock of hair at her brow blazed as she struggled against the compulsion. Zaith had been working with this Giant! That's what the dragon had been saying.

"Yes, Zaith," Tovos said. "A disappointment, in the end. His softness for you cost him his people." Lord Tovos gestured at the smoking, flaming ruin of the city of Nox Arvak as they emerged onto the veranda, where only minutes ago, Nox had played music and danced. Now it was charred, blackened, and covered in ash. "And soon it is going to cost him his life."

Lorelle's body reached the bottom of the stairs and preceded the Giant between the flickering fires, the smoke, and the sweltering heat. She stepped forward against her will into the ruined city, and she screamed inside.

Her golden lock flared, but this time her mouth made no sound.

CHAPTER FORTY-FIVE

KHYVEN

Lorelle!" Zaith said, and the name took the wind from Khyven's chest.

He stared at the Nox woman, and his stupefaction fought with his Ringer training. He should kill Zaith or secure him somehow, render him unconscious, but Khyven's sword point dipped.

Lorelle? Impossible. He blinked at the Nox woman's height, her bearing, her slender build... Everything except her midnight skin and hair looked just like...

"Lorelle?" he blurted.

She looked at him with no expression.

"Keep your wits about you, Khyven the Unkillable," Zaith warned softly, his surprise giving way to suspicion.

"What did you do to her?"

Something moved behind Lorelle. A figure rose from the smoke and shadows, coming up the back side of the hill. The man's head appeared first, rising higher as he climbed. Then Khyven realized the figure was no man. Stride after stride, his head and shoulders emerged taller and larger until he stood by Lorelle's side, towering over her.

"Um, that's a Giant," Slayter murmured.

The presence of the creature pushed at Khyven. He couldn't seem to look directly at the thing's eyes. Its glare was like staring into the sun, and the face, with its lip curling in derision, reminded him of Harkandos, the statue Slayter had brought to life.

"That's Tovos," Slayter said excitedly. "That's got to be Tovos."

"Shut up, Slayter." Khyven fought to look the Giant in the eye, but his heart hammered. Cold sweat broke out on his forehead. He grunted and looked away, focusing on the Giant's chest.

"What did you do to her?" Khyven demanded.

"She has come home," Tovos said. "She doesn't belong to the lands of daylight anymore. She belongs to me."

Khyven clenched his teeth and his knuckles turned white on the hilt of his sword. "That's what you think," he growled.

"Khyven wait," Slayter said.

Zaith slowly stood and faced the Giant, crouching on his good leg and dragging his wounded leg upright. He hadn't removed the dagger.

"You have failed me for the final time, Glimmerblade," Tovos said. "I have come to express my displeasure."

"You're a liar…" Zaith whispered. "You don't deserve to be our Lord, Tovos. You killed them all…"

"Told you," Slayter said wonderingly. "Tovos."

"Shut up, Slayter," Khyven said.

"Take care how you speak to me, Glimmerblade. I've come to pass judgment upon you for failing me. But there are worse things than death." Tovos started down the rise, his long legs covering an enormous distance with each stride. He made it to the bottom in three steps. Lorelle came after, still staring blankly ahead.

"Yes, I know that now," Zaith said, his eyes glittering.

"You released Jai'ketakos," Tovos said. "If you'd completed her bonding like I commanded, that would not have happened. Do not blame me."

"You *sent* us to the dragon's lair!"

"To bolster your weakness."

"My weakness..."

"Kneel. Take your punishment like a true servant of the Dark," Tovos said.

"I should never have knelt to you in the first place," Zaith said through gritted teeth. He leaned down and recovered his sword. "I should have fought you from the first. I should have died that day beside E'lan. I won't make that mistake again. Kill me now, you horrendous aberration. Or glance over your shoulder for the rest of your unholy life."

"Kill you? I wouldn't give you the honor of dying by my hand." Tovos sneered. He made a gesture and Lorelle leapt forward.

During the bizarre confrontation between Zaith and Tovos, questions abounded in Khyven's mind. Horrendous aberration? Wasn't Zaith Tovos's servant? Why did he suddenly seem like a potential ally? And Lorelle... Obviously she was under a spell. Could Slayter, or even Khyven, break it somehow?

Khyven's Ringer training reengaged and the blue wind swirled around the entire group. In the Night Ring, questions didn't matter unless they could be answered in the split second before he had to react. These couldn't. That meant they were just baggage.

Khyven jumped to meet Lorelle's charge, making it seem as though he was going to stop her.

At the last second, he swept past her and charged the Giant.

It worked. A half dozen dark funnels appeared all over the Giant's body. Khyven jumped high, sword cocked back, ready to plunge the point into Tovos's neck.

While in midair, a hundred spears came at him from every side, so close he didn't see them in time, so quick he couldn't dodge them. The very air of the noktum came alive, shooting forward as dark tentacles.

Khyven shouted, thrusting desperately at the blue funnel over Tovos's neck——

The point of his sword came half an inch from his target, but the tentacles of shadow yanked him up short, then slithered around him. He spun like a spindle gathering thread until he was completely bound in shadow.

"You should have stayed in your castle," Tovos said.

Khyven grunted as the shadows tightened, squeezing so hard his back popped. His right arm, trapped against his body, dropped his sword. His left, caught away from his body, dangled over his head at an awkward angle. Slayter cried out, and Khyven craned his neck to see the mage also wrapped in solid shadows.

"The rest of you are now my servants," Tovos said. "Watch closely. This is what happens to those who fail me."

Lorelle approached Zaith, who raised his sword, but without conviction.

She knocked his sword away with her blade. It broke from his grip and landed on the grass, just out of reach. Lorelle pirouetted behind him, grabbed a handful of Zaith's hair, and yanked his head back, exposing his throat. She laid her short sword against his throat.

"Lorelle, I'm sorry." Zaith didn't resist. "I'm so sorry."

"Lorelle, don't!" Khyven struggled against the grip of the shadows. He was no stranger to death, no stranger to killing. But Lorelle was. "Don't let him control you!"

Lorelle glanced at Khyven, her blade poised over Zaith's throat. Her eyes were completely black, like oil had seeped across her eyeballs.

Zaith didn't make any attempt to defend himself.

The blue wind swirled toward Khyven, around his bound body and up to his neck...

And formed into a single blue funnel over his right shoulder.

It wasn't a target, not on Khyven's enemy, at least. It wasn't at the Giant's neck or chest. It wasn't on Tovos at all. Instead, the blue funnel swirled directly around the hilt of the Mavric iron sword on his back.

The sword whined in agreement.

Free of the shadow bindings, Khyven's dangling left arm could draw the sword.

This was more than just seeing weaknesses or attacks. It was as if the wind was suggesting an alternate course of action. It had never done that before.

Khyven glared at Tovos, but the Giant was ignoring him, focusing instead on Lorelle and Zaith.

But Zaith was looking directly at Khyven, almost as though he could see the blue wind also, as though he knew what Khyven was contemplating.

"Don't," Zaith said. "Remember what I told you, Khyven the Unkillable."

"Now," Tovos commanded.

"Khyven!" Lorelle shouted in anguish, as though his name was the only word she could say. Her face, directly behind Zaith's, remained impassive.

Her single golden lock flared so bright it was almost white.

She slashed the short sword across Zaith's throat.

CHAPTER FORTY-SIX

LORELLE

A s Tovos marched Lorelle before him from the Nox palace, she felt the five little threads of her soul burning inside her. They glowed gold and the golden lock of her hair glowed as well, as though the two were directly connected. It was like it had been in Usara, no torturous burning engulfing her entire body, but that little collection of threads yearned for Khyven. More than anyone else, she wished he was here now.

At first, she'd thought the burning was just a response to Tovos and his insidious control over her. But as her body marched up a gentle rise and crested the top, her heart stopped. Those five threads were burning for the same reason they had in Usara. Khyven was here.

She quailed as she looked down at the small glade.

No! No! No!

They were *all* here. Khyven stood with his sword at Zaith's throat. Slayter leaned against a tree, stooped from exhaustion and searching his cylinder of spells.

At least Vohn wasn't here. At least…

No!

Vohn lay face up, a black-feathered arrow sticking out of his chest. His eyes were open, but he didn't move, didn't blink. She couldn't tell at this distance whether was dead or not. She couldn't see if he was breathing.

She'd left them in Usara. She'd left them safe! The whole point of her leaving them behind and going with Zaith was so she wouldn't have to lose any more of her friends. She was supposed to do this alone. They weren't supposed to be here!

"Khyven!" she called in anguish, surprising herself. She hadn't been able to say or do anything since Tovos had taken firm control of her. She hadn't actually meant to say Khyven's name. She'd meant to shout at them to leave, to run. To get away before the Giant saw them, but all that had emerged was "Khyven," as though it was spoken straight from those five golden threads themselves.

Khyven glanced up, assessing her like he'd assess an enemy, as though she was distracting him from the kill.

But then he froze. His eyes widened.

"Lorelle?"

"Keep your wits about you, Khyven the Unkillable," Zaith reminded him.

"What did you do to her?" Khyven demanded.

"Um, that's a Giant," Slayter murmured as Tovos rose to stand behind Lorelle.

Too late! Lorelle screamed in her mind. *Too late!*

Khyven, Zaith, and Tovos slung words back and forth, but Lorelle stared at Vohn lying dead in the grass. Little Vohn. Always the first with a gentle gesture or a kind word when it was most needed. Always the last to turn to violence. He hated weapons. What was he doing here in the middle of the Great Noktum? How could Khyven have brought him here?

No… she thought. *I brought them here.*

Did she really think they wouldn't try to find her? A tear snaked down her cheek, the only evidence that her body was still her own.

Then she saw Vohn move. His chest rose just a little, an indrawn breath. He was alive! There was still time to save him!

She struggled against Tovos's control again, putting every ounce of herself into breaking his hold...

But it was like trying to break a brick wall with a willow switch. Dizzy, she overheard Tovos speaking as though he was far away.

"I wouldn't give you the honor of dying by my hand," the Giant said to Zaith.

Suddenly, the grip within Lorelle tightened, seizing her, and her body leapt forward. She swung Tovos's dagger—a short sword in her hand—at Zaith. He brought his sword up, but she batted it aside and moved behind him, laying the blade against his throat.

No!

"Lorelle. I'm sorry," Zaith said.

Tovos forced her to grab Zaith's hair and pull his head back. She knew what was coming next and she tried to stop herself. The command to kill him thrummed through her, but she fought it. She screamed inside her own mind so loudly she felt numb.

Her body twitched, but she held it.

"I'm so sorry," Zaith whispered, and she saw everything he felt in that gaze. His failure to help his people. The anguish of losing his family. And love for her.

He looked past her, and his gaze fixed on Khyven.

"Don't," Zaith said. "Remember what I said, Khyven the Unkillable."

"Now," Tovos commanded. The shadows within her twisted. This time, Tovos's will came down like an avalanche.

"Khyven!" she shouted, but Tovos smashed her resistance.

She pulled the dagger, felt Zaith's throat give, saw the blood come. Zaith reacted like he couldn't feel the deadly cut. His eyelids drooped.

Lorelle screamed silently, and it rent her sanity.

She tried to reach out, to stanch the flow, to try to hold Zaith together, but Tovos didn't let her. Zaith slumped to the side and the light left his eyes.

Tovos turned her body around, taking her away from Zaith, taking her away from her friends.

Khyven and Slayter, bound by shadows, floated next to her, preceding the Giant. The mage's eyes watched everything with interest as he floated over the ground, like he was taking mental notes. Khyven thrashed and struggled, but the shadow tentacles held him tight.

"Vohn!" Khyven strained to look over his shoulder at the prone Shadowvar. "You bastard! Take him with us! He needs help!"

As Tovos forced her to continue forward, she only had a brief, final glance at Vohn. His eyes were open, glazed, and he looked dead. She couldn't tell if he was breathing anymore.

Tovos opened his cloak, a noktum cloak like Zaith's, and it swirled around all of them. Lorelle's body obligingly stepped into the Dark as she screamed denial. She felt the tingling wash of darkness flow through her and around her. It felt warm and close, comforting like the gentle rush of spring air.

The darkness parted and Lorelle found herself standing in a stone room with a dozen archways. Tovos stood next to her, with Khyven and Slayter hovering in the grip of shadow tentacles.

A dozen thick, squat men, about half the height of a Human, stood there as though they'd been waiting for Tovos to arrive. They had burly shoulders and faces that looked as if they'd been compressed, with square flat noses and squinty eyes. Their skin was the color of dark granite, not the effervescent purple of the Nox.

"Take them to the cells. Remove their weapons and lock them in," Tovos commanded. "Take care with the Mavric iron blade. If I'm not mistaken, that's Daelakos's sword."

The short men jumped into action. Three apiece pushed the floating, shadow-wrapped Khyven and Slayter through one of the archways and disappeared.

"Lorelle!" Khyven shouted. He growled. "I'm going to gut you, monster. I'm going to—"

His voice was cut off as the squat men turned the corner and slammed the door shut.

"You, on the other hand, may have a room," Tovos said to Lorelle. "I have a special purpose for you. We must discuss your friend." He walked through another of the archways and almost immediately up a flight of steps.

Lorelle's body followed like a dog on a leash. She longed to look over her shoulder to where Khyven had gone, but she couldn't.

Silently, Tovos led her up two flights of stairs, around to the left, and down a hallway. He finally stopped before a door that had an enormous handle, a lock, brackets set on either side, and a bar leaning against the wall. Tovos opened it. Inside was a bed, a rack for cloaks, a chest of drawers, and a mirror.

"This belonged to Zaith. He won't be needing it any longer. I think living here will remind you of what happens if you fail me. Zaith had a rebellious heart. I hope you can avoid that. But if not, remember this, Lorelle: If you serve well, you will be rewarded. If you serve poorly..."

Her body entered the room, walked to the bed, and sat down stiffly.

"I must return to a project that was interrupted by Jai'ketakos's appearance," he said. He held forth his hand, and her body gave his dagger back to him. He wiped the blood across a corner of his noktum cloak and the darkness seemed to lick the blood from the blade. "I will return shortly, and then we will find your friend. Like you, I seek the one who stole her."

He closed the door, leaving her alone. The moment the latch clicked shut, a tiny light swelled at the crack along the bottom, like someone had left a lantern right in front of the door. She heard the heavy bar that had been leaning against the wall sliding into the brackets. It gave a *thoom* of finality. She heard Tovos walk away and then nothing, as though he'd used his noktum cloak again and teleported.

The moment the footsteps stopped the Dark released her.

Lorelle screamed, and this time it pealed out of her, raking up her throat like fingernails. She charged the door and pounded her fists against it. She pounded and pounded until she fell to the floor. Her screams turned into a single, heart-wrenching wail, and then to quiet sobs.

CHAPTER FORTY-SEVEN
VOHN

The darkness of the Great Noktum was like a mother calling Vohn home. It always had been. He came from a people made to navigate that darkness, to thrive in it. To blend and hide and spy and kill. To become one with the blackness of the master spell that had been cast millennia ago by beings more powerful than the gods themselves.

The Giants enjoyed their creations, their castles and artifacts and weapons. But most of all, they liked the sentient creatures they had created. The malevolent minds of Giants reveled in the very idea of slavery, in lording their superiority over beings weaker than themselves. It wasn't enough for them to engineer beasts to do their bidding. No, they had to create creatures with a longing for self-destiny, and then deny it to them.

The Giants had made the Wergoi to mine pitchblende for their deadly weapons. They'd made Taur-Els to be workhorses, to haul stone and grain and steel. The Giants had made the Nox to be foot soldiers in their eternal war with each other, and that was when they'd stumbled across an interesting discovery. They had included a wisp of noktum in the Nox and it had a strange effect on their souls, forging a bond between sentient creatures and the nearly sentient Dark of their continent-spanning spell of war; the Great Noktum.

The discovery had excited them and, of course, had driven them to explore new possibilities.

They had created the Shadowvar next. A next step in the experiment. What if, instead of creating a race that could bond with the noktum, they created a race that could literally become one with the Dark?

It had been a failed experiment. Mostly.

Only a small percentage of the Shadowvar did what the Giants had hoped they would do. The Giants had mostly abandoned the project, using the Shadowvar for other tasks instead.

And then the Giants had vanished from the earth.

But that small percentage of Shadowvar who could become one with the Dark had remained.

Vohn's hometown of Nokte Shaddark had a ceremony called the Night of the Soul. Every year, every Shadowvar in the village came to the edge of the noktum with a tribute, an icon that represented a piece of their soul. The ceremony lasted all night, and every last person in the village was required to craft something from the heart to throw into the noktum.

Vohn's mother had told Vohn it symbolized, and ensured, their freedom from the yoke of the Giants. She had always been more spiritual than Vohn's father. She actually believed there were things Shadowvar could do to stop the Giants from controlling them, should the Giants ever return to Noksonon.

The myths told of how, during the many wars that flared up between the Giants and then later between Giants and the mortal races they had enslaved, the Giants would call upon these special Shadowvar to perform various tasks of war.

In the verbal legends handed down from story master to story master since the beginning of Shadowvar civilization, the details of these "tasks of war" were vague. Infiltration seemed a primary function, to scout the enemy and report on interlopers in the noktum.

The one that had stuck in Vohn's mind, after he'd studied the old histories extensively, was an entry that referred to the Human-Giant War "and the Shadowvar descended like banshees on their enemies." It made the Shadowvar sound like flying creatures, but there wasn't a single instance of a Shadowvar with wings in any of the histories.

Children were not allowed to attend the Night of the Soul until their tenth year. Shadowvar did not enter the Great Noktum anymore, and children were not allowed near it until they understood the danger. The myths talked about how Shadowvar used to live inside the noktum, but those days were long behind. Shadowvar respected the noktum, they made tributes to it like some sprawling goddess, they told stories about it.

But they did not live there.

Since then, the monsters in the noktum had gone wild, a Shadowvar was no more safe in that dark land than a Human or a Luminent.

And that was how the Shadowvar of Nokte Shaddark had treated it. Majestic. Mysterious. Dangerous. Like a cliff near the village. Everyone knew it was there, but no one would dream of jumping off.

No one save Vohn.

As a child, the noktum had called to him. When he was five, he told his mother about its inviting whispers. She had chalked it up as his overactive imagination and his boyish sense of adventure.

"Is it the idea of the creatures inside that interests you?" his mother had asked him.

That had seemed like the most ludicrous question she could have asked. Vohn had no sense of adventure and he was terrified of the monsters inside the noktum. He had no interest in meeting any of them. He didn't even like seeing renderings.

"It's not like that," he'd told her. "It's not the monsters, it's... a voice."

"Like an actual voice?"

Vohn had hesitated at that. No, it wasn't like an actual voice. He just didn't have the language to describe what it was, exactly.

"I think it's a 'she,'" Vohn had told his mother.

"The Great Noktum?"

"Yes. I think it's a she and I think she's alive."

That night, his mother had told his father about that conversation. The result? A stern talking-to. Afterward, his father had told Vohn that the subject of the noktum was closed and he didn't want Vohn thinking about it anymore.

"You don't go there, you don't think about it, and you don't call it a 'she.'"

Father's passionate rebuke had startled Vohn. Father had been a quiet, thoughtful man. As an archivist for the library of Nokte Shaddark, he believed in grave reflection as a means of solving most problems, not dramatic action or angry speeches.

Vohn respected his father, so he'd put the noktum from his mind, and for years the whispers of the noktum retreated like waves at low tide.

At age ten, though, Vohn awoke in the middle of the night, standing at his own window, staring in the direction of the noktum. His family lived at the southwestern edge of Nokte Shaddark, the part of the city closest to the noktum. But for a few houses in his way, Vohn could see the noktum from his window. The top of the black wall climbed hundreds of feet into the sky, blotting out the stars from mid-sky down.

He couldn't remember getting up from his bed, and that spooked him. It took a long time for him to finally fall asleep again, and he didn't tell his parents.

The next night, he awoke in the great empty field that separated the edge of Nokte Shaddark from the noktum. He was no more than a hundred yards from that enormous black wall with its lazy, floating tentacles.

Terrified, Vohn ran back to his house, and this time he woke his parents and told them everything. His father had just listened, just watched Vohn with a grim expression. His mother did almost all the talking, saying again and again that Vohn had had a nightmare.

The next night, Mother sat vigil in a chair next to his bed. That was the last thing Vohn remembered as he closed his eyes, but she must have fallen asleep, too.

When Vohn startled awake, he was standing before the noktum again, the compelling female whispers in his mind. His bare feet were muddy from the field, and people were shouting his name.

One of the black tentacles waved eagerly, only inches away from his ankle.

"Vohn!" his mother shrieked, running across the field with Father right beside her, holding a torch high. At the approach of the light, the tentacles redoubled their efforts to grab him, but Vohn was just out of reach.

Terrified, he stumbled backward and ran to them, hugging them and sobbing.

They sold their house that month and moved into a smaller house on the far side of the city, close to the southern edge of the Rhaeg Mountains.

The whispers were almost inaudible that far away, but Father didn't take any chances. Vohn slept in a room without a window and the door had a lock on the outside. Only when he turned sixteen, two years after Mother had died of the Orduvian Flu, did Father remove the lock and allow him to sleep on his own again.

The household was lonely without Mother, but Vohn found solace in books. He became an apprentice to his father in the library, and for a while his life became just like the lives of every other Shadowvar in Nokte Shaddark. He worked. He improved his skills as an academic and an archivist. He contributed to the community one day a week, as all Shadowvar were required to do. He attended the Night of Souls once a year. And the whispers did not return to him.

At age twenty, Vohn began thinking about those frightening nights as a child. With more than a decade of distance and the mantle of adult maturity he approached them academically now.

He studied the historical importance of the noktum in Shadowvar culture.

At age twenty-two, he began taking day trips to the edge of the noktum, recording every single nuance he could record. He didn't tell his father. But he didn't hear the whispers, either.

"Father," he said once during lunch.

They sat on the patio of the great library eating Vedok soup, a delicious stock-based broth with wheat noodles and chunks of fried Vedok, a fat grub found everywhere in the soil at the base of the Rhaeg Mountains. Raw Vedok looked slimy and disgusting, but when fried in chicken fat it tasted like softer, juicier chicken. It was a frugal man's delicacy and one of the things Vohn and his father shared a passion for.

"Yes Vohn."

"Has anyone from the library ever explored the noktum?"

Father stopped with a fork full of noodles halfway to his mouth. He set the fork in the steaming bowl. "No."

"Seems like there's a lot to know," Vohn said. "Why haven't they?"

Father chuckled, like the entire concept was a joke, but the laughter was brittle. "Fools who go into the noktum don't return."

"Who has tried?"

Father frowned. Obviously, he'd hoped his joke about the noktum would be the end of this conversation. "Years ago, a burly fool named Harguin—he was just a few years older than you, actually—went into the noktum with two of his foolish friends."

Father said nothing more and took several bite of noodles.

"What happened to him? Did he come back out?"

"Most of him. They found his head, arms, chest, and most of his ribcage in the field just beyond the range of the tentacles. He had tumbled across the grass—there were blood stains—like he'd been thrown. Everything from his waist down was missing." Father tapped his fork against the side of the bowl. He glanced over at Vohn and said, "I guess his legs were the tasty bits."

Vohn frowned. Father went back to eating, but without any apparent joy. He chewed as though it was his job, like it would keep his mouth busy with something other than talking.

They ate in silence, and finally Father said, "Are you hearing whispers again, son?"

"I thought the whispers were a dream, from when I was a child."

"Your mother certainly did. What do you think?"

"I... I don't hear them anymore, so..."

Looking unhappy, Father stood and put his bowl on the stone bench. "Come with me."

He went into the library and Vohn followed. Father ascended the elegant stone stairway that curved up to the second level of the library, then up a smaller, tight spiral staircase that went to a third-level walkway. At the end of the walkway, he turned to the stacks, looked for a moment, then selected a volume. He flipped it open to a page deep within the thick tome.

"Read this. Talk to me after."

And Father left Vohn alone.

Vohn devoured the passage, then he devoured the rest of the entire chapter. It was a book of translations, a speculation from the scholar Werliff Madresk about what the old verbal legends really meant. After reading the chapter twice, Vohn returned to find his father putting books back on the shelves.

"This sounds ridiculous," Vohn said.

Madresk had speculated that certain Shadowvar hadn't just lived in the noktum once upon a time, they had *been* the noktum. He had coined the term "Shadowborn" to encompass both Shadowvar and Nox and said that while Nox could navigate the noktum with ease, like a fish in a river, certain Shadowvar actually became the darkness. "It's a metaphor for our magical skin," he said. "That we become practically invisible in the shadows."

"Madresk is stating something particular. It's a bold conclusion," his father said.

"That we turn into shadows? You know that's not true."

"Perhaps not. But it is, to me, one more reason to never find out. If it is true, it is our past. If not, then Madresk was just a once-keen mind who lost his edge near the end. It happens."

Vohn left that meeting with his mind astir with ideas. He re-read Madresk's conclusions and, sure enough, Father could be right. It sounded like Madresk thought that some Shadowvar were extensions of the noktum, like the oily tentacles of the wall... tentacles that had broken free and learned to live alone in the world of light.

Madresk had never tested his ideas. Vohn obsessed about it for most of a year. When the Orduvian Flu returned that winter, worse than ever, it claimed Vohn's Father. Vohn began to hatch a scheme.

A month after Father was buried, Vohn went to the edge of the noktum in secret several nights in a row, preparing. First, he experimented with severing the tentacles. They looked like they were made of oily shadows, but once they grabbed something, they became as solid as flesh and blood.

With a dagger attached to a long staff, Vohn practiced to see if he could sever a tentacle with the dagger. It didn't work. The blade passed right through.

He tried flame. It was a dangerous experiment. Everyone knew not to bring torches close to the noktum. There were rumors of Shadowvar who had brought torches too close to the noktum and, crazed by the light, monsters had leapt outside just to extinguish it—and anyone who held it.

But Vohn kept a fast horse nearby, saddled and ready to go. And he had spent weeks crafting a circular piece of rough steel on a spindle set against a piece of flint. When spun with the thumb, the small device would cast a spark onto a tiny tuft of rag soaked in spirits. With this quick method of lighting a tiny torch, Vohn experimented, with his ten-foot staff, by burning the tentacles to see if they would recoil.

They did the opposite.

In a frenzy, they attacked the torch and extinguished it, but Vohn noticed something. The fire *did* hurt them. A few of the tentacles actually fell to the ground, burned away from their roots. But after the torch was a smoking ruin—in less than a second—the tentacles recovered their severed limbs and reabsorbed them.

Vohn got an idea.

On his third attempt, he heated the dagger until it was glowing hot, extended it on his staff, and cut at one of the lazily shifting tentacles. Not only did it slice clean through, but the glowing dagger didn't make the tentacles fly into a frenzy like open fire did.

Armed with his new knowledge, Vohn set up his experiment. After a week more of preparation, he had everything he needed for a brief peek into the noktum.

He found a secure outcropping of rock within twenty feet of the noktum wall. To this he tied a rope with enough slack to go ten feet beyond the wall.

He walked a good distance away from the noktum and built a small fire, keeping the flames low but the coals hot. When they were glowing red, he put them in a special, insulated steel container and capped it. The cap had a thin slit in the top, just wide enough for Vohn's dagger. He inserted the dagger into the coals, then tied the insulated container to his waist. It was unwieldy as a sheath, but workable.

He returned to his rock, tied the loose end securely about his waist, then marched into the tentacles. They wrapped around him and pulled him into the darkness.

Vohn planned to enter, see what he could see—or feel—then use the rope to pull himself out of the noktum. If the tentacles tried to stop him, he planned to draw the glowing knife and cut himself free.

Everything went to plan. He strode into the tentacles with one hand on the rope and one on the hilt of the sheathed dagger. Sweat beaded on his forehead even though the tentacles embraced him and pulled him into absolute darkness.

Vohn strained to see something, strained to hear the whispers he'd once imagined he'd heard.

And he did.

The Dark whispered to him, and this time he didn't run like the scared child he'd once been. He answered the whisper, asked her who she was.

The whisper filled him like it had been waiting for a decade. It raced through him, and all of Vohn's childhood fears, which he thought he had logically put behind him, rose like a twelve-foot wave over him. The excited whispers toppled him, spun him, churned him.

In the utter blackness, he groped for the rope, but he couldn't find it. He flailed, tried to draw his dagger, but he couldn't find that either. It was as though everything he wore, everything he'd prepared suddenly had no substance.

Or *he* didn't.

The whispers pushed him upward and he felt like he was flying. The thrill, and the fear, of freedom coursed through him. The wind rushed and just kept going and going. As he flew, his eyes slowly opened, and he began to be able to see in the darkness, to see with more than just his eyes, to see with the power of the darkness itself. The blackness resolved into a myriad of dark colors, indigos and purples, snatches of yellow and deep blue.

He didn't know how long his journey lasted. He swept through the entirety of the Great Noktum. He saw the land of the Nox. He saw a chasm that seemed to span the entire continent, its depths so dark even the noktum looked illuminated by comparison. He saw the edge of the noktum where the Lux had cracked it like a glass egg. He felt the power of an immense being hiding in a cavern near that place and avoided it at the behest of the whispers. He saw castles of old, vacant nuraghis awaiting masters who would never return. He saw the tiny filaments of the Great Noktum connected to every splatter of noktum across the entire continent of Noksonon.

It seemed like he traveled for years, perhaps for centuries, when he saw something that brought his journey to an end. A sparkle in the darkness caught his attention, a golden light on the head of a young Luminent, racing quickly hand in hand with a young Human woman. Before he could look closely at them, they left the noktum.

And that jogged a memory for Vohn. He had once lived beyond the noktum, too. That thought brought him closer to the ground for the first time in as long as he could remember. As he neared the ground where the two young women had been, he noticed sparkles there. He descended even lower to inspect them, and he found a singular amulet with the symbol of Noksonon engraved upon it. Aside from the girl with the golden hair, it was the only thing that seemed to have a flicker of natural light in this place, and it reminded him of his previous life.

He reached out with his intangible hand to touch the medallion and a lightning shock went through him.

Suddenly, he was back in his body. His indigo noktum-vision vanished, replaced by flesh-and-blood eyes, a flesh-and-blood body.

He gasped, gripping the amulet in his fist. He clutched it like it was the rope that he'd meant to use to pull himself out of the noktum a lifetime ago. With the amulet in hand, he was himself, he was Vohn and not the wind of the noktum.

He was close to the edge of the noktum, and he fled the same direction the two young women had. He burst into the sunlight of a bright day, gasping at the glorious warmth.

What he would only understand later was that he had traveled the length of Noksonon to emerge from a noktum just outside the crown city of Usara. Nokte Shaddark was nearly two thousand miles to the south.

And twenty years had passed.

But at the time, Vohn didn't know that. All he knew was his fear and the certain knowledge that he had nearly lost himself forever. If not for the girl with the golden hair and, subsequently, the amulet, he would have remained the wind of the noktum for another twenty—or two thousand—years.

The two young women, one Luminent and one Human, lean and muscled from living in the woods for half a decade, found him not long after that. They took care of him, helped him reintegrate with the world. The golden-haired Luminent's name was Lorelle, and her friend, Rhenn, claimed she was the rightful queen of the nearby kingdom of Usara.

They had a purpose, and Vohn had just lost the entirety of his life. So, he started a new one with them and soon their purpose became his purpose. While he eventually told the young women where he'd come from, he'd never told them how he'd come so far north, and they never asked.

Five years later, Khyven the Unkillable swore to chase down that golden-haired Luminent into the heart of the Great Noktum, and Vohn accompanied him into the place that frightened him more than anything else, a place where the amulet that had returned him to himself might fail. Once it did, Vohn knew he would have no protection against the whisper. That terrifying moment would come for him again, and this time it would claim him forever.

When the arrow struck Vohn's chest, that terrifying moment arrived at last.

CHAPTER FORTY-EIGHT

VOHN

When the arrow hit Vohn, he thought it was something else. Up to that moment, he'd been trying to calm the situation, find a way to keep it from becoming a bloodbath.

"Khyven," Vohn warned, trying to get the hot-tempered Ringer to stand down for once. There were too many questions unanswered to simply hack and slash. What if Lorelle had sent these sentries to look for them? Except this damned Shadowmaster was more interested in picking a fight. He needed just a few more moments of talking to draw the truth out.

"I understand my choices," Khyven said, oblivious, or uncaring, of the danger. "I don't think he understands his."

"Khyven!" Vohn warned again.

"Is that a dragon?" Slayter suddenly blurted, pointing up in the sky with his free hand. Vohn glanced that way, wondering what Slayter meant. It could have been an intentional attempt at distraction, but Vohn doubted that. Slayter was ridiculously literal for a man who had somehow been a spy in Vamreth's court for years. Most likely, the comment was a random thought that had escaped Slayter's constantly moving mind.

Or the third possibility, of course: there actually *was* a dragon.

That's when Vohn felt the sharp impact in his chest. He thought Khyven had elbowed him. The man was so hot-tempered and fast to react, Vohn assumed he'd pivoted back and wasn't watching where his big arm was flailing.

Then everything exploded into fire.

The blast knocked Vohn back and he slid to a stop on his back. Stunned, ears ringing, he belatedly realized several things at once.

First, there actually *was* a dragon.

Second, there was a fading nimbus of orange around his body and he couldn't feel the heat from the raging fire that had engulfed the forest where he'd just been. The mage had somehow protected them from the blast.

Third, it didn't make sense that Khyven had elbowed him in the chest. Didn't make sense at all. As volatile as Khyven was, the man was incredibly precise. He didn't flail. He targeted.

And finally, something long, thin, and dark was sticking out of his chest.

That's an arrow, Vohn thought. *I've been shot.*

He tried to sit up, but his body only got halfway there before he fell back to the ground. Slayter hobbled over to him and laboriously sat down next to him, awkwardly managing his prosthetic.

"Oh, well..." Slayter's hands fluttered over the shaft, but didn't touch it. "Well, that's... that's an arrow."

"Such a keen... mind," Vohn said, annoyed that his voice came out so weak. He also noticed he could barely draw a breath.

"I think maybe I could..." Slayter rifled through the cylinder of disks at his side. "I don't... I don't have anything."

"I... just need to sit up," Vohn said. Again, he tried but couldn't.

"Khyven!" Slayter called.

No answer.

"Khyven get over here," Slayter yelled again, worried this time. "Khyven!"

"I'll be fine," Vohn murmured, but Slayter's usually amused expression was solemn.

Khyven slid to his knees next to Vohn, that intense expression on his face that he always wore when in the midst of battle. He assessed Vohn and, unlike Slayter, his expression didn't change.

"I knew... I knew if I... was friends with you long enough, Khyven... it would be the death of me," Vohn joked.

"We need to get help," Khyven said. "We need Lorelle's medicine kit."

"We don't know where Lorelle is!" Slayter said.

"Then *someone's* medicine kit."

Vohn smiled. "You never give up, Khyven. I love that about you. You never give up..."

"Battle shock," Khyven growled. Something exploded to his right. Slayter winced, half-ducking his head behind his arm as bits of flame rained down on the grass around them, but Khyven didn't. He glared at the explosion like he was going to hurt it if it did that again.

Vohn giggled and his chest seized. It felt like a giant claw was squeezing it.

"I think... I've been shot," he tried to joke again, but neither of them laughed. They were so serious.

"We're going to run," Khyven said. "We're going to run like hell and hope that we can find help for him, otherwise..." He trailed off.

"Who are we going to find?" Slayter asked.

Khyven bent his lips into a smile that Vohn supposed was meant to be reassuring. "I'm going to pick you up, Vohn. You've got a... little wound here."

"Only a little one, eh?" Vohn asked. Finally, he'd got them joking.

"It's a bite. It'll pinch when I pick you up, but you stay awake, all right?"

"Stay… awake…" Now that Khyven mentioned it, Vohn felt very tired.

"Just stay awake," Khyven insisted.

"Yes… good idea."

Khyven gently put his arms beneath Vohn's knees and behind his shoulders.

"Khyven, I need a moment," Slayter said.

Khyven shook his head. "We have no moments. Keep up."

"Yes," Slayter said, casting about them. "Yes. Yes, of course." He grabbed a charred piece of the tree smoldering in the grass, winced at the heat, dropped it, then patted it with his ripped sleeve and picked it up again.

Khyven stood, lifting Vohn effortlessly, and started into a smooth jog around the burning edge of the forest. Slayter levered himself to his feet and pursued, head down and scratcher in hand. He was carving something into the charred part of the log.

"He's making a spell," Vohn murmured, but his voice came out odd, unintelligible. He wasn't sure if Khyven heard him. The Ringer stumbled, recovered, but the bounce made Vohn wince. Stars exploded in his vision.

"Stay with me, Vohn," Khyven warned.

"I'm right here…" Vohn's words came out garbled. Darkness followed the sparkles, and the world swirled away.

◆ ◆ ◆

He was jolted awake when he hit the ground. With a gasp, he felt the twist in his chest first. Pain. So much pain he couldn't breathe. He tried to look around, but he was so weak his head merely fell to the side. He blinked his eyes.

Houses smoldered to his left, burned down to the foundation. Beyond them, more structures flamed. A city. They hadn't been near a city before. The last he remembered, Khyven had been carrying him next to a burning forest. Something had happened. Vohn had lost consciousness and time had passed.

He tried to sit up, but his muscles were limp sails without a breeze. Sparkles rose in his vision, followed by sweltering black dots of unconsciousness, threatening to take him down, down, down. He felt a chilling foreboding about that. If he slipped into unconsciousness this time, it would be the last time.

He fought the sweltering black dots and managed to bring the indigo sky overhead into focus again. He tried to piece together his situation.

Vohn painstakingly turned his head and brought his hazy vision into focus.

A Nox woman was holding a dagger at the throat of a Nox man. To the right of them... Gods of Light and Dark! That towering creature was a Giant. Tovos! It had to be the Giant Rauvelos had warned them about, the one who was Lord over the Great Noktum.

The enormous creature looked at Khyven and Slayter with a sneer of disdain. Vohn's two friends were suspended in midair by some magical force holding their legs and arms pinned like they were swaddled in an invisible blanket.

"Khyven!" the Nox woman said, and she spoke with Lorelle's voice. With cold horror, Vohn realized the woman actually *was* Lorelle. What he'd rushed here to do, what he'd hoped to stop from happening had already happened. The Dark had taken her, had made her its own.

Khyven did what he always did, he fought. He struggled against the inevitable, but this wasn't some Ringer he was fighting. It was a Giant. Even Khyven couldn't fight Giant magic. Giants possessed the ability to use all five streams of magic at once. Even gods feared the Giants.

"No," Tovos commanded.

"Khyven!" Lorelle shouted, and she slashed the dagger across the Nox's throat.

If Vohn had had the strength, he would have screamed. Lorelle didn't kill people. She'd never killed anyone.

"I'm sorry..." the Nox whispered again, then his body slumped to the side. Lorelle sheathed her bloody dagger and walked stiffly to stand at the Giant's side. Khyven and Slayter also floated to the Giant, who opened his cloak.

Darkness coalesced around them, wrapping Khyven, Slayter, Lorelle, and the Giant into its folds. The darkness condensed, growing smaller and smaller, twisting into a convoluted ball.

And then they were gone.

Vohn was left alone with his predicament.

I am dying, he thought. *And no one can stop it.*

No one except me.

Again, Vohn tried to sit up, tried to roll over, tried to do anything, but all he managed to do was move his arms, hands weakly grasping at the grass. He had less strength than a newborn baby, and even that meager strength was waning. The swelling black spots returned and grew. It wouldn't be long now.

Unless...

Vohn suddenly had an idea, and a spike of fear came along with it. When he'd escaped the noktum five years ago, when he'd grasped the amulet that now rested against his chest, he'd sworn he would never take the amulet off again, never tempt the whispers of the noktum.

But the idea took hold. When Vohn had transformed into the dark wind, he hadn't aged. When he'd grasped the amulet and his physical body had reformed, twenty years had passed for the world, but not a second for his body.

That might stop my death. Becoming the wind might freeze my body in time.

The thought beat in his head like a heart, pumping, pumping...

He could become the wind, but he might lose himself forever. The terror of it gripped him, but if it worked, he might be able to do something to help his friends.

Vohn's hands trembled as he tried to make them move. He shouted, which came out as a pitiful, bloody gurgle. His shaking hands moved up, up, and grasped the chain on either side of the amulet.

Gurgling louder, blood coming from his mouth to trickle down his cheeks, he forced the amulet over his head and let it fall to the grass.

The effort sent lightning bolts of pain through him and his arms went limp. The black dots expanded over his vision. They grew and grew, covering him, and his eyes slid shut.

"Vohn…" the noktum whispered.

CHAPTER FORTY-NINE

LORELLE

Lorelle beat her hands against the door until they were bruised. She tried to escape through the window, but it was barred shut. She even tried—as loathe as she was to do it—to use the shadows to escape beneath the door. She'd never tried anything like that before, to move through a space that small, and it didn't work. The lantern just outside the door ensured there were no shadows to be seen.

Finally, she collapsed to the floor, exhausted, barely able to lift her arms. She drifted in and out of consciousness as she lay slumped against the cold stone. She didn't know how long she huddled there, the same thoughts circling through her broken mind over and over and over again.

Vohn was dead. Rhenn was dead. Zaith was dead by her own hand. She still bore the blood on her fingers, even though she'd wiped most of it on her dress.

Khyven and Slayter were imprisoned, and Tovos would never let any of them leave this place alive.

She'd come to the Great Noktum to achieve a singular goal: To collect the Plunnos and save Rhenn, to protect her family—

control the danger, limit the risk to herself alone so no one else got hurt.

It had been a long shot from the beginning, and there had been moments where she thought her quest had failed, like when the dragon had caught her, but then she had the Plunnos. She'd escaped death. All she needed was the knowledge to use it correctly. It had all seemed possible. She had envisioned returning to Usara in triumph, to show her friends she'd succeeded. To have everything go back to the way it was supposed to be.

But they'd followed her. Those beautiful fools had followed her into the Great Noktum. She hadn't controlled anything. She'd just dragged everyone she loved into a pit where they were going to die.

Lorelle had thought her life was over when Nhevaz had abducted Rhenn. She'd thought nothing else mattered. But she'd been so wrong.

Her unlikely family had been broken, yes. They'd been grieving, yes. But they'd still been there, and she hadn't acknowledged that simple miracle. And now, because of that, she'd destroyed it.

She pushed her fists against her head.

Just like she'd turned her attention away from protecting Rhenn at the most critical instant, she had turned away from Khyven, Slayter, and poor Vohn when they'd needed her most. They'd needed her to stay, to work with them, to allow them to help find Rhenn, and she'd abandoned them to do it herself.

Lotura's Eyes...

And now the Giant Tovos had her. Her bond to the Dark, so glorious at first, was actually a trap. Zaith had led her right into it. Tovos had used her.

She could still feel the jerky quivering of the short sword as she'd dragged it through Zaith's throat.

"Zaith..." she whimpered. She wanted to die. She deserved to die.

It was Vohn's voice that floated to the surface of her broken mind. Vohn's quiet voice. Vohn, whom she had killed.

"We do the best we can, and that's all we can do," she heard him say in that kindly, cultured voice of his. *"You did your best."*

"I shouldn't have run. We should have stayed together..." she murmured.

"There's still time..." Vohn's voice said.

"Not for you..." she murmured. "Not for you. You're dead."

"Not yet..."

Lorelle sat up. She'd been drifting in and out of consciousness, but she suddenly realized she wasn't just thinking about Vohn's voice. She was hearing it. It was... vibrating into her like the voice of the Dark.

It was *coming* from the Dark!

"Vohn?"

Something scratched at the door, so lightly that if she hadn't been right in front of the door she might have missed it. Something soft and light had definitely brushed against the steel.

Again, that whispering touch, and she saw the shadow of something move along the gap at the bottom.

A thin corner of black cloth slipped underneath. It rippled, as though touched by some wind. Except there was no wind.

"Take the cloak..." Vohn said in her head.

"Vohn?" she exclaimed. "Where are you?"

"No time..." Vohn said. *"Take the cloak... Tovos is coming. We have to move fast."*

She yanked the cloak under the doorway and it flowed through the tiny slit like water. She unfurled it and wrapped it around her shoulders. She felt the Dark now like she was standing in the deepest shadow, like the cloak was an extension of the noktum itself. It embraced Lorelle, flowed through her.

Except now that she knew Tovos controlled the Dark, she didn't *want* more connection to it. That connection had turned her into a slave and a murderer. What had comforted her before now made her skin crawl. The shadows oozed into her like oil and she flinched, waiting for Tovos to take control of her body again.

"Tell me you know how to use this," Vohn said through the Dark. His voice sounded much louder now.

But this time, there was no malice in the Dark. Tovos's insidious sentience didn't drive it. There was just warmth, comfort, power.

And the cloak amplified everything. Before, when she'd given herself over to the Dark, she could feel the nearest shadows, could slide from one to the other like liquid. She could feel others approaching through any shadows that were nearby. But with the cloak, it was as if an ocean of shadow lapped at the shore of her body, as though she could feel the entire noktum itself.

"By Lotura…" she murmured.

She could feel the entirety of the castle, could feel all the creatures within it whenever they touched any of the multitude of shadows within the keep as they moved about their business. She could feel Tovos high above in his tower, working magic. She could feel the stairs below her, the Wergoi moving about. She could feel the stairs going down and down into the dungeons below.

The five frayed, golden threads of her soul began to burn.

She could feel Khyven.

"Hold on," Lorelle murmured, and she wrapped the cloak around herself.

And fell into that ocean of darkness.

CHAPTER FIFTY

KHYVEN

K hyven stared through the bars. They were made of rough rock. In the noktum, of course, it was only a shade of dull gray to him, but he envisioned that the bars would be a dusky red if he could see them by daylight.

Outside the bars, an enormous creature with a Kyolar's body, skeletal wings, and the face of an owl paced back and forth. Smoky darkness wafted off its bony wings, and it never seemed to take its eyes off Khyven, as though he was the one it wanted. The thing never once looked at Slayter, who rested against the wall in the same cell.

Khyven stared back at the thing.

They'd killed Vohn. Khyven kept thinking over and over about that split second where he could have grabbed the Mavric iron blade with his free hand, but he'd hesitated because of the damned Nox. And then it had been too late. The shadows had slithered over his left arm and the opportunity was gone.

Now he wondered about Zaith's sudden realization about Khyven being the "Greatblood" the Giant was "looking for."

Had it been a genuine warning that Khyven simply didn't understand? Or had the wily Nox betrayed him, distracting him with cryptic warnings long enough for Khyven and Slayter to be captured?

Well, he wouldn't hesitate next time. If he could just get to that Mavric iron sword again, he'd see just how well it could cut through Giant magic.

Khyven leaned against the bars, glaring at the monster that glared back at him. He heard the song of violence in his mind, in his heart, and he was tempted to get up and pace just to mock the thing.

A battle with that owl-headed lion was surely coming, but the final gatekeeper in this place was the Giant Tovos. And there would be no mercy from that thing, Khyven could tell at a glance. He hadn't looked at Khyven and Slayer like they were people. He'd looked at them like they were turds on the bottom of his boots.

Khyven had known men like that. Powerful Ringers who'd looked down on Khyven when he was just a newbie in the Night Ring. Cruel masters who had tried to undermine Khyven before his bouts. Whenever Khyven had seen that same derisive expression on an enemy's face, he'd known the lay of the land. Fight your way out or die.

If Khyven remained useful—and Slayter, for that matter—to Tovos, then they would be allowed to live. But the moment they weren't, like that poor bastard Zaith, they'd suffer the same fate.

Slayter limped over to the bars. "Why are you staring at that creature?"

"'Cause he's staring at me."

Slayter raised an eyebrow. "If your goal is to intimidate it, I don't think it's working."

"How do you know?"

Slayter glanced at the monster, then back at Khyven, then back at the monster.

"That's actually a good point. I wonder if he's intelligent."

"Because that's important."

"I agree."

"That was sarcasm."

"Ah."

Khyven ignored Slayter and looked at his weapons hanging on pegs just outside the cell. The dwarves had taken away everything but Khyven's and Slayter's clothes before the shadow tentacles threw them into the cell. But they were within easy reach once they got past these bars. That was an advantage.

All Khyven had to do was get past the lion-owl.

"It would be nice if there was a door to the cell," Slayter said.

That was a disadvantage. There was no door to the cell. The shadows had somehow teleported them inside, and there was no way out except, Khyven supposed, the shadows taking them back again.

When they'd first arrived, even after they'd taken Slayter's clay disks away, the mage had tried to create a spell by tracing lines in the rough rock. He hadn't been successful yet.

"The floor isn't going to work for magic, eh?" Khyven asked.

"They took my scratcher. This rock is porous and uneven and hard. Even with my scratcher, I doubt I could have made a precise enough line. It would take me a very long time to hack something out of this stone with bare hands, and as much time to destroy it after."

"Can't you just make the design on the air?"

"Yes. But I've always been bad at that form of Line Magic. It's... sloppy."

"Maybe now's the time to get better."

"I'm saving my one spell for the right moment."

"You make a hole in the bars; I'll get that sword. Once I do, we'll have a fighting chance."

"I doubt it. I know it's your nature to dismiss physical challenges, but that's a naguil. I feel like a better moment is coming. I'm waiting for that moment."

"A better moment?"

"A better moment," Slayter repeated as though Khyven hadn't heard him.

"You think the moments are going to get better from here on?" Khyven asked.

"Well, we get one shot. It costs the same amount of energy for me to do a properly crafted spell as it does for a sloppy one. The only difference is that the properly crafted spell will be strong and the improperly crafted spell will be weak. And if it's sloppy *enough*, it might fail altogether. Writing on air requires a certain kind of imagination that... Well, my spell would be sloppy. And I'm pretty sure I'll be unconscious on the floor afterward. So, I'm waiting for a better moment."

"Fine."

"Don't be angry at yourself."

"Angry at myself?"

"I saw you hesitate. You could have drawn the Mavric iron blade back at the Nox city, but you stopped because the Nox warned you not to. You're angry at yourself for that. Don't be. He was right."

"How do you know?"

"Obviously he was trying to tell us something. Something only he knew. Something Tovos did not."

"Well, neither do we."

"Just because we don't understand the message doesn't mean it's unimportant. Tovos doesn't know it either, I'd wager. That fact alone makes it valuable. Whatever Zaith's secret is, it's powerful. Barbarically hacking at Tovos with a magic sword would have been an effort in futility. But whatever Zaith was talking about?" Slayter shook his head speculatively. "It might be an arrow pointed at Tovos's heart. It might be. When fighting a Giant, knowledge is power, Khyven."

"But you don't have any idea what he was talking about."

"Not the slightest. But I could smell the potency of it. It's making my nose twitch. Greatbloods..."

"Have you ever heard that term before?"

He shook his head. "But I've never looked, either. I wish I had my library."

"Well, I hope you're right. And I hope we can figure it out, because if we don't, then—"

A knot of darkness coalesced next to the owl-faced lion. It was about three feet in diameter with thick, dark, muscly threads. The knot expanded, then vanished and suddenly Lorelle stood in the chamber, ten feet from the monster.

Her eyes widened as she saw it. "Well, that didn't work," she said.

The monster shrieked and charged her.

Lorelle slid sideways with the mastery of a seasoned Ringer, her dark cloak flaring, and the great claws slashed through the shadows where she'd been. Khyven tried to follow her with his gaze, but he couldn't. She stepped back into the shadows near the bars and vanished.

The creature shrieked again, spinning, searching.

Khyven watched, his gaze flicking left and right. Slayter stood at the bars right next to him, doing the same.

Something touched Khyven on the shoulder and he whirled around. Lorelle now stood in the cell with them.

"That's better," she said.

The owl-faced lion shrieked and slammed into the bars.

Lorelle motioned them closer. Both Khyven and Slayter scrambled toward her, then Khyven spun around.

"Wait, the sword!" Khyven pointed at the Mavric iron blade. "We need that sword!"

She looked in the direction of the weapons hanging on the wall.

"We have to leave it," she said tersely. "Hold onto me. I think this is going to hurt." Reluctantly, Khyven grabbed one of Lorelle's arms and Slayter grabbed the other. She flung an edge of the voluminous cloak over each of them just as the owl-faced lion slammed into the bars again and shrieked.

Complete darkness enveloped Khyven. Slayter vanished. Lorelle vanished. The cell went away. He felt like he was swirling in a whirlpool of black water, spiraling down, down, head-first into a tube that was far smaller than his body.

Senji's Teeth, not this again, he thought as it squeezed him, squeezed his head into a space where a quill pen would barely fit. He screamed, but no sound came out. His body was being pulped to death, and funneled into a meaty twist of skin and blood.

Just when he thought he would go mad with the pain, he came out the other side. The darkness slid away and he stood in the place where they'd fought Tovos. The burned city of Nox Arvak smoldered behind the slumped corpse of Zaith.

Khyven held his arms out for balance. His bones felt like noodles. He staggered, teetering on the edge of falling, then his body became solid again.

He glanced over at Slayter, who wobbled, fell to his knees, and threw up on the grass.

Lorelle stood there, wincing as though she, too, was feeling the same effects. She motioned them closer.

Slayter looked up, vomit dripping from his chin. He shook his head. "A moment." He threw up again.

"Come here now, or we're dead," Lorelle said.

"We can't just leave Vohn's body..." Khyven said, then trailed off as he cast about the glade. Zaith was still where he'd fallen, but Vohn was missing.

"Where is he?"

"Khyven, come here now."

"Where's Vohn?"

She ran to him, on the verge of tears. "I know I don't deserve it," she said, "but you have to trust me. Vohn is... taken care of."

"What does that mean?"

"Khyven! I'm almost certain Tovos can track us if we use the cloak inside his castle. We just did. Which means the moment he notices what happened, he'll follow us here. But I don't think he can track us if we go from this place to another place. At the very least, it will be harder. So, we need to get away from this place."

Khyven opened his mouth, then snapped it shut. He picked up the still-vomiting Slayter around the waist with one arm. Lorelle flared the cloak around them both.

The darkness swallowed them again, and the excruciating whirlpool began all over, turning Khyven into a boneless piece of meat shoved through a straw. He screamed soundlessly.

They appeared on another field, charred woods before them. Slayter continued to throw up, dangling from Khyven's arm. Bile rose in his own throat and he shoved it down.

"One more," Lorelle gasped.

"One more?" Khyven said.

"So he can't follow us."

"Senji's Piss," Khyven cursed. Slayter moaned. The cloak wrapped around them again. It took longer this time, the swirling and the squeezing and the squishing down to paste.

Then knives sliced him. Or that's what it felt like. The tube was suddenly laced with razors.

The razors slashed. Khyven screamed and screamed without a sound. It went on and on.

The darkness vanished. The stinging, excruciating pain of the razor blades raced down his back, down his front, down his arms, and he twitched on the ground.

Slowly, the pain receded, and when he had mastered himself enough to look around, he saw Lorelle on one side of him, also on all fours, vomiting. On the other side, Slayter dry-heaved.

"I'm sorry," Lorelle breathed. "That wasn't supposed to… I didn't know that would happen. That was… I think that was the Lux."

Khyven staggered to his feet and turned, wiping his mouth with his sleeve—

His hand froze halfway across his mouth, then fell to his side. A mountain of gold and jewels the size of a three-story house rose to the high, stalactite-studded ceiling. They were in some massive treasure cavern! Wide-eyed, he looked at Lorelle, then back at the unbelievable treasure.

"Is that real?" Khyven asked.

"It's a dragon hoard."

"The dragon that just burned the Nox city?"

"Khyven, I'll tell you everything. I promise, but this isn't the place."

Khyven had never seen such wealth. He'd never even imagined such wealth. "We have a lot to talk about," he said to her.

"But first, we have to escape."

"We're *teleporting* again?" Khyven shook his head. "No."

Slayter held up a hand, nodded agreement, then dry-heaved again.

"I'm not going into that cloak again," Khyven said.

"Not the cloak." She pointed up and to her right. A stairway cut into the side of the rough walls went nearly to the ceiling, and at the top stood a Thuros, colors swirling inside, just like one in Usara.

She flipped open her pouch and withdrew the Plunnos.

"Senji's Boots, you found it…" Khyven murmured. "And it works?"

"Enough to get us back home."

Khyven let out a relieved breath. "All right. That is the best news I've ever heard. Please tell me it feels better than the cloak."

"Much better. Weird, but better."

"Weird how?"

"Like you're being dipped in oil."

Khyven contemplated that for a half-second, then nodded. "I'll take that over the slashing tube of death."

Slayter finally stopped retching and Khyven held him until he was steady on his prosthetic.

Slayter limped to the base of the treasure pile.

"Come on. We've got to get up those stairs," Khyven said.

Slayter ignored him and picked up a thick, glowing red chain with a manacle on one end. The links were big as his wrists, and the manacle was large enough to close around Khyven's thigh.

"Do you know what this is?" Slayter whispered. "I told you about this! The day Lorelle vanished. This is a Dragon's Chain!"

"Not the time, Slayter."

"I don't think we should stay here," Lorelle said, looking and sounding exhausted. Her shoulders were stooped, her head bent, and her black hair drooped on either side of her face. The noktum cloak hung around her body as though mimicking her hair. "I won't feel safe until we're far away from the Great Noktum. Tovos rules here. He is master of everything in this darkness. I don't think he can track us here, and I think the dragon is gone, but don't know any of that for certain."

"But there's so much to explore," Slayter said. He had picked up a jewel-encrusted chalice, turning it back and forth as though he was trying to look *through* it. "The magical artifacts that might be found here..." he murmured.

"Maybe we can return," Lorelle said.

Slayter eyed the treasure, his face alight with a desire to *know*. Khyven swore the mage would jump off a cliff just to see what was at the bottom. Slayter had said Zaith's secret made his nose twitch. This room had to be making Slayter's entire body twitch.

But, reluctantly, Slayter limped over to them, clutching the coils of glowing red chain against this chest. "I'm taking this."

"We'll come back," Khyven said. He looked at Lorelle, at her new face, her new hair. She was acting like the Lorelle he'd known, someone who cared about her friends, someone who would spring her friends from a prison, but...

"And what about Vohn?" Khyven asked.

"It's... complicated. But I think we might be able to save him."

"*Save* him? He's alive? Where is he?"

She gave a weary smile. "In fact, he's talking to me right now. He says you should—"

"Talking to you?"

"He says you should shut up and listen to me." She gave them a weary smile.

"Lorelle, how?" Khyven asked.

"The Dark. There's... so much we don't know about the noktum. Vohn says... He says you should trust me, that we should go. And now."

"*Can* I trust you?" Khyven asked. "Are you even still Lorelle?" He gestured at her ripped and bedraggled party dress, at her midnight skin and raven hair. "Can I?"

"I don't know," she whispered brokenly, absently pulling at the cloak. "I don't trust myself anymore. Not here in the noktum, at least. But I swear to you, I'll get you and Slayter back to Usara safely."

"And Vohn."

She closed her eyes, then opened them again. "Yes, and Vohn."

"We're going to talk," he said. "A lot. When we get back."

Tears welled her eyes. "By Lotura, I swear it. Everything and more." She reached out a hand toward him, like she wanted to touch him, then hesitated and started to let her hand fall.

He caught it before it did, held it. "You should have told me," he whispered. "About the bond. I'd have done it."

Her tears spilled over and ran down her cheeks. "I know," she whispered. "I know you would have…" She trailed off. "I… I just couldn't risk it. I couldn't risk Rhenn's life on my own hope you would succeed."

He squeezed her hand. "All right. It's all right. We'll talk about it later." He put his arm around Slayter to help him up the stairs. "Let's go home."

"You aren't going anywhere," a deep, dark voice said from behind them.

Khyven whirled, pushing Slayter away and reaching for his sword—

That wasn't there.

Stooped and gritting his teeth as though he'd just pushed out of teleportation hell, Tovos emerged from the shadows beneath the staircase.

CHAPTER FIFTY-ONE

KHYVEN

Khyven bared his teeth. The blue wind swirled around Tovos, a deep, dark blue. Every time the wind turned dark, it meant the danger was greater, the strike deadlier. Khyven had never seen the entirety of the wind this dark blue.

He wanted to leap at the Giant, to fight like he'd never fought before, to give Lorelle and Slayter a chance to escape.

But he had no weapon.

He glanced past the Giant at the mountain of treasure. Jeweled hilts stuck up from the gold. Khyven slowly, carefully sidled away from his friends.

The Giant might be powerful, but if they could flank him, they might be able to gain a tactical advantage. Now he really wished they'd spent that extra second to grab the Mavric iron sword. The way Khyven figured it, a sword forged by Giants probably had the best chance to kill Giants.

"I'm going to gut you," Khyven growled.

"You have nothing that can even hurt me," the Giant said. "You are weaponless."

The Mavric iron sword dropped from the air and stuck into the rock step in front of Khyven's foot. It wobbled back and forth, the hilt vibrating next to Khyven's hand, and it whined excitedly in his mind.

Khyven stared at the thing, dumbfounded.

Never once in his days as a Ringer had he wasted an opportunity. If an enemy stumbled into Khyven's path, Khyven didn't trip over them, he used them as a step. If a dagger spun past his face, Khyven didn't flinch, he grabbed the weapon and hurled it back. He had trained himself to instinctively push past surprise at good fortune or bad and to use it to its highest advantage, because to waste even a second might cost him his life.

But he stared at that Mavric sword, which had literally appeared out of nowhere.

Lucky for Khyven, Tovos also stared at it, like he was trying to comprehend why the sky and the ground had suddenly switched places.

Three things happened at once.

Lorelle shouted, "Vohn!"

Slayter laughed.

Khyven snapped out of his stupor and snatched the hilt.

The heat of the sword's dark power flowed into him, burrowed into his muscles and his bones. The six-foot blade leapt to guard position.

"Go!" he shouted, and he charged the Giant. "Get out of here!"

Khyven suspected he wasn't going to defeat Tovos through skill, but he didn't need to prove he was the better swordsman. All he needed to do was fight the creature long enough for Lorelle and Slayter to get through the Thuros.

And a one-in-a-hundred lucky shot might put a crimp in the Giant's arrogance.

Khyven let his eyes lose focus, keeping only a vague awareness of the steps and ground and treasure pile, so his inner eye could better see the blue wind.

The wind wove before him, different this time, more complicated than it had ever been before. Three blue spears launched from Tovos and a blue funnel opened up on the Giant's shoulder, but something new appeared, too. A glowing blue step hovered three feet in the air, just in front of Khyven.

He didn't question. He surrendered himself to the wind and leapt at the step.

Though there was no step there in real life, Khyven's foot hit it, and it was as though the air was solid beneath his foot.

He propelled himself high, spinning as two of the blue spears just missed him.

The sword whined, and the whine turned into a word.

"Good..."

Khyven flew at Tovos, and the Giant looked surprised. Khyven brought the Mavric iron sword down with all his strength, shearing through the metal plate protecting Tovos's shoulder. It cut through metal, flesh, and stuck in the bone.

Tovos screamed.

Khyven flipped over the huge shoulder, using the static blade to whip his body around and slam his feet into the Giant's back. Tovos screamed again as Khyven kicked hard and ripped the blade free. He flipped backward and landed on his feet at the edge of the gold pile.

Tovos's brows furrowed in fury, bunching inhumanly large folds of flesh above his blazing eyes as he turned and gestured at Khyven. A spell. Perhaps the same crushing, paralyzing shadow spell the Giant had used before.

The blue wind formed a shield in front of Khyven, and he instinctively whipped the sword up to align with the hovering blue light. Something Khyven couldn't see hit the sword and the blade vibrated, sending the impact up Khyven's arms.

In Khyven's mind, the sword's whine sounded suspiciously like laughter.

Whatever spell the Giant had thrown died on the Mavric iron.

Three funnels opened on the Giant. At his knee, in his gut, and on his throat.

Khyven surged forward, and the Giant's eyebrows shot up in surprise. His left arm hung limp at this side. He shouted and made another gesture.

Seven thin spears launched at Khyven, preceded by a blue wave. Another blue step appeared and Khyven jumped on it, launching himself over the blue wave.

He swayed and twisted, but three of the thin spears grazed him. An instant later, three slivers of metal cut him as they flew by. One on the thigh, one along his side, and one on his left shoulder. They all hurt; none were mortal.

Khyven flew over the blue wave. A split second later, a chunk of volcanic rock erupted from the floor like it had turned to water, then turned back to rock as it tried to crush Khyven.

It missed him, but Khyven was forced to change his course, and the blue funnels flickered and faded as he landed, rolled to his feet, and charged the Giant.

Tovos snarled, his good hand pointing at Khyven like a claw. Dozens of thin spears launched at him—

Tovos screamed. Lorelle materialized out of shadow, standing on his shoulder, a jeweled dagger buried to the hilt in his neck.

The dozens of blue spears flickered and vanished, and half a dozen funnels opened up on the Giant. Khyven stabbed at them.

There was a thunderous clash of metal on metal. A ripple of red light flashed out from the Giant. The whole cavern shook.

Khyven lost his footing and stumbled. The blue funnels on Tovos flickered and vanished. A stalactite crashed to the ground and dust sifted down from the ceiling.

"I got him," Slayter shouted. "I got him! I got him!" Khyven flicked a glance down at the Giant's feet and spotted the mage. He was kneeling next to one of the Giant's great boots, and he'd just fastened the glowing red manacle of the Dragon's Chain around Tovos's left ankle.

Tovos roared and swatted at Lorelle, but she vanished, leaving the jeweled dagger sticking out of his neck.

More funnels opened up on the Giant. Khyven circled, ready to pounce.

"No! Don't touch him! Don't touch him!" Slayter shouted, scrambling on his back like a crab, trying to get clear of the Giant.

Tovos snarled, clenched both fists, and pointed them at Khyven. His eyes blazed as he gestured, and Khyven whipped up his sword, bracing himself for the spell.

But no spears of blue wind came. No spell triggered.

"What?" Tovos roared. He made another gesture, this one at Slayter, but nothing happened.

"Get away! Get away!" Slayter said, and Khyven jumped back, giving the Giant a wide berth.

"I will crunch your bones with my teeth!" Tovos snarled, and he lunged at Khyven. A blue shape, roughly the size of Tovos, flew at Khyven. He dove to the side as the Giant swiped at him, but Tovos came to the end of the chain—which was suspended in midair, tight like it was attached to something Khyven couldn't see—and it pulled the Giant up short.

Khyven rolled to his feet, just out of range.

"Leave him. Don't touch him!" Slayter repeated.

"What did you do?" Khyven asked.

"The Dragon's Chain!" Slayter said excitedly. "I didn't know if it would work on a Giant. But elder dragons *are* Giants, so I thought it might and it did!"

Lorelle materialized from the dark next to Khyven, looking dead on her feet.

"I told you," Slayter said excitedly. "Giant magic. Made by Giant wizards. It was meant to hold a dragon."

"You're all going to die!" Tovos roared and spun about, grabbing at the glowing red chain. The links swelled, growing larger, thicker, as thick as Tovos's arms as he strained against it.

"How long?" Khyven asked.

"How long what?" Slayter asked.

"How long will it keep him chained?"

Slayter's chuckle bubbled up his throat like a burp. "A thousand years," he blurted.

"A thousand years!"

"Just don't touch him. You touch him and the spell will… Look, just don't touch him."

"What about his magic?"

"No magic. All he can use is his physical strength. And that won't break the chain."

"Slayter, you're brilliant!" Lorelle said.

"I *tried* to tell you," he said.

"So, we don't touch him. That's all we have to do?" Khyven asked.

"Yes."

"Then let's leave," Lorelle said. All three of them started up the stairs.

Tovos hauled on the chain, kicked at the air. The chain didn't budge. He tried another spell—or that's what Khyven assumed from the forceful hand gesture.

Nothing.

They were halfway up the stairs when Tovos turned his red-eyed gaze on them.

"You're not going anywhere, Lorelle of the Dark," he growled.

Lorelle stumbled. "No!" she said in a strangled voice, then fell to her knees on the steps.

"Lorelle!" Khyven knelt next to her. She crouched, twitching, as though her limbs were fighting themselves.

"I thought you said he couldn't use spells!" Khyven shot a glance at Slayter.

The mage looked worried. "I-I don't know," he said. "He shouldn't be able to. I…"

Khyven turned to Lorelle in time to see a line of blue wind slash at him. He lurched backward, another dagger, clenched tightly in Lorelle's hand, swept past his belly, barely missing him.

"Khyven!" she shouted, anguished. Her face had gone slack, but her voice was raw. She turned and started down the stairs one stilted step at a time.

"Come here, Lorelle," Tovos commanded. "Touch my hand."

CHAPTER FIFTY-TWO

LORELLE

he Dark took hold of Lorelle again, and Tovos
smothered her control.

"No!" She fell to the steps.

"Lorelle!" Khyven knelt next to her.

She fought it. Lotura's Mercy, she fought it with everything
she had, but her soul belonged to the Dark. She'd given herself
to it.

And Tovos controlled the Dark.

"I thought you said he couldn't use spells!" Khyven said.

He doesn't have to cast a spell, she thought. *He doesn't have to cast
anything. I bound myself to him. I'm part of him.*

"I don't know," Slayter said. "I-I don't know. He shouldn't
be able to. I…"

Run! Lorelle tried to shout the word. It was such a simple
word. She should have been able to shout something so simple,
but it wouldn't come out. Instead, her body jerked to life,
drawing her dagger and stabbing at Khyven. She felt Tovos's
desire to kill him, to see his guts spill out on the steps.

But Khyven was fast. Lotura be praised, he was so fast. Somehow, he saw the strike coming. The dagger slashed through air, just missing him.

Run! she tried to shout again, but it came out as, "Khyven!"

"Come here, Lorelle," Tovos commanded again. "Touch my hand."

Her body started down the steps. Now she couldn't see Khyven or Slayter anymore, and while she prayed they'd leave her and save their own lives, she knew they wouldn't.

A muffled whisper slithered through the dark, a tiny voice behind the weight of Tovos's domination. She recognized it, the only other voice that spoke to her through the Dark, vibrating in that strange way that translated into words in Lorelle's mind.

Vohn.

He was trying to help her! But he was such a small wisp compared to the thudding strength of Tovos's voice.

She focused on Vohn, made way for him, like a tunnel through the Dark, and the word became clear.

"Bond," Vohn whispered to her.

Her anger flared at Vohn stating the obvious. Yes, she had soul-bonded with the Dark. She didn't need him to explain that. She needed a solution—

Then it hit her.

Vohn wasn't stating the obvious. He didn't mean her bond to the Dark. He meant her previous bond to Khyven. He was pointing at what she had ignored. The five burning threads!

She dove into herself, found those five burning threads, that small, frayed part of her soul that remained unattached to the darkness.

They glowed fiercely, hating Tovos's control as much as Lorelle did.

Those threads still longed to reunite with the other half of her soul within Khyven. They had been screaming his name ever since that moment. That was why his name was the only word she could say when Tovos took control of her. Those threads were free of the Giant's influence. They wanted one thing: the only thing they'd ever wanted.

She felt a strong hand grab her arm.

"You can't have her," Khyven snarled, hauling her to a stop.

Her body spun into the grab, the dagger slashing out, but Khyven caught her wrist. He twisted. Nerves fired and her body reflexively let go. The dagger clattered to the steps and Khyven slipped behind her. His strong arms wrapped around her waist, pinning her left arm while his right wedged itself under her shoulder and around her neck, immobilizing her right arm.

"Kill him!" Tovos commanded.

The Dark surged inside her, and her body fought Khyven like a feral cat, twisting, thrashing, kicking. Khyven wrapped his legs around hers and they fell to the wide, flat steps.

"Not this time," he said through his teeth, immobilizing her. "I'm not letting you go this time."

"Lorelle!" Tovos thundered. "Come here!"

Tovos strengthened his hold, and her body struggled vainly against Khyven's strong grip.

"If we go, we go together," he growled. "We stay together."

Lorelle ignored him, ignored Tovos. She let him have control of her body and plunged deep inside herself, deep into her soul, into those five burning threads.

She vaguely felt Tovos making her body fight Khyven, but all she saw was darkness and those glowing threads.

And then something else pierced that darkness.

Above her, something glowed blue, something that wasn't *her* five threads, but blue threads, twisting downward, questing. There were only ten of them, and they seemed timid and thin compared to her five thick golden threads. The blue threads looked querulous, lost, searching in the dark.

It was Khyven! He was attempting the soul-bond! The blue threads were his soul reaching out to her!

Her consciousness had been huddled low around the final five threads, protecting their golden glow like she would protect a fire in the wind, but now she let them go. She released all control, letting them do what they had longed to do for weeks.

The golden threads shot desperately into the darkness to intertwine with the blue. The moment the first golden thread touched the first blue thread, all the blue threads quivered and coiled like snakes on the golden threads. Two to one, the blue threads wrapped tightly around the golden.

As soon as they twined together, blue and golden light exploded like a multicolored bonfire and chased back the shadows, illuminating the black threads of her soul, revealing the entirety of the tapestry.

The gold and blue threads wove deeper and deeper into the black threads, turning a third of the black threads gold and blue.

It disrupted her bond with the Dark, and the force of Tovos's commands shuddered under this new power.

Lorelle gasped and opened her eyes, her real eyes. She could see the cavern, the stalactites, Khyven's face above hers, holding her tightly. Lotura, she could feel *herself* again. Khyven still had his large body wrapped around hers, arms and legs and even his head against her collarbone. But her body had stopped fighting him. Her body. Hers.

"Lorelle!" Tovos shouted. The Dark surged within her, but it couldn't dominate her this time. The blue-and-gold threads rose up and fought in a way she'd never been able to before.

Tovos tried to make her limbs move. She countered him. Khyven noticed she'd stopped struggling.

"Lorelle?" he whispered in her ear. She craned her neck and looked him in the eyes, those deep brown eyes that were so similar to her own.

"Khyven..." she whispered, the one word, the easiest word to say. But she could say more now. "You bonded with me!"

"I told you I would."

"It threw off his control."

"That's what I was hoping." He winked.

"I think I love you."

A grin spread across his face. "Took you a while."

"Lorelle!" Tovos thundered. "Take my hand!"

"I really want to cut that bastard's head off," Khyven said. "But let's not touch him."

"Slayter's a smart guy."

"Let's do as he says."

"Let's."

"You'll have to carry me," she said. "He's still... so strong. I don't know if I trust myself to run."

"You hold him off. I'll hold you."

He gathered her in his arms and stood.

"We're going?" Slayter looked up from where he'd been trying to chip a symbol in the rough steps with the edge of a jeweled chalice.

"We're going," Khyven said. Slayter blew out a relieved breath and limped up the stairs.

"My pouch. The Plunnos." The Dark surged inside Lorelle. She winced but managed to fend him off. Still, her strength was waning. "Quickly."

They reached the landing and Khyven set her in front of the swirling lights of the Thuros. His hands flipped open her pouch and found the Plunnos. "What do I do?"

"Throw it at the colors," Slayter said.

Khyven didn't hesitate. He flipped the Plunnos dead center at the archway. It clinked against the colors and bounced back into his waiting palm.

"This has been educational," Slayter said, "but I think I'm done with the noktum for a while." He hobbled into the colors and vanished.

"Lorelle!" Tovos's voice thundered throughout the cavern. His black, oily presence surged over the golden threads of her soul and he broke her will for a moment.

Her body twitched, but Khyven grabbed her, hefted her into his arms as she thrashed, and charged into the swirling colors.

CHAPTER FIFTY-THREE

LORELLE

Lorelle watched the dancing flame of the candle on her nightstand. It didn't cast any shadows, she had made sure of that. Her room was filled wall to wall with bright lanterns, and only the barest hint of shadows had room to grow between the many light sources. Though the night was dark outside, there was no shadow bigger than her little finger in the entirety of her room.

She crouched in the corner, exhausted, but unable to sleep. It had been two days since Khyven had carried her through the Thuros, away from her horrible mistake. It had been two days since she'd murdered Zaith, two days since she had nearly killed everyone she loved.

She wanted to die. She thought a lot about suicide.

She'd murdered a man, had slit Zaith's throat. She still felt the short sword in her hand. Felt the thrum up her arms as it cut deep. Felt it over and over again.

Her heavy-lidded eyes stayed fixed on the candle, the guilt and remorse burning through her like she'd ripped her soul in half again.

Since they had returned from the Great Noktum, she'd refused to leave her room. Shadows frightened her. She kept expecting Tovos to emerge from them, to take control of her again and make her do something horrible.

So, she surrounded herself with lights, never sleeping, barely eating. Her friends had come by, knocked at the door, left food, tried to talk to her, but she wouldn't look at them. She couldn't face them, any of them, after what she'd done.

She even pushed away her burning desire to find Rhenn. In her blind desire to chase one friend, she'd almost killed the rest. She shrank from the idea of chasing after Rhenn like she shrank from the shadows.

She huddled into herself, clasping her knees to her chest, keeping her back to the wall and staring at the candle.

Her body ached with the need for sleep, but she couldn't close her eyes.

Every single thing she had done in the Great Noktum had been a disaster. Bonding with the Dark, giving Tovos control of her. Trusting Zaith.

And the dragon...

She'd had a chance to keep the dragon confined for another thousand years, and she'd set him loose instead. All those lives... All those innocent Nox, burning, dying. Aravelle. Maid Hoxa. Zaith's family. Everyone... All because of her.

And now, because of her, Vohn lingered in some half hell, bonded with the noktum like she had been, except worse. His body was gone. He *was* the Dark, no more than a wind and a voice.

A knock sounded on the door.

She blinked heavily but kept staring at the candle. She knew it was Khyven. He checked on her almost every hour. She felt the bond with him flare when she saw him, joyous at his nearness, but she didn't deserve joy. She deserved to die.

She expected him to be there, but she suddenly realized her soul-bond was not reacting to the person on the other side of the door. It wasn't Khyven. Slayter? But no, if it was Slayter, the knock would have been irregular, excited. The mage was always excited about everything he did, it seemed.

She briefly wondered who it might be, but the curiosity withered within her, just like everything else. It didn't matter. She didn't want to talk to anyone.

"Go away," Lorelle said quietly.

There was a brief silence, then Shalure opened the door. She squinted at the bright light and stepped inside.

Shalure?

She was the last person Lorelle had expected to see.

The baron's daughter entered and gracefully pushed the door shut behind her. She looked amazing. Her tumbling auburn hair was washed and pushed back from her forehead with a light blue bow. Her dress was of the same blue and hugged her curvy body, belted at the waist by a black belt hung with pouches.

The vague, naked woman floating on a haze of *shkazat* smoke was gone. She actually looked like her old self. Young and vital and beautiful.

Shalure squinted around the room like she was counting the bright lights, then turned a sad look on Lorelle. Shalure held up her hand. In it was Lorelle's weather-beaten little journal.

Shalure raised her other hand and carefully formed two symbols with her fingers.

Thank you.

She tucked the book into a pouch on her belt.

"You learned the language," Lorelle said.

Shalure carefully made several symbols.

I had some time on my hands.

"I'm happy for you," Lorelle said. "Now would you please leave?" She didn't want to talk to anyone right now, least of all Shalure.

But Shalure didn't leave. Her fingers were moving again. The first word took longer as she had to spell it out letter by letter.

K-H-Y-V…

"Khyven," Lorelle interrupted, supplying the name for her.

Shalure nodded, and she made more symbols with both hands.

He told me what happened.

"I don't want to talk about it."

Shalure thought a moment, then pulled out the book and flipped through the pages. She snapped it shut a moment later, looked back at Lorelle and made more hand motions.

I promise not to say a single word about it.

Shalure's lips made a ghost of a smile, and Lorelle clenched her teeth.

"Thank you for visiting me," Lorelle said, "but I don't need your help. I don't want your help."

I know.

"Then leave."

No.

Shalure crossed the room and sat on the bed near where Lorelle crouched against the wall. It was all Lorelle could do not to scream. She wanted to fling all the loathing she felt for herself at Shalure.

You gave me something, she gestured. *I've come to give it back.*

"You can keep the book."

Not the book.

Lorelle frowned. "What do you want then?"

Khyven told me what happened. He told me about your friend.

"Shalure, I'm not going to talk about…"

But Shalure's hands were moving fast, almost frantic in the effort to get the words out.

I'm so sorry. I'm so sorry that happened.

Lorelle felt the grief and sadness rise up all over again. She felt her hand on Tovos's dagger. She felt the jerk and resistance as Zaith's throat gave…

"Just go." Lorelle looked away. "If you want to pay me back for the book, then just leave me alone."

Shalure gestured, but Lorelle didn't look.

Shalure's finger touched Lorelle's cheek, and she flinched.

Please, Shalure gestured frantically. *Please… This… What I have to tell you. This is what I must give back to you.*

Shalure held up a hand as if to stop Lorelle from interrupting.

Your friend. The knife... Shalure gestured carefully.

Lorelle began to cry softly. "Just get out. Please get out."

You didn't do that, Shalure gestured.

"I can still feel the knife in my hands. I can still feel..." Lorelle said raggedly.

Shalure got off the bed and knelt before Lorelle. She took Lorelle's shoulders in her hands and squeezed.

You didn't do that. She released Lorelle's shoulders and gestured, *The Giant did. He cut into your soul.*

"I held the blade! I brought everyone I loved into the noktum!"

She shook her head. *The Giant controlled you. Your friends came after you. You didn't make those choices.*

"Please just leave!"

But you are making this one. Shalure gestured to all the lights in the room, then she reached forward and put a gentle hand on Lorelle's heart. *Your friends care about you. Let them help you.*

Shalure gave a sad smile. Those were the exact words Lorelle had said to Shalure when she'd lain in a fugue of *shkazat* smoke.

"It's not the same," she said, looking away.

Shalure caught her chin, pulled her back, and gestured carefully.

It is. It is the same.

She tapped herself on the chest, then pointed at Lorelle.

"I almost killed them!"

Shalure took Lorelle's hand and pushed her own into it, held it tight, then gestured with her free hand.

But you didn't.

"I almost did..." she whispered.

And I almost killed myself with poison smoke. But I didn't. Shalure squeezed her hand. *Because of you.*

Shalure pulled her into an embrace and the dam finally broke. Lorelle sobbed, and the woman simply held her, soft and warm and without judgment. Shalure didn't seem in any rush to let go, and they stayed that way for a long time. Lorelle cried until she had no more tears left, until the exhaustion of the past weeks overcame her. As Lorelle sagged in her arms, Shalure gently lifted her, laid her in the bed, and pulled the covers over her.

Lorelle slept.

CHAPTER FIFTY-FOUR

LORELLE

Lorelle crouched on the lip of the Reader's Library, her belly so low it almost touched the stone, her knees on either side of her head. The night was quiet and cool, an autumn stillness like it was holding its breath before the plunge into winter. The noktum cloak unfurled around her as if on an invisible wind, shielding her from any eyes watching below.

She dropped to the second story window, the cloak following her like a sea creature and settling protectively around her once again. She'd visited this exact place before, walked right into a Reader trap. She hadn't seen whatever magical alarm they'd set for her. She'd been blind in so many ways back then.

She set Slayter's disk on the sill, completed the missing line in the dried clay with a sharp fingernail. The soft orange glow spilled across the sill and up the frame of the window. A dark orange mass crouched at the upper right-hand corner.

"It's right there." Vohn's voice flowed to her from the Dark that resided inside the noktum cloak.

"I see it," she thought back to him. After a few days of practice, she'd mastered the knack of communicating with Vohn.

In his new, amorphous state, he couldn't leave the noktum, but the cloak was always connected to the noktum.

She set the second clay coin Slayter had given her on the sill next to the first, completed the missing line, then put it on the exact spot where the dark orange node had appeared.

The new coin glowed orange. There was a little flash, and the node of the alarm spell dimmed like a dying coal and then went out.

She tested the latch. It was unlocked just like the last time. She opened it and slipped inside. With her back against the curved ceiling, she side-stepped lightly along the decorative six-inch ledge and silently closed the window.

Books and scrolls and bound sheaves of paper lined every wall below her. The seven aisles of large bookcases stretched across the length of the room.

As before, the place was empty.

She dropped to the top of the nearest bookshelf and silently padded along it.

"The next row over, end of the aisle," Vohn's voice came to her from deep within the noktum cloak.

Vohn liked to talk to her, and she wasn't about to discourage that.

The upside to Vohn's transformation was that it suspended the physical body in the state it was in when the transformation happened, which meant he'd been able to suspend his own death.

The downside was that becoming one with the Dark put the Shadowvar at risk of losing his identity.

So, the more he talked, the more Lorelle liked it.

She leapt lightly from one stack to the next, never breaking stride. She reached the end, dropped to the floor, and blended with the shadows before the shelves.

The last time she'd come here, it had been to steal a Plunnos, and she'd come alone.

This time, Lorelle wasn't making that mistake. She wasn't going to try to control the situation all by herself. She didn't need to control every single thing. She had a family to watch her back. Whatever they did, they'd do it together.

Rhenn was still missing, yes, but it could wait for now. Lorelle wasn't about to leave Vohn swirling in the darkness of the noktum, possibly vanishing into nothing, when she could do something about it.

"*There it is,*" Vohn said, somehow spotting the needed volume before she did.

Lorelle quietly slid the thick volume from the shelf. *A History of Nokte Shaddark, Volume 4: The Banshees,* by Ohgonte Vanshor.

She pulled a third coin from her pouch, completed the symbol, and laid it against the volume. Both the coin and the volume glowed orange, then the glow slowly faded.

She tucked the book under her arm and left the Reader Library just as swiftly and silently as she'd come, escaping into the night.

Not a single Reader tried to stop her, and according to Slayter, not a single Reader would know the volume was missing, at least by any magical means. They'd have to discover its absence by old-fashioned happenstance the next time someone went looking for that particular book.

She and Vohn returned to the palace, descended the two flights to the basement level where Slayter had his laboratory, and slipped through the door.

Slayter sat on a tall stool, his stump propped on a stool next to him. It had been a blistered mess when they'd returned from the Great Noktum. His prosthetic, while a marvel of ingenuity, left something to be desired regarding comfort. Lorelle had salved the blistered stump and wrapped it, and Slayter had spent the last two days under orders to keep it elevated. She was pleased to see he was following instructions.

The mage worked over a small stone cauldron with a liquid the color of an orange—predictably—swirling inside.

"You have it?" He looked up. She tapped the volume lightly with her fingers.

"I felt you using the spells," he said, letting out a tired breath. "I fear I'll have to take a nap soon."

Activating one of Slayter's spells still pulled energy from him—three times as much, actually—but Slayter had insisted on the necessity of it.

She set the book on the table. She had combined her healing knowledge with Slayter's magic craft something into that could save Vohn. As Vohn explained it, when he rematerialized from the noktum, his body would be exactly as he had left it. He will not have aged a second, and his critical wound would still be critical.

Lorelle and Slayter would have to work fast when he reappeared, which meant the more they could do now, the better that inevitable moment would be. Slayter was creating a spell that could arrest time around Vohn the moment he returned. The mage had asked for the book because it was the only volume that discussed this Shadowvar transformation. Slayter hoped it would help him understand things about the transformation that even Vohn might not know. Even one tiny bit of knowledge might be the difference between life and death when they reconstituted Vohn's body.

Slayter swore he would not risk bringing Vohn back from the Dark until he was certain Vohn wouldn't die because of it.

For the first time, Lorelle suspected Slayter was actually being meticulous and not as scatterbrained as he usually seemed.

Slayter was an odd individual, and the more she learned about him, the more she wondered just how many levels he was operating on at any given time.

"How long until we try to get him back?" she asked.

Slayter blinked tired eyes and looked up at Lorelle with a weary smile. "A day. Maybe three. I am moving as quickly as I can."

"I know you are."

"I understand your urgency, Lorelle," he said. "I do. But I don't want to make a mistake." Slayter was clearly unwilling to take any chances when it came to Vohn's life. It was sweet.

"I know."

"We'll get him back," Slayter said. "Then we'll pour everything into the search for Rhenn. Now we have the Plunnos.

We simply have to understand how to use it. We're almost there."

"Yes," Lorelle murmured.

He went back to pondering the swirling cauldron, picked up a tiny vial of red powder, tapped a dash into the pot.

"So you have time." He selected another vial and considered it. "They're throwing a ball tonight," he said, seemingly at random.

She didn't say anything, but she smiled.

"Lord Harpinjur turned out to be a marvel, didn't he?" Slayter said. "We should have put him in charge from the start. He's running the kingdom far better than we did."

"Yes," she agreed.

In the short time Lorelle, Khyven, Slayter, and Vohn were gone, Lord Harpinjur had performed nothing short of a miracle. He'd not only created a plausible story as to why Queen Rhenn had made no appearances in the last two weeks, but he'd filled the kingdom with distractions to pull their attention away from the absent monarch.

"The ball is for the nobles," Slayter said, studying the vial. "And, really, anyone in the palace who likes to dance."

"You're so subtle," she finally said.

"Well, some people require more subtlety than others."

She laughed, came around the table, leaned down, and kissed him on the cheek. "Thank you," she murmured.

He pressed his cheek into her lips, then turned and winked at her. "We'll get Vohn back. Then we'll all go look for Rhenn. Together. I promise."

"Good. Because I'm not letting any of you out of my sight again."

"Like a Kyolar holding its prey between her claws?"

"Soft claws."

He went back to his labors.

She left, and for some reason she called to mind Zaith's lesson about her as a boat, slammed and jammed up against a dam of control. Sometimes the best she could do was let the boat flow with the stream.

If there was a way to restore Vohn, Slayter would find it.

So, she let the "river" take her down the hall. Sometimes she would have to paddle as fast as her arms would allow. But sometimes, she could let her friends play the parts they could far better than her.

Fighting that, she had learned, brought disaster.

She climbed the stairs lightly. Vohn had gone silent, seeming to sense her mood, and he respected the privacy of her thoughts.

She went to her room and changed her clothes, then hung the noktum cloak on the rack by the door.

"You'll be all right?" she asked Vohn.

"I am fine," he whispered through the Dark. *"Go, Lorelle. It is long overdue."*

She reached Khyven's room, raised her hand to knock, and hesitated. Her sharp Luminent ears heard him moving around inside, heard a drawer open, then close, and his soft footsteps. He moved so lightly for a Human, especially such a large Human.

Heat crept into her cheeks as she blushed, but she shook her head and knocked.

A surprised silence fell inside the room. Those light footsteps became even lighter as he approached the door; ever the Ringer, alert for danger.

When he opened the door, however, he looked relaxed. An opponent would never see anything except what Khyven wanted them to see. It was another bit of Ringer armor he always wore: the facade of relaxation, a mental tactic to make his opponents fear him, to make them believe that everything was always well within his capability to handle.

His eyes widened as he saw her.

"You look amazing." He stared at the floor-length gown she wore. "Lorelle…" he started, like he was about to say something more, but couldn't come up with it.

He'd obviously not thought he'd find her in his doorway, and his gaze roved over her face like he would memorize her eyes, her cheekbones, her ears.

Her blush deepened. Before her transformation, her pale cheeks would have glowed bright red like coals in a fire. But now she wondered if her midnight hue would even show the blush at all.

"I'm sorry," he said, realizing he was staring.

In another time, she would have shrugged, entered the room, and ignored the attention. To control the situation, to ensure her own emotions didn't get out of hand, locking them behind the big steel door in her mind.

But she wasn't at risk of soul-bonding anymore. The deed was done. It might not have been the bonding her parents—or the whole of the Luminent culture—would have wanted for her, but it was hers, and hers alone. And it suited her. She would flow with the river she was on. Lorelle was now part of the Dark of the noktum, and she was part of this man, this Ringer she loved.

"No," she said softly, forcing herself to hold his gaze. "I like it. I like you looking at me."

That surprised him. A touch of color came to *his* cheeks now, and she felt herself coming back on balance. The heat in her cheeks didn't fade, but her awkwardness did.

"May I come in?" she asked.

"Yes, please," he said, standing aside.

She crossed to the window, finally breaking her gaze with him, and looked out over the city. The Night Ring in the distance drew the eye like a slice of the noktum itself. The sun set, orange light spreading along the horizon behind the forbidding structure. She shifted and looked down at the palace below her, the courtyard with its green lawns, the fountains and sculptures. Dozens of nobles in their finery strolled toward the golden light emanating from the front of the palace.

"Lord Harpinjur has ordered a meeting for the nobles," she said. "A celebration, he's calling it."

"I know," Khyven said. "I told him he was insane to bring them all here where they could band together and upend the palace, but he told me—" Khyven switched to an impersonation of Harpinjur's gruff voice "'—Keep your friends close but your enemies closer, Khyven.'"

"There is a ball," she said softly.

"Part of the plan, I suppose," Khyven said, like they were in a council meeting. Like she had come here to discuss politics. "Something about giving a positive..." He trailed off as he realized what she actually meant. He swallowed and looked her up and down again. The ball gown. She could see it finally coming together in his head.

She faced him. "Rhenn is still out there. I think about it always. I have thought about it every moment since she was taken. I want so badly to follow her, to bring her back, but..." She swallowed. "Our journey to the center of the noktum showed me that if I don't appreciate what is right in front of me, I could lose it, too." She shook her head. "And I won't. I refuse."

Concern furrowed Khyven's brow.

"I cannot bear to lose you, Khyven. I know that now. I can't, any more than I can bear to lose Rhenn. And so..."

She smiled at him, tilted her hips, and opened her palms as though presenting her dress, and herself, to him.

"Take me dancing?" she asked softly.

"Yes," he blurted. He looked down at his clothes, the everyday clothes he wore about the palace. "Except I... have to change."

She crossed to him, stopped, and kissed him, long and lingering.

"I'll wait by the banister."

She loitered by the tall, grandfather clock at the top of the stairs. Khyven emerged from his room moments later in the royal finery Rhenn had had made for him while he was unconscious. Ever the optimist, Rhenn had the clothes tailored to him to celebrate the moment he awoke.

He approached her and extended his elbow. "You realize, I have no idea how to dance," he said.

"They didn't have balls in the Night Ring?"

"Not this kind."

She chuckled. "I'll carry you." She winked.

They descended the steps together.

That night, they danced. She taught him the steps, and Khyven picked them up quickly, as he did with everything else. They moved together like they were born to it, anticipating each other like the single soul they now were. She felt the few threads connecting them glowing, a joyous soul-bond, if a small one. Almost everyone stared at Lorelle's strange new appearance, and whispers flew behind cupped hands. But she didn't care. Not tonight. Tonight, she only cared about Khyven.

After the musicians played their last song, she and Khyven danced up the stairs. They danced down the hallway, and they danced to the door of Lorelle's room.

Her heart beat fast. It was such a wonderful feeling. Everything in the world seemed possible again, and she couldn't seem to catch her breath.

"Would you like to come in?" she asked.

"Is this where you pirouette me and I fall into your arms?"

"If you want to crush me, I suppose," she said.

He tugged her closer and she went, turning her face up to him as his arms wrapped around her. He didn't say anything. Again, his gaze seemed to drink her in, as though looking at her filled him with joy.

"Yes," she breathed, barely audible.

"Yes?"

"I want you to crush me... a little."

He kissed her, and their souls intertwined, spreading a golden light through both of them. Her single lock of golden hair shone brightly amidst the black.

Effortlessly, he lifted her into his arms and carried her into the room.

Silently, unnoticed by either of them, the noktum cloak floated up from the rack, slithered through the open door, and hung itself on the doorknob.

The door swung shut.

Epilogue

RHENN

Rhenn woke with a gasp, as though she'd surfaced from a lake. Blinking, she sat up and looked around. She was on a short bed, not quite as long as she was tall, and the mattress was little more than a sack stuffed with straw. The room was small, made of gray granite, a much lighter color than the stones of Usara, and it smelled lightly of mildew. The window to her right was no more than an arrow slit in the form of a cross. Sunlight shone through the slit, casting a bright, slanted cross on the far wall.

A man stood in the shadows next to the arrow slit. A tall man...

Nhevaz.

Rhenn reached for her sword, but it wasn't there. She was still wearing her nightgown.

"I would have given you weapons," Nhevaz said, "and dressed you appropriately, but it would have required removing your clothing. My main goal is to obtain your cooperation, and I didn't want to start our relationship by offending your modesty."

She blinked and quickly tried to get her bearings, searching for how she wanted to play this.

"So magically paralyzing me and kidnapping me is all right, but you draw the line at stripping me naked?" Rhenn said conversationally. She swung her feet around and sat on the edge of the small bed. She'd learned long ago how to control her voice, to sound casual when she was on high alert. She'd also learned that acting the opposite of the way most people acted in tense situations gave her an advantage. She had to keep him talking while she accumulated information.

She studied the room for anything that would tell her where they were, where this mysterious man had brought her. The ceiling was lower than the rooms in the palace. The arrow-slit window indicated it was a place of battle. A fortress of some kind.

"Try to see it not as a kidnapping," Nhevaz said, "but a necessary evil."

"*Necessary* evil. What a telling phrase," she said. The room didn't reveal any secrets that made sense to her. She began looking for something she could use as a weapon. A piece of metal. A rock. A loose stone.

"I didn't want to take you," he said.

"Well, I'm just glad I get to meet the infamous Nhevaz; it's exciting. Khyven has built you up as a legend in his mind."

Nhevaz turned, the bright light flashing across his face as he cut the beam. He moved toward her, lithe and silent for such a big man.

And Senji's Teeth was the man big! Khyven was a tall, wide-shouldered beast who seemed formed by the gods themselves to be a Ringer, but Nhevaz had at least a couple inches of height on Khyven, without losing any of the musculature of a born fighter.

He started toward her, and Rhenn tensed. She wished she could have found a weapon to use against him, but there was nothing near to hand. And Nhevaz himself didn't seem to be wearing any weapons that could be turned against him.

She could hike her nightgown to her ribs, give herself enough slack to twist it into a garrote. That could be done quickly, and it contained an element of surprise she liked. He'd already made a concession to her modesty. Chances were good he wouldn't expect her to flash her flesh to gain a tactical advantage. That might be a weakness she could exploit, and distract him long enough to make the garrote...

She'd have to get behind him, though. She would have to jump high enough to get her knees into his back. If she could do all that, she might be able to loop the nightgown around his neck and hang on long enough to cut off his air.

As he approached, she slid her legs onto the bed, positioning them beneath her so she could flip to the balls of her feet and launch. Her hand surreptitiously closed over the hem of her nightgown.

She kept the conversation going, kept her tone light. "You know, Khyven isn't much of a talker, but he sure talked about you all the time—"

"If you attack me, you will lose," Nhevaz interrupted as though reading her thoughts. Or her body language. Or both. "Then we'll have to start over, which would waste time, and time is always against us." He sat on the floor a couple of feet from the bed and crossed his legs. It was an insanely poor defensive position, the equivalent of baring his throat. She could fly at him a half dozen ways before he would be able to untangle those long legs.

Rhenn hesitated. Putting into action her nightgown-garrote plan suddenly seemed... well, as ridiculous as trying to garrote someone with a nightgown while you were still wearing it.

"I imagine you're scared," Nhevaz said. "Though I admit Human emotions are sometimes difficult for me to predict, even now. What makes sense to you doesn't always make sense to me."

Rhenn realized she didn't have anything to say to that, and she was abruptly chilled by the way he'd said the word "Human," like she fit into that category, but he didn't.

"I want to be honest with you," he said. "It is a gamble, but I feel that you, more than most, might be able to comprehend what I have to say without... those aforementioned emotions."

Since she'd decided not to attack him right away, Rhenn shifted into her diplomat facade. "So, we're putting our cards on the table?"

Nhevaz hesitated, as though he was trying to recall what "cards on the table" meant, then he nodded. "Exactly that."

Rhenn narrowed her eyes, wondering what angle this man was working. She tried to imagine how it benefited him to act so reasonable, to converse with her. He clearly had the power. He was physically larger. He had magic. He'd taken her to a place where she couldn't rely on friends, and he was obviously not an idiot.

Yet he wasn't trying to intimidate or dominate her. Clearly he wanted information, the kind she had to be willing to give, rather than information he could torture out of her.

She tried to imagine what kind of information that would be. Without knowing who he was or what kingdom he was from, she couldn't guess accurately. If he was an agent of Imprevar, he'd want to know about her military vulnerabilities. If Triada, he'd want to know about the political interplay of her nobles, or perhaps her intentions for marriage. But this man was connected to Khyven at least two years back, and the Ringer himself was mysterious enough. This secret-shrouded supposed "non-Human" just heightened the entire enigma to ridiculous heights. She couldn't hope to unravel that right now, not without more information.

Finally, Rhenn decided she was in entirely over her head and that the best way to play this, the only way, was to meet it head on. She had to look for those minute clues.

"Fine," she said. "Who are you?"

"My name is not Nhevaz, as you might have already guessed. My real name is Nhevalos, and I am what Humans call a Giant."

Rhenn had queued up half a dozen follow-up questions to fire at him, to try to keep him talking quickly to see if he would slip and accidentally give her something he didn't intend to give her.

Those questions dried up in her mind.

She stared at him, feeling like she should have a rejoinder to that, but nothing came. If anyone else had said such a ludicrous thing, she would have laughed and winked and played along with their obvious insanity.

Except this man had walked through a Thuros, had rendered her and Lorelle, two excellent fighters, inconsequential in less than a second, and walked back through the Thuros with her as captive. Not to mention this man had fought Khyven to a standstill. Khyven, the finest swordsman she'd ever seen, or even heard of. This Nhevaz, or Nhevalos, had held him at bay like a novice pup.

If Nhevalos was telling the truth, his comment about "Humans" made perfect sense.

Rhenn swallowed.

"Until seventeen hundred years ago, we ruled Noksonon as well as the other continents."

"Other continents?" was all she could say, and she realized she'd lost control of the conversation. Everything he was saying was completely beyond her ken, and she felt like she was stumbling to catch up, craving knowledge and playing his game rather than guiding the conversation and playing hers. She shook her head and told herself to hold it together.

"You're a Giant," she said drily, like she didn't believe him. The problem was, the more her frantic mind mulled over what he'd said, the more it actually made sense. It would explain how he'd stood next to the king all this time and gotten away with it. It would explain the Thuros. Khyven. It would explain everything.

"Yes," he said.

"Why... aren't you tall?" she blurted, then berated herself for such a childish question. She simply couldn't think of any intelligent questions.

"I worked a spell to make myself smaller. It took many years and a great deal of pain, but it allows me to walk among your kind relatively easily."

"My kind?"

"Humans."

"Of course." Her heart beat faster. "Because you're a Giant," she said in a monotone. Fear crawled up her back on cold, spidery legs as she realized she believed him.

He paused, cocked his head like he was preparing for that aforementioned Human emotional outburst. "Yes."

A new thought occurred to her. What if everything that was happening was actually happening at face value?

"You're a Giant," she said, and realized it was the third time she'd said that. "And you want my cooperation?"

"That is correct."

"For what?"

"To save your kind."

"In Usara."

"Everywhere."

"The other continents you mentioned."

"Shijuren, Drakanon, Daemanon, and Pyranon."

She swallowed. "There are four… other continents?"

"That is correct."

She felt dizzy. "And where are these other continents?"

"You are currently on Daemanon."

"I'm on Daemanon." She felt *really* dizzy, and she realized she was repeating everything. Her breath came faster; she was almost panting. "Because of the Thuros."

"That is correct."

She realized she was bordering on hysteria when she felt the urge to giggle, because if he was telling the truth, it was so frightening what could a person do except laugh?

She kept herself from doing that but sweat prickled on her forehead and her vision blurred for a moment.

"You're a Giant," she said for the fourth time. "So you can do anything. Giants are all powerful. What do you need my cooperation for?"

"If my kind were all powerful, they would have won the war seventeen centuries ago."

"You need my help because of a war seventeen centuries old."

"Because it's coming again," he said.

"I…" she panted. There wasn't enough air in this little room. She struggled to gulp it down, but there simply wasn't enough air. "I can't… breathe. I have to…" She staggered from the bed to the arrow slit and put her mouth right up to the three-inch slot and breathed the outside air.

The hard, granite aperture widened, retreating like shadows from the sun. She gasped and craned her neck to look at Nhevalos. He murmured and gestured and the arrow slit molded itself into a large, open window.

Magic. Giant magic.

She turned back to the window. Myth and magic and gods.

That's easily large enough for me to leap to my death, she thought crazily.

She leaned on the newly level windowsill and hung her head out. They were so high that the men and horses in the courtyard below looked like toys. She gazed at a green field outside the wall, a river snaking across the landscape, and a lush forest beyond with strange-looking trees unlike anything she'd ever seen before.

"What you're feeling right now," Nhevalos said, "is what most Humans feel when I tell them my purpose. But I have watched you. You have the ability to understand what must be done, the willpower to hold the magnitude of it within your heart, and the determination to act. It was for these reasons I decided to confide in you rather than manipulate you. Did I err, Rhennaria Laochodon?"

Hearing her full name snapped Rhenn back to her senses. She *was* Rhennaria Laochodon, the last of her line. She was Queen of Usara by blood and by right of combat.

She took a deep breath, straightened her spine, and turned. "You say a war is coming," she said. "Giants are coming to take over the entire world. A war that would make Usara seem inconsequential."

"On the contrary. Usara will be pivotal. That is why I have spent so much time there."

"And who are you? Besides being a Giant. Besides being called Nhevalos?"

"One of the architects of the war."

"You are trying to *create* this war?"

"To ensure your kind are the victors; Humans and the other mortals."

Rhenn blinked. "You mean Luminents, Shadowvar, Taur-Els…"

"And many others, yes."

"Other mortals on these other continents?"

"There are many races on Noksonon yet undiscovered by Lightlanders, as well."

"Lightlanders."

"Those who live outside the noktum."

"If this is a war between mortals and Giants and you're a Giant, why would you help us?"

For the first time, Nhevalos hesitated. He looked away like he didn't want to answer or wasn't going to tell her the truth, but then he looked back at her, and she thought she saw a flicker of pain in the depths of his black gaze.

"My eyes were opened," he said softly. "Long ago. So long it sometimes seems like a dream."

"What happened?"

He hesitated, then shook his head, and she knew he wasn't going to tell her. Instead, he said, "Giants do not think like you, Rhennaria Laochodon. They do not have compassion. Not for each other, and certainly not for what they see as lesser creatures. Humans, and all the other mortals, are not people to them. You are to them what a cockroach is to you. They are disgusted that you occupy the world they see as theirs, and they will crush every last one of you this time, if they can. I do not agree with them, and I intend to see that they do not have that chance. That is all you need know."

"What happens if I don't help you?" she asked.

"Then I find someone else who can."

She nodded slowly. "What happens if you lose? If this… other architect of the war wins?"

"Then you die. Everyone you love dies. Humans are eradicated or enslaved and Giants rule the world again."

"How can Humans possibly fight Giants?"

"That is my sole purpose in life. To find those ways. To expand them."

"And what can I possibly do?"

Nhevalos smiled for the first time.

"That is what I would like to talk to you about…"

INTERLUDE

(One hour before Tovos is locked in the Dragon Chain)

Tovos left the damned Luminent in her cell and swept up the stairs of his castle toward the tower room. He should kill her. He'd locked her friends in the dungeons, guarded by a naguil, but he should kill them all. He wanted to. Once upon a time, he would have. But that impulsive behavior had been his undoing long ago.

Now, he kept control of his rage. Before the Betrayer's War, he'd had none. He'd never needed it. He had been free to throttle the world as needed. It had been the purpose of the world to bend to the desires of the Noksonoi. Tovos's rage had once been reflected in the storms of the sky, the rumblings of the earth, and the cowering of the mortals who shrank from him in fear. That had been as it should be. That had been his right, the right of all Noksonoi.

And Nhevalos the Betrayer—and all his ilk—had stolen it from them all.

The Betrayer had twisted the very fabric of nature, creating an aberration wherein mortals could topple their betters. He'd given secrets to them, raised them up, made them a threat like they had never been before.

Nhevalos and the mortals had actually prevailed. Tovos wasn't even sure how it happened—that was how twisty Nhevalos was.

After the fall, the Noksonoi nearly died out. If depleted too far, Noksonoi bodies calcified and retreated into a sleep from which they would never awaken, except if awakened by another. It was called the long sleep. Drained of magic from the war, humiliated, empty of hope, Tovos's brothers and sisters slowed to a stop and become part of the hills. And if they slept long enough, they would forever become the stone they emulated.

Those who had not died in the war—Daelakos, Maeshandos, Fraedos, and Brikos—all had all gone this way. Or so Tovos assumed. Even the mighty Harkandos, the strongest of them all, had vanished. Harkandos had singlehandedly wiped out Nhevalos's largest army at the Battle of Mallorn. The great warrior had sheared off a chunk of Noksonon herself and drowned thousands of mortals. Tovos had thought—they'd all thought—that would be the turning point in the war.

It had been their downfall instead.

Nhevalos had coolly planned it all—he'd planned the death of half his forces!—so that the other half could win. He'd tricked them, attacking suddenly at every other front of the war while all eyes were on Mallorn. Somehow, Nhevalos had intentionally twisted their greatest victory into their final defeat.

Tovos had never seen Harkandos again, but he had often imagined the great warrior emerging from the rubble of that battle, the only survivor. How his triumph must have curdled to despair to look out over his great victory to find that his allies had utterly failed to hold up their end. Tovos imagined Harkandos staggering to some dark place afterward in his heartbreak, falling against hard stone, and slowly becoming one with it.

Tovos had nearly succumbed himself. He'd retreated to a nameless cave deep within the Great Noktum. But he didn't slip into the sleep. He lay there, replaying the horrible war over and over again in his mind, mystified. He could not understand how Nhevalos had done what he'd done. It simply didn't make sense, and perhaps that frustration alone kept Tovos from vanishing like the others.

He stewed. He gnashed his teeth. And finally he rose, determined to destroy Nhevalos no matter what. He put his rage aside. Nhevalos hadn't destroyed the Noksonoi with greater power; he'd done it with trickery. He hadn't rushed forward and spent his forces; he'd remained patient. He had never raged; the weasel had plotted.

And if he could do it, so could Tovos.

So Tovos had risen. He had prepared, regained his strength, and then he had dedicated himself to tracking Nhevalos. Tovos wanted to uncover every plot The Betrayer seeded and destroy them.

He passed the midway point up to his tower. To his left, a vekrin crouched in a little alcove. The vekrin had almost all died in the Betrayer's War, but a few still remained. It stood about two feet tall, humanoid, had slick black skin and a bald head with little horns poking up. But for a breechclout, it was naked, and its wings were folded tightly against its back. The vekrin's sole job was to stand in that alcove all day long until Tovos walked by, just in case he needed something. The thing got weakly to its feet and cowered in the corner of its alcove as Tovos came into view. It was particularly thin, and Tovos realized he hadn't given it leave to eat anything in two days.

"Get me the duke," Tovos growled.

"Yes, my lord," the vekrin said in its high-pitched voice, bowing and bowing again.

"Now."

It edged to the corner of the alcove, respectfully not unfurling its wings until Tovos was fully past for fear accidentally brushing Tovos.

"And eat something," Tovos added as he continued to climb.

"Yes, my lord," the vekrin nodded, and it hopped from the ledge and flapped its wings. For a moment, it seemed it wasn't going to have the strength to fly, but it sputtered and managed to get airborne, flapping erratically down the curved stairway and out of sight.

If it isn't strong enough to do the job, there's no use for it, I'm going to have to kill that one soon and replace it, Tovos thought.

He ascended the rest of the stairs to his workshop. The circular room was fifty feet in diameter with a low ceiling only twenty feet tall. Ten mirrors at equal intervals lined the walls, each in an intricately carved, wooden frame. Each mirror had a different symbol embedded in a metal disk at the top.

Each was a way of communicating with other Eldroi, and Tovos was going to use them all today. His plans on this end were shaky at best. The Glimmerblade had failed him. The Nox had all failed him.

Whatever plan Nhevalos had for Usara's queen, Tovos needed to destroy it. He'd hoped to use guile against Nhevalos, to plan the Luminent girl as a mole within the queen's circle, either to find her or to await for her when she returned. That was still viable, but since the Luminents friends had followed her, he'd either have to kill them all or find a way to use them. He'd have to think on it. If he could find a way to plant them all back in Usara under his command, that would be ideal. And there were ways, but it would require research.

For now, he needed a backup plan, just in case. Tovos would prefer to stay hidden from Nhevalos, to encompass The Betrayer's weapon with his own loyal people so that when Nhevalos went to use her, Tovos could defang him at that critical moment. So, if Tovos could outwit Nhevalos, fine. If not, then Queen Rhennaria had to die.

That was the backup.

Thumping steps pulled Tovos's attention away from the mirror he'd chosen for his first contact. The door opened and two Wergoi brought in a naked, pot-bellied Human. Tovos had pulled this man, Duke Derinhald, from Usara a few weeks ago. The duke had taken a dozen men to hunt in his favorite forest, and Tovos had made it look like bandits had set upon them. He'd slaughtered all save the duke.

"Strap him to the slab," Tovos commanded. The Wergoi dragged the struggling man to the edge of the thick stone table. He kicked at one of the burly Wergoi. It was a glancing blow, but the Wergoi took offense. He lifted the duke into the air and slammed him onto the slab. Then he punched the man repeatedly in the face until he lay there limp and moaning. They locked him into the cuffs and left.

The Human groaned, but eventually came to his senses.

"Please..." Duke Derinhalt said, looking through a swelling eye at Tovos. "I will give you anything you want. Please..."

"But you did not."

"What?"

"Give me what I wanted."

"I don't... I don't even know you..."

"Shall I be less offended for that?" Tovos lined up the stool before his chosen window. Deihmankos. On Daemanon. He knew her daughter Ihnassrios—whom the mortals called Nissra—was slowly reclaiming power on the continent, but her mother still ruled. Deihmankos would be in a good position to help him search for Nhevalos and the missing queen of Usara. She was a malevolent bitch, of course, but that was to be expected. The important thing was that she didn't hate him nearly as much as she hated Nhevalos. One of Nhevalos' champions had, after all, exacted a heavy toll during the rebellion.

"What... What do you want?" Duke Derinhalt whined.

"You failed me."

"I... How could I have failed you if I didn't know what you wanted!"

"I wanted Vamreth to stay on the throne."

"But I... So did I! I was Vamreth's greatest supporter."

"And yet you failed to stop the uprising. You failed to best Queen Rhennaria. You failed."

"But I…" Duke Derinhalt faltered. "She commanded monsters from the noktum. How could I…"

Tovos let out a bored breath. "You're going to die, Duke Derinhalt. I going to use your lifeforce to bolster my own. Since you were useless to me in Usara, I'm going to make use of you here, in this way."

Duke Derinhalt's eyes nearly bugged from his head. "No! No!" He struggled. The chains rattled.

Tovos whispered. The power of Land Magic raced through him, and the chains yanked tight, stretching Duke Derinhalt to the breaking point.

"No! Ahhh! Nooo!"

Tovos put five fingertips on Duke Derinhalt's bare chest, equally spaced apart. With the same outpouring of Land Magic, he burned those fingertips into Duke Derinhalt's skin.

The Human's screams reverberated throughout the workshop.

When he had screamed his throat ragged, Tovos stopped. He hadn't killed the duke, only marked him. Suppurating flesh bubbled in the shape of a precise, five-pointed star, Tovos's personal symbol.

"You will die here, Duke Derinhalt, unless…" Tovos whispered as the man whimpered, tears streaming down his face. "I can make use of you in some other way."

"Yes…" the duke gagged on his own pain. "Yes, by Senji, yes!"

Tovos leaned down. The duke winced, leaning his head away, but Tovos put his lips next to the disgusting cockroach's ear.

"I… want… that… kingdom…" Tovos whispered. "I want you to sit on that throne, not Queen Rhennaria."

"Yes! Yes! Please! I want that too!"

"Very well." Tovos whispered, and the chains loosened, the manacles snapped open. The duke fell to the floor, staggered toward the doorway and slammed into the doorjamb, where he managed to stay on his feet. His hands curled like claws over his burned chest, but he didn't touch the bubbling wound. His face was a mask of pain.

"You are mine, King Derinhalt. Understand me when I say this, for I will only say it once. You. Are. Mine."

"Yes."

"Also, you are king of Usara now. I have decreed it. You have one month to prove it or I will return, I will bring you back here, and I will finish what I started."

"Yes..." The king faltered.

"Call me Lord Tovos."

"Yes, Lord Tovos. Thank you."

"The Wergoi who brought you here will return your clothing. They will take you back."

"Yes, Lord Tovos."

"The next time I see you, you will sit upon the throne of Usara."

"Yes. I promise."

Tovos turned back to the mirror, but he heard King Derinhalt scrambling down the steps into the waiting arms of the Wergoi.

He concentrated on the reflection, using a combination of Land Magic, Line Magic, and Life Magic. The mirror flickered, and a hazy reflection began to resolve.

"Who dares—" Deihmankos's grating voice spoke into Tovos's mind.

"It is Tovos, son of Avos," Tovos thought to her. "I am using the mirror of Deihmankos. Open to me."

The bitch hesitated, but that was to be expected. She was always untrusting.

"I don't take orders from you... or do I have to remind of that again? What is it you want?"

"Open to me... please... and I will tell you."

Another hesitation, then slowly, Deihmankos's image coalesced into lifelike detail in the mirror. She wore a loose-fitting, sleeveless, deep-cut gown of black that barely contained her bosom. Her skin was the color of emeralds, scaly like a reptile's, with lines of bone-white spurs running over her shoulders and down her arms. Her eyes glowed crimson, with a ring of white horns surrounding her head like deadly rays of sunshine. She looked upward at him like she was looking up the hill of a mountain.

"I'm busy," she said as she placed a glittering gem onto whatever lay before her.

"This won't take long. I'm looking for someone."

"So go look."

"This someone is on your continent. I ask for permission to come there, to look for him."

Deihmankos's face soured. "You're joking."

"It is important."

"You want me to let you into my realm and roam around, interrogating my people, no doubt using magic in Daemanon?"

"Yes."

"I see no reason to help you, and even if I did, you wouldn't pay the price I would exact. The old accords still stand, the last time I checked. Unless you wish to challenge me." She almost purred the last.

"Do it, Deihmankos. It is in all of our benefit for you to aid me. We will need to help each other if we are to survive what is coming. Or should I be talking to Ihnassrios instead? She seems to be gaining power quickly, and right under your nose."

"Ihnassrios does nothing that isn't part of my design, whether she knows it or not. I don't need your help. I never have."

"You will."

"Will I, now?"

"Nhevalos is moving. He is scheming. He is in your lands."

The bitch went silent for that.

"Nhevalos is dead," she said with icy certainty. "Harkandos hunted him after the war was lost."

That stunned Tovos. He'd never heard that story, and a chill of fear went up his back. If Harkandos had hunted Nhevalos, and Nhevalos was still alive, then surely Harkandos was dead. But how?

Frustration rose within Tovos. Nhevalos wielded barely a fraction of the power Harkandos had. How could that weasel have bested him?

Because Nhevalos did not fight with strength. Somehow, he must have tricked Harkandos, like he had at the battle of Mallorn. Somehow...

"Nhevalos lives," Tovos said, trying to keep his surprise from his face. "He plots again."

Deihmankos remained silent for a long moment. Finally, she said, "How do you know?"

"His footprints are all over one of my kingdoms here. Usara."

"I remember Usara," she replied grimly.

Of course she did. She'd lost a hand in that battle. Tovos had seen it cut from her body by one of Nhevalos's champions. She'd grown it back later, of course, but that was not an easy, quick, or pleasant spell to endure.

"Then let's work together to ensure we don't face that again. Let me visit your Thuroi. Let me look for signs of Nhevalos's passage."

"I will do it myself," she offered. He could see the loathing in her eyes. Her hunger for Nhevalos's blood was almost as strong as his.

"You will never find him."

"And you will?"

"I have been studying him and his ways for two millennia. No one knows Nhevalos like I do."

"Then why haven't you killed him by now?" Her smile bordered on a sneer, and he knew she was goading him... testing the rage she knew always boiled just beneath his surface.

Tovos drew in a breath, exerting all his control. He wanted to crush her throat with his bare hands, but he calmed himself.

"Ask Harkandos," Tovos said. Her sneering smile faded.

"If you come into my realm, I will destroy you," Deihmankos said.

"This is how we lost."

"Your memory may be mired in the Betrayer's War, but I remember the wars before, the wars of the Eldroi when my father trusted yours, trusted all you slithering Noksonoi, and he died for it."

"If you don't let me follow him, and yours is the land where he's chosen to hide, you'll regret it. Nhevalos plots against all of us, not just me."

"You're not coming here."

"Deihmankos—"

"I will allow you to send an agent." She cut him off. "I will give you aid in your fruitless quest and exact a toll of my choosing when it suits me. Agreed?"

Now it was Tovos's turn to hesitate. "That will suffice," he finally said. "I will start in the east."

"Hapreth's Nuraghi, then."

"Yes."

"Fine."

"Thank you, Deihmankos."

She cut the connection.

Tovos drew a deep breath and moved his stool to the next mirror.

I am coming for you, Nhevalos, he thought. Soon, there will be nowhere you can hide from me.

THE DARKEST DOOR

BONUS SHORT STORY

This is it." Rhenn held up the huge silver key to Lorelle in the yellow light of the lantern, turning it so it was sure to glimmer, like it was magic.

Rhenn had brought Lorelle here, to her father's study, because it stood at the end of the hall—the furthest room from the bedrooms of the royal wing. In the study, it was less likely their parents would wake at their whispered voices. Rhenn loved Father's study; it smelled of oiled wood, leather, and old paper. It smelled like secrets, and a future queen should know secrets. She should know more of them than anyone else.

Books lined the walls, rising to the ceiling, and a thick wooden desk stood at the back of the room with Father's cushioned leather chair behind it. Of course, Father had told Rhenn a hundred times that his study was not a place to play, but a warning like that was just another way adults hid secrets from children.

Lorelle, Rhenn's best friend, looked wonderingly at the key. The beautiful Luminent already stood taller than Rhenn by half a foot—a fact that annoyed Rhenn. Princesses really ought to be taller than those who weren't.

Of course, Luminents were taller than humans. That's just the way it was. Luminents were also lighter and more graceful. They could tiptoe along the edge of a rooftop and never fall. And even if they did fall, it wouldn't hurt them like it would hurt Rhenn. They also had beautifully pointed ears and hair that glowed when they got excited. Or scared.

If Lorelle hadn't been so perfectly made to be Rhenn's best friend, Rhenn suspected she might have hated her. But the Luminent girl had proven herself right from the start. She'd happily joined all Rhenn's adventures, and she'd kept every secret Rhenn had ever told her. And perhaps most importantly, Lorelle deferred to Rhenn's leadership.

"What does it unlock?" Lorelle asked.

"A noktum," Rhenn said.

"Senji's Boots, it does not!" Lorelle blurted.

"Hsst!" Rhenn sliced her hand down through the air, looking nervously at the door. Her parents, brothers, and sisters weren't far up the hall. "Do you want them to catch us?"

"A noktum, really?" Lorelle whispered wonderingly.

Everyone knew about the otherworldly patches of darkness that blotted out more than a tenth of the Kingdom of Usara, remnants left over from the mythical Giant wars, they said. The Giants of those wars had been so powerful that, even though they'd died out almost two thousand years ago, their noktums still stood.

"Which door does it open?" Lorelle asked.

Of course that was the first question Lorelle would ask. It was the first anyone would ask because, while the noktums were spread at random across the countryside, there was only one place within the Crown City of Usara where actual doorways opened into that tentacled darkness: the Night Ring, where Rhenn's father held contests and feats of arms to entertain the public.

The Night Ring had five deadly doors: the Fire Way, the

Dragon Pass, the Daemon Portal, the Night Door, and the Lore Gate, and each opened into a noktum. Huge, locked iron gates made sure no one went in...and also that nothing emerged. In the noktum, it was said, living people drew monsters like candlelight drew moths.

No human who'd entered a noktum had ever emerged. And no Luminent, for that matter.

"Which door does it open?" Lorelle prompted, jolting Rhenn from her reverie. "The Daemon Portal?"

"Not the Daemon Portal, not the Dragon Pass," Rhenn said. "None the Night Ring's doors. A different door."

"Different?"

"This key—" Rhenn turned the big silver key in her hand, trying again to catch the flickering glow of the lantern on the desk, "—opens a noktum inside the palace."

"It does not!" Light shimmered down Lorelle's long, golden braid like a single strand had caught a ray of sunlight, and Rhenn smiled in satisfaction. That glimmer meant Lorelle was excited. Or afraid. Or both.

"Where in the palace?" Lorelle whispered.

With a smug smile, Rhenn pointed at one of the bookcases to the left of her father's desk.

A look of confusion came over Lorelle's face, and the brief glimmer in her hair died. She glanced back at Rhenn.

"You read about it?" Lorelle asked, not understanding.

"Not exactly. I discovered something."

"In a book?"

Rhenn ignored the question and said, "What if the adults have been lying to us? What if they've been lying to everyone?"

"What do you mean?"

Rhenn's chest was about to burst with excitement. She walked to the bookcase, removed a thick tome entitled The Theology of Senji the Warrior Goddess, and set it on father's desk. Holding up the key, looking directly at Lorelle, Rhenn reached her arm into the hole left by the missing book.

"I don't understand—" Lorelle began, and then her mouth

rounded in a gigantic "O" as the bookcase swung silently outward.

Behind it, a dark stairway went sharply downward.

"Gods and monsters…" Lorelle murmured, covering her mouth with one elegant hand. Golden light flickered through her entire braid, and this time it stayed, a barely-perceptible glow.

Rhenn chuckled. "Indeed. We might find both down there."

"There's a noktum down there?"

"That's what Father said."

"Your father told you?"

"He was talking about it with Mother. They almost caught me this morning, but I hid behind the Kuldraha tree." She pointed at the squat, mysterious tree in the corner of the study. It only rose about eight feet into the air, but its wide limbs reached out sideways. Its wide, midnight leaves—limned in moonlight silver—obscured some of the books lining the walls. Mother claimed it was unique, and it was obviously magical like the noktums. The pot itself was made of black-fired clay inlaid with gold leaf. It was five feet in diameter at the top, sloping to about three feet wide at the bottom.

The eerie Kuldraha tree didn't shed its leaves in the fall like normal trees. Instead, it shed one a day, every day. The leaves dried up, crinkled, and then drifted down. When they hit the circular plate atop the pot, which had been fitted around the trunk—the soil beneath couldn't be seen—they clinked like metal, turning into liquid darkness that spread out across the surface, creating a little pool as dark as a starless sky. Father had tried to capture the metal as it hit, but it always turned into that inky black liquid. He'd tried to study the liquid, but if taken more than a dozen feet from the tree, it evaporated. The little tree was a mystery, but Mother had told Rhenn it was one of the Laochodon family's most prized possessions, as well as one of its more tightly guarded secrets.

"You hid in the Kuldraha?" Lorelle asked, staring at the dark pool filling the metal plate beneath its leaves.

"Not in the tree, silly. Behind the pot." She pointed. Four

feet tall and five feet wide, the space was plenty large enough to hide a ten-year-old girl.

So when Mother and Father had unexpectedly entered the study this morning—when Rhenn was in here reading about the devious Bericourt family—Rhenn had ducked behind the pot just in time. To her surprise, her parents had begun talking about the secret entrance to the noktum downstairs. They'd also mentioned something called a "Thuros," but Rhenn didn't know what that meant.

"I want to see one up close," Rhenn said.

"One what?"

"A noktum, silly."

"No you don't!" Lorelle's eyes got wide.

"Of course I do. I'm a princess, aren't I?" Rhenn raised her chin. "Father refuses to let me see the doors in the Night Ring up close. I need to know about the things in my kingdom."

"Your kingdom?"

"Yes, my kingdom. I'll be queen someday, and I need to know everything."

"You have two brothers and a sister in line before you."

Rhenn set her mouth in a straight line. Lorelle, to her credit, flushed. Rhenn hated it when anyone talked about how far she was from the throne, and Lorelle knew that.

"We're going," Rhenn said firmly, "to the noktum."

Lorelle bit her lip, and her hair glimmered even brighter. "It has tentacles," Lorelle protested.

"I know it has tentacles."

"Well, they grab you and pull you in."

"Are you my best friend, or aren't you?"

"There are monsters in there, Rhenn. They eat people."

"If you're scared, I'll just go on my own." Rhenn started down the stairway.

Lorelle caught her arm. Her fingers were light, but strong. "I can't let you go down there—"

Rhenn yanked her arm from Lorelle's grasp. "Just try and stop me." Rhenn balled up her fists. It was bad enough when adults told her what to do, but Rhenn lost her temper when children tried.

Lorelle held up her hands pacifyingly. "Alone. I was going to say I can't let you go down there alone."

Rhenn relaxed a little. "Oh. All right. That's good."

Lorelle craned her long neck to peer down the curving stairway, as if, if she got too close, she might fall.

Rhenn came up alongside Lorelle, and they both stared into that dark, spiraling hole.

"You're not saying go into the noktum, right?" Lorelle asked. "You just want to see it up close."

"Inside the noktum?"

"Yes."

"Lorelle, that's suicide."

"I know. I just wanted to hear you say it."

"We're going down there," Rhenn agreed. "See what they don't want us to see."

Lorelle's hair shone brighter, and her large brown eyes fixed on Rhenn. She picked up the lantern from the desk and held it in front of them.

"Come on." Rhenn went through the dark doorway and down the first few steps. She glanced over her shoulder at Lorelle, and the stalwart girl was right behind her. Best friend material.

The light from the lantern cast a long, bent shadow across the curving wall of the spiral stair. Lorelle's slender hand slipped into Rhenn's as the doorway vanished behind them around the curve of the wall. Butterflies leapt in Rhenn's belly, and she clenched the large silver key in her hand, reminding herself that queens weren't scared of the dark.

Rhenn heard a distant thumping overhead, like booted feet. Lorelle stopped and turned back the way they'd come. All they could see was the turn of the spiral staircase falling into shadow below and above where the lantern's light ended.

Lorelle's hand tightened on Rhenn's.

"Rhenn...." she murmured.

A scream ripped through the air, and both girls jumped. That hadn't come from below. That had come from above, from the royal chambers.

And it had sounded like Rhenn's older brother, Whendon.

Rhenn pushed around Lorelle and sprinted back up the steps. Another scream tore through the air. Shouts. Swords clashing.

"Senji's mercy!" Rhenn pushed her burning legs harder—

Lorelle caught up and yanked on her hand, bringing her stumbling to a stop. The lantern slipped from Rhenn's grasp, hit the floor, and crashed down the steep steps, crunching and banging, glass shattering. The oil spattered from inside and caught fire, bathing the right half of the stairway and wall in sudden flames. They shielded their eyes, then spun about as more screams and shouts came from above.

"Stop it!" Rhenn shouted, trying to pry her wrist from Lorelle's grasp.

"Rhenn wait," Lorelle begged.

"Whendon is screaming!"

"That's steel. Swords on swords. They're fighting up there!" Lorelle said urgently.

"Someone is hurting my family—"

"Yes." Lorelle yanked Rhenn so they were face to face. "What if they want to hurt you, too?"

"Your parents are up there, Lorelle."

Lorelle jerked like Rhenn had poked a pin in her. Her friend seemed not to have considered that. Her eyes went wide, and her hair shone so bright Rhenn squinted. Lorelle leapt past Rhenn and vanished up the stairs, her light fading with her.

"Lorelle! Wait!" Rhenn shouted, launching herself up the stairs again. Lorelle weighed less than half what Rhenn did, and she just couldn't keep up. Horrible visions flashed through her mind. Whendon hurt. Mother and Father hurt. Lorelle rushing into danger....

Two more screams ripped from the chaos above, the first high and piercing, then dying out as a second one began. Those sounded like Rhenn's sisters.

Rhenn's legs burned as she forced them harder, faster. She burst into the study, which was bright with the light from Lorelle's hair. The Luminent stood at a crack in the open door to the hallway, but she'd stopped there, frozen in place. There were no more screams, but Rhenn heard the booted feet of many men, the creaking and clinking of armor.

Gasping and huffing, Rhenn grasped the door to fling it open when Lorelle stopped her.

Rhenn followed Lorelle's gaze and looked through the barely-open door to the hallway—

Two bodies lay on the hallway rug in a pool of blood. They were long and tall, stretched out as though they'd been cut down while running. Both had golden hair. Lorelle's parents.

"No..." Rhenn whispered, and her heart wrenched. She wanted to charge into the hallway and demand an explanation, but Lorelle hauled her back from the door. If Lorelle had been a human of the same size, such a grapple might have thrown Rhenn to the floor, but because of their weight difference, she only pulled Rhenn back a little as Lorelle's boots skidded on the floor. "Lorelle—"

She clapped a hand over Rhenn's mouth.

"They're dead," Lorelle whispered through a tight throat, as though she didn't believe her own words. "My parents are dead."

Rhenn tried to shake Lorelle's grip off and reached for the handle, but Lorelle yanked back and swept Rhenn's legs out from underneath her. The slender Luminent picked Rhenn up and ran back to the secret passage.

"Let go of me! You don't know they're dead!" Rhenn struggled. Lorelle put her back on her feet, but kept hold of her arm.

"I overheard them talking," Lorelle whispered. "They killed your mother and father. They killed...everyone. Now they're looking for you. And me."

"You don't know my mother and father are dead yet—"

"Rhenn, I heard them! I heard your mother scream."

Rhenn couldn't believe it. Even though she'd seen the bodies, she simply refused to believe it. Things like this didn't happen. You didn't just walk halfway down a stairway with your parents alive and asleep and safe, and then walk back up the stairway to find them dead. They had to be alive.

"I have to get to them!" Rhenn said.

"They will kill you," Lorelle said adamantly.

That single statement hit Rhenn like a slap to the face, and she realized Lorelle was right. Somebody had attacked the palace. The stomp of boots and clink of armor. The clash of weapons. The screams of her brothers and sisters....

"But I have to help," Rhenn said in a small voice. "How...can I help them if I run away?" She felt tiny, powerless. She wasn't a queen at all.

"Live," Lorelle said in a broken voice. She was crying quietly now. "You have to live. And that means we have to run."

Rhenn looked at the barely-open study door, a thin barrier between them and slaughter. She suddenly realized it was astonishing someone hadn't already burst through.

"We...have to run," Rhenn said numbly.

"Yes."

"But...that's the only way out," Rhenn said.

"No." Lorelle looked at the open painting, at the dark stairway.

Rhenn desperately wanted to believe her parents were still alive. She wanted to fling herself into the hall and search frantically for them, to claw out the eyes of anyone who would dare hurt her family, but she froze.

Rhenn had once asked Father what it meant to be king, to rule over so many people, and he'd answered her.

"When you're a ruler, your life doesn't belong to you. You cannot choose to die selfishly, because your life doesn't belong to you alone. It belongs to those you protect, and you must guard it for those who need you."

If Rhenn's parents were dead—if that was really true—it

meant she really was the queen now. She had to look after the kingdom, after her subjects. She had to look after Lorelle.

Rhenn squeezed her eyes shut. She drew in a deep breath and opened them again. She saw the open painting and the dark stairway with sharp clarity.

Her fears calmed, and she saw what she needed to do.

She couldn't spend her time being afraid. She couldn't spend it being angry. She had to be like Father. She had to be smart. To make good decisions. She had to look at what was in front of her with clear eyes.

"They're coming for us," she said in a monotone.

"Rhenn—"

"Those who killed our families are going to come for us," she said, and each word felt like a little hammer strike on her chest. That was the truth. That was what was real. That was seeing clearly.

Lorelle didn't protest this time. She swallowed and nodded.

"But we won't let them. We're going to hide." Rhenn shoved the giant key into her belt and snatched a long, thin dagger from Father's desk, the one he used to slice through wax seals on scrolls.

"Yes. We hide," Rhenn repeated emphatically. The guards in the palace would come eventually; they would kill these horrible murderers. Maybe there was a battle taking place right now, loyal guards fighting fervently to get to the royal wing. Rhenn had to keep them safe just long enough for reinforcements to arrive.

Rhenn took Lorelle's wrist and entered the hidden stairway. She turned and carefully closed the painting behind them. It clicked shut with finality, as though their new world was this stairway, and only this stairway. Rhenn swallowed her fear and led the way down.

The oil from the lamp Rhenn had dropped was almost burned out, flickering weakly up the wall. It barely lit the spiral staircase. They stuck close to the inner curve of the spiral and stepped quickly past the burning oil.

Around and around they went, down and down, until even

the burning oil was a dull, orange flicker behind them. Finally, Rhenn stopped. They both breathed loudly in the silence, listening.

A thump came from above, then angry, arguing voices, but Rhenn couldn't make out what they were saying. More thundering noises, as though someone was pulling books from the shelves and throwing them to the floor. Lorelle's hair brightened.

"That doesn't sound...like someone who's coming to help us," Lorelle said.

"Come on," Rhenn said. They wound around and around the staircase, but this time Rhenn didn't feel the exhaustion in her legs. She didn't pay attention to the burn in her lungs. The stairs ended abruptly at another door. Rhenn pushed the latch, and it opened on well-oiled hinges.

The room beyond looked like something out of a myth about the Giants. The stairway ended in the middle of a circular room. To the right, an enormous arch with strange markings upon it glowed in the center, smears of many colors slithering across the plane that should have shown the darkness of a hallway beyond.

Directly ahead stood another archway, this one human-sized and closed with a thick, cross-banded iron gate. The lock was enormous and looked like it was a perfect fit for the tarnished silver key in Rhenn's belt.

"That's..." Rhenn pointed at the larger archway. "That must be the Thuros."

The two of them walked around the circular room. The ceiling was twenty feet tall, and the walls were made of the same dark, chiseled stone as the stairway. There was no other way in or out except the stairway or the iron gate. Or the slithering rainbow Thuros. Rhenn ascended the dais and put her hand on the swirling colors. She half-expected her hand to go through like water, but it felt like a smooth stone wall. There was no way out there.

They approached the iron gate. Lorelle's glowing hair pushed back the shadows until they resolved into dark, oily tentacles. They drifted forward lazily, as though looking for something to grab. Under the direct shine of Lorelle's light, the tentacles turned grayish, fading from the deep black to something that Rhenn could almost see through. The further out from the radius of Lorelle's light, the darker the noktum became, a supernatural darkness that threatened to devour anyone who came too close. It oozed evil.

"Do you see what your light is doing?" Rhenn asked. "It's...I can almost see into it. Do you see that?" Rhenn had never heard of that. Noktums swallowed light. All light. No light had ever pierced a noktum, not even bright sunlight. But somehow the light from Lorelle's hair did.

"I don't want to go in there," Lorelle murmured.

"We're not going in there. We're not even opening the door. We're just going to wait here until the palace guards—"

A loud bang came from the doorway to the stairs. They both jumped. Lorelle's hair grew brighter, and tears welled in her eyes. She clenched Rhenn's hand and looked more scared than Rhenn had ever seen her. Rhenn felt the same way. That didn't sound like guards coming to help them. But Rhenn had to think of something. She had to think clearly. She had to give Lorelle courage.

"All right. We are going in after all," Rhenn said.

"Rhenn!"

"Not into the noktum. Just...inside the gate. We'll hide there. They don't have the key, and if we blend with the shadows, they'll never see us. They'll come in, find nothing, and they'll leave."

Tears stood in Lorelle's eyes, like diamonds in the bright light from her hair. "How are we going to hide?" She gestured to her hair, brighter than a torch.

Rhenn pushed the naked dagger into her belt and pulled out the thick silver key. She shoved it into the lock and tried to twist it. It didn't budge. She tried harder. Nothing.

"Help me," she commanded.

Lorelle put her hands on Rhenn's. They both twisted with all their might.

It didn't budge.

Booted steps echoed on the stairway, coming closer.

"Rhenn!" Lorelle whispered urgently.

"Open!" Rhenn commanded, twisting futilely. Tears of frustration streaked down her face. She yanked the stupid thing out and slammed the key into the lock again and again. "Open, open, open!"

Something crunched in the lock, and when Rhenn withdrew the key this time, flakes of rust came with it, sifting and falling to the floor. Rhenn jammed the key in harder and tried to twist it again. This time, it did turn a little, and a little blue flash of light flickered inside the keyhole. Magic!

Lorelle grabbed Rhenn's hands again, and they both twisted, grunting with the effort. The lock screeched, and the key turned. Blue light flashed within the keyhole, tumblers clicked, and something inside clanked. The gate jolted half an inch forward.

The girls hauled on the door, and it ground open.

"What are we doing?" Lorelle asked hopelessly as they went into the tunnel and stood on the other side of the gate.

"Help me close this," Rhenn commanded.

Together they pulled the screeching gate back into place. Turning the key from the other side was hard, but it had loosened up a little. With both of their hands working on it, they managed to lock the gate. If the gate was locked, the murderers couldn't reach them. That was something, at least. It was hard to kill someone with a sword if they were twenty feet behind a steel gate.

"We have to cover your hair," Rhenn said, trying to keep her voice steady. She pulled her tunic over her head, leaving only her nightshirt to ward off the bone-deep cold of the tunnel. "If we cover your hair, they won't see us," she said. Together, they wrapped Lorelle's hair in the tunic, securing it tightly with a knot. The tunnel plunged into absolute darkness, and the hair on the back of Rhenn's neck prickled, knowing how close the tentacles were. Senji, they could be inside the noktum now for all she knew!

"There's no way out," Lorelle whispered, echoing Rhenn's desperate thoughts. "We're trapped."

"We'll be all right," Rhenn said. Surprisingly, her voice sounded strong. She pushed the key back into her belt, yanked out the knife, and held it with both hands.

The booted feet sounded from the stairway louder. Eerie blue light flickered at the bottom of the door.

"They're coming," Lorelle squeaked. The darkness around Rhenn retreated, giving a slight illumination to the tunnel and the gate. At first, she thought it was the new blue light, then she looked over her shoulder and realized Lorelle's hair had become so bright, it shone through the cloth of the tunic.

"Lorelle!" Rhenn whispered harshly. "Your hair—you have to calm down."

"I-I can't!"

The door banged open, bathing the circular room with blue light. An armed man emerged from the stairway, and Rhenn froze, feeling horribly exposed. How had she ever thought they could hide here?

The man peered into the dim room, gripping a bloody sword in his hand.

"What is this place?" he said, his deep voice loud in the cavernous room. Rhenn recognized him. It was Baron Tybris Vamreth!

The bright blue light followed him, growing stronger. A woman in mage's robes emerged, holding the blue light in her palm.

Vamreth stared at the Thuros, cocking his head in curiosity. The swirling colors had pulled his gaze away from the tunnel, and Rhenn and Lorelle. He hadn't seen them yet.

Reflexively, Rhenn retreated and bumped into Lorelle. Lorelle desperately grabbed Rhenn's arms to steady them both. The tunic, which Lorelle had been trying to tie tighter, unraveled and fell to the ground. Bright, buttery light filled the tunnel.

Rhenn twisted, reaching down to snatch at the tunic—

She sucked in a breath and froze. Behind Lorelle, the reaching tentacles of the noktum had lengthened. Somehow, they'd sensed the girls, and their tips wriggled like hungry tongues, inches away from Lorelle's legs.

"Your Majesty!" The mage with the blue light said as more armed men poured into the room. Vamreth tore his gaze away from the Thuros and followed the pointing finger of the mage.

This time, he saw the girls.

Baron Vamreth smiled a horrible, smug smile.

"Open it," he said to the mage.

"It's…bound," the woman replied.

"Bound?"

"The key is the only way," she said. "This lock cannot be picked, and it cannot be forced by any spells I possess."

A flood of relief flowed through Rhenn. If they couldn't get inside, they couldn't reach the girls. Maybe that would be enough. Maybe the palace guards would come, and these murderers would have to flee.

"Then what good are you?" Baron Vamreth snarled. He looked over his shoulder at the dozen men who'd entered the room. All of them were looking around. "Crossbow!" Vamreth snapped.

Rhenn's heart sank.

The baron's men looked at him like he'd said something indecipherable, and Vamreth rolled his eyes. "Senji's Teeth, get yourselves together. Somebody give me a crossbow."

After a shuffling moment as murmurs went through the crowd of fighting men, one of them passed a crossbow forward. Vamreth fitted a bolt and turned to the girls.

"You're in a bit of a spot, aren't you?" he said, approaching the gate.

Rhenn and Lorelle's hands clasped together, fingers intertwining. Lorelle began crying softly, looking back and forth between Vamreth and the noktum's tentacles, which had nearly reached them. Rhenn clenched her teeth, and a high-pitched sound escaped her. She wanted to leap at these murderers, tear their throats out with her bare hands. She felt utterly helpless.

"You…" she said, choking on the words. "My parents…"

"Are dead." Vamreth carefully put the tip of the arrow between the slats of the gate and leveled the crossbow at her.

"Nnnnno! Nnnnno!" Lorelle said through her sobs. Her hair brightened like a miniature sun. Vamreth squinted, peering at them as he aimed.

The crossbow twanged, and Lorelle yanked Rhenn backward. "No!" Lorelle shouted.

White hot pain stabbed into Rhenn as the bolt sank to the feathers in her arm. She screamed.

The girls stumbled back together—

A single shadowy tentacle brushed Rhenn's cheek like a feather. It twitched as though in ecstasy…and then all the tentacles lunged for the two girls at once. They coiled around and around the girls. Rhenn's heels skidded on the rough-hewn ground as the tentacles pulled her and Lorelle backward.

The last thing Rhenn saw was Vamreth's surprised expression. Then the entire room vanished as Rhenn plunged into utter blackness…

For the first moment, she couldn't breathe, couldn't think. She felt like she was floating, like she'd been plunged into a cool tub of water.

Am I dead? she thought. Is this what it's like to die?

"Rhenn?" Lorelle's frightened voice pierced the darkness.

Rhenn's sense of weightlessness vanished. Her feet hit the ground, and she stumbled, flinging out her arms to catch her balance. Her arm screamed in pain, and she lost her grip on the dagger, heard it clatter somewhere in the dark.

Slowly, the dark retreated around a single glowing light. In the midst of the light emerged Lorelle's face, tight with fear. Her hair could pierce the noktum. Rhenn could see!

Rhenn cast about, fingers fumbling, and grasped the dagger she'd dropped.

Lorelle's hair revealed their surroundings in a ten-foot radius.

Beyond that, it was just blackness, but they appeared to still be in a tunnel, just as before. Rhenn didn't know what she'd expected. Tumbling forever in a weightless blackness with bat-like terrors trying to take a bite of her? So far as she could tell, this was just an extension of the tunnel, except now everything was utterly dark except for the ten-foot radius of light provided by Lorelle's hair that showed the world in shades of gray. And if that went out…

Rhenn shuddered.

"Keep shining," she murmured. "Don't stop being scared."

Lorelle gave her a look like Rhenn had gone insane. Rhenn forced a pained laugh.

"Where are the monsters?" Lorelle whispered. "Legends say they attack light immediately."

"I don't know," Rhenn said, pushing her fist—still gripping the dagger—against her arm beneath the arrow sticking out of it. It hurt so much, it made her dizzy.

"We should…find a way out," Lorelle said, looking up the tunnel. Behind them, the tunnel ended in a flat black wall. Going back would put them into Vamreth's hands again.

But the other way led deeper into the noktum.

"Yes," Rhenn said, and she led the way. A queen should lead the way without fear. But with every step, she waited for a monster to leap out of the darkness.

Time passed as the tunnel wound on and on. Abruptly, the cave widened, and they reached the end of it. Lorelle's light grew suddenly brighter as they looked out onto a flat landscape. Her light now reached twenty feet out, but Rhenn could also see a kind of sky overhead. It was dark gray instead of black. A stand of trees began to her right, and all of them seemed to be made from darkness. No greens or browns, only shades of gray and black. Black tufts of grass grew just outside the cave atop the dark gray of the ground.

The girls stood there, staring, for a long moment.

Lorelle looked over at Rhenn. "What do we do now?"

"I don't know—" Rhenn stopped herself. No. She was the

queen now. She didn't get to "not know" what to do. She cleared her throat and stood up straighter, thought the pain in her arm lanced through her. "An hour ago we were children, but we can't be children anymore. We survive. We live. That's what we do."

A flicker of hope crossed Lorelle's face. It encouraged Rhenn, so she continued.

"We start walking." She looked to her right. "Into those trees. The noktum...south of the city... it runs through the trees. Everybody knows that. So we walk until we find the edge of it. It can't be far."

"How do you know that's the right direction?" Lorelle asked, pointing at the trees. "How do you know that's northeast?"

"Because...." Rhenn hesitated. "Because the palace is at the western edge of the city, right up against the wall." Rhenn dredged up half-forgotten memories, things she knew, and things she'd been told, linking them together like a chain. "If we'd come out to the east, we'd be under water. To the north or south, it'd be plains. So that's the Laochodon Forest," she said with conviction. She pointed at the trees. "Which makes that north. And the noktum barely comes as far north as the city. Which means we won't have far to go to get out—"

An insidious purr drifted from overhead.

Rhenn craned her neck to look upward, and her breath caught in her throat.

A long, sinuous creature crept into the light of Lorelle's hair, coming down the cliff above the cave entrance. It clung to the rock face six feet above them. Its sleek, black-furred body was longer than both girls stacked on top of each other, with claws that crunched into the rock and looked strong enough to crush a person's head easily. The thing had a large, black nose at the front of a blunt muzzle, and beady black eyes on either side of its round head.

It peeled back fuzzy lips to reveal fangs as long as Rhenn's dagger.

"Nnnnooo..." Lorelle keened.

The thing leapt upon her.

It happened so fast, Rhenn didn't even know the creature had moved until it landed on her friend, driving Lorelle to the ground with a thump.

Rhenn screamed in rage and jumped on the thing's back, stabbing wildly with her knife. Rhenn's parents had died tonight. Her brothers and sisters had died.

This monster couldn't have Lorelle, too!

The thing shrieked. It whipped about, giant fangs snapping at Rhenn. She leaned back from the snapping jaws, but she kept stabbing. The teeth barely missed her arm and closed on the arrow sticking out. The beast thrashed, yanking on the arrow, perhaps thinking it was part of Rhenn's body.

She screamed.

The arrow tore free, and the force of the creature's yank threw Rhenn sprawling to the ground. The enormous fanged otter slithered into the air—hovering! It forgot Lorelle and leveled its deadly gaze on Rhenn. Rhenn scrambled to her feet, gritting her teeth at the pain, and held the dagger before her protectively with her good hand.

The thing's short legs folded back against the long body as it hovered. It seemed to be preparing to launch itself like an arrow.

Lorelle rose up behind it, blood trickling down her forehead from where the thing had scored with its fangs. She raised a fist-sized rock clenched in both hands. The monstrous fanged otter sensed her and twisted.

She brought the rock down on its nose. Something crunched, and black blood spattered the ground.

It twitched, floating backward, and Rhenn charged, stabbing the dagger into the beast. It sank to the hilt, and the creature screamed.

Apparently, that was enough for it. The beast whipped back, flying away. It shot up into the sky, wriggling through the air like a water snake through a pond. It went up and up…

…and into a cloud of beasts just like it. The throng of monsters writhed in the sky like a mass of black worms.

"Senji's Spear…" Rhenn murmured, and Lorelle gaped.

"Run, Rhenn. We have to run now!" Lorelle said.

They turned and sprinted into the forest. Rhenn spared a glance over her shoulder, through the gaps in the branches, and saw the horde of creatures turning their direction.

"They're going to catch us," Lorelle said.

"Not both of us," Rhenn huffed. "You're fast enough. Run ahead, Lorelle. Make it out of the—"

"I'm not leaving you!"

"Go!" Rhenn cried. "Find the edge of the noktum!"

Lorelle hesitated, then leapt ahead like a bounding deer, outdistancing Rhenn in seconds. No sooner had she vanished into the trees than her voice floated back excitedly.

"Rhenn! It's here! It's right here! Hurry!"

Rhenn heard branches cracking behind her. Feet pounding, lungs burning, she glanced backward and glimpsed the massive fanged otters tearing through the forest to get to her. She ran harder, gasping for breath.

Lorelle's light glowed ahead. Rhenn headed for it. Trees whipped by in a blur, Lorelle's light flickering between them, and then suddenly Lorelle appeared. She stood before a flat black curtain that wound through the trees: the edge of the noktum.

Lorelle gripped her rock. She stepped forward and threw it hard at Rhenn's head.

An insidious purr sounded just behind Rhenn's ears at the same moment—

Lorelle's rock just missed Rhenn's head and smacked the creature in the eye. One fang scraped Rhenn's neck as the creature howled and jerked away.

Rhenn reached Lorelle at a full sprint, and they dove through the flat black curtain.

They burst into a bright world beneath stars and a silvery moon, and the two girls tumbled across the ground. Though the curtain of the noktum was flat from the inside, on this side it was covered with those insidious tentacles that quested toward them, seeking to draw them back in.

Lorelle pulled Rhenn to her feet, and they staggered back, out of reach.

They held onto each other, staring at the lazy tentacles, waiting for the fanged, floating otters to burst through. But they didn't.

Compared to the dull gray light inside the noktum, it seemed like the sun was shining here. Rhenn could see everything: the green and brown of the pine trees, the green grass beneath them, even the wall of the city through the branches, with the tall Night Ring and the towering palace poking high into the sky.

Heart thundering, Rhenn clung to her best friend. They watched the tentacles, safely out of reach. Rhenn expected the giant fanged otters to burst through and finish them off at any moment.

But the creatures never emerged.

Finally Rhenn said, "So…that was a really good throw with the rock. I think you have a true talent there."

Lorelle looked down at her and laughed. That single laugh turned into two, and then they were both laughing. The laughter became uncontrollable, they staggered back into a tree, and fell to their butts, still holding hands. They laughed and laughed until it became sobs, and they just held each other.

The sobs eventually turned to sniffles, and then to silence.

"What are we going to do?" Lorelle finally asked in a small voice. The question rang loudly in Rhenn's mind, too. Their families were dead. They'd escaped a bloody coup. They'd escaped the noktum. She could barely comprehend all they'd just done. But now that it was over, they still weren't safe. Where could they go now? To one of Father's loyal dukes or barons? How could she know which was which? She'd thought Baron Vamreth was loyal.

Rhenn stared at the forest. The crying had left her feeling hollow. The storm of fear and grief inside her had blown itself out. She just looked at the tentacles of the noktum, at the trees, and at the Crown City of Usara in the distance.

A ruthless calm settled over her. Below the fear and grief, a molten layer of rage bubbled in her soul.

Yesterday, if Rhenn had found herself alone in the woods with no parents to protect her, she'd have been terrified. No food. No shelter. Wild beasts.

Strangely, she wasn't afraid now.

She thought about Baron Vamreth. In one murderous instant, he'd taken away everything that mattered to her. Everything except Lorelle.

Rhenn wanted to charge back up to the city, knock down the gates, rage into the palace, and kill Vamreth, kill all his murderers.

But a queen had to see clearly. Two girls against an army that had just sacked the palace? She would only be giving Vamreth exactly what he wanted: placing herself and Lorelle under his butchers' knives again.

"What do we do now?" Rhenn repeated Lorelle's question steadily, glaring at the palace.

"Yes," Lorelle said.

"We just went into the noktum, and we emerged alive. We've done the impossible," Rhenn said. "And if we've done it once, why not twice?"

Lorelle glanced at the palace, then back at Rhenn. "What...do you mean?"

Rhenn drew a deep breath and let her anger flow into her, making her stronger. She let it burn away the last of her fear and grief like a rising sun. "In a handful of seconds inside the noktum, we learned secrets no one else knows. Your hair illuminates the noktum. The monsters within can be fought. They can bleed. What other secrets might the noktum give us if we search?"

"You mean go back in?" Lorelle asked incredulously.

"Yes," Rhenn said. "Not now. But soon. Now we learn the secrets of the forest. We make this our home. And then we take the noktum, too. We use its secrets."

"Take the noktum...." Lorelle said, as though trying to understand. "And...what'll you do with these secrets?" Lorelle asked.

"Take back my kingdom, of course," Rhenn said.

"You mean, use the noktum…as a weapon somehow?"

"What a weapon it would be," Rhenn murmured.

Realization dawned on Lorelle's face. She pressed her lips together in a firm line and nodded. "Yes," she said, and Rhenn's heart felt warmer. Whatever else happened, Rhenn wouldn't be alone. And she knew if she wasn't alone, she could do this. Somehow. She could do the impossible. She could make Baron Vamreth pay for what he'd done.

"Together," Rhenn said.

"Together," Lorelle echoed.

ABOUT THE AUTHOR

Todd Fahnestock is an award-winning, #1 bestselling author of fantasy for all ages and winner of the New York Public Library's Books for the Teen Age Award. *Threadweavers* and *The Whisper Prince Trilogy* are two of his bestselling epic fantasy series. He is a winner of the 2021 Colorado Authors League Award for Writing Excellence and two-time finalist for the Colorado Book Award for *Tower of the Four: The Champions Academy* (2021) and *Khyven the Unkillable* (2022). His passions are fantasy and his quirky, fun-loving family. When he's not writing, he teaches Taekwondo, swaps middle grade humor with his son, plays Ticket to Ride with his wife, plots creative stories with his daughter, and plays vigorously with Galahad the Weimaraner. Visit Todd at toddfahnestock.com.

AUTHOR'S NOTE

Lorelle of the Dark was written because I was getting too fat. Okay, let me back up a little. I'm addicted to sugar. Like, it's a true-blue addiction. When I'm riding high on the sugar train, I will literally talk myself into believing irrational things to convince myself to gorge on confections.

"I have to have a Coke to get me back into the writing groove. 'Cause, y'know, I read somewhere that sugar fires up the neurons. So really, I *need* this to do my job today."

"It's Easter! You're *supposed* to have a chocolate bunny on Easter. It's practically mandatory."

"If I don't eat that Halloween candy now, it's going to make me fall off my diet tomorrow."

"The dog farted. I think that deserves a Chocodile!"

So, as 2021 trundled to a close, the holidays stirred up its typical flurry of friends and family activity, and I took it upon myself to add Christmas cookies to my baking resume.

I already know how to make chocolate chip cookies. I mean, I don't want to brag, but my chocolate chip cookies are *legendary*. Labeled "crack cookies" by my New York City crew of friends, they are everything a true connoisseur of chewy, melty, chocolatey cookies craves. In fact, they are the first thing I ever learned to bake, all in an effort, of course, to catch the attention of a super-cute actress I met in New York way back in the late 1990s. It worked, by the way. Well, sort of. But that's a different story.

So, there I was buying cookie cutters, edible eyeballs for cookie snowmen, and the octo-compartment cookie decorators with their colored sugars (green and red, of course), and star-and-dot sprinkles. I invested in the flour and sugar (which is almost all that goes into a Christmas cookie) by the pound, stocking up our baking storage containers. With such an outlay, I think my subconscious was already hatching a plan. When my second batch actually turned out awesome (I give myself lots of room for mistakes when I undertake a new baking endeavor), I began to give some thought to what I was going to do with all these new things I'd purchased.

That's when the plan came into focus.

At this juncture, it's important to note: baking is the perfect mental vacation from writing. Writing is all about pulling creativity from the depths of the imagination, which is all about change and surprises, and making a truckload of decisions every day, all day, which is mentally exhausting for anyone.

For me, baking is about a proscribed rhythm that, once I've achieved my desired product through trial and error, just repeats and repeats. No surprises. I follow the recipe, make no new decisions, and fall into a rhythm of measuring and pouring, mixing, and dolloping, timing the flow of my operation and making sure the cookie sheets spring from the oven at that apex of chewy/crispiness (for chocolate chip cookies) and whiteness/brownness (for Christmas cookies).

All this is relaxing to my beleaguered brain.

So, as I contemplated the wealth of cookie-making resources, I decided I wasn't just going to make cookies for me. I was going to make cookies for everyone I knew. The assembly line began. And I loved it.

Make the dough. Taste the dough. Have some more dough.

Make the cookies. Taste the cookies. Have an extra cookie. Throw some milk in a cup and drink it down. Now I need *another* cookie.

I think you see where I'm going.

As the manic Christmas activity settled into the big day and gave way to that restful, contemplative week between December 25 and January 1, I began to look forward. What did I want to accomplish in 2022?

Well, those of you who follow everything I write will know that I released a book called *Ordinary Magic* last year wherein I chronicled a 5-week, 450-mile hike over the Colorado Trail with my 14-year-old son during the summer of 2020. During that trek, I lost 25 lb. (along with sizable chunks of my ego), which proved to me that I *could* lose 25 pounds (true), and strangely also proved to me that I could eat anything I wanted and still lose 25 pounds (False. *Unless* you're burning 7,000 calories a day because you just hiked 18 miles. Every day. For 5 weeks).

But my rebellious, irrational sugar-mind latched onto this halcyon notion that I could eat what I did on the trail while back in the posh relaxation of city life and still lose weight.

The result? I returned to civilization and within six months gained back those 25 lb.

So, as I approached the end of 2021, in the wake of my cookie-gobbling, I formed a plan to shed those 25 lb. again, this time in a sustainable way.

Here's where writing comes into the mix. Managing my weight was not the only issue plaguing me last December. I had hit writer's block for the first time in my life, and it was ripping me up inside. You see, I'd accrued a bunch of attention for my work early in the year.

And the positive press had paralyzed me.

I had begun working on *The Slate Wizards*, the third book in the Whisper Prince series, and I was so paranoid that this story wouldn't live up to my latest, award-winning books that I second-guessed myself all over the place.

"The novel is a hot mess…"

"This steaming pile of self-indulgence can't possibly compare to *Tower of the Four*…"

The anchor of expectation got heavier and heavier around my neck. I started. I stopped. I backtracked. I deleted and added. And I finally swirled to a halt in late November in utter despair. I tried to shake it off, failed. So, I chucked the half-baked novel into the trunk and made cookies instead.

But as I headed toward New Years, as my resolve to get back in shape burst forth, burning like a thousand pounds of ignited fuel, I hitched my writing woes to that same rocket.

January, I decided, was going to be a tribute to willpower. For my health, I was going to hold myself accountable for striking sugar and alcohol from my diet, eating primarily vegetables, and moderating my intake of everything else. For my profession, I was going to write an average of 1,000 words a day. (As an aside, I'm capable of writing 2,000 to 3,000 words a day, but I wanted a goal that was readily attainable so as to fend off discouragement.) I was going to build a rhythm. I was going to be relaxed, easy, and methodical. I was going create a "new normal."

I was terrified of *The Slate Wizards*.

The very idea of going back to the book that had thrown me seemed like tempting fate. I mean, I supposed it was just because I'd had mental vapor-lock, but what if the novel was like quicksand? What if it pulled me back under and I spent the next six months like I'd spent the last?

I couldn't risk it. I had to start fresh. I had to give myself a clean slate and the opportunity to "write a crappy novel."

The sequel to *Khyven the Unkillable* wasn't due for nine months. It was nowhere near the top of my priority list and perhaps because of that fact, it felt safer. I mean, if I totally screwed it up, I'd have a lot of time to get it into shape, right?

So, I started.

Immediately the fears rose inside me. This was supposed to be the sequel to Khyven's story, but Lorelle jumped forward as the lead character. She had the arc. She had the transformation that needed to happen. Khyven had come through his fire and made himself better. Now it was her turn.

In the early days of January, I struggled with this, trying to turn the book back into being Khyven's book, but Lorelle wouldn't let go.

January passed. I averaged 1,500 words a day and totaled 45,000 words for the month.

Finally, I gave up trying to force it to go as expected. Khyven was going to be a supporting character this time. Lorelle had the reins and I let her run. She led us deep into the noktum. She showed us the civilization of the Nox. She took us face to face with a Giant and a dragon.

So. Clearly. The right. Decision.

It was once again that same old bit of writerly wisdom. My subconscious was screaming at me to get the hell out of my own way, to let my expectations drop and let the story unfold.

February passed. I averaged 2,353 words a day, totaled

65,874 for the month, and *finished* the rough draft. "Khyven II" got renamed *Lorelle of the Dark*, and it was official. Not only did it create a better story, but it set a new direction for this collection in Legacy of Shadows.

March and half of April passed. I cut 22,000 words and added 16,000 more, and then I was done. Done and done. After telling Lara I suspected the novel sucked (to which she replied, "That's nice, dear."), I sent it out to my alpha readers.

The feedback came back positive, and I breathed a sigh of relief. My writer's block was, apparently, over.

So that's how me feeling too fat led to the production of *Lorelle of the Dark*. Although I suspect losing weight wasn't exactly my main drive heading into 2022. I suspect it was a feint by my subconscious, which stepped in and helped me out, kept me from looking at my real problem head on, and crafted a "list" of things to accomplish where "oh, writing is just a part of that list…"

The subconscious can be crafty, no?

But incidentally, as of this morning, I've lost a total 12.5 lb. since January 1. Gonna work on the other half in May.

And probably start *Rhenn the Traveler*…

Also By Todd Fahnestock

Eldros Legacy (Legacy of Shadows Series)
Khyven the Unkillable
Lorelle of the Dark
Rhenn the Traveler
Slayter and the Dragon
Bane of Giants

Tower of the Four
Episode 1 – The Quad
Episode 2 – The Tower
Episode 3 – The Test
The Champions Academy (Episodes 1-3 compilation)
Episode 4 – The Nightmare
Episode 5 – The Resurrection
Episode 6 – The Reunion
The Dragon's War (Episodes 4-6 compilation)

Threadweavers
Wildmane
The GodSpill
Threads of Amarion
God of Dragons

The Whisper Prince
Fairmist
The Undying Man
The Slate Wizards

Standalone Novels
Charlie Fiction
Summer of the Fetch

Non-fiction
Ordinary Magic
Falling to Fly

Tower of the Four Short Stories
"Urchin"
"Royal"
"Princess"

Other Short Stories
Parallel Worlds Anthology — "Threshold"
Dragonlance: The Cataclysm — "Seekers"
Dragonlance: Heroes & Fools — "Songsayer"
Dragonlance: The History of Krynn —
"The Letters of Trayn Minaas"

Want More Eldros Legacy?

If you enjoyed this story and the world it's set in, then the creators of the Eldros Legacy would like to encourage you to don thy traveling pack and journey deeper into the mysteries of the world Eldros and all the myriad adventures set therein.

The mortal world of Eldros is coming apart. The Giants, who once ruled its five continents with draconian malice have set their mighty designs on a return to power. Mortals across the globe must be victorious against insurmountable odds or die.

Come join us as the Eldros Legacy unfolds in a growing library of novels and short stories.

More Novels in Noksonon

Relics of Noksonon Series by Kendra Merritt
The Pain Bearer
The Truth Stealer
The Death Bringer

Worldbreaker by Becca Lee Gardner

Founder Series in Eldros Legacy

Legacy of Deceit by Quincy J. Allen
Seeds of Dominion
Demons of Veynkal (Forthcoming)

Legacy of Dragons by Mark Stallings
The Forgotten King

Legacy of Queens by Marie Whittaker
Embers & Ash
Cinder & Stone (Forthcoming)

Other Eldros Legacy Novels

Other Eldros Legacy Short Stories